MW01234133

THE BEAT OF MY HEART

AVERY MAXWELL

That's What She Said Publishing, Inc.

www.AveryMaxwellBooks.com

ISBN: 978-1-945631-96-2 (ebook)

ISBN: 979-8-88643-000-4 (paperback)

082923

DISCLAIMER

& TRIGGER WARNING

While Burke-Mountain is a very real place in Vermont's North-East Kingdom, everything else in this book is a work of fiction. All characters, scenes, and other settings, including Waverley-Cay, were all created in my imagination.

*Domestic abuse and eating disorders are mentioned, but not described.

National Domestic Violence Hotline: https://www.thehotline.org/

Or, the National Eating Disorder Association: https://www.nationaleatingdisorders.org/help-support/contact-helpline

A NOTE FROM AVERY

The Beat of My Heart is **Book Two** in the **interconnected series The Westbrooks**. While it can be read as a stand alone, Avery believes they are best read in order.

PLAYLIST

1. Bibia Be Ye Ye, Ed Sheeran
2. One Night Standards, Ashley McBryde
3. The Wolf, Mumford & Sons
4. Bluebird, Miranda Lambert
5. Catch, Brett Young
6. It Won't Kill Ya, The Chainsmokers
7. Give Me Strength, Snow Patrol
8. Say Goodbye, Dave Mathews
9. The Man, Taylor Swift
10. Raise Your Glass, Pink
11. Circus, Brittany Spears
12. Done, Chris Janson
13. Holding Out For The One, Tenille Towns
14. Guiding Light, Mumford & Sons
15. Fifteen Minutes Old, Snow Patrol
16. One Of Them Girls, Lee Brice
17. Sweet Caroline, Dave Matthews Live @ Fenway
18. Weak, AJR
19. Life Changes, Thomas Rhett
20. Break Things, Kylie Morgan
21. Inside Out, The Chainsmokers

22. Life On Earth, Snow Patrol
23. To Hell & Back, Maren Morris
24. American Pie, Don Mclean
25. One Beer, Hardy
26. What I Never Knew I Always Wanted, Carrie Underwood
27. Daddy, Coldplay
28. Count On Me, Bruno Mars
29. Good Love, Shy Carter
30. Monster, Imagine Dragons
31. Grace is Gone, Dave Matthews
32. Smile Like You Mean It, The Killers
33. Lonely If You Are, Chase Rice
34. On Top Of The World, Imagine Dragons
35. Believer, Imagine Dragons
36. Even My Dad Does Sometimes, Ed Sheeran
37. Every Other Memory, Ryan Hurd
38. Stand By You, Rachel Platten
39. Tell Your Heart To Beat Again, Danny Gokey
40. The Luckiest, Ben Folds
41. Single Saturday Night, Cole Swindell
42. With A Little Help From My Friends, The Beatles
43. Monsters, Eric Church
44. Not Afraid, Eminem
45. Counting Stars, One Republic
46. Hey Brother, Aviici
47. Memories, Maroon 5

Extended Epilogue) 7-Years, Lukas Graham

PROLOGUE

JULIA

"Bed of Lies" by Nicki Minaj featuring Skylar Grey

Stepping into the sunlight, my body rejects its warmth. Instead of raising my face to the sun, I look down and shiver from the inside out. The granite steps of the courthouse reflect my every step.

"Julia," I hear Cora yell. I pause so she can catch up. "We did everything we could. I'm sorry, I know this isn't the judgment you were hoping for."

"I get it, Cora. Honestly, thank you for all your work. The truth is, I do this for a living. I should have seen it coming."

"Jules, he conned you. He cleaned you out and ran a debt so high it's crippling. Plus, you loved him. No one would have seen this coming." I know she's trying to comfort me, and I wish to God her words could have the desired effect.

"I should have. I watch for this shit daily. God, if this gets out, I'll lose my job, then I'll never be able to repay this debt."

"We'll file an appeal, but I need to tell you this one more

time. Jules, I wouldn't be a good lawyer or friend if I didn't. Your parents are literally two of the best attorneys on the East Coast. Confide in them and ask for help. If anyone can find a way out of this, it's them." Her eyes are pleading, so I glance at my feet.

We've had this conversation once a week for at least a year. My parents owned a highly successful firm in Boston up until they had me. Once I was born, they decided they wanted a slower life for me. They sold McDowell & Co. and moved us to Vermont, where they opened up a much smaller office.

"Cora, please drop it. I can't and won't do that. This is my mess, not theirs. I'll fix it."

Realizing my words have come out more harshly than I intended, I roll my shoulders, willing myself to calm down.

"Julia, you'll be paying off this debt for years. You'll have to put your life on hold because you won't be eligible for a line of credit for almost ten years."

I've explained this to her so many times, and I don't feel like doing it again. This will affect my lifestyle for the next five or so years, I get that, but I make good money and I'll take care of it on my own. I'm done relying on anyone.

"Cora, it isn't like I'm hanging out at the Packing House bar riding the bull every night. I haven't even tried to take a vacation since spring break in college. Let's just put in the appeals and go from there, all right? If the judgment falls to me once again, I'll figure out how to deal with it. On my own. I appreciate everything you've done, but I'm exhausted. I'm going home. I have so much shit I need to clear out."

"Erick's stuff?" she asks, cringing slightly.

Nodding, so she doesn't hear my voice waver, I turn to go.

"Jules?" she stops me. "Is Lanie going to help you? I can come over too if you want? We can burn his shit in the fireplace."

A laugh escapes despite my foul mood. "No, thanks, Cora. I've got this. I appreciate it, though."

She leans in for a hug, and involuntarily, I roll my eyes.

"Just call if you change your mind."

"I will, thanks."

When I turn toward my car, I'm thankful she could stop the creditors from putting a lien on my house and my new car. That would have made it impossible to handle this mess myself. As it is, I hated having to tell Cora that Erick left me. Not only did he leave me, but he wiped out my savings right after he racked up hundreds of thousands of dollars in debt. In my name.

Lanie: Hey, lady! Wanna wine and Netflix tonight?

I haven't told anyone that Erick won't be returning, but after so much time, I assume it's obvious. I don't know why I've been hanging onto something that never existed in the first place. I've been putting it off, too embarrassed to tell the truth, but the time is coming. What's one more lie, right?

Julia: I can't tonight. Erick's coming over to talk.

Lanie: The jerk. Want me to come give him a piece of my mind?

Her text actually makes me laugh, and I almost drop my phone. Lanie hasn't sworn out loud since she was ten years old. Her idea of giving someone hell has a lot of PG-rated vocabulary and even some made-up swear words that are just so Lanie.

Julia: I got it covered, but thanks. Raincheck? Maybe tomorrow?

Lanie: You got it! I'll be over with pizza around 6 p.m. See you then. Luvs.

Lanie: Call if you need backup tonight.

Julia: I will. Luvs.

Stopping by Golden City on my way home, I order a giant to-go bag of General Tso's chicken, pork fried rice, scallion pancakes, wonton soup, and egg rolls. It's more food than I can eat in a week, but I figure I'll need it to get through tonight. I already had my wine delivered a few days ago, so I officially have every break-up-clean-out item necessary. *Except for your friends, you twit.* My conscience often sounds a lot like Lanie's grandmother, GG. It's annoying as fuck.

The second my front door closes behind me, I unhook my bra, pull it off through the sleeves the way us girls do, and toss it on the couch. I'm headed straight for the kitchen, but something on the fireplace mantel stops me in my tracks.

The framed picture of Erick and me from graduation stares back. Mocking me. "Goddamn it." It slips from my mouth as I swipe angrily at a stray tear. Hefting the bag of food to my hip, I grab the picture, and storm off to the kitchen for a garbage bag.

After placing the food on the counter, I reach under the sink and pull out a giant green contractor bag, then chuck the picture—frame and all—into the bag with such force I hear it crack when it hits the ground. I quickly realize the sound is cathartic, and I'm ready to do it again. And again.

"Okay, Jules. Let's do this." Pushing up my sleeves, I strip out of my skirt, too. It's my house, and if I'm going to rid my home of my ex, I'm doing it in comfort. I run to my room, toss my tank top aside, and grab my extra-large Red Sox T-shirt. Pulling it over my head, I sigh. *What's better than giant, cozy T-shirts?* It's so big, it comes down to my knees, which is probably more acceptable should someone stop by.

I rub my hands together, then take the garbage bag with me and start at the front of the house. I'm going through every nook and cranny of this place until I've destroyed every last memory of Erick. *Just like he did to your life.* "Oh, for fuck's sake! Shut up, GG."

Once I finish in the entryway, I'm a little sweaty. Who knew emotional stress could affect your body so much? Dragging my long, dark hair into a ponytail, I walk to the kitchen for a bottle of wine. I give the wine glasses the side eye, then shrug. "Screw it. Who needs the added clean up? Not this girl!"

"Glad we're on the same page then." Spinning in place, I find my best friend, Lanie.

"You scared the living shit out of me. What the hell, Lanes?"

Grabbing her own bottle of wine, she uncorks it and clinks her bottle with mine. "Cheers."

"Wh-What are you doing here?" I ask, embarrassed at being caught in a lie.

"Jules, how long have we known each other? I know the second you're even thinking about lying to me, so as your best friend, I'm here. You don't have to tell me anything, but by the looks of the bag I just stepped over, we're cleaning Erick out of your life tonight, right?" She takes a very unladylike gulp from her bottle, and I grin.

Unable to make eye contact, I stare at my hands. "Yeah, we're done."

"Okay then, let's get started." She doesn't question me, just gets her own bag from under the sink. Standing upright, I watch as she unhooks her own bra, slides it out from her armhole, and tosses it onto the kitchen chair. "Sisterhood and all." She winks.

All I can do is raise my bottle to hers. "To sisterhood. And, Lanes?"

"Yes, my darling?" she sing-songs.

"Thank you."

She kisses me on the head—because she's literally an entire foot taller than me—and I watch as a slow smile creeps across her face. "Anytime, chica. Let's do this. Can we break things?"

"I'm hoping so." Once again, she forces a laugh from my cranky face.

For the next three hours, we rid my home of all things Erick. I know when Lanie goes home I'll cry. Mourn the loss of what I thought we had. Then I'll pick up the pieces and move on. Men will not be a part my life for a very long time. Who needs the heartache when I've got great friends and a vibrator?

PART I
THE FIRST VERSE

CHAPTER 1

JULIA

"Bibia Be Ye Ye" by Ed Sheeran

"*I* can't believe I let Lanie talk me into this. I mean, seriously. What the hell is she thinking?" Walking across my bedroom floor in the highest heels I own, I turn to stare at myself in the full-length mirror. "Okay, fine. She has a point. My ass looks freaking fantastic."

"I told you it would." Lanie smirks from the doorway.

Practically jumping out of my skin, I spin to face the door, catch my heel in a groove of the old, hardwood floors of my one-hundred-year-old farmhouse, and face-plant right at Lanie's feet.

Lifting only my head, I scowl. "What the actual fuck, Lanes? You couldn't knock at the front door like a normal person?"

"Jules, when have I ever knocked? Plus, you don't even have locks on your doors. It's like a town law or something." Laughing, she leans down to help haul me up.

Where Lanie is a six-foot tall blonde goddess, I'm pushing five foot two on a good day with chocolate brown hair. We could not be more opposite. With my emerald-green eyes boring a hole into her crystal-clear blue ones, I mumble again. I do that when I'm uncomfortable. Speak my innermost thoughts out loud. It's not something I can control, no matter how hard I try.

"Why do you insist on this shopping trip? I'm only going to Boston for a conference. Which, by the way, is totally unnecessary. I probably know more than everyone giving presentations combined." I'm not bragging but telling her the God's honest truth. My IQ is higher than most—they say it's up there at genius level. The only good it does is give me an excuse for my rambling. Sometimes.

"Why, why, why do I let her talk me into these things?" I'm trying to kick off the shoes when Lanie's fit of laughter lets me know I spoke again. "Why can't I keep those thoughts to myself? It's fine when I'm with you, but honestly, at twenty-four, this is getting embarrassing. Thank fuck I don't have to work in an office very often. I wouldn't be able to hold down a position anywhere."

I used my giant brain to land a job before I had even finished college. Since schoolwork came easy for me, I started at my company full-time in the summer of my junior year while also finishing my third degree. I became so good at it, in fact, that when I said I was going home to Vermont after graduation, they made me an offer to work remotely. It's been the best thing possible for my overcrowded mind.

Shaking her head, Lanie pulls my arms until I'm standing. "Keep the shoes on; you need to practice wearing them."

"Listen, I know I was the one complaining about finding a guy and being horny as hell, but I really don't think I need to put so much effort into a one-night stand." She twirls her finger, and I continue to prance around my room. "Shouldn't I just be able to go to the Dog House and pick someone?"

"Ugh, Jules. When is the last time you actually set foot in the Dog House? Just because they sell cheap drinks doesn't mean you can be a cheap date. No, absolutely not. Plus, do you really want to hook up with a townie who has known you since birth? Running to the grocery store will become an exercise in the walk of shame. Is that what you want?"

I feel a mumble coming on, and the words tumble out of my mouth a second later. "Easy for you to say. You only have to sneeze and you have guys lining up to wipe your snot."

Lanie snorts. "You certainly have a way with words, Jules. I already told you, I have no use for dating. I just want to work and grow old with you. Love is overrated anyway. I think."

I know Lanie is a closet romantic, but her childhood sucked and has left her a little tainted as an adult. Growing up, she did have GG, her grandmother, and my parents, who love her like their own. Unfortunately, Lanie's mother liked to use her as a prop, so when she decided she needed Lanie around, there was no telling what kind of abuse she would be subjected to.

"Lanie, it's September. I'm not walking around the mall in three-inch heels. It's just not going to happen."

If you have never been to Vermont in the fall … first, you're missing out because it's breathtaking. Second, prepare yourself for any season because one minute it could be seventy degrees, and the next, it could be snowing.

"You know the saying … if you don't like the weather in New England, give it five minutes? Yeah, well, I'll stick with sneakers if you insist on shopping."

Sighing and dropping onto my bed, Lanie looks up at me with puppy dog eyes. "Jules, this will be fun, okay? I promise! We'll just get you a few stylish suits to wear at the confer-ence, and some super sexy outfits to wear to dinner and drinks." She can't help but wink at me.

Rolling my eyes while heading for the door, I give in. "Fine, let's get this over with. I'll drive."

"Jules, my car isn't that bad, you know?" Lanie stares at me with a furrowed brow.

I'm not trying to hurt her feelings, so I march toward my car. "I know, but mine is newer, and since we have to travel for two hours to get to a freaking mall, we might as well put the miles on mine."

Lanie is a social worker. She graduated at the top of our class, just like me, from Boston University. She always knew she wanted to help kids, ones like her who had a difficult start in life. As you can imagine, that doesn't pay very well, and as much as I love her, I'd rather not ride for hours in her ten-year-old Corolla. Instead, we hop into my lovely little blue Volvo.

If Lanie only knew how much money I pay every month in restitution, she'd probably faint.

"Fine," she says, "but I'm in charge of the music."

"Awesome, Madonna and Mumford for four hours." The sarcasm in my voice is all for show. Secretly, I love that we'll blast music and sing at the top of our lungs like we're thirteen again.

"Who are you kidding? You love it and you know it! You'll be singing along to the beat with your own words like you always do." Laughing, she plays with the volume.

She isn't wrong. As much as I love music, I've never gotten the lyrics right. *I like my versions and I'll sing them if I want to,* I say it to myself, but grin when Lanie laughs again.

"I know it drives everyone nuts, but it's another thing about myself I can't control. Plus, I like my Julia-tized lyrics better, anyway. It's not my fault you can't pick up the song from my perfectly executed melody."

"Jules, no one on Earth could name a song you sing even with your perfect rhythm." I can actually hear her rolling her eyes. "And if you do happen to find someone, they just might be your soulmate."

∾

"HOLY GEEZ, Jules. I think we got stuck behind every leaf-peeper on Route 2," Lanie states the obvious while getting out of the car and stretching.

"Three fucking hours to buy some slutty clothes," I grumble.

Coming up beside me, Lanie hooks arms with me. "I didn't say slutty clothes, Julia. I just think the one suit you have for the random meetings you attend in person will not cut it for an entire week. Especially if you're planning on a little debauchery happening."

"Ugh, I guess she's right. I do need more than one suit." I sound like a sullen teen even in my head.

Laughing, and now doubled over, Lanie holds up a hand to stop me. "Jules …" She's trying to catch her breath, and I know I was talking to myself again.

"Yeah, yeah, I know. Now I do it just so you can hear how unhappy I am without hurting your feelings." I fight a smile and lose.

"Come on, grumpy-pants, let's get a move on. We have some shopping to do." Without waiting for a reply, she drags me behind her.

That's how I end up in a dressing room at Neiman Marcus with my arms secured above my head by a dress I have somehow gotten tangled in. Lanie knocks on the door, and I squeak, but the dang dress I'm choking on muffles my voice. "Ah, who is it?"

"Jules? Why do you sound so funny? What's taking you so long?"

"Um, ah, noffing." As soon as I say it, I know I do, in fact, sound strange.

"Jules, open the door. What's going on?" I hear the door handle jiggle, but thankfully, I remembered to lock it.

Starting to panic, I wiggle and writhe, trying desperately to get the strap that's around my neck off so I can loosen whatever fabric has my arms locked together around my ears.

"Julia, open up right now or I will crawl under this door like a six year old." I can tell by her voice that she's serious.

Bending at the waist, I try shimmying my arms free from the dress. Somehow, though, it tightens its grip. With my arms standing straight up behind my back, locked together at the wrists, and bound to my shoulders, I'm really and truly stuck. *Gah!*

Feeling something hit my ankle, I know it's Lanie crawling under the door. *Fucking hell.* Thank God this devil dress covers my face, because I do not want to see her reaction when she stands to help me.

I hear the laughing first, then the telltale shutter of a picture being taken.

"Lanie Heart, don't you dare! Don't you dare take pictures of this clusterfuck you got me into," I all but scream. I know she could barely understand me, though, because I'm still being gagged by the chemical-tasting fabric. I hear her trying really hard to control herself, but snorting instead. Finally, she pulls herself together.

"How in the world …"

"I don't know, okay? Just get me out of this damn thing." I'm louder than I mean to be, but I'm really starting to sweat under here, and the material is cutting off my circulation.

"Okay, okay. Hold still and let me see what the heck you have done to this dress."

"This is stupid. I told you this was stupid. If they don't want me for my brain and my yoga pants at this damn conference, they can go straight to hell—"

Lanie cuts me off, "You know I can't hear or understand a word you're saying. Just calm down and let me figure out where your head should be. Did you … did you put this on upside down?" The laughter in her tone isn't helping my mood.

"For Christ's sake, Lanie! Cut me out of the damned thing and I'll buy it. We can use it as rags."

"I will not cut you out of a dress that costs more than my rent. Just give me a minute and hush up," Lanie tells me, using the voice I imagine she uses with insolent children. "I've almost ... hmmm. Yup, here we go. Arm through here." Her words halt as she pulls my arm through the fabric, turns me around, untangles my neck, and finally lifts the dress free.

"Holy cow, Jules. Look at your bra!"

I'll admit, I love a bra and panty set. I don't spend money on much—I can't, thanks to Erick—but lovely lingerie is a splurge of mine. Glancing down, I see a violet lace bralette and matching panties. Shrugging, I say, "I like beautiful underwear, so sue me. Now get that death trap away from me. Seriously, Lanes, I'm done. No more shopping! Pick out whatever you think I'll need, and I'll buy it. We can figure it out at home." Pointing my finger at the dress in her hand, I snap. "Except that one! Never come near me with that again."

Shaking her head, Lanie turns the dress right-side-out while I pull on my yoga pants and Henley. "You know, Jules, shopping is supposed to be fun."

"It is fun when done from the comfort of my bed, or couch, or anywhere else. Because you know what you can do now? Shop online, Lanie. It's the best thing since sliced bread."

Lanie sighs to display her unhappiness. "Yeah, for a hermit that never wants to leave her house."

I slap her on the ass like football players do. "Damn right, now hurry up. You have ten minutes to pick that shit out, then we're out of here. I'm starving." Exiting the dressing room, I make my way out to the couches that line one wall. Lord knows Lanie will never decide in ten minutes.

While Lanie shops, I pull out my phone and check all of my accounts for the seventh time today. Ever since Erick, it's become a habit I don't intend to break. Thinking of him and

17

my stupidity makes me shiver. *I'll never be taken advantage of again.* It's my cross to bear. I was the idiot. I was the gullible one. I'm the one who thought he actually loved me. *Never again, Jules. Never again.*

Close to an hour later, I'm helping Lanie carry the shopping bags to my car. All of them. "Lanie, I love you, but seriously, this was exce—"

I'm cut off as we step outside because the sky chose that moment to unleash on us. Running through the parking lot, I already know it's impossible to keep up with Lanie and her gazelle-like legs, but I try. I reach into my pocket, pull out the keys to unlock the car for her, and attempt to jump over the last puddle as she had. Something I guess you should know about me; I am a certified klutz.

Landing on the opposite side of the puddle, my foot hits something slick, and before I can think, my feet are in the air. I fall on my back in the pool of rainwater, but hold the bags in the air so I can hopefully return some of it later.

Motherfucker.

"Oh my God, Jules. What in the heck happened? Are you okay?" Concern and mortification are written all over Lanie's beautiful face.

"I'm fine," I snap. "Just take these freaking bags so I can get up."

Lanie, always the sympathetic friend, hurries to my side. Taking the bags in the hand holding an umbrella she found in my car, she pulls me up with her other. "Geez Louise, you're going to have to change. You can't ride all the way home soaking wet." She wrinkles her nose. "Your car will smell like a wet dog by the time we get there."

Grumbling but intentionally biting down on my lips so she can't hear me, I trudge through the murky water and into my car. Once inside, I blast the heat because … remember what I told you about the weather in New England? Yeah, it's now just above freezing.

"Aw, Jules. Here," Lanie says, handing me her sweatshirt. "Let me look through this stuff back here and pull out something you can wear. Do you still want to go to dinner?" The way she asks has me lifting an eyebrow at her. She has something up her sleeve.

"I-I dooo ..." I draw out. "Why are you asking like that?"

A smile too perfect to be real plays across Lanie's lovely face. Clapping her hands like a child, she dives into the back seat. "This will be perfect, Jules. Absolutely perfect."

"Perfect for what, Lanie? What the hell are you talking about?"

"We're going to practice your flirting skills at dinner, and you just bought the perfect outfit for it."

I can only shake my head since I have no clue what's in any of the bags.

"No. Oh, definitely not. Lanie, I'm putting my foot down," I tell her as I slip out of my wet shoes and yoga pants, followed by my favorite Henley. Reaching for her sweatshirt, I pull it over my near-naked self. Luckily, it's dark. I wasn't really paying attention when I started stripping.

Folding her hands in her lap, I can feel her disappointment before she ever speaks. "Jules, it'll be good for you. I promise. Plus, you're starving."

Lanie is the only one who has ever settled me. She places a gentle hand on my arm, and it's all the support I need to calm myself. Taking a deep breath, I turn to look at her.

"Lanes, you know I love you, but I've had my fill today. Tomorrow will be a long day of driving, and I still need to pack. I promise, when we get back to my house, you can give me all the pointers I'll need, but right now, I'm going to drive through Al's French Frys, order us some burgers, and drive us back to Burke Hollow. Okay?" My body deflates as I run out of steam.

Lanie squeezes my arm one more time before wrapping me in a hug. "Of course it is, Jules. You know I'm only pushing because you asked me to, remember? Last week? You begged me not to let you get out of this. You even made me pinky promise, which I did. Plus, it's about time you moved on. You broke up with Erick almost two years ago."

"Right," I grumble. "Two years." And don't I fucking know it. Two-hundred and twenty thousand dollars down, only one-hundred and ninety-four to go.

Leaning back, Lanie gapes at me and laughs. "Are you really going to drive home in my old sweatshirt and nothing else?"

Putting the car in drive, I smile at her before pulling into traffic. "You know I am."

CHAPTER 2

JULIA

"One Night Standards" by Ashely McBryde

I wake to a constant beeping sound, and I know immediately that it isn't coming from my phone. Rolling over, I notice the curtains in my pale-yellow bedroom are drawn wide open. *Lanie.* Turning to my stomach, I pull a pillow over my head. I'm almost back to sleep when the covers get ripped from my body.

"Rise and shine, chica! We have to finish getting you packed up!"

"It's way too early in the morning for that kind of perkiness," I grumble.

"Oh, stop being such a puss. Come on, get up. I've got your coffee ready for you."

Ugh, Lanie knows the way to my heart.

"Okay, fine." Sitting up in my bed, I can barely open my eyes as I'm blinded by the morning sun.

Why the hell does the master bedroom in this house face the rising sun? Someone should be shot for this. Holding my hands out in a gimme-gimme kind of way, I ask her, "Did you sleep here last night? You know you should just move in with me and save money on rent."

Lanie completely ignores me. I've told her this at least a hundred times, but she flat out refuses. She thinks she has to live on her own to prove something; I don't know how to make her understand she can lean on those of us that love her.

"No, I didn't sleep here. You watched me walk out the door. Did you drink more wine after I left?" She smirks, knowing it wouldn't be the first time.

"Fuck no. I was so worn out from our little shopping excursion I took a Xanax and passed out. If you didn't sleep here, then why the hell are you here so early?" I can't help the grumpiness in my voice. Glaring at the clock, I see it's eight-thirty a.m. "Ugh, Lanes. Seriously, I don't even have to leave until one this afternoon."

"I know, but it'll take us a couple of hours to go through these outfits. Unless you want another dressing room fiasco on your hands with no one to rescue you this time?"

"Always a freaking comedian." I throw a pillow at her. "Fine, show me what you think I need."

And she does. For the next hour, Lanie places outfit after outfit in front of me, taking pictures with a Polaroid so I'll know how to put everything together when I'm on my own.

I'm about to pull my hair out when I hear my front door open and slam shut, followed by my new rescuer calling out, "Lanie? Julia? Where the hell you two at?"

Lanie and I make eye contact and start laughing.

"What's GG doing here?" I hiss.

"She brought us breakfast. If we don't hurry, she'll have the entire town out looking for us."

This is not an exaggeration. For someone in her eighties, GG has taken to texting better than most adults. She has the entire town in a group text. She says it's a safety measure, but really, she just figured out gossip can spread faster this way.

Jumping up, we both scatter to the door, tripping over each other as we race down the stairs.

"You two numbnuts had best quit all that ruckus before ya kill ya-selves," GG scolds.

GG is Lanie's grandmother, and I've called her GG since we were kids. When Lanie's aunt died, we were all around two years old, and GG took in her cousin, Lexi. Lanie told me once she thought that was the reason her mother went off the rails. She never really had a normal childhood after that.

"Sorry, GG," Lanie and I say at the same time.

"Oooo, GG, what did you bring me? Did you know your granddaughter has been torturing me with clothing for the last twenty-four hours?"

"Nah, but by the looks of things, ya could probably use some help in that department if ya wanna find a man," GG says flatly.

"No way, GG. I'm not looking for a man, just a man for the night, if you know what I mean." I wait for her eyes to meet mine, then wink.

GG cackles in the way only she can. "Good Lord, you lil' hussy. Good to know someone is getting somethin' these days." She stares unabashedly at Lanie, who holds up her hands in surrender.

"Oh no you don't. You two will not gang up on me. I'm perfectly happy just the way things are. I have no interest in relationships. You both know how that has worked out for my mother."

"That's a bunch of bullshit, Lanie Heart, and you know it," GG admonishes. "You're not and never gonna be your mother." Before Lanie can respond, GG turns her attention back to me. "Now, you," she says, pointing a crooked finger my way. "I know you're gonna get a man's attention, but I've been touchin' with the ladies, and we need to talk about safety before you go bumpin' bones down there in Boston, ya know."

Jesus. GG may text like a pro, but she still can't get the name right. 'Touchin' with the ladies' as she calls it, means she's been texting with the town gossips.

"This cannot be happening, GG!" I yell, knowing full well that she doesn't filter her messages, and that means my mother has been getting updates on my plans for a one-night stand. Groaning, I place my face in my hands. "After everything that went down with Erick, the only thing I want to do is get laid in peace. Is that so much to ask for?"

"Don't you go GG-ing me. I'm all up to date on these one-nighters. That floozy Jillian Carter taught us all about them last night at card group. How it goes is, you don't need no …"

Lanie and I burst out laughing.

"GG! Jillian Carter aside, that's a country song. Listen," Lanie says while pulling up Apple music. "It's called 'One Night Standards' by Ashley McBryde."

"Well, I'll be damned. I wondered why I was singin' it. Must have heard it on the radio. Anyway, it's all settled. We got you some of these." GG throws an entire pack of condoms on my kitchen table, and I about die right there. "We also decided that you'd better get practicing that secret code you girls used to write in so you can email Lanes to get you out of trouble if there are any issues."

Whack. Whack. Whack. "That's my head hitting the kitchen table."

"Well, of course it is. I can see that, you silly child. Now knock that shit off."

GG has never understood when it's my inner dialogue escaping.

"You know, that might not be a terrible idea, Jules," Lanie chimes in. "We could use that old email address you created in college. The one for the fake business."

In college, I created an elaborate rescue plan in case one

of Lanie's dates turned out to be a serial killer. What? It was a totally responsible thing to do. It was better than a fake phone call. We had an entire system worked out. She would text me in full view of the guy if he was a creeper, letting me know she had arrived safely, and that would be my cue to send the work message. A few minutes later, she would get an email that came with alarms and buzzing, alerting her to a work emergency. She would open the message, and he would see the company logo front and center. *I know what you're thinking. A phone call from a sick friend would have been faster, but whatever, this worked for us.*

"Lanie, are you serious? We're adults now; we don't need to be making up bullshit."

"It's this or I'll come with you," GG informs me, knowing full well that would put an end to my one-night stand mission.

"Ugh, fine. Fine! Lanie, do you remember how to decipher the code if I have to write it?" We had also come up with our own secret coding language years before, and I knew tossing that out there would get GG off my back for a while.

"I've got my cheat sheet at home," Lanie says, laughing and bouncing on her toes like a sugared-up toddler.

"Good, I reckon I've done my bit then. You girls get to eatin' before it gets cold." GG stands and gives me a swat to the head—her version of a hug. "Be safe out there, Jules. And, Lanie, I'll expect some touchin' updates."

"Texts," Lanie and I both yell after her.

She merely raises her hand and shuffles out the door.

There's always a sense of what the hell just happened after an encounter with GG, but this one might go down in the record books. Sitting across from Lanie at the table, neither of us moves. We're both a little shell-shocked. Then she grins.

"Back to the one-night stands," she sing-songs. "So, the rules. No actual names. Never leave the bar unless you're one-hundred percent sure you want the guy. Never go back to your own room, and sneak out as soon as you possibly can."

"You know a lot about one-night stands for someone who's never had one," I say skeptically.

"I've been doing my research. If you're hell-bent on having a little fun while you're down there, we'll do it right." Lanie is grinning so broadly now, it makes me nervous. "Let's get moving, it's almost time for you to hit the road."

CHAPTER 3

TREVOR

"The Wolf" by Mumford & Sons

Glaring up one last time at the house that had once been my heaven and my hell, I put the car in reverse and back out. My knuckles are white as I grip the steering wheel, but I just need to get the fuck out of here. The shitstorm in my head is threatening to take over and I can't let it. Not yet. I realize the monster thinks he's won, but I know differently.

"He'll get what's coming to him," Loki says, stirring me from my thoughts. Glancing over, I notice he's already on the phone. "Magnet phi, I need ears on target alpha. We're expediting this package."

Truthfully, I don't really understand what any of that meant, but I know Loki. He's been my friend since middle school. He, Dexter, Preston, and I have been a tight unit ever since. After college, he went to work in intelligence but has never really explained what he does. I'm not sure he can. These days, we just get a text from him saying he's 'going dark' for a while, and he'll be in touch when he can. When we don't hear from him for weeks on end, it's a fucking nightmare. I often wonder if he knows how much we worry about him.

This last time, Loki had been gone for about three months when he showed up on my doorstep.

"Dude! You're back," I say, opening the door and embracing my friend. The worry I'd been carrying around while he was away vanished instantly. "Why didn't you let us know? Should I call Dex? Get him and Pres over here for a beer?"

"It's good to see you, Trev, but I think we'd better talk before we reach out to the guys."

Something in Loki's demeanor tells me I won't like what he has to say, and I'm on edge immediately. Waving him in, I take a deep breath and steel myself for what's to come.

"Trevor?" Loki questions, and I realize I've yet to pull out onto the main road.

Nodding once, I pull into traffic and know that, from this day forward, my only goal in life will be to bring an end to my very own father.

"I'm good," I tell him. "I have to get to Dexter's. I promised to stay with Tate so he could get the papers processed with the attorney. You want to come?"

"Had I known how badly Bitchzilla would fuck our man up, I would have been more of a dick to her from the first time I met her." Loki's voice is full of well-deserved disgust.

Meeting him over the center console for a fist bump, I nod in silent agreement.

"Who the hell can walk away from their kids like that? What's she thinking?"

"I don't know, man." I shake my head, trying to focus on my friend and the nightmare he has brewing now that his soon-to-be ex-wife dropped the bombshell of wanting a divorce, ten-thousand dollars, and no contact with her own kids.

"Dex will be even more messed up because this is what

his mother did to him," Loki says, speaking a truth we know all too well.

The four of us are all close, but Dex and I have been there for each other since we were barely walking. My mother treated him like her own until they took her from us. Now it's Preston's mom who's adopted us all.

"I don't know that he'll ever be the same," I admit. I'm trying not to focus on the hell my own life will be for the foreseeable future, because I can't bring my shit down on Dexter. Not now, not ever. "Loki, I-I want to make sure all this stays as far away from Dex and Preston as possible. Can we do that? Is it even possible to separate my life into fragments like that? To keep them safe?"

"I'll do what I can, you know that. I get that Dex feels like his world is falling apart, but if he had an inkling of what you were about to get yourself in—"

"No, Loki. Fuck!" I yell, cutting him off. I don't mean to lash out at him. I know he's only trying to help. "I'm not bringing this evil down on them. I won't allow the mistakes of my father to hurt anyone else that I love. I couldn't save my mother ... I'll rot in hell before I let him or his goons get their hands on anyone else. That's the end of it, Loki, I mean it. Keep Dexter and Preston out of this. Please," I add more softly.

"He'll be pissed, Trev, and hurt. You know that, right? We could find a way to clue him in, just so you have someone on your side you can talk to. When I go dark, you'll be all alone in this until hell breaks free. Please, just reconsider bringing him or even Preston in."

"No," I say again, more calmly this time. "Thank you for looking out for me, Loki, but I can do this. Once Dex finishes with the divorce attorney, Mrs. Westbrook will come to stay for the week while I'm in Boston. Hopefully, he finds a nanny soon, but Preston's mom will be the perfect distraction for

29

them all. I just want to check in with him and Tate before I head out."

"Okay, let's go. I'd like to see them before I take off, too. But since this will be our last face-to-face before then, let's go over Boston one more time."

Sighing, I finally release the death-like grip I have on the steering wheel. I'm going to this conference in Boston to run tests on Mantra, my software the military just purchased. As a bonus, it also allows me to be *seen* in Boston.

"I'll attend the conference like any other rich fuck but run Mantra in the background. I'll go to all of the cyber-security seminars I can, announcing myself to the industry, and force the Black family to take notice." We've gone over this plan so many times, it makes my eyes burn.

"You must appear to have already made a killing off Mantra," he tells me for the tenth time. "Trevor, this is your shit. This conference is like Disneyland for you, so try not to focus so much on what I'll be doing. Your one and only job is to run the software, schmooze, and take these seminars that give you a semi on any other day. Maybe find a girl to spend some time with or something. Just be sure to project a confident, successful man without a care in the world."

I can't help the laugh that escapes. "Dude, this is a cyber-security in actuarial sciences conference. Do you know what that means? It's a conference for math and science geeks. Do you really think I'll find a woman at this thing who is even remotely capable of keeping my mind off the fact that the actual mob will be following me?"

Laughing, Loki shakes his head, holding his hands up in surrender. "Hey, you never know. Those math geeks can be hot."

If that's true, I've never met one. Being born into money, even if it turned out to be dirty money, gave me some perks. I have the all-American good looks people associate with money. I'm straight out of a J. Crew catalog from the 90s with dirty blond hair and bright caramel eyes. My mom always said they were the color of whiskey and fireflies. Thinking of my mother brings the reality of my life to the forefront again.

"Yeah, I'll pass. I'll be doing my best not to end up at the bottom of the Charles River. Women are not on the agenda." I fear the truth of that statement at my very core.

"Hey, we'll have your back. It'll be a shitty time for you, though. Which is why I wish you would consider telling Dex everything about your dad. You'll need someone you can trust, and more than anything, you'll need a sounding board to keep you sane," Loki says earnestly.

"Thanks, man. I wouldn't be able to get through this without you. However, I will not bring this down on anyone else. I lucked out that you ended up with this assignment, though I'm still not convinced that was a coincidence. This is a job for you, and I'm thankful to have you, but you're trained for this. Dexter? His family? Preston? They're not. I can't bring this to their doorstep, regardless of the fallout it's likely to cause when it's all over." I pull into Dexter's townhouse and turn to my friend. "Thank you, but I hope you understand."

Placing a hand on my shoulder, Loki sighs. "I'd do the same thing. I just want to make sure you fully understand what this will mean for you."

I stare my friend straight in the eyes. "I know. I've gone over every possible angle, left no stone unturned. If there was another way, I would have found it by now. I have no other options."

With one last glance, Loki turns to open his door and I do the same. I have a pit in my stomach as I walk into my friend's home. I take everything in as I make my way through his space. I can't help but wonder if today will be the last time I ever see them.

Behind me, I hear Loki's voice—low and controlled.

"Don't go there, Trevor. It won't do anyone a bit of good. If anything, it'll just take you off your game. Pack it away. I won't let anything happen to you, but you have to be on point." I turn to look at him just as he says, "Trust me on this."

Sucking in a deep breath, I make my way to the kitchen in search of my godson, Tate, Dexter's ridiculously cute four-year-old boy.

"Hey, Dex?" Loki calls out. "Where are you guys?"

"I'll be right down," Dex hollers from the second floor, followed by three enormous trash bags full of shit.

"Whoa, dude, what the hell is all this?"

Dex huffs and tosses another bag over the railing. "Her shit."

Loki and I exchange a worried glance. This is worse than I thought. "Do ... ah, do you need any help?"

"Nope." *Thud.* "This is the last bag," he informs us as he tosses another one that lands with a crash. Whatever was in there wasn't clothing.

Scratching his head, Loki stares from the bags to Dexter and back again. "Okay, dude. Where are they going? Your car or the driveway?"

"Car," Dex says, walking down the stairs, adjusting his tie as two little arms hold his neck in a choke hold. "I don't want her anywhere near the house."

In silent understanding, I walk toward him and talk to his back. "Where is my main man Tate? I was hoping he would help me find your secret stash of cookies in the kitchen, but I can't find him."

Soft little giggles erupt, and I see Tate's head jump up from his hiding place buried in between Dexter's shoulders.

"Hey, man, you scared the June bugs out of me. You ready to find some cookies?"

Just then, the door opens, and Preston walks in, followed by his familial entourage. "I want some cookies," he tells

Tate just before we lose him to Dexter's shoulder blades again.

Fucking Preston.

"Great timing," I grumble as he and his four brothers enter the crowded foyer. "I thought you were all coming over with Sylvie later?"

"We were, but Halt and Colton were wrestling and broke her newest favorite vase, so she kicked us all out. She'll meet us here in a couple of hours," Preston's youngest brother, Ashton, tells us.

"Don't you guys ever grow up? How on earth she made it this long with all you animals is beyond me."

Preston howls at the ceiling. "You guys are part of the pack, too, don't forget that. Sylvie has eight boys as far as she's concerned, so welcome to the chaos. And you'd better shave that scruff off before she gets here or you'll never hear the end of it, you cheap fuc—"

"Preston!" Dexter and I scramble to interrupt the F-bomb he was about to drop in front of Tate. "Come on, Pres, language. When are you going to remember that?"

Preston ruffles Tate's hair as Easton, yet another Westbrook brother, grabs Tate and hauls him onto his shoulders. "Sorry, little dude. I'll do better."

At least he sounds sincere.

Absentmindedly rubbing my hand over my unshaven face, I wait for Dexter before picking up a bag and carrying it out to the garage.

"I have an extra razor in the master bathroom," he tells me, and I laugh. He knows I don't want to disappoint Sylvie —neither of us do. She's been a mom to us both for years now. "Hey, Trevor?" he asks when I turn to grab another bag from the house.

"What's up? You okay?" I ask, realizing for the first time just how terrible Dexter looks. Usually considered one of the more handsome among our group, he has big, black circles under his eyes and his skin seems sallow. My body tenses as I wait for his answer. Dexter and I are always there for each other. My stomach turns at the thought of not being able to help him when he needs it most.

He leans against his car and hangs his head. "Tate stopped talking, almost completely. The twins will be here before you know it, and I can't even handle one kid. How am I going to take care of three?"

"What do you mean he isn't talking? Have you gone to the doctor?" I already know he has them on speed dial.

"Yes, the pediatrician said it's his coping mechanism with all that's going on. I mean, what the fuck, Trevor? How could she leave Tate the way she did? Not to mention that she's pregnant with twins. My twins, my daughters, and she wants nothing to do with them as soon as they're born. This is the bullshit he has to deal with now. I'm failing him, Trevor. I don't know what to do." The pain he's feeling makes his voice raw with emotion.

Moving to stand next to him, I weigh my words. Do I promise him I'll always be there for him and these kids I already love so much, even though there's a genuine possibility I'll never return home? Or do I appease him, this friend that's been my brother for over twenty years? Do I do that to him?

His wife ripped the rug out from under him, leaving him to pick up the pieces alone. In some ways, I guess my father has done the same to me. It's this realization that spurs me into action. I know at this moment I'll never let Dexter, Loki, or the Westbrooks down. They're my family, not the asshole who shared my DNA. I'll do whatever it takes to keep us whole.

"You keep living, Dex. You keep giving him and showing him a happy, healthy home life. Love him when he needs it, hug him often, and never give up on him. We're not giving up on any of you. We're your strength when you need it, and together, we will get through this."

When Dex raises his head, his signature smirk is in place. "When did you turn into a Yoda-loving hippie?"

"Fuck you." I laugh with him, but that was some serious self-reflection, even if I can't admit it to him.

"You ready for Boston?" he asks. "Your app will kill it, man. You have nothing to be nervous about."

He mistakes my guilt for fear. I had to tell him I was going to sell an app, not some secret cyber-security software the military has already retained. I've never lied to him before, and I hate that I'm doing it now. I have to remember it's for his own safety, though.

"Thanks, Dex. I'm sorry I have to leave in the middle of this."

Dex sighs, and I can feel exhaustion rolling off him in waves. "After today, it'll all be over. I probably won't even have to see her at the birth of the girls. She has it all planned out. They'll take the girls straight from labor and delivery to me in the maternity ward."

"I'll only be gone a week, Dex. When I get back, I'm here for you. Whatever you need." For the first time in months, those words don't feel like a lie.

Leaning in for a one-armed man hug, Dex chokes out, "You'll kill it up in Boston, I know it. You deserve this. Don't worry about me, I'll figure it out."

With a lump in my throat, I force the words to come. "I'll see you next week?"

"Next week! Pizza movie night with Tate on Friday. We're getting them in before the girls arrive, so stop by when you get home."

Saying nothing, I nod and head outside to my car. *Here goes everything.*

CHAPTER 4

JULIA

"Bluebird" by Miranda Lambert

*D*riving in Boston is like sitting with your grandfather after a baked bean eating contest. You know he's going to blow, you just don't know exactly when. Five hours, four middle fingers, three wrong turns, two wrong-way signs, and one speeding ticket later, I finally pull up in front of the Four Seasons in Boston's Back Bay. *Watch out, world, I'm going to blow.*

After putting the car in park, I search everywhere for the valet. "Where the hell is this guy?"

As I'm packing up my crap that got thrown all over the car when Mr. Policeman pulled me over, "Girls Just Wanna Have Fun" starts blaring through the car speakers, sending all my shit flying again.

I press the button on the steering wheel. "Hi, Lanes," I sigh. "I'm here. I just pulled up to the valet but I'm waiting for someone to come get the keys."

"Eesh, that was a long ride. You doing okay?" The thing about Lanie is she's always looking out for me. It makes me smile even when I'm ready to scream.

"Yeah, Lanes, I'm fine. Oh, let me call you right back. The valet is here."

"Sounds good. Luvs." She hangs up before I can respond.

I grab the rest of my crap, step out of the car, and tell the valet the keys are in the ignition. After making my way around to the passenger side, I remove my suitcase, my garment bag—*Thanks a lot, Lanie*—and my work bag. It's a lot of stuff, and I'm trying to maneuver it all and give the valet a tip when the guy shuts the door in my face.

"What the hell?" I screech, stepping back and tripping over my giant suitcase in the process. Before I know what's happening, I'm sailing through the air, preparing my ass for the hard landing it's about to receive when two powerful hands grab my waist and haul me back to standing. My hair is wild, a mass of nests I didn't bother taming today, so I can't immediately see anything. Finally, collecting my wits and swatting at the hair in my face, I slowly turn in a circle, trying to find my hero. All I see is the retreating form of a rather expensive suit and a very nice ass.

"Great. Just freaking great," I say, stomping my foot like a child. "Stinking rude ass people. First, the valet knocks me on my butt, not to mention the assholes giving me the finger for the last hour. News flash, I'm not the awful driver here! Then, someone rescues me and doesn't even bother waiting so I can thank him." *Ugh ... inner monologue, Julia! Inner monologue is supposed to remain inside.*

I take out my AirPods and stick them in my ears even though they died on the drive down here. At least I'll be able to get through the lobby without people thinking I'm talking to myself. *So what if I am? They don't need to know that.*

"Oh my God, I cannot believe I have to be here and present in front of a bunch of entitled assholes. They probably won't even be able to comprehend what it is I'm showing them. The last time I did this, I spent the final two hours of the presentation explaining what my job even was.

Forget about the software they had no chance of understanding."

"Hi, checking in. Julia McDowell," I say, handing over my license and credit card, and holding onto my AirPods to let the girl know I'm on the phone ... or pretending to be anyway. My rambling only gets worse as more and more people close in around me, waiting to check-in.

"This was a colossal mistake. I hate crowds. Why the hell couldn't I have caught whooping cough or something? Whooping cough is still a thing, right?"

The poor girl behind the counter shrugs like one would when encountering a crazy person. "Ah, not sure, miss. You're on floor thirty-two. I've written your room number right here along with the Wi-Fi password. If you need anything at all, just call the front desk and someone will be happy to assist you."

"Thanks," I mumble and follow her directions to the elevator. "Please don't let some pregnant lady get on the elevator with me. Or a really, really old person. Maybe just let me have the elevator to myself? That would be best. Ugh, I already want to go home. Who even likes going to these things, anyway? Not me, I can tell you that. I'd much rather be home in my bed. Oh, and this one-night stand business is just out of control. My poor mother must be having a heart attack. Fucking GG and her touchin' with the ladies. Jesus."

I feel someone come up behind me at some point in my latest rant, so I bite my lip until I taste copper and stare at my phone, willing my craziness to stop for just five minutes so I can get to my room without further incident. *Lanes!* Quickly pressing the FaceTime button, I call Lanie back.

"Hey, girl. How's it going?" For such an awful upbringing, Lanie sure as shit has a sunny disposition most of the time.

"This is the worst," I tell her. Most girls would get whiny, I get bitchy. "Why do they insist I present at these things?

Every single person in my company has witnessed one of my epic meltdowns. Why do they keep doing this to me?"

"Jules, you know why. You're the smartest person I know. If they say they need you, it's because no one else understands what the heck is going on." She laughs.

Hearing the ding of the elevator, I stick my phone into my bra-strap and attempt to shuffle my bags onto the elevator.

"Ooh, I love the lacy pink bra, lady! This one is sexy as heck! You'll totally be able to have a one-night stand wearing this stuff," Lanie exclaims as I pull the phone back out of its confinement.

Laughter escapes unbidden. "I can't do this ... I can't have a one-night stand. I have been muttering nonstop to myself, pretending to be on the phone since I walked into this hotel. Now I have to figure out how to match these outfits for a dinner I don't even want to go to. I'll be a walking boner-killer."

"Ah," Lanie starts and stops multiple times, so I hold the screen right up to my nose to scrutinize her. She never fumbles with her words.

"What's going on?" I demand. "Why are you stuttering? Do I have boogers on my face? It wouldn't surprise me. I got so many middle fingers waved at me for no reason. I even snorted, laughing at two of them. Don't do that, by the way, they get even more pissed, especially when you're in stop and go traffic."

"Ah, hun. You do realize you're not alone in that elevator, right?" Lanie whisper-yells and points to my right.

"Oh, fuck."

"And he looks really hot ... well, the quarter-inch I can see on my phone," she whisper-yells again.

My cellmate, who has obviously been watching on in horror, lets out a bark of laughter that echoes through the small, enclosed space, causing me to jump and nearly fall again. A steady hand wraps around my bicep, righting me, and I know for a fact that he's the one who kept me from falling earlier.

"Fuck me," I say to the ceiling with my eyes closed.

Ding.

The elevator doors gracefully slide open, and I shove, kick, and push my crap through them. I refuse to even look at the elevator man. I mumble a thank you and push forward into the hallway as quickly as my short, little legs will allow. This causes him to laugh again, and I shiver at the velvety rich sound.

"You're welcome. And, for what it's worth, this is the last place I want to be, too," he says as the doors close behind me.

"Holy hell. Lanie, are you still there?" I yell into my bra strap, where she's face planted once again via my phone.

"Geez, Jules. That guy was so stinking hot, I wish I could have seen his entire face and not just a portion of his profile. Please tell me he was as hot as he sounded?" Lanie pleads.

"What? You think I looked at him after that? Are you out of your goddamned mind? Lanie, he heard my entire spiel, probably from the time I checked in. Who knows what the hell I said? I was seriously on a roll. Like graduation day, pre-speech roll. I can't be held accountable for the shit that just flew out of my mouth. Hell to the no did I look at him."

Silence.

I push the key into the door of my hotel room and shove everything, myself included, inside. Immediately, I flop down on the bed and grab my phone. Lanie is sitting there staring at me blankly.

"What?" I ask tentatively, not at all liking where I think this conversation is going.

"You're scared to have a one-night stand, aren't you?" Lanie asks with a giant smile on her face. "This isn't just about the conference or having to speak, you're nervous about having to entertain a gentleman friend all on your own."

"Entertain a gentleman friend? Lanie, who are you, GG?" I spit, knowing there may be some truth to her statement. Sighing, I eventually admit defeat. "Okay, maybe a little. I've always had you as my wing-man, and let's face it, when you're around, there's no shortage of male attention."

"Julia McDowell," Lanie says in her best teacher's voice. "You're a beautiful, smart, amazing woman, and you will go down there and own that conference. Don't worry about what anyone thinks about you, okay? Honestly, Jules. You're the most amazing person I know, and if someone doesn't see that, they don't deserve you, anyway."

"Thanks, Lanes."

"I know we were putting a lot of pressure onto this one-night stand business, but it was mostly just for fun. Just go down there with no expectations and have a drink or two. Get yourself ready for your first presentation tomorrow. You'll do great, I know it," Lanie soothes.

"You're right. I'll be better off if I stop worrying about a hook-up. Maybe it's time to order a new vibrator. It'll definitely cause me less anxiety than this … even if Al at the post office tells GG that I got a naughty toy again," I say, laughing.

"Oh my gosh, Jules. Only in this town would you getting a vibrator make front-page news." We're both laughing so hard now, we're nearly in tears.

Looking up, I realize it's getting late. "I should go get ready. The cocktail welcome party starts in forty-five minutes, and if I get stuck in a damn dress again, I'll need time to call someone." This has her laughing all over again.

"Okay, Jules. But, hey? If you do have hot, wild monkey sex, I want to hear all about it immediately. Luvs." She hangs up quickly, so I can't argue.

"Luvs," I reply to an empty room. "Fuck, she better not have stuck that death trap of a dress in my suitcase."

Opening my laptop, I want to scan my accounting software before I leave to make sure there have been no new accounts opened in my name. I've become somewhat obsessive about it, I know, but when the man you love up and leaves with one hundred thousand in cash from your savings, only to find out he's been opening cards and lines of credit in your name for almost six months, it tends to make you a little paranoid.

Glancing around while my computer boots up, I take in my surroundings and am glad I'm not paying for this room. Everything about it screams money. "You're at the Four Seasons, moron. Of course, everything is expensive here," I snort.

Satisfied that nothing seems amiss, I go about unpacking all the outfits Lanie had me buy and hope like hell I can find something to wear that won't try to kill me.

CHAPTER 5

TREVOR

"Catch" by Brett Young

*L*eaning against the wall of the elevator, I let the doors close even though this was my floor, too. That crazy woman was the same one I kept from falling beside her car. The thought makes me smile. She had no idea I was behind her this entire time, and the diatribe that flew from her mouth was entrancing. I had to bite my lip to keep from laughing more than once. The best part is, she wasn't even talking to someone for half of it. That bit of comic relief, I realize, is just what I needed to start this week off. I told her I didn't want to be here either, but she doesn't know the half of it.

I ride down to the lobby, then back up to our floor. *Our floor?* The thought causes me to misstep, but unlike my little pixie friend, I catch myself. I stare at each door as I pass, wondering what room the fiery, little angel is in. *What the fuck? Pixie? Angel?* Those are not words in my vocabulary and have me seriously regretting not taking Loki's advice to talk with Dex before I left.

My room is at the end of the hall—one of the two suites on this floor. Holding my phone up to the keypad of room 3206, I hear the slight clicking sound and push the door open. I don't have much time before my reservation in the hotel bar, so I quickly unpack and change. I would have liked a shower, but there's no time.

Remembering what Loki told me, I take my phone from my pocket and start the app. Setting it in the safe, I grab the one left there by his team and feel the sweat trickle down my spine. I'm not a wuss by nature, but when you're trying to take down the mob and the monster who killed your mother, all bets are off.

Taking a deep breath and physically shaking out my arms, I crack my neck from left to right and move once again toward the elevator. I can't help it. As I walk through the hallway, I listen for her voice. *Perhaps I will find a distraction here, after all.*

Entering the hotel bar, I head to the table in the corner. It's a rounded booth that faces the lobby of the hotel. Sitting in the middle of it allows me to see everyone that comes and goes. The large, potted tree to my right also helps keep me concealed. I notice I have an unobstructed view of the elevator, so I watch that spot more than anything else.

"Welcome, sir. My name is Anthony, and I'll be taking care of you this evening. Will you be joining us for dinner or just drinks?" the waiter standing in front of me asks. I'm about to answer him when something catches my attention, and I wave him aside.

"Just a Macallan, neat, for now, please," I tell him, my attention on the elevator and the tiny, little package that just exited.

Until now, I hadn't fully seen her face. She was always a mass of wild hair and sweatpants four sizes too big. But there's no doubt in my mind the woman who just stepped off the elevator is my angel, and I'm hypnotized. Gone are the sweatpants and long-sleeved Henley. Now she's wearing a form-fitting, navy dress that hits just below mid-thigh. I can tell from here that she hates it. Watching her tug at the hem, stomp her foot, then stare at the ceiling, I grin.

Angel steps to the side of the elevator, seemingly to plot her next move, and I lean back in my booth to observe her. She's mesmerizing in the strangest of ways, but she's gorgeous. Her green eyes sparkle even from twenty yards away, and her chocolate brown hair falls around her shoulders in waves. She's holding her bottom lip between her thumb and forefinger, but even from here, I can see her lips moving. She's spewing something that I desperately wish I could hear. As she takes a step forward, I lean in, hoping I'll get a full view of her in that dress, utterly aware of my stalker-ish tendencies here.

She takes a step forward, then two back. It's a dance all of her own. I feel a need to put her out of her misery. I'm about to go talk to her when the girl jumps a mile, bobbling the phone in her hands. The scowl followed by relief that washes over her face has me in a trance. She darts left, then right, and now she's heading straight toward me, stopping on the other side of the potted tree I'm hiding behind. She's positioned herself so far into it that anyone passing by would be hard-pressed to even see her. What she doesn't realize is she's backed herself up so far, I could reach out and touch her from my booth. *God, her ass looks fantastic.*

"I can't do this," she hisses into her phone. "Seriously. I think I should just go back to my room, order room service, and watch Netflix."

Oh no. She isn't getting away that easily.

"I don't think one-night stands work like that," she tells her partner in crime. I wish I could hear the other side of that conversation.

"One drink. You hear me? I will order one drink and then I'm going to my room. I don't even want to go to this thing."

Funny, I notice she doesn't ramble nearly as much when she's actually talking to someone. I see her jam her phone back into the little clutch she's carrying, then tug on her dress again.

"Come on, you pussy. You can do this. Who cares if you're standing in a bush outside of your hotel bar talking to yourself? You don't know anyone here, and it's only a week." She exhales. "What were you thinking, you dumbass? You're not someone who has a one-night stand. No one sticks around once you start babbling anyway," she murmurs.

Angel snorts and starts laughing at herself. She's back to mumbling, and even though she's this close, I can't make out the last words.

Angling my face toward her, I keep my voice low. "I'm listening, and I'm not leaving anytime soon."

"Ah-kkkk," is the only way to describe the sound that comes out of her. My angel has once again tried to jump out of her skin. This time, her clutch gets hooked to a branch of the tree she's hiding in. She then proceeds to wrestle with it.

"Motherfucker, what the hell?" she screeches. "What the hell?"

Angel has a mouth on her. Oddly, I like it. With her arms and legs flailing wildly, I realize we're drawing a crowd, so I move swiftly to her side.

Placing my hand on the small of her back, I lean in. "Shh, Angel. Let me help." Her entire body goes rigid, and I don't know if I should expect a slap to the face or not. Peering around her body so I can see her face, I have to stifle a laugh. Her eyes have gone cartoonishly large and unblinking.

The second I remove my hand, she talks again, but not to me.

"Oh my God. Seriously, how is this happening again? What the fuck is wrong with me? I told her. I told her I shouldn't have come down here. Now I'm stuck in a goddamn tree with Mister Sexy trying to free me. It wasn't bad enough he had to save me from the valet, then listen to my rambling in the elevator. Now he's here to get me out of a tree, too? Ugh. Is he a fireman? Or just an unlucky bastard who's on my schedule? Why, oh, why do I do this shit?" she asks, followed by a muffled, "Geez, please stop talking. Just shut up."

I still don't think she's blinked, and I'm not entirely sure if I'm supposed to answer her, so I compromise. "Just hold on one more second, I've almost got you out of this thing."

"Muphhed-er-gabbled."

Startled, I take a step back, worried she's having a seizure. Looking her over, I realize she's fine, but she has her lips pierced between her thumb and forefinger, forcing herself not to speak. Hence the mumbled sounds from a moment ago. Cocking my head to the side, I watch her.

"Blink, Angel. Breathe," I coo.

In slow motion, she comes back to life, and her mouth takes no time playing catch up.

"Are you a guardian angel? No, a fireman? Unlucky bastard? Why did you call me Angel?" she asks in rapid succession.

I try to answer, but she's not done.

"Just my luck. The one time I let her dress me up, and I literally stumble into Mr. Sex God himself, multiple times, and I'm running my mouth like a lunatic. Oh, hey, yup, that's me, just call me Loony. Good Lord, I need a freaking drink. Okay, well, thank you again for saving me. Again. I said that, didn't I? Well, I mean it. Who knows how long I would have hidden out in there until I could free myself. Sadly, I can't even say that's the first time it's happened. Just before I came here, I got stuck in a dress in a department store, and my best friend had to slide under the stall door to get me out. I'm really a mess. Anyway, gotta go."

I watch in amusement as she attempts to side-step me. I

move in tandem with her, then take her hand in mine. A gesture that's so foreign, I pause to stare at the connection.

"Ah, I was just kidding about being a lunatic. If you're planning to turn me in, it's okay. The front desk has already been witness to my kind of crazy," she says, rolling her eyes but slightly less manic.

I glance at her over my shoulder. "I'm not turning you in, Angel."

"Well, I'm also not a missing child. I mean, I know I look like I could be a child, but I'm an adult many birthdays over. I'm actually here for the conference, so you don't have to go searching for some frantic parents missing a teenager."

This makes me stop completely. "Has that happened to you before?" Something about the way she said it makes me think it has, and I'm biting my tongue to keep from laughing.

"Ugh, you don't even want to know how many times. So, why are you holding my hand then? And why do you keep calling me Angel? Oh my God, are you meeting an escort here? It's not me … I mean, I'm not a hooker," she rambles, shaking free from my grasp.

I've been very patient, but I can't let her leave thinking I'm picking up a prostitute. Placing both hands on my hips, I lower my face to just inches from hers. "I am not, nor have I ever, ordered a hooker. You said you needed a drink," turning her to face my table, I say, "that's my table right there. Let's get you a drink."

Angel nods, but says nothing at first.

"Hmm, I do need a drink. This has been a clusterfuck of a day, but I don't remember telling you I needed a drink. Maybe you're the crazy one?" As she speaks, I can literally see the wheels begin to turn.

I think she's about to get on another roll, so I place my hand on the small of her back and gently guide her toward the table, but she stops abruptly.

"How do you do that?"

I stop again to stare at her because I'm not sure if she's talking to herself or me, but after a minute of silence, I realize she's allowing me to speak. The thought puts a genuine smile on my face.

"Do what, Angel?" I ask softly.

"Calm my thoughts," she replies, looking confused. "Only my best friend has ever done that." She seems upset by the knowledge.

"What do you mean? How am I calming your thoughts?" It's embarrassing how badly I want to know.

"Ah, nothing. Never mind. Let's get a drink, shall we? I really need to get to bed before I make another spectacle. I hate ordering drinks at places like this, though. They always have stupid names. Why can't they just say what's in the drink instead of a copper-headed turtle or whatever the hell it is that they call them?"

Holy shit, this girl's mind really does work a million miles a minute. With no filter, it's fascinating to watch. Taking her hand in mine again, she slows.

"I really only drink vodka sodas or Mules these days. Sometimes wine, but usually only red and only in the winter."

It only takes a few steps to reach the table, and I hate letting go of her hand, but I realize it's highly inappropriate since I don't even know her name. Not to mention physically impossible to slide into the rounded booth holding hands.

Settling into the high-backed booth, she starts again. "You know, you should probably just cut your losses. Most people can't handle me for lengthy periods of time. Well, except my best friend, but in all honesty, she has a way of getting me to shut up. Something about her presence. She just places a hand on my arm, and suddenly, I can control the chaos going on up here," she says, pointing to her head.

I stare at her, raising my hand at the same time to signal

the server who scurries to my side. One benefit of having money, I guess. "A vodka soda, please. Tito's, if you have it."

"Yes, sir. Anything else? Appetizer, perhaps?" He sure does work the upsell like a pro.

"Not right now. Thank you," I tell him, but continue to stare at my angel.

He takes the hint and backs away.

Placing my arm along the back of the velvet-covered booth, I lean into the cushions, never taking my eyes off of her. I know it's coming; I want to see how long she can go without combusting. Within thirty seconds, her lip is back in her fingers, and she is mumbling intelligibly. Leaning into her personal space, I take her hand away from those gorgeous lips.

"Don't bottle up the chaos, Angel. I want to hear it." It comes out as a growl, and her eyes go wide again.

"What are you, a sadist?" Her response flies from her painted pink lips, causing a bark of laughter to erupt from deep within me.

"No, Angel. No sadist here, I just don't want to miss a second of what's going on in that sexy little head of yours." I end with a wink and love the slight blush that plays across her cheeks.

When is the last time I flirted like this?

There's a reason, Trevor. You're dangerous, don't get caught up in attraction. This is not the life you get to lead.

My conscience is loud tonight.

Letting go of her hand, I lean back into my own space, and she immediately starts again.

"Why do you keep calling me Angel? No, wait, you shouldn't answer that. The one-night stand rules say no telling your actual name. So, you call me Angel, and I'll call you …" She pauses, thinking, then claps her hands together, bouncing in her seat like the child she said she wasn't. "Got it, I'll call you Charlie." She sits back in her chair with a smile that could melt glaciers.

"Charlie," I say, then it hits me. "Charlie's Angels."

"You got it!" She beams.

"I do." Leaning over the table, I watch as her eyes darken. "My angel."

CHAPTER 6

JULIA

"It Won't Kill Ya" by The Chainsmokers

J'm biting the inside of my cheek so hard I taste blood. *Jesus, Jules. Do not speak. Do not do it.*

Before I can embarrass myself further, the waiter interrupts us with our drinks. Reaching for mine quickly, I mumble, "Thanks," then inhale half of it. Lifting my gaze over my glass, I find Charlie watching me with a raised brow.

Feeling slightly defensive, I sense the chaos turning in my head. "What? I needed this," I say a little too loudly. "I needed that. I …" *Oh shit, here it comes.* "I hate these things, you know? I mean, really? For once they couldn't find someone else to speak at a convention? My giant freaking brain." I shift in my seat, hoping and praying my mouth will shut up. "Plus, I have to wear these stupid suits when I'm much happier in my leggings and sweatshirts. These shoes I'm wearing? They are *the* worst. Seriously, it's like someone has my toes in a Chinese pincher. Do you know what those are? I got one once at the fair when I was a kid. It was the cheapest piece of crap, but I loved it because I knew the secret right away. Then there's actually being back in Boston— gah, what are you doing?"

In one fell swoop, Charlie has grabbed my hand and slid me closer to him. "I think you said I calmed your thoughts. And I believe it happens when I touch you," he says, reaching for my foot. Removing my shoe, he places it in his lap.

My mouth opens and closes multiple times like a fish.

Chuckling, Charlie says, "Blink, Angel. Breathe."

"Easy for you to say. You don't have your feet in the lap of a sex god," I grumble. Realizing what I just said, I sit up, trying desperately to pull my feet away.

Charlie tightens his grasp. "Let's talk, Angel. Just talk. Your feet are hurting, and while feet are usually the last thing I find sexy, I'm very excited to be holding yours. If this calms your chaos, let it be, and let's talk." The timbre of his voice has already relaxed me. It's deep and smooth with a hint of a southern accent.

I snort, because, well, I'm me. "Have you not heard me talk enough in your few brief encounters with me? Most people are trying to shut me up by now." That's it. I don't continue about how people usually find me weird or how my ex would get embarrassed going out with me. I just stop talking like I do when Lanie's next to me.

Judging by the expression on Charlie's face, he expects me to continue as well. Thankfully, our waiter has impeccable timing and shows up with another round of drinks I hadn't seen anyone order. I'm not a big drinker, mainly because I'm not a big person, but I'm liking this insane interaction I'm having with my handsome stranger, so I take another sip.

After the waiter leaves with our empty glasses, Charlie turns his focus back on me. "No."

"No? What are you talking about?" I ask him, confused.

"No, I have not had enough of hearing you speak." He looks me up and down, and I swear my panties melt right off.

"Or watching you fidget. Or feeling the energy you bring to the room. So, tell me, Angel, why is it you're so set on having a one-night stand?"

I'm mid-swallow, and before I can catch myself, my drink sprays from my mouth across the table and lands all over his beautiful face. "Oh my God, I'm so sorry," I say, reaching for napkins on the other side of the table. I'm spiraling, and somehow, he knows it, because he squeezes my right foot.

"Relax." It's a one-word command, and I respond hypnotically. Laughing again, this time definitely at me and not with me, Charlie grabs a handkerchief from his suit pocket and wipes his face. "That's one way to swap spit, Angel."

Burying my face in my hands, I shake my head. "Listen, you have been so lovely to me, but I'm entirely socially inept." I reach for my clutch and try to grab a twenty, but Charlie lays a hand across mine.

"Angel?" he asks so softly I'm compelled to look at him. "Do you want to leave? Or are you leaving because you're embarrassed?"

"Both. This is not my scene," I tell him honestly. "I'm here because I have to be for work, but normally, I'd be at home on the couch with my best friend watching a Hallmark movie or something." *Again, no rambling.* "To be one-hundred percent honest, I'm also a little thrown. For whatever reason, I'm not babbling, and generally, that only happens two other ways. Either my best friend is with me, or I'm at work talking about numbers and security threats."

"Hmm, so what you're saying is I have the magic touch." I don't miss the hint of naughtiness in his voice.

"I can only imagine what kind of touch you have, Charlie, but I should go."

He removes his hands from my feet, and his voice stills me when he says, "I'd like you to stay."

Immediately, I miss his powerful hands. "You're really a glutton for punishment, aren't you?" I eye him, trying to figure out the game he's playing, but I'm at a loss. Sighing, I give in. "Okay, let's talk."

Resting his hand back on top of my feet, he observes me.

"What?" I self-consciously smooth my hair with my fingers while I wait for his response.

"I have so many questions for you, Angel. I don't know where to begin." I see the truth of his statement reflected in his whiskey-colored eyes.

"Okay, well, start wherever you want. Just remember the rules. No proper names and nothing too personal." I'm actually proud of my sudden ability to speak like an adult. The day I walked out of the courtroom with a half-million-dollar debt, I decided I would have no relationships of any kind until I have cleared my name and my credit. That means Charlie, too.

"Ah, yes. The rules. Let's go back to that. No drinks this time." He has the audacity to smirk. "Why the one-night stand mission?"

Staring at the ceiling, I debate how honest I should be. Since he doesn't even know my name, and I'll never see him again, I figure telling him bits of the truth couldn't hurt.

"Where I come from, there aren't a lot of options for dating, unless you want to date your third cousin once removed or your best friend's ex. Everyone there has known me since I was a kid, and you probably can't tell, but I'm not really everyone's cup of tea. Most people tune out after the first ten minutes with me, and well, I was horny as hell. So, I told my best friend La— ah, my best friend, that I would have a one-night stand while I was here. I mean, guys do it all the time, right? Plus, I haven't had the best of luck in the relationship department. I think I'm better off not expecting anything from anyone."

Wow, that was more honest than I intended.

"Sure, some guys, I suppose." His words cover me like a weighted blanket, and he never takes his eyes off of me. I can tell he's debating asking about the relationship part of my spiel, but he plays nice and follows my rules instead. "Tell me about this friend who has dressed you up in the devil's clothes that can also calm your chaos?"

Smiling, I relax into the cushions, thankful that we won't be talking about my one-night stand escapades any further. "That's easy. She's been my best friend since we were kids. She once gave a girl a swirly for spreading lies about me to the basketball team. That's just her, though. She never let anyone mess with me. I've always been the odd man out, but she never once made me feel that way, even though she could have easily dumped me for the cool crowd as we got older. She's my family."

Charlie seems to be lost in thought, but he's smiling, and for once, I don't feel the need to fill the silence with chatter.

Never taking his eyes off of mine, he takes a deep gulp of his drink. "My family is chosen, too," he says cryptically, but since he agreed to my rules, I don't push for more information.

"Why don't you want to be here?" I blurt.

I watch as a lazy smirk covers his handsome face. "There isn't anywhere I'd rather be than right here, with you, Angel."

"But it was you on the elevator, r-right? You told me you didn't want to be here either. How come?" I watch as something dark crosses his face and I feel myself recoil. "There's an energy around him I can't figure out. I don't feel like he's dangerous, but there's a darkness, a sadness to him."

He shifts, visibly uncomfortable, and I wonder what's bothering him.

"You truly have no filter when you're uncomfortable, do you?" he asks, making me scrunch my nose in confusion. "You just told me I'm not dangerous, but there's a darkness to me." As he says it, I realize he's more sad than dark.

Pinching the inside of my thigh, I attempt to have some self-control, and fail miserably. "Do you? Have a darkness?"

He squeezes my inner ankle, shaking his head. "Not by nature, no."

Again with the cryptic talk.

"I thought we were playing by some rules here tonight, Angel? Have you forgotten so easily?" He's trying to ease the tension that settled around our table, and I appreciate it.

"Ah, the one-night standards you mean. It's a song, you know?"

"Angel, I'm a southern boy. Don't let this forced boarding school vocal training fool you. I'm a country boy through and through. If I didn't know an Ashely McBryde song, I'd have to turn in my southerner card." He winks. Again.

Who freaking winks this much, and why does my tummy turn to lava when he does?

Just like that, he has me relaxing into the booth cushions again.

"You never answered me. Why don't you want to be here?" I ask again.

"Well, at first I didn't want to be here because it's work and not the kind of work I'd like to be doing. But now, my opinion has changed because there's an entirely new reason to love coming to work this week." He signals the waiter.

"What can I get you, sir?"

"Could I have some bottles of water and a charcuterie board? I'll also have another Macallan. Angel?" He directs the waiter to me.

"Oh, no, I'm all set, but thank you. Another drink and I'll be on the bar dancing like a freshman in college." I slap a hand over my mouth because even I know I just said that out loud.

Blushing, the waiter quickly retreats, and Charlie falls victim to a full-on belly laugh.

When he's able to compose himself, he wipes a tear from his eye and puts his full attention on me. "As much as I would love to see you dancing on the bar top, your dress is far too short, and I'm too much of a selfish asshole to let that happen. If anyone sees those lacy pink panties your friend mentioned earlier, I want it to be me," he growls.

In an instant, the mood has shifted again.

"Actually, because of this damn dress, I wasn't able to wear any panties." I shrug as if it's no big deal that I just told a virtual stranger I'm going commando.

Charlie moves so fast I don't even have time to squeal. He's pulled me even closer, so now I'm sitting right up against his side. My feet that were in his lap now dangle between his legs. My dress has ridden up on my slide across the bench and he notices. Gently grabbing the hem, he attempts to pull it down. Not too much, but enough that I'm not giving any X-rated shows.

My breathing is rapid. The chaos is coming.

Placing a hand on my thigh, Charlie whispers into my ear, "Calm down, Angel. Relax."

"Shockingly, I do."

"I know," he says, chuckling.

Motherfucking inner dialogue.

His arm that was resting on the back of the booth wraps securely around my shoulders. From this angle, I have no option but to lean into him as they deliver the charcuterie board.

"Tell me, Angel, what does your one-night stand look like?"

"Wh-What do you mean?"

"I mean, tell me how you envision your first one-night stand to go?" His voice causes a shiver to run through my body.

A nervous giggle escapes me. "Oh, I hadn't really thought about that, I guess."

Tucking my hair behind my ear, he growls, "I don't believe you. So, tell me, would it start with him running his finger along your collarbone and down your arm? Would he

58

watch the goosebumps that fall into place as he slides along your body?"

I gulp as he does everything he's saying. I can only nod as my eyes get lost in his. "Your eyes are the most unique color I've ever seen." *I guess I can speak after all.* "They're like whiskey and …"

"Fireflies," he adds.

Shocked, I say, "Yes, how did you know that's what I was thinking?"

"I don't know, Angel, I just do. Dance with me."

It isn't a question, and I don't have time to give an answer. Before I can speak, he's slid us out of the booth and is walking us toward a makeshift dance floor that has filled up while the ominous beat of The Chainsmokers "It Won't Kill Ya" begins to play.

CHAPTER 7

TREVOR

"Give Me Strength" by Snow Patrol

What the hell am I doing? Standing from the table, I intentionally leave my phone, hoping my shadow will use that time to make his move.

Marching through the hotel bar that has become crowded, I have to slow my gait, realizing Angel's little legs are no match for my six-foot-three frame. I usually hate to dance, but I had to think of something quickly. I was losing control with her sitting in my lap, and I can't do that tonight. I wonder briefly if I'm putting her in danger by spending time with her, but push that thought aside as quickly as it came. I won't see her again after tonight. I can't.

Standing above her, I finally get a feel for her tiny frame. Even in her four-inch heels, I tower over her. If I was a dick, I'd feel powerful, but instead, it makes me want to protect her. I want to dominate her, I realize, in the most carnal of ways.

"Charlie, I-I'm not really a dancer—" she starts, but I cut her off.

Wrapping my arm around her waist, I haul her into me.

The way we're standing, bodies pressed together, I work my thigh between her legs, and we start to move. She's so short, I don't think she can even hook her arms around my neck. Instead, she hangs on tightly to my biceps as I sway, the bass pumping so loudly I feel it through her body.

"Just dance with me, *mon amour*. It won't kill you," I sing into her ear.

"This is like the scene in *Dirty Dancing*. I'm not sure if that makes me Baby or Penny—" she says, but again, I interrupt her.

"Will your one-night stand move you like this, Angel?" My hands find her hips, and I move her against my thigh in time with the music.

Every inch of our bodies is touching, and I'm growing harder by the second.

"Oh, I …" Angel's eyes go cartoonish again.

"Yes, mon amour, I want you, but I can't have you, so dance with me." I see the confusion in her eyes. Possibly the hurt, but I look away. I'm a selfish prick because I should walk away, but the thought of her with anyone but me has my gut raging. Instead, I pull her close again.

"Would your one-night stand nip your neck, Angel? Would he throw you over his shoulder and carry you to his room?" I pause, glancing down at her. The fire in her eyes is almost my undoing. *Fuck me hard.* "Would he grab the hem of your dress and rip it up the center to see that fucking sexy as hell pink bra I know you have on? Would you let him? Would he lick and nip and suck from your ear to your navel? Ghost his fingers over your stiff peaks, Angel? Would he be as hard for you as I am right now? Hard as fucking steel and about to come in my pants in a room full of strangers?"

Her breathing is ragged, and her face is flushed. Her lips part when I pull away slightly to stare at her, and all my will power goes out the window. Just as I'm about to kiss her, the song changes and she tries to break free. *Not yet. Please, not yet.* I hear a song by Dave Matthews start, and I wonder who the fuck the DJ is. I recognize the song, "Say Goodbye".

How fucking fitting. In true Dave Matthews fashion, the first minute and a half of the song is un-danceable.

"Just wait, keep moving with me, Angel." I take a moment to breathe her in deeply.

"This is my favorite song," she whispers. "We can always be friends, mm mhm, tonight we'll be lovers," she attempts to sing along with Dave and fuck me to hell if I've ever wanted something so badly. I've also never been so damn close to laughing as I am right now.

"Angel, you do know that isn't how the song goes?" Our dancing has changed along with the song. It isn't as crazed, as dirty, but it's just as sexy. Our bodies are moving in perfect sync. I know this cannot leave the dance floor, and I'm all too aware that our song is ending.

"This evening …" Angel sings. "Yes, I know. I can't help it. I love music, but my lyrics always sound better. It drives most people freaking crazy, but it's just me," she says, and it makes me want her even more. I want her babbling, lyrically screwed-up, uncoordinated body like I've never wanted anything before. I know I have to send her on her way. Keeping this up will only put her in danger, and I have the distinct feeling that losing her is not something I would recover from.

Unable to speak to her ear the way I want with our height difference, I lift her right off the floor and hold her as tightly as I can. "I want more than anything to take you upstairs and do wicked, wicked things to you until the sun comes up. I want to hear all your noises, all your words. I want to be the lover that makes you moan and scream and writhe in ecstasy. I want to taste you and fuck you, then roll you over and do it again and again."

The gasp she emits has me second-guessing my every intention.

Our song is winding down, and I feel the anxiety building, knowing I have to let her go. Setting her carefully on her feet, I lean in and take her lips in mine. I'm frantic, and I know it. My tongue pushes at her seam, and she opens on a breath.

Her eyes are open, as are mine, and she nods imperceptibly, granting me permission.

As I take control of her lips, her hands wrap around my neck, and I'm pulled closer. My hands tangle in her hair while I explore every inch of her mouth. She tastes of mint and ginger. I'm starved for her. I'm about to say fuck it to every messed-up thing my father has done to put me in this position when my watch goes off, alerting me to a text.

Resting my forehead on hers, I covertly read the message.

Unknown number: Package acquired.

My body goes rigid as I attempt to stay calm. I knew they were here. I knew they were watching me and that they would try to gain access in this way. What I wasn't expecting was Angel. As much as I want her, I can't have her.

"Wh-What's the matter? Did I do something wrong?"

Standing to my full height, I pull away. God, the look in her eyes; it's burned into my memory for eternity and will follow me to the depths of hell. Leaning in, I kiss her cheek.

"No, Angel. You're perfect, however, it's time for you to go. I can't be your one-night stand, and I'm also too selfish to let you leave with anyone else. There are things beyond my control, but know this, in another time, I would have taken you and never let you go."

"Wh-What? Are you fucking kidding me?" she seethes.

Grabbing my left hand, she inspects my ring finger with her small hands.

"What are you doing, Angel?"

"I'm looking for a wedding ring indent. I knew it, you're married, or engaged or something, aren't you?" She's a spitfire, and mad as hell.

I can't help but chuckle. "No, Angel. I'm not married, engaged, or seeing anyone. I haven't even dated anyone in a very long time. This has nothing to do with anyone else. It's about things that are out of my control. I want you to know I'm sending you away for reasons I can't explain, but if there were any other way, you would be mine."

Narrowing her eyes, Angel pokes me in the chest, hard. "Fuck. You. Charlie." And she storms off, stopping at the table to grab her purse.

My gut clenches, knowing that very dangerous men were just in that exact spot.

It's better this way, Trevor, I repeat over and over again in my head. I chuckle, realizing Angel is probably cursing every thought she has out loud right now. I'm saddened knowing I won't hear her feelings anymore. *You should have controlled yourself better and never brought her to your table.*

Dragging a hand through my hair, I watch her make her way to the elevator, then I head back to the table. Raising my hand, I signal to the waiter.

"What can I get you, sir?" he asks, trying to hide the fact he just saw my companion storm off.

"Johnny Walker, blue label. The bottle this time," I demand.

"Ah, sir, that's five-hundred dollars a bottle," he informs me.

Trying not to be an asshole, I grind my teeth before answering, "I'm aware, just bring it, please."

"Yes, sir." He scurries off, no doubt excited about the tip he knows he's about to get.

Rolling my shoulders, I try to relax, but feel myself stiffen as someone stops at my table. Forcing my gaze up, I relax, seeing Loki.

He takes the seat across from me with a shit-eating grin. "No hot girls at a math and science conference, huh?"

"Not now, Loki. I'm not in the mood."

"It seemed like you could have been. What happened?"

"I sent her away, and she got pissed, end of story."

Shaking his head, Loki reaches for a glass the waiter just set in front of him and pours himself a drink. Reaching over for my phone, he casually palms it, and I see he's stuck something to the bottom. No other person would have noticed.

"Scrambler," he informs me, and I realize the device he placed is so we can talk freely without being picked up through my phone. "I will only say this once, Trevor, so listen carefully. You have spent the last ten years barely living. You have to cut this shit out. We will right all the wrongs of your past, I promise you. But, if you don't figure out how to let the past go, what's the fucking point? Your mother wouldn't want you living this way, and you know it."

"Fuck you, Loki," I say, downing a fifty-dollar glass of scotch.

"Yeah, fuck me. But fuck you, too. This is not your fight, Trevor. I told you that from the beginning. I appreciate you helping us like this because it makes it a hell of a lot easier, but the sins of your father are not your own."

Fuck me. That sentence repeats in my head a hundred times a day. The sins of your father are not your own. Except, this time, they are.

I realize I zoned out in my own thoughts for a few seconds, but Loki has kept talking.

"You have to live your life, and not just for yourself but for your mother's memory. If you clam up like you did when you received that text message on the dance floor, you will fuck this up for us all," he scolds.

This gets my attention. "What are you talking about?"

"Everyone reads body language, Trevor. Anyone watching you on that dance floor saw your demeanor change as soon as I sent the text. You can't do that shit ... it will alert them to what's going on. Once can be played off, but you do it again, and they'll be on to you faster than you can say fuck it."

"Jesus, Loki. Am I cut out for this?"

"In any other situation, I would say you're too close, but I know you, and I know your determination. That's why you're here right now. This is personal to you. Use that to keep yourself in check. Think about the end goal here."

"What do I do? How do I make it through this week?"

With a grin, he tells me what I don't want to hear. "You seemed relaxed with that girl, what's her name?"

"I don't know, I just call her Angel." I know damn well he was listening to every second of our conversation, and it pisses me off. It feels like a betrayal, and as fucked up as it sounds, I hate the idea of betraying her.

"Did you fuck it up with her, or can you see her again?" he asks like it's a challenge he's throwing down.

"No. I'm not endangering her, Loki. What the hell? Why would you even suggest it?" I'm pissed. He's the professional here. What the hell is he thinking?

Sighing, he takes another sip of his scotch. "Trevor, spending time with her will not endanger her. Especially not right now." Leaning in, he lowers his voice. "Do you have any idea how many agents are stationed in this city right now? Jesus, she's safer with you than she would be walking the city on her own."

I stare at him, dumbfounded. Fuck, did I just ruin my chances of having Angel? *For how long, asshat? She doesn't even want your name. She's just looking for a one-night stand!* If she only wants a one-night stand, it'll be with me then. God, she's already rubbing off on me. When have I ever held a conversation with myself? The thought has me grinning like a goddamn fool.

"I don't even want to know what just played out in that head of yours," Loki says, laughing.

"You honestly think it's safe to spend time with her this week?" I need him to confirm it one more time.

"Yes, Trevor. I do." His confidence gives me hope.

Pulling at my neck, I let the smile I've been holding in break free. "Shit, I have to find this girl."

"I know someone that can help with that." Loki smirks.

"No, thank you. I don't want you or your guys anywhere near her. She has her reasons, I have mine. I don't want you looking into her at all, okay?"

He raises his hands in surrender. "All right, man, it's all you. I'm out!" Finishing his drink, he stands and claps me on the back. "See you around."

"Yup," I reply, already lost in thought. I signal the waiter. "Can I have the check, please?"

"Yes, sir. Here you go."

I don't even look at it, just hand him a credit card. My mind is already making a list of ways to get Angel to talk to me again.

Stepping off the elevator, I swear I can smell her. I don't know if her scent is stuck to me or if she leaves a trail wherever she goes, but the knowledge that she's on this floor has me walking at a snail's pace through the hall. I'm hoping to hear her, so I pause for a second at each door. *When did you turn into such a fucking stalker?*

My shoulders sag as I get to my room at the end of the hallway. I didn't find which room was hers, and it upsets me. Holding my phone to the lock, I hear her, and my entire body freezes. *No fucking way.* Glancing to my left, I pause. Is it possible she's in the room next to mine, or am I hallucinating?

"Can you believe that shit? Who the hell does that? Motherfucker! Seriously! He got me all worked up, then sent me on my way like a toddler. I bet he has a small pecker, anyway. Oh, who am I kidding? I totally felt it when we were dancing. That fucking thing would have broken me for sure. Gah! That's it. I hate him. Yup, he's off my list. I don't care if I see him again or not. My mission is on. Tomorrow, I'm having a one-night stand with someone, anyone. But not him. Nope, not Charlie. He's a douche canoe. I hope he has to sit through all my presentations and watch as I fucking kill it. Then I'll walk right by and ignore him. Yup, that's my plan ..."

She's on a roll, so I let myself into my room because I know there's a door connecting our rooms. Grabbing a glass and the bottle I bought at the bar, I pull up a chair to sit at the entrance to listen. I know it's wrong, but I want to know everything I can about this girl, and I don't have much time. We'll both leave Boston at the end of the week and go our separate ways because we have to. I need this week with her, and I'll do whatever it takes to make it perfect.

Realizing she said she was presenting, I'm tempted to pull up the list they gave me when I checked in, but don't. I kind of like the game we have going on. No one can get hurt this way. It seems like a win-win. I know I'm lying to myself, but I do it anyway. I told her if things were different, I wouldn't let her go. The truth in that statement scares the living shit out of me.

CHAPTER 8

JULIA

"The Man" by Taylor Swift

Beep. Beep. Beep.

"Nooooo," I moan. I hate mornings.

Beep. Beep. Beep.

"What the fuck?" I can't help but spew when I realize it isn't even my alarm going off. Rolling over, I grab my phone. 4:45 a.m. "Who the hell gets up this early?" I have forty-five minutes before my alarm goes off, so I try to go back to sleep.

Click.

I hear my neighbor leave and sigh in frustration. Kicking at the crisp white sheets tangled around my legs, I attempt to free myself from their confines. I sit up in bed, knowing I'm not getting back to sleep now, and reach for the room service menu.

"I freaking love room service." Picking up the phone, I place my order.

"Hi, can I please have an omelet with sausage and fresh tomatoes, a blueberry pancake, and the biggest pot of black coffee you can find?" Thinking I should probably eat some fruit, I add, "Also, some fresh berries or something?" I order them, knowing they'll sit in their bowl untouched. But my mom would be proud of me for trying.

"Today is a big day, Jules. Big, big day!" I give myself a pep talk on the way to the shower and think of the presentation I'll be giving in a few short hours. Reaching inside of the shower stall, I'm interrupted by a knock at the door, which startles me. I know it can't be room service yet, so I grab the big, fluffy robe that's at least twice as big as I am and walk to the door.

Checking the peephole, I don't see anyone, so I crack the door open slightly and stick my head out, looking left, then right. No one's there. *Assholes.* I'm about to close the door when something catches my eye on the floor.

"What the fuck?" Sitting at my feet is a giant, and I mean probably the biggest Starbucks coffee cup I've ever seen in my life. Thinking it's intended for someone else, I'm about to close the door when a note attached to the cup catches my eye. "Angel."

Stomping my foot, I growl. "Okay, Charlie. Are you stalking me now? Seriously, get out here. I know you're here somewhere, and let me just tell you something. I will not play games with you. I've got my own shit to deal with today, so you can take your coffee and shove it right up your hot as fuck ass. I ordered my own coffee, and the last thing I need is a man-child fucking with me."

Satisfied, I slam my door. Well, I try to anyway. Freaking hotel doors and their suspension. I press on the door with all my weight, and it still only closes with a soft click. "Humph. That'll teach him."

Wiping off my hands like I just took out the trash, I go to take my shower.

Knock. Knock.

"Room service," I hear someone call. Luckily, I just finished my shower.

Rushing to the door, I swing it open.

"Thanks so much, I'm starving," I tell the delivery man. Grabbing my wallet, I pull out a five-dollar bill and hand it to him.

"Have a wonderful day, miss."

"Thank you. You too," I reply, already plopping down on my bed to eat.

Picking up my phone, I pull up my kick-ass playlist and am immediately rewarded by Pink's "Raise Your Glass". Stuffing my face with an enormous bite of pancake, I hop up and go to my closet. "I mean, can you really sit still when Pink is blasting? I think not. Okay, what are we going to wear today?"

The beat picks up and I'm dancing around my suite now, stopping every few minutes for another bite. "Who needs the gym when you have Pink?" I laugh to myself. "Singing, dancing, and eating are probably not a good combo, but I don't give a rat's ass. I have to prepare myself to present in front of four-hundred suits, and I'll get ready however I please." Now I'm laughing hysterically, thinking about what all those men would say if they saw my pre-game routine. "Raise your glass. Hells yeah, Pink!" I shout, singing every other verse in between bites.

Lanes: Good luck today, chica! Kick butt!

Julia: Thanks, biatch.

Lanes: Have you started your pre-game routine yet?

Julia: You know it. Just rocked out to Pink. I probably should have done this pre-shower because I'm all sweaty now and have to get dressed.

Lanes: It's all good. Guys give off testosterone or something, right? You give off your strong woman vibes and show all those stuck-up suits who's the smartest of them all.

Lanes: What are you wearing today?

Julia: I'm not sure I want to be giving off my sweaty stank, but I get what you were going for ;)

Julia: I'm thinking about the red pantsuit?

Lanes: Ooh yes! That's hot! You'll own the room for sure! Make sure you match it with the killer black heels I stuck in that bag. And, remember, minimal makeup and jewelry, let the suit do the talking.

Julia: You are so fucking weird.

Lanes: But you love me.

Julia: Always.

Lanes: Good luck, call me later. Luvs.

Julia: Luvs.

Throwing my phone on the bed as Britney Spears' "Circus" comes on, I dance with jazz hands and shrug my shoulders. "I'm in the circus, ah huh, ah huh." I really should work on my dance moves, but my lyrics are on fire. Lanie once told me I dance like a forty-year-old white man to this song, but whatever, I'm good with it.

Placing my hands on my hips, I stare at the closet like snakes will jump out at me. Here goes nothing. Taking the picture Lanie attached to the garment bag, I pull out the pantsuit. She's right, this will look freaking hot.

I lay it all out on the bed, unable to help the dance-shrugging happening with my shoulders. Dancing on my toes, I scrunch my nose and dance to the ugliest painting I've ever seen. *Why do all hotels hang this shit?* I lift my shirt over my head and twirl it like a stripper. "Let's go, Jules. Let me see what you can do. All eyes will be on me at the conference, just like the boss, ah huh, ah huh," I sing. Catching myself in the floor-to-ceiling mirror, I laugh. I had better tone it down or everyone in this hotel will know what a shit-show I am.

Thirty minutes later, I have everything on, just as Lanie had instructed. Taking a quick picture, I send it to her.

Julia: Good?

Lanes: Hot! You got this! Have you done your grand finale yet?

Julia: Just about to. I wanted to make sure I had everything right with the clothes first.

Lanes: Perfect. Go get them!

Julia: Luvs.

Lanes. You're the man ;) Luvs.

Stepping into the torture device Lanie calls shoes, I make my way back to the mirror. I have a routine when I have to give presentations like this. It includes a lot of badass female musicians, and I always end with Taylor Swift's "The Man".

"All right, Julia. You have this. You know your material better than anyone in this building, and you know that's not an exaggeration. You're smarter, faster, and the queen in the room full of jokers. Don't let them dictate. Don't let them talk over you. Never let them talk down to you. Put them in their place when they need it. Take their balls in your hands and crush them! Oh, yeah!" I fist-bump the air for good measure and press play.

"Everything I do shows you I'm the boss," I sing just before putting my AirPods in. I know I'm probably shout-singing now, but I can't control it. This is my pre-game pep talk, and I'll do it my way.

Dancing around the room, I collect all my stuff for the day. Once I've gathered it, I give myself one last glance in the mirror and smile. Lanie can be a pain in my ass, but she knows her stuff. I will slay these meetings.

Opening the door, I'm still singing, "I'm the man, I'm the man, I'm the man," and I walk right into fucking Charlie.

With one hand, he removes an AirPod.

"Hey!" I screech. "Never, ever touch the AirPods. Especially when I'm in pre-game pep talk mode. Do you have no couth? Seriously, Charlie? What the fuck are you doing here? You sent me away last night, I went. End of story. Nice to know you." I attempt to push my way past him, but he stands firm, putting my AirPod into his own ear.

"I am beyond happy that you're not a man, Angel. To answer your question, that's my room." He points to the door next to mine.

"Of freaking course it is." I slap my forehead with my hand. "Your stalking knows no bounds."

"Actually, I've been in that room since yesterday morning, so technically, you would be the one stalking me." His voice carries that calm, rich tone that makes me want to throat punch him.

"Whatever. I don't have time for this or for you. I've got work to do. You made your position very clear last night, so again, nice knowing you." I try again to get past him.

"I made a mistake, Angel. Spend time with me this week. We can extend your one-night stands to one week. What do you say?" The look of hope on his face almost makes me falter.

"No can do, Romeo. One-night stands are one night for a reason. Whatever your reasons were last night, you didn't think twice about them when I was standing there. I'm not one to put myself in the position to get shot down twice." *What are you doing? You want to bone this man so hard, just go with it.* For once, my inner dialogue stays inner.

"No, not Romeo, just Charlie. Your Charlie. Okay, so one-nights stands aside, spend the week with me. Whenever you're not working, be with me." It wasn't a question, it was a command. And while it should piss me off, I find my panties getting wet.

What do I have to lose?

"Fine. You have one more chance, but we play by my rules. No names, nothing too personal, and you have to pass my test tonight. If you can get dirty, I'll consider spending more time with you the rest of the week." His smile tells me he has no idea what I mean by getting dirty.

74

"Oh, I can get dirty just fine, Angel. Tell me when and where," he challenges.

Smirking, I take him all in. From the tailored suit that even I can tell costs a small fortune to his wingtip shoes that are so shiny I can probably see my reflection. "Do you even own a pair of jeans, Romeo?"

Growling, he cages me in against the wall, making me drop my bag. "Not Romeo, Angel. Charlie. Your Charlie."

Pressing against his very firm chest, he finally backs away. "Fine, I didn't realize you were so touchy. But seriously, do you own a pair of jeans?"

The sly smile that crosses his face makes me shiver. I feel like he's about to say checkmate, and I'll once again be his pawn. When the smile takes over his entire face, my curiosity outweighs my need to flee.

"You'd be surprised by what I own, Angel. What time should I pick you up?" My mouth wants to drop open at his words, but I force it to remain neutral.

Picking up my bag, I start down the hallway. Charlie's so close I can feel his breath on me, but I keep walking. "I'm not sure yet. I'll leave a message on your room phone. So, what do you have on your schedule for today?"

He takes my elbow, escorting me into the elevator before he speaks. "Nothing interesting. I told you, I didn't want to be here either. There's only one presentation I'm interested in seeing, but it's at the same time as the one I'm forced to go to. I'm hoping to sneak out early and at least catch the end of her presentation though. I hear she's fucking phenomenal. One of the smartest minds in the business right now."

Genuinely curious, I ask, "Who is it? Maybe she's on my schedule, I can give you notes."

"Julia Murphy. Do you know her? I tried to Google her last night, but literally, nothing comes up. No high school pictures, college awards, nothing. Even her bio on their company website only gives the minimum. She's also the only one without a picture. It's so bizarre, she must be extremely homely or something."

I can't help the choked giggle that comes out of me, and I'm back to pinching my lips together with my thumb and forefinger. The last thing I need is for Charlie to find out his homely, brilliant mind is me. Because of the nature of my job, I had taken to using my mother's maiden name at these things.

"Yup, I've heard she's great. She must be homely, though … that's the only explanation I can come up with," I say, laughing.

"Well, Angel, not everyone can be as fucking hot as you are. You're killing me in this suit. I have never once found a pantsuit on a woman sexy, but you've outdone yourself with this one," he whispers, leaning into my personal space again. His mouth is so close to my ear, I can feel damp heat every time he breathes. "I'll be ready and waiting whenever you say to be tonight, Angel. But let me tell you this, it won't end like last night did. Tonight, I want to see, feel, taste, experience every single inch of you."

Ding.

"Ah! Saved by the bell. I guess?" I squeak as I slide down the wall and under his arms. I quickly make my escape, feeling his eyes on me the entire way to the concierge.

"Hello, Miss McDowell, how can I help you today?" the concierge asks, and I cringe, hoping Charlie is far enough away that he didn't hear my name. Tony is here every time I come to one of these things. He's gotten used to my shenanigans, even if I've never bothered him directly.

Thinking quickly, I ask, "Actually, Tony, could you inform the staff not to address me by name? Since I'm giving so many presentations this week, I'd rather not draw attention to myself any more than necessary. I'm sorry, that's probably a strange request, but I just really like my privacy."

"Of course, miss. I apologize. I will make sure to inform everyone. Was there something else I can do for you?"

"Yes, actually. Is there any way I could get a Red Sox T-shirt and two baseball caps delivered to my room before four p.m. today?" It's the first time I've used my position to request something like this, and it makes me ridiculously uncomfortable.

"Absolutely, miss. That's no problem at all. What sizes?" If he's thrown by my request, he doesn't show it.

"You probably get all kinds of odd requests, don't you?" I blurt without thinking.

He laughs jovially. "You have no idea, miss. This is nothing, trust me."

"Okay, thanks. Um, let me think. I already have my shirt, but I'll need a baseball cap, probably a youth-sized one if you can. I'll also need a men's shirt, maybe an extra-large? Hmmm, I'm not really sure." Standing on my tiptoes, I reach as high as I can and ask, "What size do you think someone this tall, maybe a little taller, would wear? He's about, maybe this wide across his shoulders." I make size estimations using my hands.

Trying desperately to suppress his laughter, he says, "I think an extra-large would be just fine, miss. And a hat to match?"

"Phew, that was easier than I thought it would be. Yes, a hat, too. Thank you," I tell him sincerely.

"Anytime, miss. Have a wonderful day. Do you need help setting up for your first group today?"

"No, thanks, I have it. They set most of it up last night. Now I just have to hope I can explain it so a room full of people can understand me."

He smiles kindly, reminding me of Lanie's grandfather. "Good luck, miss."

CHAPTER 9

TREVOR

"Done" by Chris Janson

*M*y day has been hell. I haven't been able to focus on anything except a certain little pixie with a fire engine red suit on today. I found myself watching doors, scanning crowds, checking rooms all day for a glimpse of her, but she was nowhere to be found. To top it off, I never made it to the presentation I wanted to see. I heard a few people talking about it after lunch, and I'm even more pissed that I missed it. I've spent the last two hours stalking this woman online and have come up empty. Even hacking the DMV website didn't turn up anything. *How does this woman have no online presence at all?*

Sometime around three p.m., I checked out mentally and went back to my room, hoping there would be a message from Angel. Entering the room, I immediately know something's wrong, something's out of place. That's when I see him in the corner—the devil himself: Romero Knight, my father.

"What the hell are you doing here, Romero?" I spit, throwing my phone onto the table and standing guard in front of the door connecting me to Angel's room. *Please, God, don't let her be in there.* The last thing I want to do is scare her off before we even begin.

"Romero? Tsk, tsk, since when do you call your father by his given name? I'm still Papa, you know?"

"No, you haven't been Papa for a long time. Not since you killed my mother."

He sighs heavily. "I didn't kill her, mio figlio."

"My son? I'm not your son, Romero. I told you we were finished the last time I left your home. We. Are. Through."

"You are mio figlio," he bellows. "I've made mistakes, but you will always be mio figlio, and don't you forget it. Our family is in too deep for you to be anyone else. It's time you came into the business, Trevor. I cannot protect you forever, you must make your move."

Stepping into his personal space, I realize for the first time how old and tired he looks. This man who was once my hero is now, and forever, my enemy.

"I will never enter your business, Romero. I don't give a fuck about the consequences; I'm not a criminal. I've sold my software and made my money, I don't need yours ... not that I ever did. The trust you set up is still intact, in full, and will never be touched by me. I will not be suckered into your life that way. I have my eyes wide open to you and your crew, and I'll never be part of it. So, whatever it is you thought you could accomplish by being here, you're wrong. You'd be smart to leave now."

There's a knock at my door that neither of us are expecting. Romero moves faster than I thought him capable.

"This is not over, mio figlio. I've learned the hard way, this will never be over." With that, he walks to the door and sweeps it open.

Fuck. Angel stands at the door, holding a bag in the air.

"Um," she starts, gaping between my father and myself, the tension so thick it's suffocating. Seeming to sense my distress, she says, "Ah, the concierge delivered this to my room by mistake ... I believe it's for you." She's staring at me.

When I step forward to take it, she practically throws it at me and hurries off to her side of the hall. If I wasn't scared shitless that my father would see through her, I'd comment on how fucking adorable she is. Instead, I nod in thanks and escort him out of the room while she slips into hers.

"Do not come to me again, Romero. We're finished. We're no longer family, and I'm no longer your son. Do what you must, but do so with the knowledge I'll never join you."

"Trevor," he begins, but I've already turned on my heel to enter my room once again.

Hurrying to our shared door, I knock. "Angel?" I question as I try the door handle and am relieved to find it unlocked. I find her sitting on the edge of her bed where she's swinging her legs below her because they don't reach the floor. Her hands are tucked under her thighs and her eyes are downcast.

"Sorry, I-I didn't mean to interrupt. I was getting ready to deliver your stuff for tonight and I heard someone yell. It seemed pretty intense. I just wanted to make sure you were okay," she whispers—no rambling, no mumbling, just stating facts.

Kneeling down in front of her, I loop my hand under her chin and lift her face to mine. "You were trying to protect me, Angel?" My chest is so tight, I worry I may be having a heart attack. It's like the devil himself is squeezing my heart and I'm finding it hard to breathe.

Enveloping my large hand in her much smaller one, she leans into my palm, and I suck in a large gulp of air. The devil released me. *Fuck, it's her*! She fought the devil inside of me.

Before I even realize I'm moving, I have her laying back on the bed, me on top of her. I haven't touched her yet. Our bodies are pressed together from the waist down, but my gaze is focused on her face. Her bright green eyes stare back.

"I don't need protecting, Angel. I just need you." Lowering my head to meet hers, I allow myself to get lost in her. Cradling her head with both of my hands, I rest my weight on my forearms. She's so tiny that I have to take care not to crush her. That self-control lasts until the second our lips touch.

Fuck me. I think I'm ruined. This tiny pixie of a woman is destroying me, and she doesn't have a clue.

Shifting my weight to one side, I let my right hand ghost down her neck until my thumb lands on her pulse point. I don't press, just hold it there, feeling her react to me as I kiss her, loving the way her heart rate speeds up as I deepen the kiss.

Lowering my lips to her jaw, I nip gently. "Fuck, Angel, what are you doing to me?"

"I-I-I—" she tries.

I interrupt her by rubbing the pad of my thumb back and forth across her bottom lip. She shocks the fuck out of me when she pops it into her mouth and sucks. Hard.

Unable to control my most basic instincts, I grind my cock into her, and she groans. "I love that sound, Angel. Shall we see what other sounds I can wring from your tight, little body?" I ask as I pull my thumb from her lips with a pop.

"Y-Yes, I think we most definitely should," Angel breathes out.

Her answer causes me to chuckle, but staring down at her, I become serious. "This won't be a one-night stand, Angel. I won't be done with you after one time. Promise me we'll have all week to explore, or I won't be able to leave this room until I'm done with you."

"Holy hell," she blurts.

"I'll take that as a yes?"

She nods emphatically, and I shift my weight again,

grinding against her pussy in just the right place to make her moan. I don't remember the last time I got such satisfaction from dry humping like a horny teenager. Taking both her hands in one of mine, I place them above her head. I stare into her eyes just before I slide down her body.

"You're so beautiful. Do you know that? I walked around with a hard-on all day thinking about those fucking tight red pants."

"How uncomfortable for you," she snickers.

"Oh, you don't know the half of it, Angel. During one of my sessions today, my mind wandered, and I had to excuse myself in the middle of some poor schlep's presentation. That was very bad form on my part. I never get distracted." Leaning in, I lick her neck where her pulse is racing.

"Very bad form indeed," she teases, so I bite down on that sensitive flesh.

"Do you know what I was thinking of, Angel?" I whisper huskily as I snake my free hand under her shirt and skim her bra line.

"Um, I'm guessing not actuarial science?" she says cheekily.

"You're full of banter today, aren't you?"

"In case you haven't noticed, I don't seem to own a filter, and never once have I been accused of being quiet."

This time she blushes from embarrassment. I don't like it.

Reaching under her, I unsnap her bra and relish in the sounds of surprise that escape her. "In case you haven't noticed, Sweetheart, I fucking love all your sounds. Now, let's see what new ones we can make."

Quickly, I raise her shirt and bra above her head, caging her arms in, and I see a moment of panic cross her face. "I've got you, Angel. All you have to do is say stop and I will, okay?"

"Yeah, it's not that. This …" she says, shaking her arms at

me, "just reminds me of the shit-show I got myself into while shopping for this trip."

It's so far out of left field, that I stop my perusal of her body and stare into her eyes. With a raised eyebrow, I encourage her to continue.

"Hmm, is this going to count as telling personal information? That would be against the rules. But then, I'm not going to tell him where we were—"

"Angel?" I interrupt. "Inner dialogue is escaping again. If you want to tell me, just tell me. Fuck the rules. We can make our own. I agree; this can't go anywhere after this week … I-I just have a bunch of shit I can't bring you into."

She quiets me with a finger to my lips. "Okay, we'll make our own rules. Don't think beyond this week. We both have our reasons. Just please promise me I'm not becoming the other woman here, okay? I couldn't live with myself if that's the case."

I can see how troubled this idea makes her, and I nip it in the bud quickly. "There is no one else, Angel. There hasn't been in many years. I promise you that. So, new rules. We tell each other what we want the other to know when we want them to know it, with the understanding that we have to part ways in five days. What do you think?"

Realizing her arms are still restrained above her head, she laughs. "All right, well, last week, my best friend took me shopping. Since I had to give so many presentations this week and I usually work from home, she was probably right. Anyway, she gave me all this crap to try on, and the quick version is, I got stuck in a dress. I mean, like really stuck. She had to slide under the stall because I couldn't move or even see to open the door for her. Of course, she took pictures, but ugh, why am I even telling you this?" She closes her eyes and tries to shake her head, but I capture her face again with a kiss.

"I fucking love that you can't stop talking. I never have to wonder where I stand with you, and I think it's cute as hell. Now, tell me, do you want me to set you free?" I ask.

Biting her bottom lip, she shakes her head, causing me to growl and pounce. Share time is over for now.

Keeping eye contact for as long as I can, I lower my mouth to her breast and hear her hiss in pleasure. Lightly, I lick around her nipple, then flick the taut peak as her eyes begin to close. I trace my fingers over every indent of her rib cage, down to her pant line. Skimming my fingers just beneath the hem, I see her shiver. Glancing up, my cock twitches when I see her eyes have darkened watching me.

"You like to watch, Angel? Do you like to watch me touching you?" Lowering again, I lick a line from her belly button up her center until we are face-to-face once more. "Do you want me to touch you, Angel? Every part of you?"

"Yes," she pants, and I grin against her neck.

"Keep your arms there, don't move," I instruct. I've never been into the whole domination thing, but fuck me if I don't want to own every inch of this woman.

She nods her head, watching as I slide my hand down her body. With a flick of my fingers, I unbutton those fucking sexy pants and lower myself to the floor between her legs. Waiting until her eyes find mine again, I lean up and grab her zipper with my teeth.

Angel expels all her air in a whoosh, and I realize I love shocking her.

Slowly, I lower the zipper as far as it'll go, then run my nose up her center, grinning like a fool as she tries to wiggle free.

"Stay," I command, and am shocked when she does. I thought for sure she would argue, but searching her face, I see the truth. She's calm. Her brain isn't working on overdrive, she's just feeling, and that makes me fucking nuts.

Standing, I tuck my thumbs into the waistband of her pants and slowly lower them down her legs. Once she's naked, I scan her body and feel my cock grow harder than it's ever been before. It's so hard it's painful, so I shuck my clothing as well and watch as her eyes do their cartoon thing again. Smirking, I stand with my arms crossed as she checks me out.

Before I know what's happening, she's flailing her arms wildly, and I'm about to freak the fuck out. Placing a hand on her stomach, I ask, "Angel, what the hell? Are you okay?"

She pauses to look at me, and I see her calm down from my touch. Reaching up, I grab the shirt she's wrestling with to set her free.

"Finally," she says, jumping up to her knees and shaking her arms out. She uses all her might to push me onto the bed, and it takes my brain a second to catch up.

"What are you doing, Angel? Are you okay?" I ask, hating how concerned she has made me.

"What? Yeah, I'm fine, why?" She moves so quickly, I feel drunk. Now she's straddling me, and my dick is bobbing like an apple on Halloween. "You can't stand there all sexy-like and expect me not to touch you, too."

"Holy fuck," I say, shaking my head as I watch her take in my chest. I'm so shell-shocked I don't even have the where-withal to puff up a little. Thankfully, my hours at the gym take care of that for me.

I feel her delicate hands roam, and I struggle to control my breathing. Shit, it's been a long time, and I'm worried I won't be able to hold out very long. When I feel her hands squeeze the base of my cock with one hand and cradle my balls in the other, I shoot up to a sitting position and watch in awe as she strokes me.

This fucking girl.

Her delicate hands can barely wrap around my hardened shaft, and I can't take my eyes off of her. Licking her hand, she moves it to my base, and I almost fucking come right there. Holy hell, my dirty angel. Watching her lick her lips as she jerks my cock off is too much. I fall back to the bed on my elbows. With my head hanging behind my shoulders, I work on steadying my breathing. When I feel her tongue hit my tip, I know I can't let her continue.

Before she knows what has happened, I've hauled her back up to the bed. I'm straddling her, watching my cock bounce against her tiny frame, tapping her mound, begging for entrance. *I have to calm that little fucker down.*

Leaning over, I whisper in Angel's ear, "I will eat your pussy until you come all over my face. Then I might do it again. I want to hear you, Angel. I want to hear you screaming my name, screaming incoherent nonsense. Whatever the fuck you want, just let me hear you. Can you do that for me?"

Her response comes flying from her mouth in an instant. "Fuck, yes."

Shaking my head at her dirty mouth, I make my way down her body, stopping to kiss and nip wherever I can. When I reach her pussy, I want to shout to the gods myself. Cupping her, I feel her heat and I groan. "Angel, are you already wet for me?"

"It would be impossible to see you naked and not be wet, Charlie." For the first time since I've met her, the use of my nickname irks me. I know it has to be this way, but fuck if it doesn't piss me off.

Trying to ignore it, I lower my mouth to her pussy and watch as she lifts up on her elbows to watch. "God, yes, Angel. It's so fucking hot to see you watching me."

With my eyes trained on hers, I stick my tongue out and run it up her seam. I groan as I see her eyes roll to the back of her head. I do it again and again before taking her clit into my mouth and sucking hard. I enter her with my index finger, and finally, I hear her moan. It's low and long as she tries to gyrate against me. Using my free hand, I pin her hip to the bed.

"Don't move, Angel. Not until I'm done with you."

"Charlie, I-I need …"

"What do you need, Angel? This?" I question as I add some pressure to her clit and curl my fingers inside of her, searching for that secret spot.

"Yes, oh, God! Yes," she screams. Her hands have a death grip on the sheets around her, and her entire body is flushed with a light sheen covering her skin. "I-I'm going to come," she moans, attempting to rock from side to side, but I hold her steady.

"I'm not done, Angel. I want to wring every ounce of pleasure I can from you. How far can I push this tight little body?" Lowering my head, I suck her clit into my mouth one more time and feel her entire body go off.

"Charlie," she screams. "I-I …"

Releasing her clit briefly, I wait until her gaze finds mine. "Just feel, Angel. Just feel me."

Her slight frame spasms all around me, and I have never been prouder of anything in my life. I stroke her gently until she comes back to earth. Watching as her eyes come into focus, I see a beautiful smile take over her face.

"Oh my God, that was … fuck, that was …" She doesn't need to finish, I saw her come. I know how it was.

Crawling up her body, I take her bottom lip with my teeth and pull gently. "You're amazing, Angel. I've never seen anything sexier in my entire life." Laying here naked with her, my dick makes himself known and jerks against her stomach.

With a crooked grin, she reaches between us and grabs hold of my cock, giving it a gentle squeeze. I'm about at my limit, so I close my eyes and try to think of the least sexy things I can like old man balls, saggy tits, dirty socks. *Fuck*. It doesn't work. Her petite hand on my shaft overrides every other brain cell I own.

That's when it hits me. "Shit, Angel, stop. I-I don't have

any condoms. I meant to grab some from the front desk but got distracted earlier."

Fucking Romero, ruining something else.

Angel sits up quickly, head-butting me really freaking hard.

"Jesus, that hurt," she says, holding her head, and I realize it must have hurt her just as much.

"Are you all right?"

Shaking her head, she slides out from under me. "I'm fine. Don't worry about the condoms. Luckily, I come from a very … let's just say eclectic town, and all the old ladies chipped in to buy me these." She reaches into the drawer and pulls out a giant, Costco-sized box of condoms.

"Hold up," I say, holding my hand out for the box. "You're telling me a group of old ladies from your town got together and bought you these? Why?"

Laughing, she climbs back onto the bed, which takes some effort on her part because she's so short. Shrugging, she responds, "Miss Rosa wanted me to be safe. She started touchin' with the elders, and she showed up one morning with breakfast and this box of condoms."

There's so much to unwrap in that sentence, I don't even know where to begin. Luckily, I don't have to think long because Angel moves stealthily and is straddling my lap before I can ask a single question.

I enjoy holding her here like this. I shouldn't like it as much as I do, that's going to be a problem. As I run my hands up and down her smooth back, she slowly rocks against me. Anchoring her with one hand on her hip, I guide her against me as she slides along my erection. Dropping my gaze between us, I watch as her lips part, making way for my shaft. She grinds again, coating me in her wetness, and I push down on her hip, holding her still while I reach for the box of condoms.

Working together, we rip one open. She rolls it on my

raging head, and my cock twitches with every movement. I have to focus so I don't embarrass myself. Leaning back on my thighs, Angel inspects her handiwork. Apparently happy with what she sees, she gazes up at me under thick lashes, and it's my undoing.

Grabbing hold of both her hips, I lift her over me. In this moment, I realize the vast size difference between us. "Are you ready?"

Without answering, Angel lowers herself onto my cock and it takes every bit of restraint not to go off like the motherfucking Fourth of July.

Halfway down, she pauses. I hadn't thought about my size being too much for her. This position might be more than she can handle. "Are you okay, Angel? Do you want to try another position? You may not be able to take all of me like this."

Furrowing her brows, she asks, "Is that a challenge?"

I almost laugh, but I can tell she's serious. "What? No, it's not a fucking challenge, Angel. I don't want to hurt you." Before I get the sentence out, she impales herself on my dick, and all thought leaves my brain.

"Uhhh-ohhh," she moans, letting her head hang back.

I'm clenching my teeth, trying to fight my instinct to move. "Angel?" I grit out. "Are you all right? Do you want me to move?"

Raising her head, her eyes are still closed, and I take a moment to memorize every inch of her face. Knowing I only have a few days with her has the devil clawing at my chest again. As if she senses my distress, she opens her eyes and places her hands around my neck. Just like that, the devil recedes.

"I'm going to move," she informs me.

"Thank fuck." It slips out, but I mean it. I don't know how much longer I could have handled feeling her tight pussy gripping me and not be able to move.

Slowly, she rotates her hips, and we both moan. I don't know that anything has ever felt this good before. Gradually, she picks up the pace, and I let her have control for as long as I can. When I feel as though I'll combust, I grab her hips and slide us both to the back of the bed. Laying down, I keep her on top of me. Grabbing her arm behind her back, I hang on to it for leverage.

"Are you ready, Angel? I'm going to fuck you now. If it's too much, you have to tell me."

"Gawd, yes, please," she whines.

With one arm holding her midsection and the other arm holding onto hers, I lift her slightly to her knees just before I pound up and into her, again and again.

"Ooh, Angel. You're fucking heaven. Every goddamn inch of you is perfection. Do you feel how we fit together?"

"Holy hell," she pants as I pick up my speed.

"Never, Angel, have I ever felt something so perfect." I'm thrusting up and into her with such force I feel the entire bed move.

"Charlie! Fuck, Charlie, harder. Please," Angel moans.

Suddenly, I despise the name Charlie, but knowing I'm the one making her moan and beg has me pounding into her at an unnatural pace. I feel her body quivering, and I know she's close.

"Don't come yet, Angel. Not yet," I warn her.

"Charlie, I-I can't hold it," she pleads.

"Yes," thrust, "you," thrust, thrust, thrust, "can." Thrust. "Come, come now, Angel," I demand as I thrust one last time, feeling my balls tighten and my spine tingle. I blackout for a minute, that's how fucking insane it is. When I come to, Angel is leaning over me, searching my face with concern.

"Are you okay?" she asks.

"No, Angel. I'm not. I think you just ruined me for anyone else. I have never come that hard in my entire life."

She smiles so sweetly I feel the devil at my chest again, and I wonder for a moment if I should see a doctor.

"Ah, well, glad you're okay," she says as she tries to slide away from me.

"Stay," I tell her. "Just for a minute. Just lay with me."

She hesitates for a second, and I can see the wheels moving again. Something's brewing in that pretty head of hers, but until I can form a coherent thought, I won't be able to figure out what. Pulling her into my side, I position her so she's lying with her head on my chest. I sigh, feeling relieved. Relieved for what, I'm not sure.

I don't know how long we stay like that—her head on my chest, me stroking her back, her arms, her hair, pretty much anywhere I can reach—but I know it'll end soon. Angel is becoming fidgety; something isn't sitting right with her. I keep waiting for her dialogue to start, but so far, it hasn't happened.

CHAPTER 10

JULIA

"Holding Out for the One" by Tenille Townes

*O*kay, this is the longest inner monologue I've ever had. I've been lying on Charlie for at least fifteen minutes, and as far as I know, nothing has escaped my lips. My mind is running like a jacked-up race car, though. I don't know how much longer I can hold it in. I'm about to go into full crazy mode.

That was, hands down, the best sex of my life, and now I don't know what the hell I'm supposed to do. Just as I start to pull away, my phone rings, saving me, and I lurch out of bed like my ass is on fire.

The telltale ringtone of "Girls Just Wanna" have fun tells me it's Lanie, so I forgo the greetings.

"Hey, what's up?" I ask, turning in circles, trying to decide what the hell I should put on. Finding nothing, I end up at the foot of the bed, naked, staring at a grinning Charlie.

"Jules? What's the matter? You sound funny."

Lanie and I've known each other our entire lives. I should have known better than to answer.

"Huh? Nothing, nothing's wrong. Why do you ask?

Everything's just fine … just fine. I've had a busy day, is all. I gave a speech today, you know? It was about, uh, it was about … well, you don't care what it was about." I watch wide-eyed as Charlie climbs out of bed and stalks toward me. Grabbing me around the waist, he pulls me down onto his lap. The yelp I exhale has Lanie worried, though.

"Julia, what the heck is going on? You're babbling and yelping, and you just sound funny. Let me FaceTime you, so I can check you out for myself."

"*No!*" I scream. "I-I can't FaceTime right now. I'm, ah … I'm naked." I notice I've stopped babbling and stare wide-eyed at Charlie, who is still grinning at me. He does have the magical touch. I scowl, thinking about it.

Lanie notices I've stopped babbling, too. "Jules, are you sure you're okay? You were just in the midst of a babble fest, and now you're not. That never happens unless I'm with you."

Sighing into the phone, I involuntarily lean into Charlie's chest. "Yes, I'm fine. I promise. More than fine. Today went well." Shifting my gaze to stare at Charlie, I smile. "Really well, actually."

Charlie rests his chin on my head while I finish my call with Lanie. My mind is cloudy with confusion as I hang up, but Charlie makes no attempt to move. Instead, he sits and waits.

When it becomes apparent that I don't know what to say, he tilts my head to look at him. "What's going on in this beautiful head of yours?"

"Trust me," I snort, "you don't want to know."

"I think I've proved more than once that I do, in fact, want to hear all your noises, Angel."

I can't help the blush that forms at his words. The chaos is coming. Standing up, I take a few steps away from him and start pacing while I gather my thoughts.

"Well," I start, "here's the thing … what do we do now?

One-night stand rules say I should never have you in my room so I can sneak out as soon as you fall asleep. But, we're in my room so I can't exactly sneak out and it's only, what? Five p.m.? Unless you have geriatric sleep habits, what the hell am I going to do for six or seven hours while I wait for you to fall asleep?" I'm pacing with my hands waving wildly through the air as I speak.

Finally, I pause to glance up and find him following my every-single-move. That's when I realize I'm buck ass naked and his dick has grown three sizes again. *Holy fuck.* Make that four sizes.

Stalking me like the cat about to get the cream, Charlie glides across the room, his thick cock bobbing with every step.

"Angel, if you keep staring at him like that, we'll never leave this room. I thought we decided we would make our own rules?" Taking my hand, he leads me toward the bed but veers to the left at the last minute and sits in the chair, pulling me down with him. "I want to make something very clear, right now. If you ever sneak out of my life without a proper good-bye, I will find you, Angel. I understand we have our reasons for not carrying this on longer than a week, but don't cheapen it by thinking I won't want a proper good-bye. I want every second you can give me, and that means sleeping in the bed with me. Not sneaking out in the middle of the night, okay? Is that why you were itching to get out of the bed earlier?"

"Well, sort of. I was actually waiting for you to kick me out. Then I realized it was my room. Then I remembered that if we're going to make the game, we need to leave soon. We won't be able to tour the green monster now because we're so late, but a game at Fenway is something everyone should do once."

"Hold up," he says, sitting up straighter. "Is that what we're doing tonight? Going to a baseball game?"

"That's what I was planning, but honestly, you need jeans. You can't go in a suit. Do you even have any?"

He laughs like I'm missing the joke. "Yes, sweetheart, I own lots of jeans. What was in the bag you brought over earlier?"

"Your gear." I smile. "You cannot go to Fenway Park unless you're suited up."

Lifting me off his lap like I weigh nothing at all, he hurries into his room.

"Oh no. I can't wear this, Angel. It's blasphemy. I'm a southern boy," he yells from the other room. "I'm a Brave's fan through and through."

Laughing as he walks back into my room, holding the Sox shirt like it has cooties, I place my hands on my hips. "Well, I'm a New England girl, born and raised, and when you go to a Red Sox game *in* Fenway Park, you dress for the home team, especially since they're playing the Yankee's tonight. If you're not wearing your Red Sox stuff, you'll be mistaken for a Yankee's fan, and you'll likely end up wearing a beer or two."

He stares at me wide-eyed. "I've heard you Boston fans are crazy, but are you kidding me?"

I shrug my shoulders. "We like our home teams. So, what's it going to be? Red Sox shirt I bought just for you, or wear your crap and stink like beer for the entire game?"

"You're serious?" he asks again.

I grin. "You have no idea. You should also know that I'm no fair-weather fan, so if you're not prepared to last the entire game, I'll just go alone."

"Fuck that. You're not walking around the city by your-self," he fires back, and while I want to scold him for thinking he can tell me what I can and cannot do, I can't help but feel touched he cares, so I let it go.

"Okay then, you'd better hurry and shower. We have to leave in fifteen minutes."

"You expect me to believe you'll be ready to go in fifteen minutes?"

"Listen, buddy," I scoff. "I don't think you understand. I don't walk around carrying my high heels," I sing, Julia-tizing the lyrics to a new country song.

"Or yesterday's little black dress," he sings back with a wink. "Yeah. You forget, I'm a southern boy. Country music is in our blood."

Standing, I stare at him with my mouth agape. I'm shocked. "Holy fuck, he just got my song lyric reference. No one ever gets my music lyrics, not even—"

Stepping into my space and cradling my cheek in his hand, Charlie cuts me off, "Not even your BFF?"

I shake my head and whisper, "No, not even her." Lifting my head to look at him, I see a grin that makes him seem like a shy teenager.

My heart rate accelerates as his face leans in for a kiss. "I'm glad I'm the only one then." Patting my ass, he ushers me toward the bathroom. "Now, hurry up. I don't want to be late for this big game."

Silently I enter my bathroom, wondering what it all means.

I wasn't kidding when I said I don't mess around when it comes to baseball. Ten minutes later, I'm sitting cross-legged on my bed, waiting for Charlie. I heard his shower shut off a couple of minutes ago because he left our connecting doors open. *I wonder if he did that on purpose?*

I grab a pen from my purse, and scribble pros, cons, and questions. Under questions, I write: ask Lanes how to handle the open door. In the pros column I add: he's fucking hot. I'm about to write I'll end up hurt in the cons row when I feel a hand on my arm. I'm so startled I jump right out of my skin.

"What the fuck?" Flies from my mouth as I tumble backward and almost roll right off the bed when Charlie's unyielding hands steady me.

"You really have a strong startle reflex, don't you, Angel?" Even when I'm embarrassed, the humor in his tone warms me.

"Jesus, stop sneaking up on me," I sulk.

"Okay, I'll try." Now he isn't even trying to hide his laughter. "Imagine my surprise when I walk in here, fully expecting to be waiting on you, to find you ready to go, and lost in that gorgeous head of yours. Tell me, Angel, what has you so lost in thought there?" He grabs for my list, but I don't react quickly enough.

We both refuse to let it go, and the page rips in half. Luckily for me, all he has on his piece is how to handle open doors.

"Do you do this a lot?" he asks.

"Do what?" I volley, wrapping my arms around myself as I feel my defenses rising.

Is this where he'll realize what an odd duck I am and be on his way?

Sitting beside me on the bed, he places my hand in his. "Relax, Angel. I'm just asking if you make lists like this a lot?"

Not sure why he's asking, I shrug. "Yeah, it's kind of my crutch. At work, I never second guess myself, I don't have to, I'm the best at what I do. I'm in complete control. In life? Not so much. I need to see things in black and white to work them out most of the time. Why? Do you think it's weird?"

Rubbing his thumb back and forth across the top of my hand, he stares from it to me, and I see the honesty written in his eyes. "No, I don't think anything about you is weird, Angel." Kissing the side of my head, he hands me his piece of my list. "Hold on, I'll be right back."

My eyes are glued to his ass as he enters his room, but he's back within seconds, a leather-bound notebook in his hands. He sits down next to me, and my body shivers as he opens to the last used page. In bold, scratchy writing, I see two columns: pros and cons. My eyes snap to his.

"You only beat me getting ready because I made my list before I showered."

I stare at him open-mouthed like a blowfish. Folding the paper in half lengthwise, he hands me the notebook. "I want to show you my pros. I wish I could show you the cons just to prove it has absolutely nothing to do with you or another woman. I just can't, Angel. But it's important you see my pros."

Taking the notebook from his hands, I stare at his handwriting. I'm barely registering his words as I run my fingertips over his penmanship.

"It's just a coincidence. It doesn't mean anything ..."

"I beg to differ, Angel, but given the circumstances, meaning something isn't enough." His voice is thick, and I wonder what darkness binds him.

"Does it have something to do with your father?" I blurt out.

"What?" he asks in an unnerving tone I've yet to hear from him.

"The man in your room earlier? He was your father, yes? You have his eyes. I've never seen anything like them before, so they were a dead giveaway that you were related."

"Fuck." Charlie curses as he runs a hand through his hair just as his foot taps the floor like he's trying to pump the brakes in a car that has none.

I place my hand on his knee, and he calms. *Interesting. Maybe I have the same effect on him?* "It's okay, Charlie. I'm not asking you to tell me. I was just making an observation. Your demeanor changed when he was here. Whatever darkness haunts you, I'm sure it comes from him."

Resting his head against mine, he breathes me in before speaking. "You have no idea."

Leaning into him, I register his words for the first time.
Pros:
-She's smart as hell.

-She's the most gorgeous woman I've ever met.

-She keeps me on my toes.

-I never know what she'll say.

-I don't have to wonder, she always tells me what's on her mind.

-I love listening to all her noises.

-She calms me.

-She makes me feel less alone.

Peering up at him, I study his face. "I make pros and cons lists to answer a question. What's your question?"

He swallows roughly before answering. "If I can make it through this week without breaking or breaking you."

"What?"

"Angel, please don't ask me to explain. I can't." He sounds pained, and something in my chest aches for him.

"Okay. Um … okay. Well, did you come up with an answer?"

He nods his head a few times, seeming to weigh his next words. "I did."

"What is it?" I ask, even though I'm afraid of what he'll say.

"I decided you're too incredible to let go. I'd be a fool not to spend the little time I have with you. So, I put all the other shit aside because I want to get to know you. I want to spend time with you in this game we are playing, as much as I can, for as long as I can. Is that all right with you, Angel?"

"Uh-huh." Apparently, not only can he calm me, but he can also stun me into complete silence.

"Good. Now, about your list. You make them to answer questions you need to see in black and white. Does seeing my list clear things up for you? I want the door to stay open because I want to spend every second of this week that I can with you."

"Okay, let's go." I jump to my feet like I was shot out of a cannon.

"Okay? That's it?" he asks.

"Yup, the chaos is coming. I need to walk, and we need to get to the game, so let's get moving."

I'm standing in front of him, trying to wrestle my hand free from his, but he holds firm, pulling me in between his legs.

"Let the chaos come, Angel. I want to hear it. You know, my friends actually welcome people to the chaos all the time." Charlie places both of his hands on my hips, and I feel a zing when his fingertips skim the hem of my T-shirt.

"I-I can't," I stammer.

"Why not, Angel?" His words are low. Comforting and dangerous at the same time.

"I'm not sure. It just doesn't come when you're this close." I'm shocked by my honesty.

"Good, that's what I want to hear. Let me calm your chaos." He gives me a smile that could be featured on the cover of *GQ*, and I melt.

"And I'll keep your darkness away." I'm not sure what makes me say it, but by the look on his face, we both know it's the truth.

Sighing, he lowers his gaze. "I don't know that anyone can do that, Angel. But you certainly bring in the light." Standing up, he kisses me chastely, then drags me through the room to the door. "Let's get to this baseball game you keep talking about."

The moment has passed, but I want more than anything to chase his darkness away.

"I don't think I've ever known a woman who can get ready faster than me." He's teasing, but there's also something else in his voice. Amusement? Appreciation, maybe? I try not to dwell on it.

"Shit, shower, and shave, as Miss Rosa would say. What else do you have to do?"

He laughs. "This Miss Rosa sounds like a character."

"She's definitely one of a kind." *If he only knew the half of it.*

Stepping out of the hotel onto the sidewalk, Charlie looks both ways, like he's lost. That's when I remember this is my city. I'm playing tour guide today. The thought has a calming effect. I'm in control here. Or at least I can pretend to be.

I grin as Charlie walks to the edge of the sidewalk. He holds a hand in the air like he's flagging a taxi.

"Ah ... what are you doing?" I ask him, fully amused.

"I checked the map, Angel. Fenway is quite the hike from here, so I'm getting a cab."

Poor misguided man.

"Is that right?" I hum. With his attention on the road, I drink him in, appreciating his low hanging, well-worn blue jeans for the first time. I love that his shirt says Betts on the back. Mookie Betts is one of my favorite players, and I'm willing to bet Charlie has no idea who he is. "I hate to break it to you, Mr. Bigshot, but this is Boston at rush hour, on game day. If we take a taxi, we'll arrive just in time for the seventh-inning stretch."

Taking his hand in mine like it's the most natural thing in the world, I drag him toward the public gardens. "The scary thing is just how natural this feels."

"I couldn't agree more, Angel," he whispers, kissing the side of my head.

"Crap, I said that out loud? I can't keep anything to myself."

"Angel, our time is limited. I'd be fucking ecstatic if you let every little thought spill from those sexy lips. Stop trying to keep things from me." It's a command issued with a smile.

I know he's teasing, but he doesn't understand how tempting that is for someone like me.

"Okay, my New-England girl. Tell me, where are you taking me if we can't take a taxi?"

Smiling, I lead the way. "We'll walk two blocks through

the public gardens, then we're getting on the Greenline. It'll drop us off right at Kenmore."

Charlie's steps falter. "The Greenline? You mean the subway?"

Turning to look over my shoulder quizzically, I stop, too. "Yes. The subway. Don't tell me Mr. Fancy Pants is too good for the subway."

"It's not that," he starts. "Fuck, this is embarrassing. I hate being underground. We don't have subways where I'm from. To be honest, growing up, I always had a car service. It's the only option I was given."

Somehow, knowing this is something he needs a gentle push on, I take his hand. "Luckily for you, I became an expert at the subway when I was in college. We can walk to the Back Bay stop, then it's a quick hop to Kenmore. We won't be underground long. I'll chase away your darkness, Charlie." Stepping on my tiptoes, I kiss him gently. It's such a familiar gesture already, I feel my heart cracking. *This will suck come Friday.*

"Even in the darkness, you're still my guiding light," he sings, and I'm confused for a second until realization hits me like a wrecking ball. He's playing my game.

"I'm always in awe of you," I sing.

"My angel, and my guiding light."

"I thought you were a country boy? You're a Mumford fan, too?"

We continue walking for about a block before he answers. "Music has always spoken to me. My dad and I never seemed to be on the same page." He stops and studies me. I can see a debate going on in his head.

"Tell me anything you want me to know, remember? We're making our own rules," I add with a shrug.

"That we are, Angel. That we are." He inhales sharply before continuing, "Well, my mother loved music. She could hear a song once and know every word. Music was always blaring throughout our house when she was home. I guess I got my love for it from her."

Not wanting to interrupt him, I squeeze his hand to let him know I'm listening.

"As I got older, it was my escape. I could connect with it even when I couldn't connect to my father." He laughs, lost in thought. "My best friends and I started going to live shows when we were thirteen. We'd sneak out of each other's houses and use fake IDs to get in."

We arrive at a crosswalk at the end of the public gardens and have to wait to cross. Turning to me, his eyes soften. "The music died for me for a long time. My head has been silent for years. There's something about you that brings it back. From the very first time I saw you beside your car, and again when I realized you were talking to yourself, I felt the music." He laughs. "Do you want to know what I heard?"

"Ah, I don't know. Do I? If it's a song about a crazy lady, the answer is no, I don't want to hear it." I'm not even joking. I already have enough people in my life that think I'm crazy. I can't handle it from him, too.

His shoulders shake with laughter. "There's nothing crazy about you, Angel. I heard Ed Sheeran. Tell me what's going on in your head," he sings.

"Get the fuck out of here." I shove his chest harder than I intended, causing the people on the street to turn and stare. "'Bibia Be Ye Ye'? That's my theme song," I shout, not because I'm mad but because I'm excited and a little freaked out. "I've never told anyone that. But it's my theme song. It seems to fit how my brain works when I have to be social. It's like I'm floating around, never really fitting in, but I'm happy." Throwing my hands over my face, I peer out through my fingers. "I'm totally crazy, you know?"

Charlie chuckles and grabs my hand. It's like we both crave the contact. "You're not," he promises. "And if you are, then I am, too, because I called your theme song. Are we

103

crossing?" he asks, gesturing to the blinking man telling us it's safe to cross.

"Yeah, come on."

Making our way to the Back Bay station, I notice Charlie clamming up. *He really doesn't like being underground.* I'll need to distract him.

"What would your theme song be?"

He doesn't hesitate, "The Wolf."

"Again with Mumford. I like it. It's all about frightened hearts. Do you know what I like about that song?"

"What?"

"The beat is dark, and dangerous. But the lyrics? The lyrics are full of hope and love. He wants to learn to love like he's been loved. It's the juxtaposition of those two things that make a whole person. You just have to figure out how to come to terms with both sides."

Knowing that was way too deep for what we are, I'm thankful when I hear the muffled voice of the conductor announcing Kenmore station. On game days, they pack these trains wall to wall. Tonight's no different. Floating with the sea of red and blue Red Sox gear, we make our way to Brookline Avenue.

"Okay. We have a few mandatory stops before we make it into Fenway," I say, grinning. Fenway Park is one of the few places where I feel truly at home.

Feeding off my enthusiasm, Charlie motions for me to continue. "Lead the way, Angel."

CHAPTER 11

TREVOR

"Fifteen Minutes Old" by Snow Patrol

*A*ngel walks us up Brookline Avenue toward a line at least fifty people deep. It's a bar called the Cask 'n Flagon, and as much as I want to let her lead, I'm not waiting in this line. She shocks the hell out of me when she marches us right to the front door.

"Babycakes. What are you doing here?" an old man who I estimate to be in his sixties asks, wrapping her in an embrace so tight he lifts her right off the ground.

What the fuck?

Angel's laughing as he whispers something while staring at me, and they have a conversation I can't hear. Balling my hands into fists, I take a step forward. These caveman instincts are new for me, but he can get his goddamn hands off of her right the fuck now.

Sensing my distress, Angel turns and places a hand on my chest. "Relax, Charlie. This is Teddy. He's friends with my dad and has worked here for longer than I've been alive."

Thrusting my hand out, I shake his. "Nice to meet you, Teddy."

He replies in the thickest Boston accent I've ever heard. "Ya too, Charlie. You got your hands full with this spitfire here, huh? You ever been to a game with her before?"

"No, sir, first time," I grind out.

Both he and his colleague double over, laughing. "Wh- Where are you sitting, Babycakes?"

Why the fuck does he keep calling her Babycakes?

"Third base dugout," Angel replies sheepishly.

He starts laughing so hard I can't understand most of what he's saying, until he composes himself. "Oh shit, honey. Is Reggie umping tonight? Or am I going to get a call to pick you up at the gate again?"

Scowling and looking embarrassed, Angel huffs. "You listen here, Teddy. That was one time. One. Time. And they didn't even kick me out of the park, they just reseated me."

I have no idea what she's talking about, but I get the distinct impression I'm in for one hell of a night.

"You better keep good tabs on her, Charlie. If you haven't been warned, she takes her baseball very seriously." His words sound ominous.

"Whatever, Teddy. Can we go in? Charlie has to experience the Cask before we head over to BeerWorks," Angel interrupts.

"Sure thing, Babycakes. I'll let Mikey know you're headed his way. Do you want a table at BeerWorks, or are you just getting a blueberry?" Teddy asks.

I'm thoroughly confused.

Staring at me, then Teddy, Angel says, "Just blueberries, I think. Charlie needs to experience the sausage guy, too."

"Sounds good. Have fun, Babycakes. I'm heading to the park in five, so call if you need backup." His full belly laugh drowns out the surrounding crowd.

Rolling her beautiful green eyes, Angel grabs my hand and drags me into the dim bar with the people behind us grumbling about waiting our turn. Once my eyes adjust to the darkened atmosphere, I have a look around and am shocked by the sheer amount of people here—every single person in head-to-toe Red Sox apparel.

She yells so I can hear her over the crowd, but I still have to bend almost in half to make out her words.

"You have to experience the Cask at least once when you come to Fenway. Come on, we'll get a shot here, then head over to BeerWorks."

Following her through the bar, I admire her appearance. Tight, dark-wash skinny jeans hug her ass. She has the legs rolled up to mid-calf, showing off her delicate ankles that flow into her pink Chuck Taylor's. Earlier, I noticed a worn hole just under her front pocket, and I've been itching to rub my thumb along the exposed skin. No matter how close she is, it doesn't seem to be enough. Her faded, well-loved T-shirt is as soft as it looks from being washed so many times.

Mine says Betts on the back, and I had to Google it. At first, I thought she was playing some kind of trick on me. I was pleasantly surprised to find that Mookie Betts is an all-star right fielder. Her shirt says Varitek, and while the name is familiar, I don't recall much about that specific player. Glancing around the bar, I notice most of the girls Angel's age have dressed to the nines. Full faces of makeup and sky-high heels showing off excessively exposed legs. My eyes trace Angel's retreating form once more. Her Chuck Taylor's are frayed, and she's pulled her hair into a high ponytail. If she has any makeup on, it's minimal enough that I can't tell. She's gorgeous.

I stand back as she leans over the bar to hug the bartender, but my hands ball into fists again. This guy is young, good looking, and I immediately want to rip his goddamn head off.

"Two red-headed sluts, please, Jimmy," Angel yells.

Sliding in beside her at the bar, I give a death glare to the fuckwad beside me, who was trying to invade Angel's space. "Do you know everyone in this city, Angel?" I grumble.

Either missing my attitude or ignoring it, she shrugs. "Just near Fenway. I used to work here in college. My dad got me a job with the grounds crew. It was so freaking awesome."

Well, I guess that explains why she knows all these guys.

"Here you go." She hands me a shot.

Clinking glasses with her, I down the shot and immediately want to vomit.

"What the hell was that?" I choke out.

"Red-headed slut," she giggles. "I know they're not great, but it's part of my pre-game ritual. Come on, I'll show you around, then we'll head to BeerWorks. You'd never tell from the outside, but this place is huge."

Walking from the bar, I follow her into a room that opens up to a dance floor.

"Dance with me, Angel?" I command.

I don't wait for an answer. I drag her to the middle of the room just as "One of Them Girls" by Lee Brice comes on. Pulling her in as close as humanly possible, I move. Every time we dance, the world fades away.

I'm usually the last one on the dance floor, but I can't help myself around her. Our bodies move in sync to the beat. As Lee sings about trading your whole life for a girl, I know I'm in trouble. I'm in a lot of fucking trouble because I know without a doubt I would trade my entire world for more time with this girl in my arms.

The song ends, and Angel pulls away, grinning. "I never dance. What are you doing to me?"

I'm trying not to fall for you, a voice in my head shouts. "Just trying to make sure you never forget me."

Sadness washes over her face, and I want to kick myself. As quickly as it came, it's gone. She's smiling again but it doesn't quite reach her eyes.

"Let's go. We have just enough time for one more Fenway staple before we head into the park."

"Angel," I begin. *What? What do I want to say to her?*

"No worries, Charlie. We both know what this is." Turning her back, she walks toward the front of the bar. I have no choice but to follow behind.

"We both know what this is," plays on repeat in my head. I hate it.

Out on the street, we say our good-byes to yet another fan of hers. I didn't even attempt to get this guy's name. When she finally separates, I take her hand even though I'm not sure what direction we're headed. I'm feeling out of sorts.

"This way," she says, pulling me in the opposite direction.

"Why aren't you looking for forever, Angel?" I ask, stopping her in her tracks.

"Who said I wasn't? Someday, it'll happen. I know it will, so why force the issue? Especially with someone I meet in a city I visit every few months. I'm not planning to move, are you? Love happens when you don't expect it. I spend my entire life learning what to expect, that's literally my job. And, I have responsibilities at home." Her eyes shift anywhere but on me. "You have shit going on, too. I don't need to know specifics to know that. So, the way I see it, you can take this for what it is and have fun, or you can move on, but I'm going to this game."

Breaking free from my grasp, she marches toward the street. I see it happen in slow motion. As she's storming off, she misses the step down from the sidewalk. My angel, who is the least graceful person I've ever met, also has no self-preservation whatsoever. She sweeps her arms like a windmill to keep from falling, just as I reach her. Pulling her to my side, I breathe her in deeply. *I need to stop doing that.* As I exhale, I try to let my shit go so I don't ruin the small amount of time we have together.

"Okay," I relent. "Show me this blueberry thing I need to try. But I swear to God if it's as bad as that red-headed slut, I will definitely spank you later."

Sucking in air, she gulps audibly, and I laugh.

Leaning in so my lips touch her ear, I ask, "Would you like that, Angel? To be spanked right before I fuck you? Would you like to feel my hand meeting the flesh of your ass, just enough to sting? Then feel me soothe it as I kneed the pink flesh?"

Her entire body is flushing pink, and I feel ten feet tall, knowing I did that to her with just my words.

"Tonight, Angel. Tonight, we'll experiment."

She blinks rapidly before leading us to the front of the line at BeerWorks. I can't help the smirk on my face as I watch a flustered Angel trying to hold a conversation with Mikey, the guy at the front door.

"Hi, Mikey. Nice to meet you, I'm Charlie."

"Nice to meet ya, man. I hear this is your first game with Babycakes here. You're in for a real treat. Don't let her fool you. She seems all sweet and innocent, but she can get kicked out of the park with the best of them," he laughs.

Shocked, I train my gaze on Angel, who shrugs, looking bored.

"What?" she asks. "I told you I'm not a fair-weather fan."

"That's one way to put it," Mikey chimes in. "This pint-sized girl has brought more than one professional baseball player to his knees."

Wide-eyed, I volley between Angel and Mikey. "Surely, that's not true?"

"Once. It happened once. I was a kid, and it was *the* game of the century. I mean, come on! Schilling's sock was soaked in blood. What did that guy expect? He should have worried about his at-bat anyway, not what some kid in the stands was saying."

"Like I said, good luck handling Babycakes in that stadium." Mikey chuckles. "Where are you sitting, anyway?"

I'm not going to lie, I'm getting nervous.

Angel grins. "Third-base dugout."

"Oh, shit!" Mikey barks out. Clapping me on the back, he says, "Good luck, man. You better chug a few beers. You're going to need them."

Rolling her eyes, Angel takes me by the hand and, once again, drags me inside.

Using her little body, she worms her way through the densely packed room, somehow clearing a path for me in her wake. Once we reach the back wall of the industrial-themed room, she weasels herself up to the bar where the bartender automatically hands her two beers. There's no way she had time to even order them, so I assume the man behind the bar is another friend of hers.

"Here you go." She hands me a beer with floating blueberries in it.

"What the hell is this?" I ask.

"A blueberry beer, another ritual. I'm not superstitious, except when it comes to baseball. Drink up."

Taking a sip through my teeth, I attempt to avoid the berries.

"Honestly? I'm not really a fan of the floaters," I admit.

"Why? They're blueberries," she explains like I didn't hear her the first time.

"I know, and I like blueberries, but I can say confidently that I dislike them in my beer."

She stares at me like I have three heads, then takes the drink from my hand. I'm in shock as she sticks her little fingers into my beer and scoops them all out into her own glass.

"That was both disgusting and sexy as hell. Thank you for saving me from the floaters." I laugh.

111

"That's what I'm here for," she bumps her shoulder into my side before continuing, "to save you from yourself."

I pause with my beer mid-air at her words. She doesn't understand how true that statement is, and it's scaring the shit out of me. Trying to shake it off, I ask, "So, do I have something to worry about at this game tonight? Should I run to the ATM to make sure we have bail money?"

"Ugh, they all exaggerated. I'm not that bad." She doesn't sound convincing, though.

"Famous last words If I've ever heard them," I joke. "Have you always been a die-hard baseball fan?"

The smile that takes over her face tells so many stories. Stories I want to know so badly but realize I can't. *You're only her now, not her forever.* My chest tightens at the thought.

"As long as I can remember. My dad loves the Sox. My parents have had season tickets since before they had me. We drive down for as many games as we can now. When I was a kid, my parents used to pick my best friend and me up from school, drive down for the game, then drive home after so we wouldn't miss school the next day."

"Sounds like you're close with your family?" It slips past my lips, but I like knowing she has people looking out for her.

"Very. My parents and my best friend are all I have. I've never been very social. My best friend I was telling you about? She's this tall, beautiful goddess that everyone loves, so I've always had people around by proxy, but her and my parents are my peeps." Her smile while talking about family disarms me.

"That sounds really nice," I say, shocked that I mean it.

"What about you? I know, well, we don't have to talk about your father, but what about your mom? Friends?"

Normally, this is a sore subject, but knowing how much my mother would have loved Angel has me opening up. "My mother passed away when I was in college, but before that, I counted on her for everything. Not in a momma's boy kind of way," I clarify.

Angel laughs as I hoped she would. "Of course not."

"I just mean, she was the constant in my life. The one who always stuck by me and encouraged me. It was hard when she died, for my friends and for me. She was like a surrogate mother to them."

"I'm so sorry for your loss." She places a hand over mine, and my gaze lingers on the connection. She doesn't ask how she died, thank God; she just holds my hand, passing me her strength.

This girl!

Urgently needing to change the subject, I blurt, "Tell me something about yourself. Something real."

She hesitates, tapping her chin while she thinks. Her brows lift when she has an answer. "My middle name is Grace."

I almost drop my glass and have to swallow multiple times before I can speak again. "That was my mother's name," I force out. "Grace Juliette." Lifting my gaze to Angel's, she seems as flustered as I feel.

"Huh. Wow, that's an … ah … a coincidence, isn't it? Funny how life works out. Well, we should finish these beers. The game will start soon. Do you watch baseball? I mean, I know you're not a Sox fan, but in general? Did you play any sports growing up? I'm not athletic, but you've probably figured that out already. I'm not super graceful. Huh. Grace. There it is again. So …"

Placing my beer down, I pull Angel into me. "What has you spiraling, Angel? What's happening in this beautiful head of yours?"

Biting her bottom lip so hard I can see the indent forming, she shakes her head.

"You don't want to tell me?"

She shakes her head again.

"Okay," I say, taking half a step back so I can see her fully. "Did I say something wrong? Are you all right?"

She sucks in a large gulp of air and holds it for a few seconds before answering. "Yes, sorry. It's nothing like that. It's just, well, we still have rules, right? But it sounds like your mother and I probably had a lot in common. I'm sorry I'm being weird. The superstitions all make me a little nuttier than normal. My mind is just wandering to crazy places."

You and me both, Angel.

CHAPTER 12

JULIA

"Sweet Caroline" by Neil Diamond

*G*race Juliette? Grace freaking Juliette? Coincidence, Jules, that's all. Just because your name is Julia Grace, it doesn't mean anything! I scold myself, thankfully able to keep these words in my head.

"Angel?" Charlie's voice makes me jump. *Shit, I must have spaced out in my thoughts.*

"What? Sorry, what did you say?"

"Are you sure you're okay?" he asks again.

"Yup, totally. You ready? We have to get to our seats. Chris Sales is pitching tonight, and he has been on fire! I need to watch his warm-ups to see how the game will go. Plus, Christian Vazquez is catching. I love catchers."

Chuckling, he sets my empty beer glass on the table beside him and takes my hand. "Lead the way, Angel."

Walking through Fenway is like coming home. A home that thousands of people consider theirs. "Are you hungry?" I ask.

"Always," he says, but his eyes stay locked firmly on my lips and I shudder.

Pulling myself together, I drag him through the throngs of people. "One more stop, then. You have to meet the Sausage Guy."

Charlie laughs but follows along. I walk up to George and give the big, sweaty guy a fist bump.

"Babycakes, long time no see." He is the epitome of Boston, and I love it. "What can I get you?"

"Two, please. Loaded." I reach into my pocket and pull out my money, but Charlie places a hand over mine.

"I don't think so, Angel. You got away with buying the beers because you didn't give me another choice, but I'm paying from here on out," Charlie whispers in my ear.

After handing George the money, he takes the two sausages in one hand and offers his free one to me. When I place my hand in his it seems different, but I couldn't tell you why. Trying to shake off this feeling, I pull him into the underbelly of Fenway.

Finding our seats is easy. I know this place like the back of my hand. "We can get settled, then I'll run up and grab a couple of beers. They just started selling Sip of Sunshine. It's a beer from Vermont. If you like IPAs, this will be your new favorite," I say confidently. "I don't know how they do it, but it's the best IPA you'll ever have."

"You surprise me at every turn, Angel." His tone is full of reverence. "Sit your cute, little butt down and try not to get thrown out before the game starts. I'll grab the beers."

He leans in and kisses me quickly, then makes his way back up the concrete steps toward the concession stands. *How did I end up here with this man?* I've never seen a more attractive guy in my life.

Sitting back, I let the sights and sounds of Fenway cover me in happiness. The Green Monster that's across the stadium, Pesky Pole, even the Citgo sign. They're all reminiscent of happy times. I wonder how many people here see these things and have the sense of nostalgia I'm having right now.

Scanning the crowd, I take in the smiling faces of everyone around me. Children and adults alike. All here for America's pastime in one of the most iconic stadiums in the world. I'm relaxing into my surroundings when my eyes land on ones so familiar, yet so cold, I immediately go stiff. *Whiskey and fireflies*, Charlie had said, and that's exactly what's staring straight at me. Charlie's eyes in the face of a much older, angrier looking man.

"Jules, Jules!" I hear my name being called. Glancing around, I spot Reggie standing by the dugout.

I jump out of my seat, take a step forward, and lean over the railing. "Reggie!" I cry. Reggie has been a friend of my dad for years. Before I was born, he was a client at my parents' law firm. Over the years, he and my dad have formed the most unlikely of friendships.

Reaching up, Reggie pulls me into a hug. "Hey there, Babycakes. How are you?"

"I'm good, Reg. How are you? How's MaryAnne?" I ask. His wife, MaryAnne, has been going through cancer treatments at Brigham and Woman's Hospital.

"Oh, you know her. She's good, and giving the doctors hell," he says, smiling. Motioning behind me, he asks, "A friend of yours?"

Righting myself, I turn to see Charlie standing a few feet away wearing a scowl. I can't help but grin at the jealousy written all over his face.

"Yup, that's Charlie," I tell my friend. "I should get back. Please tell MaryAnne I said hello. My mom wants to come down next month to check on her, too."

"That would be great, Babycakes. We sure miss you guys," he adds with a wink. "Please don't make me throw you out of here tonight, huh?"

"Don't make any terrible calls, and we'll be just fine," I respond, only partially joking. Friend or not, I'm not messing around with my Sox.

"I'll do my best, Babycakes. Good to see you, hun."

Taking the few steps back to Charlie, I stop right in front of him. "What's with the face, Charlie? You swallow some lemons or something?"

"Do you know every man in this stadium or what? And why do they all call you Babycakes?" he asks, sounding like a sullen teenager.

"Why, Charlie, are you jealous?" I tease.

"Yes," he bellows, then quickly tries to backtrack. "I mean …" He lets out a heavy sigh. "Here, Sip of Sunshine, just like you requested. I even sprang for the matching koozie."

"Ooh, I love koozies. Come on, let's get to our seats, and I'll tell you all about Babycakes."

Placing his hand on the small of my back, he guides me to our seats and we sit. With my eyes trained on the field, I force the words to come. "My dad has taken me here forever, but I wasn't always an easy child. The noises sometimes bothered me. I didn't like people getting too close, and I hated when people sat behind me, which, as you can imagine, made these seating arrangements a little tricky."

"Why would he bring you, then?" Charlie asks, sounding concerned. "I mean, it doesn't sound like it could have been enjoyable."

"He brought me because I loved it. I hated everything else, but I loved being here. I think more than once, it broke him to see me struggle with wanting to be here in my mind, but physically crawling out of my skin. I was the kid with those big headphones on that would rock in my seat when things got to be too much. I saw my father cry in these seats for reasons that had nothing to do with baseball," I admit.

"Anyway, if I could make it to the seventh-inning stretch, I was in the clear, but getting there was tough sometimes," I say, swallowing hard. "I don't know how I didn't end up weighing three hundred pounds as a child, but my dad figured out the fried dough would distract me during my episodes. I liked to watch the powdered sugar float through the air with every bite. When I was really little, I called them babycakes." Pausing, I peek at Charlie as understanding takes place. "All these 'guys' you met tonight? They're all friends with my dad or people that had season tickets next to us. All people that just wanted to help a little girl enjoy something that meant the world to her. They became friends who would go sprinting through Fenway to find the funnel cake guy as soon as I started rocking in my seat. After a while, my dad never even had to ask. Everyone around us got used to my cues. Some of them got so good at reading me, I'd have a babycake in my hands before I even realized I needed one. It only took one season for the name to stick. I've been Babycakes to them ever since."

Leaning in to press his forehead to mine, Charlie whispers, "I'm glad you had all these guys, Angel. It sounds like you have an amazing family. But, what would happen in the seventh-inning stretch?"

I smile because I do have a fantastic family, but thinking of them reminds me of Charlie's dad, and I pull away quickly.

Not sure where to start, I answer the easy question first, "During the seventh-inning stretch they play my song, you'll see." I smile. "Um … Charlie?" I'm so nervous and I have no idea why.

"What is it, Angel?"

"I know we have our rules, but—"

"Fuck our rules, Angel. Remember, we're making our own." His words are firm, but gentle.

"Right, well, ah, I mean, it's just that …"

Charlie places a hand on my knee and I relax. Staring into his whiskey and firefly eyes, I ask, "Would you be okay if your father was following you?"

His hand squeezes my leg, almost to the point of pain, before he gets his bearings and eases up. "Sorry, Angel," he says, rubbing my leg where his hand had been. "Why would you ask that?" He's glancing around us now, visibly shaken but trying to control himself.

"When you went to get the beers, I saw him. He was sitting five or six rows up at your eleven o'clock."

I watch as Charlie nonchalantly takes in our surroundings, focusing his attention where I told him to look, but not finding what he is searching for. Pressing a button on his Apple watch, he barks, "Eyes on me, eleven o'clock, fifteen minutes ago."

Training my eyes on the beer in front of me, I realize I'm wringing my hands. Something is very, very wrong here. My foot taps in time to my thoughts as I make mental lists, trying to figure out what I've gotten myself into. Without thinking, I blurt, "Are you dangerous?"

Taken aback, Charlie appears hurt, but seems to understand my need for information.

"No, Angel. I'm not dangerous. I'm not married. I'm not a liar. I'm not a criminal. What I am is a man trying to make his own way in this world but have family ties that are trying to drag me under. I won't let that happen," he says.

I think he's about to elaborate when a man I don't know sits down beside him. Charlie's body language changes instantly. He obviously knows the stranger.

"Charlie," the man says in acknowledgement. Leaning over Charlie, the man offers his hand to me. "Nice to meet you. I'm Lance Jacobs. I've been friends with Charlie here since elementary school."

"Ah, I'm … Angel? Angel McDowell," I tell him. "It's nice to meet you as well."

Why did I use my real last name? Fuck.

A smile that seems genuine takes over the stranger's face.

"The pleasure is all mine. Do you mind if I borrow our friend here for a moment?"

"Ah, sure?"

"Lance," Charlie warns, barely controlling his temper, "I'm not leaving her here." He grumbles the words under his breath, but I hear them.

Nodding in understanding, Lance speaks in fragments. "Eyes have vacated. The mark is untraceable. I've tried it."

They're talking in code, and it's exhausting trying to follow along, so I train my attention back on the field. After a while, JD Martinez takes the field, and I jump out of my seat like the fangirl I am. Then, I chant along with the other thirty thousand fans, "Let's. Go. Red. Sox."

When Christian Vasquez throws out a runner trying to steal second base to end the third inning, my voice is hoarse and I'm a little sweaty. I've gotten so lost in the excitement of the game that I forgot who I was with. Glancing down, I see Charlie sitting back in his chair, his long legs spread wide to fit in the compact space. He isn't watching the game. Charlie is watching me. His eyes have gone dark, intense, *smoldering*. Sitting down, suddenly shy, I can't take my eyes off of him.

It only takes a second for him to wrap one arm around my middle. "You're the fucking sexiest woman I've ever met. I don't know how I can get my fill of you in just four days, but I'll try. And you'll go home feeling me inside of you for weeks."

I gulp. "Mhm." I'm unable to form sentences. Reaching for my now lukewarm beer, I chug it, causing him to chuckle.

"Goddamn it, woman. You'll be the death of me." He's running circles around my neck with his index finger and my brain short circuits.

For the first time in my life, I sit watching the rest of the game without actually seeing it. Charlie's hand on my neck has all my nerve endings doing the Cha-Cha, and my clit throbbing.

I'm heading for heartbreak for sure.

Finally, it's the seventh inning. Turning to Charlie, I grab his hand and help him stand. Together, with thirty thousand others, we sway and sing along to Neil Diamond's "Sweet Caroline" hand in hand.

CHAPTER 13

TREVOR

"Weak" by AJR

We're both quiet as we make our way back to the hotel. Angel isn't chatty, but I can see her brain working overtime. I hate that she has doubts about me. I hate even more that my father put them in her head. It's yet another thing he's ruining for me.

I spent the entire game watching her. I have every inch of her memorized for when we have to part. It's the knowledge that no matter how much I want things to be different, there can be no other ending with her.

Why couldn't I have met her after my father was in jail?

It's taking every shred of decency I have not to ask her to wait for me. *What kind of asshole would that make me?* I can't be with you right now, but wait for me? I can't even tell her why.

My father showing up at the game tonight brought me back to the present in the harshest of ways. As much as I want to pretend the devil isn't on my tail, he was right there to remind me he's coming. If not him, then someone like him. It's only a matter of time. I cannot, no matter how much

I want to keep this woman, bring her into this world. Not when everything in me is screaming that she'll end up like my mother.

When Loki introduced himself as Lance, I thought my time with Angel was over. I was sure he was there to escort me home. Thankfully, that wasn't the case. But it was a reminder that my time with Angel is limited, so I need to take advantage of every fucking moment.

The door closes softly with a click, and I watch as Angel sits on the bed to untie her sneakers. Knowing I have to address the elephant in the room, I walk to her and stand between her legs. I place my finger under her chin and bring her eyes to mine.

Lowering myself to the floor until we're face-to-face, I tell her what I can. "Angel, my father is a vile human being. He probably always has been and definitely always will be. He's my reason for agreeing to play your game. Until he's out of my life, I can't have a future. He's not a good man, Angel, but he will not hurt you. No one knows who you are. The man you met tonight, Lance? He's one of the good guys, and he assured me that no one can find you. If he can't find you, men like my father won't be able to either. I know this is all cryptic and scary sounding. Fuck!" I sigh, raking a hand through my hair almost violently. "If you want me to leave, I will, but I really hope you don't, because I like you, Angel. More than I've ever liked anyone, and I want to get my fill before we're forced to go our separate ways. I'm sure whatever your reasons for the rules are, they're nowhere near as crazy sounding as mine. I'm just trying to be as honest as I can with you. Y-You're special to me."

"You make it sound like he's in the mob or something." She laughs.

I inhale sharply, but she doesn't appear to notice.

She moves to stand, but I don't budge. It forces her body to connect with mine, and there's no missing my arousal.

Reaching up on her tiptoes, she grabs my neck to bring my mouth to hers.

"Thank fuck," I groan, ripping her T-shirt over her head and tossing it to the floor. The red lace that greets me is exquisite. Ghosting my palms over her nipples, I feel the heat radiating off of her. She moans before I've even touched her, causing a growl to escape from deep within me.

"Charlie," she whispers, the name growing on me. I feel more alive as Charlie than I've ever felt as Trevor.

"I know, Angel. God, I know." It's all I can say. There's so much that has to be left unsaid between us, and it fucking makes me hate myself. This girl deserves the world. She deserves love, a life I know I'm incapable of providing at the moment. I hate myself because even with that knowledge, I'm too goddamn selfish to walk away from her. I'm connecting to her in a way that, until now, I never would have believed existed.

Slowly, I lower her to the bed, cherishing, worshiping every inch of her. I'm committing every freckle, every indent to memory, knowing I'll have to leave her. This line of thinking has my chest aching so painfully I fist a hand over my heart, willing it to stop.

"Are you okay?" Angel asks, noticing my distress.

I stare at her for a moment, contemplating how to respond. Hating that I'm about to lie to her. "Yeah, Angel. I'm fine. I-I just get lost in you sometimes." The last part was the truth, at least. I'm getting lost in her so fast, my brain doesn't have time to catch up.

Hovering over her delicate body, I lower my lips to hers. I'm praying everything I want to say to her is emitted through this kiss. As my tongue seeks entry, my eyes close, and I'm lost to the sensations of her. The softness of her lips, the sweet taste of mint from the gum she was chewing on our way home. The way she moves under me, seeking the friction I know she needs. It's all enough to break me. I'm weak to her.

Grabbing her hips, I roll her to her stomach in one quick movement, and she shrieks. After lifting her to her knees, I reach up from behind and cup her tit with one hand. I lean in, letting my cock grind into her ass as I run my other hand down her spine, stopping at her bra strap to undo the clasp.

Angel wiggles her ass into me. "You're good one-handed, Charlie," she teases.

"You haven't seen anything yet, Angel." I groan into her ear as I slide her bra straps down her arms.

She's about to say something else, undoubtedly something sassy, but I cut her off when I use my hand to flick open the button on her jeans, and she gasps. "Something you'd like to say, Angel?" I growl.

"Ah, nope, nothing at all. Just keep on carrying on," she says a hundred miles a minute.

"I like that plan, Angel. I think I'll do just that." Leaning over her again, I unzip her jeans, then use both hands to pull them from her body, loving the view I get as she pushes her ass in the air so I can get the jeans past her knees. When her pants are off, I wrap one hand around her waist and bite her ass cheek. Not hard, just enough to hear her squeal and try to pull away from me.

Remembering our conversation from earlier, I run my hand along her ass, skimming my thumbs along the seam of her thong. She remembers our conversation, too; I can tell because she tenses momentarily. Rubbing rhythmic circles on her backside, I whisper, "Shh, Angel. I'll never hurt you." And I mean it with every fiber of my being.

"Charlie," she whines.

Without warning, I smack her ass with my open palm and listen as she moans, burying her face in the pillow to muffle the sound.

"Oh, Angel. That isn't going to work," I say, reaching

above her to pull the pillow away. "I want to hear you, remember?"

"Holy hell," she gasps as she pushes her ass into me again.

"Impatient tonight, Angel. I like it, but we're taking this nice," I pause, linking my thumbs into the corner of her thong, "and slow," I finish as I tug her panties free.

"Fuck! Angel, you're soaking wet for me."

"Yes," she pants.

Chuckling, I'm surprised by her one-word response. "Have words finally escaped you, sweetheart?" The endearment rolls off my tongue like it was branded there, just for her.

"Yes," she says again, sounding more desperate this time.

I place both hands on her ass, angling it toward the ceiling, giving me the perfect view of her glistening pussy. *Holy shit.* I know I said we were taking this slow, but I've turned into a wild animal. Turning my hand palm up, I cup her pussy, tapping my middle finger against her clit, causing her to moan. Painfully slow, my finger enters her channel. Warm heat envelopes me, and I have to count to ten.

When I briefly pull away, Angel whines in protest. After shucking my clothes so fast I rip a hole in the arm of the Red Sox shirt I was wearing, I'm back to her in seconds. Gripping my cock in one hand, I place the other back inside of her warm lips.

"Fucking hell, Angel," I force out through gritted teeth. I'm stroking my angry, weeping cock, trying to keep him from going off on his own accord. Curling my fingers inside of her, I place my other hand on her hip and pull her into me, letting my dick press into her backside.

"Charlie, I want you inside of me. Please," she begs.

"Not yet, sweetheart. I need you to come first, and I'll lick every last drop from you before we continue." Spreading her legs, I lay down underneath her, pulling her throbbing clit to my face. The surprised gasp she emits has me smiling like a goddamn fool again.

With my hands on her hips, I press her lower so she's straddling my face, and I set the beast free. Hanging on to her tightly with one hand, I use the other to cup her tit, pulling and pinching her nipple as she grinds involuntarily on my face. It's the single hottest moment of my life, and I pray to God I remember every single second of it.

"Charlie, I-I'm, oh God," Angel starts, then pulls away so suddenly I'm left bereft. Before I can protest, she has turned herself around and is lowering her mouth to my cock.

"Jesus Christ, sweetheart, what the fu—" My brain cells have all died and gone to heaven.

Unable to keep my hips on the bed, they lift to meet her sexy mouth. Using her hand as a guide, she licks a line from my base to tip, paying extra attention to the underside of my head, and I'm fucking gone.

Lifting her hips, I raise her body over my head. Before she can protest, she's landing on the bed behind me. Then I'm on top of her again, pushing my tip to her entrance. I try to slow down, but when I look at her face, all my willpower evaporates. Using her heels as leverage, she pushes up, and her walls claim my cock with a squeeze so tight I'm panting.

"Fuck me, Charlie, please. I need you now," Angel implores.

Rolling my hips, I thrust up and into her, hard. Again and again. Once I'm seated fully inside of her heat, I grind my pelvis against her clit, never letting up on the friction. I'm deep, and she's so tight. I'm grinding my teeth so fucking hard I'll be surprised if they aren't ground to dust by the time I finally come.

Her pussy's pulsating, squeezing my shaft tighter with each thrust, and I know she's getting close. Leaning down so my torso is in line with hers, I kiss her. The kiss is full of the feelings I can't say. I snake a hand between us and put pressure on her clit just as I pick up the pace.

"Angel, I need you to come. I want you to come on my cock so hard my dick will feel your walls strangling him for days," I growl.

My spine tingles, and I have to clench my ass cheeks. *You will not come before she does, you little fucker*. Her pussy vibrates, and I know she's about to go off.

"Let me hear you, Angel. Let me fucking hear you," I remind her through clenched teeth.

And then I'm gone. Unable to hold back any further, I unleash, pounding into her tight, little body like I'll never have this feeling again. I see stars. I'm grunting like a wild animal, and I'm covered in a sheen of sweat when I finally come to.

Glancing down into Angel's face, my breath gets caught in my lungs. *I think I could love this girl*. Twenty-four fucking hours and I think I'm in love.

We stare at each other for what feels like an eternity. Neither of us speaking. Neither of us blinking, just staring into the other's eyes, seeing what forever could look like.

Angel is the first to break. "Holy shit. That was …" She can't finish.

"That was devastatingly amazing, Angel. That's what that was." I kiss her tenderly, then pull back and watch as my dick slides out of her pussy. Watching my come flow from her entrance, I want to pound my chest like a motherfucking caveman. Then I meet her eyes, and the color drains from my face.

"*Fuck!*"

Angel sits up quickly, banging her head against mine. "What the hell?" she shrieks, holding her forehead.

"Sweetheart, if you're going to head butt me every time we have sex, I'll need to invest in a helmet. But, seriously, we have a problem."

"Wh-What's the matter?" she asks, searching the room for danger, and I hate the uncertainty in her voice. If anything in my life were different, I'd vow right now to make sure she never sounded like that again.

"God, I'm so fucking sorry. I got carried away. I ..." I'm so ashamed of myself. Guilt has settled deep in my gut, and I feel sick, but not for the reasons I should. I feel guilty because the thought of her pregnant with my child flashed before my eyes and I didn't panic. I didn't fight it. I reveled in it. In a split second, I envisioned her pregnant with my baby, and I felt a happiness I didn't know existed. A happiness I don't deserve. A happiness I can't have. "Fuck, I forgot the condom, Angel. I'm so sorry. Tell me what to do. I'm out of my element here. I have never, not even once, had sex without wrapping that fucker up tight."

Unable to look at her, I lower my head. I'm afraid she'll tell me to get the hell out and I'll never see her again. That's when I know Friday will never be enough. I'm fucked seven ways to Sunday, and there's not a goddamn thing I can do about it.

I startle when I feel a gentle hand rest on my shoulder. Angel is in front of me, on her knees, so she's eye level with me. Completely fucking naked and so gorgeous it hurts.

"Charlie?" she asks quietly.

When I turn to face her, I'm gutted. "I'm so sorry, Angel."

Putting her hands gently on each side of my face, she pulls me to her chest. She just holds me. Comforting me when it should be the other way around, or at the very least, mutual. Wrapping my arms around her, I hug her back; the gesture so innocent, yet so powerful, that my eyes sting. I don't fucking cry, and yet here I am. Not because Angel might be pregnant, but because instead of freaking the fuck out, she's holding me.

"I'm on the pill, Charlie, and while no condom isn't ideal,

I think we'll be okay. I can call my doctor and have her call in Plan-B to be safe."

"I'm such a fucking idiot, Angel. I promise you, I've never done that before," I plead because I need her to believe me more than I need my next breath.

"So, what you're saying is, I'm your first?" It takes me a minute, but when I catch on, she's smiling.

Just like that, she's pulled me from the dark. I'm laughing when, moments ago, all I felt was despair. "You're my guiding light, aren't you? And to answer your question …" I pause to pull her into my lap. I need to hold her close. "Yes, you're most certainly my first."

*My first unprotected sex, my first love, my first broken hear*t, screams the voice inside of my head.

"I like being your first," she whispers.

"Me too, Angel. More than you could know."

"I'm going to go call my doctor. You okay?"

Why the fuck is she worrying about me?

"Yeah, sweetheart. I'm all right. I'll go take a quick shower so I can go with you wherever we have to go."

"I think it'll just be a pharmacy," she says like I'm crazy.

"Angel, let me be very clear about this. I *fucked up*. I'm not a *fuck-up*. I'll be going with you." I leave no room for discussion.

"D-Do you think I wouldn't do it? Don't you trust me?" Her gaze drops to the floor, and she's biting her lip. She's so insecure, and I hate that I've caused it.

I lift her so she's straddling me, and we're face-to-face. "Angel, that has nothing to do with it. For reasons I can't explain, I think I trust you more than anyone I've ever known. This is about me being there for you."

I want to tell her that if circumstances were different, I'd tie her to the bed and hope and pray she was pregnant with my child—something I've never once wanted before. But I don't. Because I can't. She can't be part of my fucked-up life.

131

"Okay," she says, but her voice wobbles and I know I haven't convinced her yet.

"Call your doctor. I'll be back in five minutes." My heart screams to reassure her, but the words won't come.

Nodding, she stands, and I watch as she trips over herself trying to make it to her phone. *My clumsy Angel, what am I going to do with you?*

Nothing, ass-fuck. Get your goddamn head on straight. This isn't forever.

CHAPTER 14

JULIA

"Life Changes" by Thomas Rhett

I wake up, severely overheated, and in a vice. I can't move a muscle. Rolling my head to the side, I see Charlie has me tucked into every nook and cranny of his hot, delicious body. And by hot, this time I mean actual temperature hot.

"Charlie," I say, trying to wiggle myself free, which only causes him to grasp me tighter.

After I got off the phone with the doctor two nights ago, I told Charlie that she didn't think I needed the emergency contraceptive. We were both relieved, I guess, but the rest of the night was a little strange. He made it very clear that he was not leaving my room, so after a quick shower, we climbed into bed and held on to each other until we finally fell asleep. He's been within arm's reach ever since.

"Charlie?" I try again, this time poking him with my elbow.

"Oomph," he says. I guess I elbowed him a little harder than intended.

"What the hell, Angel?" he asks, sounding sleepy.

"Sorry, I have to pee and get ready for work. I have the early presentation today."

"I keep hoping I'll walk into one of these seminars and see your hot ass up in front," he says, drawing a line around my hardening nipple.

"Seriously, I have to go to the bathroom." I wiggle to let him know I'm serious.

"Are you kicking me out, Angel?" He's laughing, but I can feel his dick growing hard.

"Yes. I have a routine, and I have to stick to it before every stupid presentation." Now his interest is piqued, and I fear I may never get out of here.

"Ah, yes. The Pink and Taylor Swift montage I heard yesterday. Will you let me watch this morning, Angel?" His voice is full of sex and trouble.

"Fuck no. Are you nuts? I'm not letting you see that kind of crazy," I tell him honestly.

Pulling me under him, his eyes dance with mischief as he speaks. "How many times do I have to tell you? I want to see all your crazy. I want to hear all your crazy. I want all of you, Angel."

I can't help the snort that escapes. "You've seen all of me, Charlie. Trust me, there isn't anything left for you to see."

Suddenly serious, and so freaking sexy, he leans in within inches of my face. "Oh, sweetheart. That's where you have it wrong." Rolling his hips, he grinds his hard cock into me. "I have so much more exploring to do." He kisses my neck, and my bathroom needs are forgotten. "So many more positions to try," he says just before he sucks my earlobe into his mouth. I try to rub my thighs together for relief, but he has me pinned. "So many places to experiment with on your sexy little body, sweetheart." When he nips the sensitive spot on my neck, I swear I almost come.

As quickly as he started, he pulls away, shooing me from

the bed. "Out you go, Angel. I think you said you need the restroom and to get ready for work."

I feel the pout forming on my face, but I can't stop it.

Standing, he captures my lips with his. When he allows me to come up for air, he asks, "Do you have to go to the dinner tonight, Angel?"

"Dinner?" I question, all brain cells exploding from just a kiss. Shaking my head, I come to my senses. "Oh, dinner. Yes, tonight."

"I'll escort you then."

"Oh, you will, will you? What if I already have a date?" I tease and immediately regret it.

His beautiful features turn dark. "Then you'll cancel it. You're mine for as long as I can have you. Do I make myself clear?" Charlie seems as surprised by his declaration as I do. "I … fuck. I'm sorry, that was such a dick thing to say. You're making me crazy, Angel. So fucking crazy."

I know I should be pissed—after all, I'm an independent woman—but fuck me. I want to be his.

"It's okay." I'm shocked because I actually believe it is.

"Let me try that again, though. Will you allow me to escort you to dinner tonight, Angel?" This time his smile is genuine.

"I'd like that very much."

"All right then, I'll let you do your thing, but don't leave without me. I want to see you again before we start our day. Just knock on the door whenever you're ready," he calls over his shoulder as he walks to the door that connects our rooms.

When I hear the door click, I run for my phone and call Lanie.

She answers on the second ring. "Hey, there, lady! What's up?"

"Lanes? I only have a few minutes. I've been having hot monkey sex with the elevator stranger; I named him Charlie, by the way. Like, serious monkey sex. We went to the Sox game and have been spending all our time together. But then we forgot the condom, and even though I'm on the pill, I thought the responsible thing to do was to call Dr. Foley for Plan-B. Well, Dr. Foley decided, since I always take my pill at the same time and never miss, I didn't need Plan-B. This is only until Friday, but I-I think I like him. But there are all kinds of messed up things going on with his dad, like scary stuff. And I don't even know where he's from so there's no way this would go anywhere. I can't leave Vermont. I've got responsibilities and my parents, and you, and—"

"Whoa, whoa, chica. Slow down. Wow. Just wow. Let's break this down, okay? So, the sex is good?"

"Holy shit, Lanes. You don't understand. It's like some *Fifty Shades* of good, and it keeps getting better." My cheeks flush at the admission.

"Holy hot pockets, Jules! This's awesome. Well, not the unprotected sex part. What were you thinking?" she scolds.

"Obviously, I wasn't. It's kind of hard to think when he's making me orgasm before, during, and after sex," I whisper-yell while rolling my eyes.

"Why are you whispering?" she asks.

"Because his room is next door to mine. Like right next door and there's an adjoining door connecting our two suites, too."

Lanie laughs. "Well, isn't that convenient?"

"Lanie, I swear to God. Do not mess with me today," I warn.

"Okay, okay, so what's the problem?"

Sighing, I wonder how truthful I want to be. Then I remember it's Lanie and she'll know before I even try to lie. "I'm going to end up with a broken heart," I finally whisper.

"Ah, Jules." Lanie is nothing if not empathic. "Sweetie, you do realize you're the one who made these stupid rules to begin with, right? Nothing's stopping you from exchanging numbers. This doesn't have to end on Friday unless you want it to."

"I know," I say, still feeling defeated. "B-But what if that's not what he wants?" And there it is. My old insecurities are creeping up to strangle me yet again.

"Well, then he isn't worth it, Jules. This is all really fast; just try to take it day by day, okay? Don't put so much pressure on yourself. For once, just ride the wave and see where life takes you."

Glancing at the clock, I realize I'm running late again. "Oh, shit. I gotta go, Lanes. I'm late."

"Okay, luvs. And for crying out loud, use those stinking condoms!" Lanie yells just before I hang up.

"Yes, mom. Luvs," I say, running to the shower, stopping only to press play on my kick-ass playlist.

Trevor

I'M SITTING in the chair outside of our door, listening to Angel sing off-key and possibly knocking over every piece of furniture that's not nailed down. *God, she's fucking adorable.*

Checking my phone as I wait, I see another message from Loki.

Unknown Number: We're in. Package secure.

Unknown Number: You're free to go anytime.

Trevor: Thanks.

Unknown Number: See you at home.

Trevor: I think I'll stay for the rest of the conference.

Unknown Number: Understood. Eyes will be present.

Trevor: Thanks.

Well, that makes this week a little more interesting. If Loki says the package is secure, that means they've infiltrated

Black's system. Thank fucking God. Maybe this nightmare will end before anyone else gets hurt.

Crash.

What the hell?

Bursting through the door, I find Angel half on the bed, half off with one leg in the air.

This fucking girl.

"What's going on, Angel?" I can't help but tease.

"Ah … nothing," she says, trying to stand herself up. In the process, her skirt rides dangerously high.

After crossing the room in three quick strides, I reach down and pick her up, straightening her skirt as I go, using the excuse to run my hand up her smooth leg.

"Nothing?" I ask, not bothering to contain my laughter. "Looks like something." Glancing at the bed, I notice she has pictures laid out showcasing different outfits.

"Ah …" She scrambles to pick up all the pictures. "I … oh, fuck it." Before I know what's happening, she's thrown the photos in the air. "Gah, I hate getting dressed."

"Well, Angel. Um, I hate you're getting dressed, too, but if you don't, I'll end up in jail for murdering all the assholes who gawk at you." I smirk, but know it's the God's honest truth. "What exactly is going on here?"

"Ugh. I was trying to figure out which shoes I'm supposed to wear with that dress," she says, pointing to a garment bag hanging on the door.

I swallow, hard. "That's the dress you're wearing tonight?"

"I have to. My best friend tricked me and snuck it into my bag. She didn't pack a back-up. That," she says, disgusted, "is the dress I got stuck in while shopping. It's the devil."

"Holy fuck," is all I can manage as I make my way to the dress. Picturing Angel in it has my slacks going tight in a hurry. As I peer at the scarlet hued gown with the plunging neckline and slit up the leg, I have to adjust my tie to breathe. Fingering the silky material inside of the garment bag, I turn it over and notice the back is open with crisscrossing thin straps.

"Yeah, holy fuck. That damned thing nearly murdered me the last time I tried to put it on. How the hell does she expect me to get that thing on by myself?" Angel pouts.

Closing my eyes to get the image of fucking her in this dress out of my head, I cross the room and pull her into me. "Good thing you're not alone then. I'm not going to lie, though. I might rip that thing to shreds when we get home so no other fucker can see you in it," I growl.

"That's fine with me. Are you ready? I have to get down there to set up. What seminars are you in today?"

"Nothing fun," I tell her, not wanting to lie. Now that I don't have to be here, technically, I don't need to attend any of the seminars. Instead, I'll use the time in my room to work on my next app.

Making sure the door closes behind us, I ask, "Do you have time for a coffee before you check in?"

Glancing at her watch, she grimaces. "Not really, sorry. I like to be the first one there to make sure the systems are all running properly before I have to speak."

I place my hand on the small of her back and escort her down the hallway. "Tomorrow, I'll have to plan better then. You'll need your energy for what I'm going to do to you after I see you in that fucking dress." My voice is strained, and I feel my composure slipping. I've never been a jealous asshole, but there's no controlling my reactions to her.

"Promises, promises," Angel teases as we step into the elevator.

Once the doors close, I cage her into the corner. "Yes, Angel. Promises I intend to keep." Then I pounce, taking her lips with mine as if I own them, and at that moment, I do. She submits, and I control the kiss for thirty-two floors. When the elevator slows, I pull back and adjust my cock just as the door pings open.

"Have a good day, dear," I say, smirking as I step off the elevator in search of coffee.

"Good day? What the hell? Does he have any idea how many brain cells he just fried?" I hear her mumbling behind me. The bark of laughter that sneaks its way out makes me feel lighter than I have in years.

That is what she's doing to you, asshat. She's your light in the darkness.

My conscience needs to shut the fuck up.

PACING the suite for the hundredth time today, I stare at our connecting door. My mind asking questions I won't answer. *How easy would it be to invade her space? Find out about Angel? Where's she from? What's her name? What's she hiding?* But I don't—I can't. I know that if I find out her real name, I won't be able to stay away. This shit with Romero may never end, and I won't bring my sweet angel into the depths of hell with me.

Unable to stand it anymore, I pull out my phone and text the guys.

Trevor: Hey.

Preston: Missing us, asshole?

Dexter: How's Boston?

Trevor: Fuck off, Pres. Boston is fine. How's Tate? Any news on the girls?

Thinking about Dexter's kids, I smile. I've never wanted them myself, but Tate is an amazing little guy. Angel and I would make fucking exceptional kids. The thought should scare me, but it doesn't. It makes my heart hurt.

Dexter: Tate's good. His new nanny started today, but I think he would prefer it if Sylvie stayed with him.

Preston: You know she would have, dickhead. She even offered.

Dexter: I know, but I have to handle this on my own.

Trevor: Letting us help is not a failure, Dex. Remember that.

Dexter: Thanks. The girls are growing. The doctors forwarded me the new ultrasound this morning. I'll show you when you get home.

Preston: You getting any ass there in Boston douche bag?

Trevor: Why are you such an asshole?

Preston: Is that a yes?

Trevor: Fuck off.

Dexter: Wait, are you getting ass?

Trevor: Wtf is wrong with you two?

Loki: I happen to know for a fact that he is.

Trevor: What the actual fuck, Loki?

Dexter: What the fuck, Trevor?

Dexter: Who is she?

Preston: Is she hot?

Dexter: Once or more than once?

Preston: He isn't hitting it more than once unless she was hit with the ugly stick.

Trevor: Watch it, asshole.

Preston: Protective? Hmmm, isn't that interesting?

Dexter: Who is she, Trev?

Trevor: No one.

The biggest fucking lie I've ever told. No one. *She's* every-one, I want to scream. *She's* everything *I can't have because my father went to work for the mob and allowed them to kill my mother.*

"Fuck," I scream, throwing my phone against the tiled wall of the bathroom and watching as it shatters into a thousand pieces.

∾

Julia

"Knock-knock," I say as I tap on the door to Charlie's room. Entering, I find him asleep on the bed. I stand there for a few minutes, unsure of what to do.

"Don't just stand there thinking, Angel. Always, always come to me if that's what you want." His sleep-filled voice fills the space.

Crossing the room, I stand at the foot of his bed. "Tough day?"

"You could say that," he says, reaching for me.

"Anything I can do?"

"You're doing it, come here." When his hand finds mine, he pulls me onto the bed with him.

Resting my head on his chest, I breathe him in. He smells like teakwood and summer; it's something I've never noticed on anyone before. It's so distinctly him, I commit it to memory. He rubs his hand up and down my back lazily.

Peeking up at him, I ask again, "You okay?"

"I am now." He smiles, and the butterflies in my belly take it up a notch.

We lay there for a long time, just enjoying the closeness. I'm drifting off when he speaks.

"I spent all day debating entering your room to snoop around. I didn't, but fuck if I didn't want to."

He did? "Why?"

"I go back and forth, longing to know everything about you and knowing that's a selfish fucking thing for me to want."

I stay silent, waiting for him to explain. He doesn't.

"How long do you need to get ready tonight, sweetheart?" he asks, changing the subject.

"It depends on if that stinking dress tries to kill me again." I'm not even joking.

Kissing my head, he nuzzles his nose into my hair. "I won't let anything happen to you, I promise."

I know he's talking about more than dresses. I feel unsettled, and Charlie's lost in thought.

"Hey," I say. "I'm going to get ready, but if you … if you need someone to talk to, I'm here, okay?"

He nods, but lets me go.

O-kay then.

CHAPTER 15

TREVOR

"Break Things" by Kylie Morgan

*W*hy the fuck did I just go there with her? I know what this is, what it can only ever be. I proved the day they killed my mom that I can't be trusted.

I hear Angel turn on her shower, so I shove out of bed. I have to get out of my head. Going to my own shower, I turn it on as hot as it can go. As I stand under the stream of near scalding water, I pray for it to burn the monsters away. I can't let this go too far. The last thing I want to do is break my beautiful angel.

Fifteen minutes later, I walk through Angel's door with my shirt hanging open to find her standing in a black lace thong with thigh highs and nothing else.

"Fuck. Me," I say, almost dropping the tumbler of amber liquid I just poured. I'm frozen in the doorway with my mouth hanging open. Angel turns to me and scowls.

"Don't just stand there," she snaps. "You promised to help me into this death trap, remember?"

"Uh-huh." *Close your damn mouth you fool.*

"Charlie?" she screeches, stomping her foot, which makes her tits bounce.

I swallow and try to find my voice, but I'm like a teenager seeing boobs for the first time. The vision in front of me will be spank bank material for the rest of my fucking life.

"I'm serious," she says, sounding slightly hysterical, snapping me out of my reverie. I can't help but laugh, and I know that's the wrong reaction. I've never seen Angel mad, but her face is turning red, and she could shoot daggers from those sexy, green eyes.

Holding my hands up in surrender, I say, "Okay, okay, sweetheart, what do you need me to do?"

I walk to her, set my tumbler down on the nightstand, and press my front to her back. Resting my chin on her head, I watch her in the mirror.

"I don't know, but last time that thing seriously almost killed me," she huffs. "Look, I have the picture to prove it." She shoves her phone into my face.

Taking it from her hands, I stifle a laugh. I don't know how the fuck she got tangled up in it as she did, but studying the picture, my cock stands at attention. She looks fantastic. The dress binds her hands behind her, forcing her tits up and out. Her head is slightly bowed from the angle of her arms.

"Jesus, Angel. You are so goddamn sexy." Leaning in to nip her earlobe, I whisper, "Will you let me tie you up like this tonight?"

I watch in the mirror as her neck works to swallow and her eyes dilate with need.

"Will you trust me to tie you up like this and have my way with you, Angel?" I repeat.

Turning to face me, she asks, "Will you trust me to tell me what was wrong earlier?"

We stand, facing each other for a few moments—too long to be comfortable—before I answer.

"I'll tell you what I can, how's that?"

Placing her hands on her hips, she nods. "Fine, that'll work. Now help me into this nightmare."

"Sweetheart, the only nightmare will be me trying to make my dick behave watching you prance around in that dress."

"Ugh, I don't prance," she scoffs, but has her eyes on my shaft.

Cupping it, I wait until her eyes find mine. "You keep staring at him like that, sweetheart, and we'll never get out of here."

"Ah-uh," she backs away, "I have to go tonight. I take my job extremely seriously."

"I see that, Angel. And it has me so curious about what it is you do. You seem to be in high demand."

"I'm very good at what I do," she says noncommittally.

"You're very good at everything you do, I'm sure." I mean the words, but I'm still watching her tits. Shaking my head, I say, "We need to get you dressed or I won't be able to walk. Let me see that dress."

Examining it, I'm beginning to understand how she got stuck in the first place. All these silky strands that are supposed to crisscross her back look like a torture device. "Maybe I can slip it over your head?" I offer.

"Maybe." She's still staring at it as if it'll bite her.

"How did you get into it last time? Let's do the opposite tonight," I say, only half-joking.

"Yeah, that's a good idea. I tried to step into it at the store."

"Okay, over the head it is. Arms up." She follows my command, and I'm momentarily distracted by the sway of her breasts.

Thirty minutes later, we're both sweaty and a little annoyed. That freaking dress was a nightmare to get on, and now it's a fucking nightmare because I have to watch her move around the room in it. Every guy in here has noticed her, and it pisses me off.

As soon as we entered the ballroom, we were separated by people wanting her attention. Angel is rubbing elbows with some very influential people here, and if I'm not careful, my curiosity will win out.

"She's a beautiful creature," a man to my left says, making every hair on my body stand to attention.

Fucking Romero. He isn't alone, though, and that has me worried. Trying to keep an eye on my girl without him noticing, I position my body so they have to turn if they want to continue the conversation I want no part of.

"What do you want, Romero?" I ask.

"Do not disrespect me here, son," he threatens.

"Would you prefer I call you a murderer?"

His body tenses as he attempts to keep himself from lunging for me.

"What will it take to get you to fall in line, boy?" questions the man to Romero's right. A man I now know works for Antonio Black.

Motherfucker.

Seething, I square my shoulders. "I'm not a boy, and I will never fall in line with a murderer."

"Tsk, tsk, Romero. The boy still thinks his mother's death was your doing? I thought we spoke of this?" the man says, causing my head to whip around so fast I'm surprised I don't have whiplash.

"What," I demand, "the fuck are you talking about?"

Suddenly, I'm surrounded by men in black and know immediately they are not the good guys. I know they're Antonio's men when they flank my father and his friend immediately.

"Trevor, there you are." I hear Loki's voice, but I don't take my eyes off of the men in front of me. "I've been looking for you," he tries again. "Hello, Mr. Knight. I didn't know you would be here." He's addressing my father this time, but I still haven't shifted my gaze.

"Loki? What are you doing here?" my father asks, staring between his companion and Loki.

"I'm here as Trevor's council. His software is all people are talking about, so I convinced him to take me on to make sure he has all his ducks in a row on these contracts. You must be so proud of him?" Loki continues. He's known my father most of his life, which means he also knows how to play him.

"Speaking of which, I'm sorry to interrupt, but there's a gentleman over there from the IRS that is very interested in speaking with Trevor. Do you mind if I snag him for a bit?" Loki asks, already leading me away.

"What the fuck was that?" he demands under his breath.

"What did you hear? My father's comment on Angel or the fact that Antonio Black's man said I didn't know who killed my mother?" I bark.

Loki, who's always controlled, missteps. "What are you saying?"

"I don't fucking know what I'm saying. All I know is they've noticed Angel, and I will not let them get to her like they did my mother."

Taking me by the arm, he drags me to a secluded area of the ballroom. It's much harder to monitor Angel from here, and he notices. "I've got eyes on her, Trevor. Focus."

"I thought you left?" I ask, suddenly realizing not only did he just save my ass, but he was close enough to step in at a moment's notice.

"I told you I had your back, Trevor. That means while you're here, so am I. But it's not always helpful to have you aware of my comings and goings."

"You're lucky my father doesn't know you never sat for the bar," I bark.

"Yeah, except I did, asshole."

148

"What?" That's news to me. Loki went to law school with Dex, but as far as we knew, he'd never taken the bar.

"Listen, you need to make some decisions, and you need to make them fast. It will not be safe for you to stay here in Boston much longer. We've intercepted some communications through Mantra. Your program is running like fucking clockwork, but they're moving fast. They're also becoming excessively uncomfortable with the fact that you have not joined ranks," he says as his eyes survey the area.

Glancing over his shoulder, I catch sight of Angel laughing with another man, and my stomach clenches painfully.

"Dude, you've known her what? Four days? What's going on with you?"

That's the million-dollar question, isn't it?

"If this were any other situation, if I were any other guy, she's the woman I'd marry," I say confidently.

Rocking back on his heels, he searches my face. "Holy shit."

"Yeah, holy shit," I repeat.

"Trevor, man, I know what you're thinking, and now it makes sense why you've been playing this game with her—"

"She wanted these rules," I interrupt.

"I know," he says, more subdued this time, "but I think you're using them as an excuse to push her away, too."

Watching Angel as she moves around the room with a confidence and grace I've only seen her have when we're alone, I tell Loki the truth, "I can't have her."

"Fuck you," he shoots back.

"What? You of all people know the fucked-up mess I'm in right now. You of all people know exactly what happened to my mother, and you of all people should be the one telling me to run away as fast as I can before I break her," I spit.

"I know what kind of mess they've thrown at your feet, asshole." Loki gets in my face in a way he's never done before. "I know what kind of man you are, what kind of man your mother raised you to be. I've also seen what kind of man you've become since she passed. A part of you died that night with her, and it's time to wake the fuck up."

Taking a step forward, we're now nose to nose. We have never come to blows before. In twenty years of friendship, this is as close as we've ever come, but I'm about to lay him the fuck out.

"If I had gone with my mother that night like I should have, she'd still be alive. She died alone because I was too selfish to be bothered. You're out of your fucking mind if you think I will drag my girl into the pits of hell just to have her taken from me, too."

"Trevor, if you had gone with Grace that night, you'd also be dead. That's a fact. It's a fucking miserable thing to live with, but that's the truth. There's nothing you could have done. Your father has taken so much from you already, don't let him take your future as well."

Stepping back, I scan the room for Angel. When I find her, I lower my voice. "I have no future until Romero is in the ground." It's an ominous warning, but it's also the truth.

"Trevor," he says, waiting for me to meet his eyes, "you love her." It isn't a question, and I don't answer at first.

"I've only known her for a few days, Loki."

"And you love her," he repeats.

Swallowing a bowling ball sized lump that has suddenly taken up residence in my throat, I admit my biggest fear, "I think I could." It's as much as I'm willing to give. If I admit I love Angel now, I'll never be able to let her go.

Loki claps me on the back and pulls me in close. "Listen, put an end to this bullshit with her. Get her name, explain what you can. I'll do what I can to keep her safe until you can tell her you love her."

Shaking my head, I feel my eyes stinging. I choke back the tears. "I can't. I just can't bring her into this, Loki. I have to let her go, but I'm a selfish prick because I'm hanging on to every moment I have with her here. Please, just let her have her anonymity. I can't be what she needs, and I know if I have access to her, I won't be able to stay away."

"You know I love you, man, but mark my words, you're making a giant fucking mistake. You'll regret this decision for the rest of your life."

"I know," I tell him. "I already do."

TONIGHT HAS BEEN a true test of my fucking character. I'm wound so tight that when Loki pats me on the back to tell me he's leaving, I jump out of my chair and almost take out a waiter.

"Jesus, man. Calm the fuck down," he warns.

"I'm about to lose my goddamned fucking mind," I whisper-yell.

"Trevor, I told you, I have eyes on her. Why aren't you in the other room with her, though?"

"Because they split this thing up into two groups of people. Whatever the hell she does for work granted her access to the other part of the ballroom. The only time I see her is when I catch a glimpse of that siren red dress float by on the dance floor. I'm trying really hard not to kill someone, but if one more man tries to play grab-ass with my fucking girl, you'll have to bail me out of jail."

"I can have someone look into her, Trevor. Just because I couldn't find her, doesn't mean my crew can't figure out a way."

My fingernails bite into my palms as a reminder of why I can't have her. "No, I'm not going over this again, Loki. I can't have access to her once we leave here. I won't say it again."

"Just think about it, Trevor. You have a couple of days left with her, but think about what your life will be like always wondering if she was the one. It seems like a pretty fucking miserable life if you ask me."

"I won't wonder, man. I already know, but this is the only way."

Shaking his head, he mumbles, "Stubborn asshole," and walks away.

In my head, I hear, *"Don't fall too hard ... I'll break you."* Angel has brought music and light to my life in just a few short days. I know in only a few more, the music will die, and I'll plunge headfirst into the darkness again.

CHAPTER 16

JULIA

"Life on Earth" by Snow Patrol

I feel him before I see him. My body is so in tune with his that I know he's behind me before he's even spoken a word.

Peeking over my shoulder, I see a man on the edge. Six-feet-three inches of muscle held together by a tightrope. Whatever has him worked up has to be significant. I can see every muscle, every tendon pulled tight across his body, ready to explode. A storm he can barely contain. It should scare me, but like a moth to a flame, I'm drawn to him.

Excusing myself from the group, I go to him.

"Angel," just one word, one breath, and I feel his control slip.

Cupping his face, I lean in. "Open your heart so I can reach you," I sing.

Pressing into my touch, he replies, "You'll start a war."

He gets me.

Continuing to Julia-tize The Chainsmokers, I whisper, "I want to see your darkness and your light—"

I don't get to finish because the next thing I know he's dragging me from the ballroom.

"Is there anyone you need to say good-bye to, Angel?" He sounds desperate.

"No." *Just you*, my heart weeps.

We arrive at the elevator before Charlie speaks again. "I need you tonight, Angel."

"You have me," I say without hesitation, but confusion lacing my voice.

The elevator door chimes, and he ushers me inside. We stand on opposite sides of the elevator, staring at each other. His breathing is heavy and erratic. His hands have turned white on the railing he's holding on to.

I stroll across the compact space and place a hand on his chest. "Charlie, what is it?"

His breathing slows almost immediately as he covers my hand with his own. My palm is splayed across his heart; I feel it beating rapidly through his suit jacket.

"My life is not my own at the moment, Angel. No matter what I want, there are rules I have to follow," he says sadly.

"You speak in riddles sometimes, Charlie. I don't know what to make of it." My words drip with honesty and heartache.

The elevator opens to our floor, and we exit, side by side. At the end of the hall, Charlie breaks. Taking the key from my hand, he kicks open the door and hauls me through, slamming the door behind us. His hands are everywhere at once.

"Lift your arms," he commands.

Doing as he asks, I don't break eye contact with him. In the depths of his soul, I see pain, hatred, love, and confusion. This beautifully broken heart is shattering before my very eyes.

In one fluid motion, he lifts the dress over my head and

tosses it to the floor. Charlie's breathing so heavily, he's panting, and I see him trying to gain control.

"Let go, Charlie. With me, let go."

"There's so much I want to say, Angel. So many things I wish were different." His voice cracks, and I feel a tear fall down my face. Rushing to me, he wipes my tears with his thumbs. "Angel, what is it, sweetheart? Did something happen tonight? Why are you crying?"

Shaking my head, trying to speak through the pain that's settled in my throat, I bury my face in his chest. I need a minute to collect my thoughts. I'm not a crier, and I don't know how to explain what I'm feeling. Finally, taking a deep breath, I gaze into his eyes.

"You're broken, Charlie. Here," I place my hand over his heart, "I feel it deep in my soul."

"Yes," he says. "I-I—"

I place a finger over his lips. "Shh, Charlie. Come, let me hold you tonight." I walk him toward the bed. I unbutton his shirt, pull it from his pants, and slide it over his broad shoulders. Before I can think better of it, I place a tender kiss over his heart.

Charlie inhales a breath, as if I'd branded him.

Lowering to my knees before him, I hesitate for a moment as I look at him. His head is hanging low, eyes shadowed, haunted, but entirely on me. His shoulders droop forward. Gone is the domineering man of the past few days. This is just Charlie, baring his all, and it ruins me.

I undo his pants, letting them fall to the floor, and he steps out of them. Sitting back on my heels, I watch him, waiting for his command, but it doesn't come. He's fighting the darkness, and it's my job to bring him the light. Raising up on my knees, I lower his boxer briefs and watch in awe as his cock springs free. Even on my knees, I'm too short to do what I want, so I stand.

I'm unsure of how to handle the quiet, conflicted Charlie, so I gently set him on the edge of the bed and lower to the floor once more. With my hands on his thighs, I drop my mouth to lick his tip and watch as it bobs in response. Placing one hand around his base, I use the other to stroke him slowly as my tongue circles his crown.

His hands fist into my hair, almost to the point of pain, and I like it. He doesn't guide me, doesn't force me, just hangs onto my hair as if his life depends on it. Lowering my mouth to take as much of his length as I can, I gag when it hits the back of my throat, but I hold it there for a second when a broken cry escapes his throat.

"Fuck, Angel," he screams. His voice is ragged, wounded. He pulls at my hair, and I release his dick with a pop.

Climbing his body, I find his lips and kiss him with all I have. His hands wrap around me, kneading my ass cheeks. There's something about this kiss, this experience with him right now that feels so much more intense than anything I've ever experienced. There's an emotional urgency we're playing tug of war with.

Unable to breathe, I pull away from his kiss. Turning myself so my back is to his front, I lower my pussy to his lap and hear him groan as his tip finds my entrance. With my hands on his thighs for leverage, I move.

Neither of us speaks except for the occasional moan. This isn't how it's been before. This is something else entirely. Using our bodies to express what neither of us can say, I raise and lower my body against his. Over and over again, I move while his hands wind around my body, teasing and pinching my sensitive nipples.

"Charlie," I pant, leaning back into him as my feet come off the floor and he takes control. Sliding us farther up the bed, my back still flush against his front, he gracefully slides his hand from my nipple to my mound. Making slow, torturous circles around my clit, he rolls us to my side.

Lifting my leg over his hip, he moves within me. There's nothing frantic about what we're doing. He's loving me with his body, that I'm sure of. Again, working my clit, he picks up his pace and I'm a goner. My belly is trembling, and I know I won't last very long.

Charlie leans in, so we're almost cheek to cheek as he whispers, "Mon amour, mon amour, mon amour," repeatedly. It's all I hear as the world shatters around me.

I've never experienced an emotional orgasm before, never had a connection so deep with someone that every nerve ending in your body explodes—until now. I didn't understand when people would say an orgasm was so intense it brought them to tears, and yet, here I am. Wholly incapable of controlling any part of my body, heart, or mind.

The last thing I'm aware of is Charlie cleaning me with a warm cloth, then wrapping his body tightly around me. I don't know where his body ends or mine begins.

Trevor

MY BODY ENVELOPS MY ANGEL; I don't dare to let her go. She's been asleep for hours, but sleep eludes me. Our evening is playing on repeat. I'm a fucking mess. This is not a connection you walk away from. Loki was right, but I don't know what to do.

Mon amour, I'd said. My love.

I love her, or I could? Do I even know what love is? I'm reminded of a letter Dex wrote to me when we were teenagers, and my father had sent me to summer camp in England. He was always the bleeding heart of the group; it kills me that his ex-wife has broken him like this. But I'll never forget the letter he sent me when I asked his advice about a girl.

July 10th

Dude,

Why so formal? Are they monitoring your letter writing, too? It wouldn't surprise me. I looked up the camp yesterday. Who has a dress code for summer camp? It must be so stuffy and boring as hell.

I've included as many snacks as I could fit in the box. I hope they get to you, and they don't confiscate this stuff. It cost me a small fortune.

Okay, about the girl. Do you realize you never even told me her name? I need names and descriptions to give you advice, dude, but this sappy heart will improvise just this once.

Here are Dexter's rules for knowing you're in love:

Are you willing to do anything to keep her safe, like from snakes and big ass spiders?

To see her happy?

Can you always put her first, even if that means leaving in the middle of the most epic game on Xbox?

Think about her dating someone else. How does it make you feel?

Are you happier around her than when you're not?

Does she make you want to do better? Be better?

I know we aren't old enough to have fallen in love a bunch of times, but I know you, dude. You'll always run from it. When you find the girl that makes you feel all the feels, don't be an ass.

Go for her. You deserve to be happy. You always have. When we grow up, we'll make sure we're all happy, always. We're family, remember that.

Pretty deep for a couple of twelve-year-olds, right? I believe in love, Trev; I have to. I know we'll all find it someday. If I ever forget, you remind me, and I'll do the same for you.

Get your ass back to Waverley-Cay. Summer sucks without you.

Dex

For some reason, I'd hung on to that letter all these years.

I've read it and re-read it to the point of having it memorized. I'd always admired Dexter and his ability to love so freely, but now his questions are haunting me.

Am I happier when she's around? *Fuck yes*. Does she make me want to do better? *So goddamn much*. She's brought back the light, the music—she's brought me to life. But what kind of life can I give her?

My father has ruined so much in my twenty-eight years. I can't let him ruin her, too. Loki said I couldn't have saved my mother, but it'll always be a question in my mind.

Brushing hair away from her face, I stare at my angel. Her long lashes splayed over her fair cheeks that have a smattering of freckles. I've memorized each one in the last few hours. As the first light of morning cracks through the drapes, the world around me is suddenly in slow motion. She calms me, and I'll be damned if I let her go without a fight.

Angel mumbles, "This doesn't have to be the end of us." I think she's awake, but looking down, I see her eyes fluttering in sleep.

I chuckle. Even in sleep, we're in tune. She can be my home, my life, something I haven't had in many, many years. *Will she want that, too?* There's so much I have to figure out. So much I'll have to tell her, hoping and praying that she'll understand. I'll have to put all my trust into Loki and his ability to keep her safe. With sudden clarity, I know I'll never be able to walk away from her.

Kissing her gently on the lips, I slip out of bed. I've got shit to do. I smile—the first genuine smile I've felt through my entire body in over ten years. Grabbing a piece of paper and a pen, I write Angel a note.

Angel,

I had to take care of some stuff this morning. Have dinner with me tonight. Meet me in the hotel lobby tonight at 7 p.m. Wear whatever the hell you want. I happen to think you look adorable in your sweatpants.

~Charlie

There's so much more I want to put into that letter, but it needs to be said in person, so I refrain. I tiptoe to my room, change, and slip out into the early morning light. Loki is my first stop.

CHAPTER 17

JULIA

"To Hell & Back" by Maren Morris

*R*olling over, I stretch and immediately know something's off. "Charlie?" I ask an empty room, already knowing he's gone. My stomach sinks until I reach for my phone and see his note. Running my fingers over his neat handwriting as I read, I smile. I had hoped we could spend the day together since my schedule was open after my morning meeting, but dinner will have to do.

I go through my morning routine thinking about last night. It was intense on every level. Sitting at the desk, I take out my notebook but just stare at the empty page. Instead, I pick up my phone and call Lanie.

"Hey, lady, what's up?" she asks in the cheerful tone only she can have at seven in the morning.

"I'm going to tell him my name," I blurt. "I'm going to tell him I like him and I want his number and that I want to see him after this week is over and that I've never felt like this with anyone in my life ever before. I'm going to tell him that the sex is out of this world, but it's our connection that I don't want to live without. I want to see where this can go, Lanes. I-I think I love him," I say in a single breath.

Silence.

Staring at my phone, I bang it on my hand. "Lanes? Are you there?"

"Hold on," she says before she hangs up. Seconds later, my phone rings with a FaceTime from her.

"Let me see your face," she demands.

I don't try to contain the grin that covers my entire face. "He gets me, Lanes. When I ramble, he listens. When I speak in Julia-tized lyrics, he finishes them. Last night … well, I'm not exactly sure what happened last night, but I know if I walk away, I'll never be the same. I'm going to tell him and hope he feels the same, but somehow, I just do, Lanes. I know he feels the same. Last night was fucked up in so many ways, but it was real, it was us, and I-I need him."

"Oh my God," Lanie says with teary eyes. It's as close to a swear as I'll get out of her, so I take it.

"Holy fuck, Lanie. Holy fuck," I scream.

"Yeah, Jules … just, please be careful? This is all so fast. You say you're sure he feels the same, but protect yourself, okay? I've never heard you talk about anyone like this, so just be careful," she warns.

"Lanes, I sat down to make a list, and I can't. I can't do it … nothing comes," I tell her, knowing she will understand how monumental that is for me.

"Nothing?" she questions.

Shaking my head, I confirm, "Nothing."

We sit, smiling at each other through our phones for far too long.

"You think he's your puffin?" Lanie finally asks.

"You'll always be my puffin," I tell her.

We've been each other's puffin since the sixth grade when we had to do a project on Maine and found out they mate for life. As soon as Lanie read that they find one partner and stick by them forever, she was hooked.

I think I've finally found my puffin.

"Think Charlie is okay with a threesome?" she jokes.

We laugh until tears fall. Lanie composes herself first. "Jules?"

"Yeah?"

"I'm really happy for you. I can't wait to meet him."

"You'll love him. I know there's still the possibility he won't want to know me, Lanes. I am preparing myself for it, but for the first time in my life, I want to take the risk. I think he's worth it. He has some serious shit to work out, but so do I, right? I'm going to tell him tonight. He left me a note this morning asking me to meet him for dinner."

"Yay!" She pauses. "What are you going to wear?"

I roll my eyes, because of course that's her question.

"Who the fuck knows! I'll call you tonight when I'm getting ready, okay?"

"Sounds good. Talk to you later. Luvs."

"Luvs," I say before hanging up.

Noticing the time, I see I don't have long before my first lecture starts, so I shower and dress in record time, then grab my purse with what I'll need for the day and rush out to the conference center.

JUST BEFORE I reach the double doors, I see a hotel phone in the hallway. On impulse, I rush to it and press the four-digit number to Charlie's room. "Oh, hey, it's ah … it's Angel? So, listen, there's something I want to talk to you about tonight." I start to panic and think maybe I'd better give him an out. "I-I don't want to play this game anymore, Charlie. I mean, I still want to see you, but I want to see you as me, so when I come to meet you tonight, I want us to introduce ourselves, for real this time. I know there's a bunch of shit going on, but I want this to be real." I pause again, all the confidence leaving my voice in a rush. "Please, if you don't want the same thing, just maybe don't come to dinner. I-I don't think I can handle the rejection in person, but I'm hoping we're on the same page. I have some very big and scary feelings for you, Charlie. It'll break me if this ends without ever really knowing you. Okay, well, bye."

Hanging up the phone, I rest my head a little too hard against the wall a few times. I try to remember what I had said, but it's too late to worry about it now. I head into the conference room, just as they call my name.

THE DAY DRAGS ON, and I'm glad I didn't make plans with Charlie after all. My boss has been up my ass all day about a new client he's stuck me with. No matter how many times I explain things to this guy, he just doesn't get it. Finally, as tactfully as I can, I tell him I'll send him a report because sometimes it's easier to see on paper when, in reality, I'll have to go Sesame Street on his ass and put everything in pictures.

Peeking at my phone, I see it's already five-thirty p.m., but thankfully, that'll give me plenty of time to get ready for tonight. I guess being so busy has been a blessing in disguise because I haven't had time to freak out about what I'm going to tell Charlie. If you'd asked me a week ago if love at first sight was an actual thing, I would have said you're fucking nuts, but now? How can I not believe it?

I'm about to put my phone back in my bag when it rings. Noticing my dad's name, I smile. I haven't talked to him all week when, usually, I talk to him multiple times a day.

Smiling, I answer, and my world crashes and burns.

"What do you mean she was attacked?" I cry. "I just spoke to her this morning." I'm walking in circles around the conference center. "No, Dad, no. She'll be okay! She has to be."

Someone comes up beside me, trying to calm me down. "No," I scream. "Don't tell me to calm the fuck down."

"Daddy," I choke. "Is Lanie going to be okay? Please tell me she'll be okay?"

Through tears of his own, he tells me the truth. "I-I don't know, sweetie, I-I-I, you just have to come home. Now. Reggie is waiting out front. He'll drive you home. I've told him to hurry."

My legs cannot hold me anymore, and I crumble to the ground. "Daddy, please, please don't let her die. I need her. She's my puffin, please. Please!" I scream as my body rocks in place.

"Babycakes?" Glancing up with blurry eyes, I see Reggie, and he has police officers with him. His own face is tearstained. He's known Lanie almost as long as he's known me. Leaning down, he scoops me up like a small child, and they usher us at breakneck speed to my car. We're escorted to the Massachusetts border by the highway patrol. Reaching New Hampshire, their state police take over, and they escort us all the way to the Dartmouth trauma center.

At some point during the drive, Reggie explains his brother is an officer and arranged to get us to New Hampshire as quickly as possible, but I'm numb. I only hear bits and pieces during our two-and-a-half-hour drive.

I'm rocking in my seat, my arms cradling my middle, just like when I was a child. "Please, please, let her be okay. Dear God, please don't take Lanie from me. Please," I chant the entire way.

It isn't until hours later that I realize I just gave up one puffin for another.

Trevor
"American Pie" by Don McLean

7:30 p.m.

Checking my watch one more time, I tip the waiter and take my drink up to our room. I'm actually concerned she's gotten herself trapped in another dress. The thought has me laughing out loud. I feel lighter than I have in years.

Entering the unlit room, dread sets in, but I try to tamp it down. *She probably got stuck in a meeting,* I tell myself. Walking through her room, I feel an enormous sense of relief when I notice her stuff scattered everywhere. She must have had one hell of a morning. There are pictures everywhere. I'm sad I missed her morning routine. That sentiment tells me everything I need to know. I have to make it work with her.

Heading back to my side of the suite, I notice the message light blinking and walk toward it much faster than is reasonable. Pressing the button, I'm relieved to hear Angel's voice. I love the message but hate that she thinks for even a second I'm not on the same page. She will be mine. Not wanting to miss her, I head back down to the lobby bar with an extra spring in my step.

8:30 p.m.

I'm pacing our suite. *Where the fuck is she?* My phone rings and I dive for it.

"Angel?" I ask irrationally. I know she doesn't have my cell phone number. Why the fuck doesn't she have my cell phone number?

"Ah, Trevor? What's going on, dude?" Preston asks.

"Nothing. I-I have a situation here. Do you need something?"

"Does the girl have your panties in a twist or what?"

"What the fuck do you want, Preston?" I yell.

"Jesus Christ, man. What the hell is your problem?" he snaps back.

Taking a deep breath, I try again, "I'm really in the middle of something. Is everything all right?" Preston never calls, so it has me trying even harder to calm down.

"Anna is having some complications. The girls are fine, but Dex is kind of a mess. I was just wondering how long your trip is or if I should call my mom and have her come back to give him a hand?"

"Fuck." Running a hand through my hair, I tell him, "Call Sylvie. I'll be back as soon as I can."

"Sounds good. Are you sure you're all right, Trevor?"

"Yes. I gotta go," I tell him and hang up.

Where the fuck are you, Angel?

10:30 p.m.

"She's gone, Loki. She left me a message this morning telling me she doesn't want to play this game anymore, she wants to know the real me. We had plans tonight at seven, and she hasn't come back. All of her stuff is here, something's wrong, I feel it." A desperation I've never felt claws at my chest.

"I'll get my guys on it. Just try to relax, okay? We'll find her."

"They took her, I know it. I should have fucking known better, Loki. What did I do?"

I break.

3 a.m.

I'm pacing her room while Loki works on the computer in front of me. I've already broken down so many times I've lost count. She's gone, I feel it deep in my heart, she's gone.

Turning to me, Loki takes his headset off. "The Blacks don't have her, Trevor, but I don't have much more information than that."

The air leaves my lungs and I collapse to the ground. "Then, where is she?"

"We have security footage from one of the conference rooms. It's pretty hard to watch."

"Show me," I bellow.

Turning the screen, I see Angel appear. She's pacing, then collapses to the ground. When she raises her face to the ceiling, I see the pain etched all over her beautiful, tearstained face.

"What upset her?" I choke out.

"I'm working on it," he says as the video feed continues. I see the man from the baseball game appear along with several of Boston's finest. I watch as he scoops her up, and they all hurry from the room.

"We think she's in a car that hit tolls through Massachusetts up into New Hampshire with a police escort. I don't have any other information yet."

"But she's all right?" I ask.

"It appears that way. Something happened, Trevor, but not to her." His promise sits empty in my soul.

I don't remember crying this much, even when my mother died. I was too angry. Hatred is powerful—it dried my tears—and I've been full of rage ever since. Until I met Angel. With the knowledge that the devil hasn't taken her, I find myself on my hands and knees sobbing in a way I've never done before. Crying because she's safe, and crying because this just confirmed that I have to let her go.

Without saying a word, Loki helps get me cleaned up. Once we've packed up all Angel's belongings, he turns to me. "Trevor, this doesn't mean—"

Holding up a hand, I stop him. "Yes, it does. She's gone, and she has to stay that way." I never even took a picture of us, I realize, and my chest constricts. "Can I have that footage?"

"Trevor, don't …"

"Can I fucking have it or not?" I scream.

"Sure," he sighs, "I'll get you a copy."

"Thanks." Gathering my belongings, along with Angel's Red Sox T-shirt I couldn't part with, I make my way out of the hotel.

It's time to make Romero pay.

CHAPTER 18

JULIA-3 MONTHS LATER

"One Beer" by Hardy

"*L*anie! What the hell do you think you're doing?" I ask, walking into her hospital room. "Stop reaching for the computer. You have stitches and staples everywhere. Are you trying to bust them open again?" Sighing, I walk over and hand her the laptop. "You're supposed to be resting."

"I have been," she says sheepishly. "That doesn't mean I can't keep searching for Boston while I'm stuck here."

Inwardly, I cringe. I had to ask her to stop calling him Charlie because it was too painful, not that I'd tell her that. Now, we refer to him as Boston, but even that's more painful than I'd like to admit. The guilt she feels is immeasurable, so I never talk of my heartbreak.

"Lanes," I turn my back so she can't read my face, "we've searched for him everywhere. I've even broken a few laws hacking into various systems," I whisper. "He's gone."

"I'm so sorry, Jules. I'll make this up to you, I promise. I will find him," she vows, and my heart cracks a little more.

Walking to her, I take the laptop away again. "You have physical therapy in half an hour. You need to rest." I'm trying my best, but I can't hide anything from this girl, and before I can turn away, she sees the first signs of a tear.

"God, if I had only called the police when I got to that house instead of entering," she starts.

"Stop, Lanie! Right now, just stop. You did the right thing. There was a small boy in that house. I would have done the same," I tell her for the millionth time.

"We'll find him, Jules. I promise we'll find him," she whispers.

A knock at the door saves me from this conversation. A nurse enters, bringing Lanie lunch. As she passes by, I'm hit with a wave of nausea so fast and furious I barely make it to the attached restroom.

Fuck.

Once I'm cleaned up, I enter Lanie's room to a circle of concerned faces. My parents have joined us, and they saw me get sick yesterday.

Shoulders slumped, I just nod my head as the tears come, letting them all know what they suspected anyway. With Lanie in the hospital fighting for her life, I had confided in my mom in the first few weeks after I returned home. She's known my private pain. Securing me in a hug, she pats my hair and tells me it will all be all right.

My father, who's sitting comforting Lanie, speaks with the kind voice he's known for. "We'll get through this, all of us. That's what families do."

Making eye contact with Lanie, I'm immediately worried. I know her. She won't be able to recover from this guilt. Trying to ease her worry, I say, "Okay, puffin. You ready to be a dad?"

She smiles, but it's not sincere.

Am I ready to be a single mom? Hell no. But I'll manage.

Will my heart recover from Charlie? Doubtful, but I'll also figure that out. Lanie's already lived through hell her entire life. I can't let her carry this burden, too.

CHAPTER 19

TREVOR

*T*en months. It's ten months post-Angel, and there's no music. There's no light. I spend every waking moment waiting for the day I get the call saying they've taken my father out. The longer this goes on, the darker my thoughts become.

At night, I'm haunted by images of Angel. Loki told me he's found her, but he can fuck off. The night she disappeared, I thought my worst nightmare had come true. I lived it, thinking they'd taken her, killed by the same bastard that killed my mother. The fact that she's alive is a blessing I don't deserve, but won't take for granted. God was telling me something that day. I can't have her in my life while my father is still breathing. And trust me, the thought of being the one to take his last breath has crossed my mind more than once. If it wasn't for Dexter and his children needing me, I probably would have ended Romero myself.

Dexter: Are you close?

Trevor: Be there in 10.

Dexter: The fucking nanny doesn't know how to change a diaper.

Trevor: WTF.

Dexter: I fired her, now I'm fucked.
Preston: Was she at least hot?
Trevor: Fuck you, Pres. Where the hell are you?
Preston: Getting laid.
Loki: Your dick is going to fall off.
Dexter: GUYS.
Trevor: Pulling in now.
Loki: Me too.

Walking up the steps to Dexter's townhome, I hear Loki call out. Turning, I cringe as he takes in my appearance.

"What?" I demand.

"Fuck, Trevor. Call her."

Ignoring him completely, I ask, "Any news?"

"Your father called me this morning."

What the hell? "Why?"

"My guess is he thinks I'm still running contracts for you. I'm thinking they'll try to force me in."

I can't help but laugh. "Fucking hell. They think they'll turn a federal agent?"

"They think I'm just a schmuck lawyer mooching off the rich boy."

It makes sense, but I don't like it.

"You'll have to go undercover, Loki."

"That's the plan."

"Jesus, man. There has to be another way," I insist.

"Listen, we're not talking about Preston going in. This is me. I'm trained for this, okay? But I'll be blind for a while, and I have to know you can hold it together. If ever there was a time to bring Dex in on this, it's now."

"No fucking way. He has newborns and a four year old, Loki. I can handle this. Do not bring them in," I warn.

He's about to argue when the front door is ripped open. "Thank fuck, guys. Here," Dex says, handing me one of the girls. I'm ashamed to say I can't tell them apart yet.

"Hey there, Babycakes." The endearment falls from my

lips without my consent. It's like a sucker punch to the solar plexus.

Loki pats me on the back in silent comfort. I don't want to know how much he heard from my time with Angel, but the fact that he knows about Babycakes tells me a lot.

"You okay, Trevor? You're looking a little rough," Dex says.

"This coming from the father of three with no nanny?" I retort.

"Exactly. What's going on with you, man?"

"Yeah, Trevor, what's up?" Loki goads.

"Just work," I mumble. "Who do I have here?" I ask, holding up the baby.

"Ah, oh hell … check her diaper. Sara has a birthmark on her hip bone."

"That just sounds wrong on so many levels," Preston says, walking in behind us.

Laying the baby girl down, I do as Dex instructed. "This isn't Sara, and holy Christ. What the hell did you feed her?" I ask, gagging.

"Oh, yeah. Harper is brutal on the diapers," Dex says, throwing a diaper bag at my head.

"Jesus Christ," I grumble, but staring at this little face, it's hard to stay mad. If I'm being honest, it brings me right back to Angel. The first and last time I ever considered fatherhood.

"I'll just have to be the best freaking uncle in the world then," I whisper to the baby.

"Hey, dickwad, where's Tate?" Preston asks.

"He's in the family room watching *Jake and the Never Land Pirates* or something on Disney," Dex yells as he tries to find something in the closet.

Glancing around, I notice he's made no headway on packing. Not that I can blame him with the kids and all, but fuck. "Ah, Dex? Aren't the movers coming next week?"

"Yeah, they'll be here Tuesday."

"Did you call us here to help you pack, dude? I wasn't kidding about having a date," Preston whines.

"No, you asshat. I need help with the kids so I can call the nanny agency. Again."

"How the fu— how do they send a nanny that has no idea how to change a diaper?" I ask.

"It's just my luck, Trevor. You don't understand the women they've been sending over. I thought Molly would drag one girl out by her terrible weave," he tells us, laughing.

I can just picture his assistant, Molly, too. She doesn't have much of a tolerance for stupid. "At least you can laugh about it," I say. "What moving company did you go with?"

"Ah, Olympic or something, I think? I can't remember. It's on my desk somewhere," Dex replies.

I hand Harper to Loki and excuse myself, heading that way.

I'm not usually one to rifle through my buddy's shit, but Dex is in over his head. Finding the receipt, I call the number at the bottom.

"Hi, this is Dexter Cross," I lie. "I have you scheduled for next week and I'd like to add packers to my order."

"Hi, sir, I'd be happy to sort that out for you. Is there anything else I can do for you?" the woman asks.

"No, but a friend of mine, Trevor Knight, will stop by tomorrow to give you additional payment information. He'll also give you the new billing address then," I tell her.

"Very well, have a wonderful day."

"Thanks, you too." Dexter isn't hurting for money, but Jesus does he have his hands full. Picking up that tab is the least I can do.

Walking down the hall, I hear the TV on, so I follow the sounds to find Tate. This kid will always hold a special place in my heart. "Hey, Tate buddy, I've missed you," I say honestly as I sit next to him.

He looks at me and smiles but says nothing. I guess the little guy is still having a tough time since his bitch of a mother up and left.

Slowly, he crawls across the couch cushion and into my lap. This isn't abnormal. I've known him his entire life. Other than Preston's mom, I was his first babysitter, and he's my godson, but tonight when he climbs into my lap to cuddle, I feel a pain deep in my chest. Something that's never been there before attempts to cut me from the inside.

Wrapping my arms around him, I hold him in close to my chest. His pirate pajamas cling to his little body, and I breathe in his scent. *Do all kids smell like this? Would my kid smell like this?* Shaking my head, I try to shut that thought down because I know it leads straight to Angel. I'm tempted to pull up the security footage of her—it's all I have—but I don't. Instead, I let myself get lost in Tate and a show about Never Land.

CHAPTER 20

JULIA

"What I Never Knew I Always Wanted" by Carrie
Underwood

otherfucker. My water just broke. It takes me a minute to realize since no one freaking tells you that you piss yourself all the freaking time when you're pregnant, but pushing aside the covers, there's no mistaking it.

"Okay, Julia. You can do this. You've got it. Your bag is packed, and Jimmy from the fire station loaded the car seat. You've got this! You'll be a badass mother … AAAR-RRGGGG, Nope. I don't have it. Not at all."

"Mom!" I yell, thankful that my parents insisted on staying over for the last two nights because I was having back pain. I'm trying to stand when Lanie and my mom come flying around the corner, fighting to get through the door first. My dad and Lanie's grandmother, GG, are close behind them.

"Jesus Christ, do we need the whole goddamn town here?" Although I'm glad they're here, I feel another contraction coming and it brings me to my knees.

Rushing to my side, Lanie grabs one arm, and my mother takes the other.

"Motherfucker," I scream.

"Jules," my dad warns.

"Pete, you don't want to mess with that child right now," GG warns him. "She's likely to rip your balls right off just for having them."

"Rosa!" my mother scolds.

If something wasn't splitting my insides wide open, I'd probably laugh.

"Well, don't just be standing there, Pete. Go call Dr. Foley and let her know we'll be on our way," GG tells my dad.

I'm not surprised when he follows her directions without question, but I am amazed by the intense pain that has me cussing out every person in the room.

"I read about this. They're coming pretty close together, though, aren't they? Didn't she just have one?" Lanie asks, panicked.

"Lanes, I love you but shut the fuck up and get my bag."

"Oh, right, your bag. Okay. You got her, Mimi?" she asks my mom.

"Just get movin', Lanes," GG scolds, taking my other arm.

I look at her, shocked by how strong she is in her old age.

Winking at me, GG says, "Come on, ya sinner, let's get ya to the hospital." She'd taken to calling me Sinner or Sinny since I got home from Boston. You learn quickly with GG that you'll never win, so it's best to just go with it.

We arrive at the hospital twenty minutes later, thanks in no part to my father's crazy driving. Once I'm checked in, I sit up waiting for the epidural. But suddenly, I need to stand up. "I think I'm going to shit myself. Get me out of this bed," I yell. I'm starting to hyperventilate, and it's getting ugly.

"Julia," Dr. Foley says authoritatively, catching my attention. "You're going to be just fine, honey, but you have to calm down. I'll have the nurses help you to the bathroom, then we need to get you hooked up to the monitors. Someone wants to make you a mom in a hurry."

"A mom?" I repeat, stupidly. *Holy fuck. I miss Charlie.* I can't help it. The tears come. I've tried to shield Lanie from it, but at this moment, it all comes out. These damn hormones have me crying like a drunk girl at a party.

"Charlie will never get to know he's a dad. I'm never going to tell him I love him, and I need to shit," I sob as the nurses help me to the toilet. Once I'm seated, I cry. I cry for Charlie, I cry for my baby that won't know their dad, I cry for myself, and then I cry because it fucking hurts.

Looking around the room frantically, I see a window. It's a little high, but I can make it. Somewhere in the recesses of my mind, I know I'm not making any sense, but until you've had your uterus squeezed by some torture device, you don't get to judge. I'm going to make a break for it and come back tomorrow. "You hear that, little angel? You have to wait and come tomorrow. Mommy's not ready today."

Grabbing a wad of toilet paper, I go to wipe and almost pass out.

"H-Help me, I think it's escaping," I scream at the top of my lungs, which sends the nurses and my family running. They bust through the door. I'm sitting on the toilet with my legs spread eagle as I point in the toilet. "I think there's an arm sticking out. Hurry up and grab it, make sure the baby's okay."

The nurse, thoroughly confused but nervous, rushes to my side and looks in. "Oh, dear. That's just your mucous plug. Reach in there and give it a good pull and it'll come right out."

"Fuck you, I'm not doing that. I didn't come to the hospital to deliver my own kid. If I wanted to do that, I'd have some hippie-dippy doula sitting in a bathtub with me," I scream hysterically.

"Jules," my mother tries to calm me. "That's not the baby, you just need to pull it out."

"No, it looks like a bloodbath. I'm not fucking doing it," I say, crossing my arms over my chest just as another contraction hits, making me sway on the toilet.

"Holy shit, this hurts. It hurts so goddamn much. Am I being punished? Is this me being punished for something?" I scream. Poor Lanie's standing off to the side, looking like she might pass out.

"Oh my God, I need to shit again," I screech, but the nurses are already lifting me off the toilet and carrying me back to the bed. "No, I have to shit," I scream again.

"Julia, your baby's coming. You feel the urge to poop because your body is telling you to push," the nurse explains.

"What? Noooo. I'm having an epidural, I told you that," I say stubbornly just as Dr. Foley walks back into the room.

"Hi, Jules. Let's take a peek, okay?"

"Ah, no, I'm getting the epidural first, remember?" *Am I the only one that remembers the birthing plan we made? Jesus.*

"Yes, I remember. You've told us all at every appointment, and we all got your lists every day this week," she teases. "But I still have to look. How long have you been having contractions?"

"Um, I'm not really sure. My back has been killing me since yesterday, but I guess I felt the first real one a couple of hours ago. Where's that guy with the epidural, anyway? Ugh," I moan, "what the hell was that?"

"Sorry, I was checking your cervix," Dr. Foley tells me. "Honey, it seems like you've been in labor for a while. Let's get you strapped up to a fetal monitor, but I'm not sure you'll have time for an epidural."

"Get the fuck outta here," I wail. "I'm having that epidural, or I'm going home. I'll come back tomorrow. Actually, maybe that's better anyway. I'm kind of tired. I think I'll just go home and come back later." I move to unhook the IV as the mother of all contractions hits and I'm left screaming obscenities at everyone in my line of vision.

Within seconds, the nurses have all kinds of wires attached to me, and the doctor is wheeling in a portable machine I recognize as an ultrasound.

In the next few minutes, everything happens in slow motion, yet I still don't catch everything. I'm aware of my family being ushered from the room, and me being wheeled to a sterile, chilly room as bits and pieces of conversations float through my conscience.

"He's breach."

"Emergency C-section."

"Clear the room."

"Will she be okay?"

"What about the baby?" is the last thing I hear before they place a mask over my face and the world goes black.

∼

Trevor
"Daddy" by Coldplay

GASPING, I wake with a start, clutching my chest. "Angel," I whisper, even though I know it's pointless. I can't explain it, I just feel her. In my heart, I feel her needing me. Clumsily, I swat at the nightstand, searching for my phone. Once I find it, I swipe up to see the time, causing the music app to open, but I jab it off more forcefully than needed. Music breaks my soul without Angel in my life. It's 3:07 a.m. I turn the light on, trying to remember what I was dreaming about, and come up with nothing but an empty feeling in my chest.

Opening my nightstand, I pull out her T-shirt. I know it makes me a creeper, but something is wrong and I need to feel closer to her. Holding her shirt, I do something I said I would never do again. With it clutched to my chest, I climb out of bed, fall to my knees, and pray. I pray that she's all right. I pray that I'll be okay, and I pray that someday, I'll be whole again.

PART II
THE MELODY

CHAPTER 21

LOKI

"Count On Me" by Bruno Mars

*L*eaning back in my chair, I read over the reports my assistant gave me last week: Lanie Heart and Angel herself, Miss Julia McDowell.

Listen, I don't make a habit of interfering in my friend's lives like this, but Trevor is losing his goddamn mind, and I'm afraid he'll do something stupid before I get this case closed.

Then there's Dexter. Fucking Dexter and his kids. These guys have been as close to brothers as I've ever had. I feel guilty for deceiving them for the better part of ten years, but it was the only way. As far as they know, I work for the "Agency," though no one has ever come out and asked which one. In all fairness, I've made it nearly impossible for them to do so.

Someday, I'll be able to tell them about my life … maybe. Eventually, perhaps they'll even forgive me for all the lies I've had to tell, but today isn't that day. In some ways, everything I've told them is the truth, at least in part. I'm one of the good guys, and I'm on their side, but everything else they know about me is a lie.

I work behind the scenes to bring down the monsters. When it came to light that Trevor's dad was one of the biggest demons, I had to come forward. Knowing I can be the one to set Trevor free, I'll do whatever the fuck I have to. It's the least I can do. It is, after all, my fault he's in this position.

Sifting the file again, it seems like a perfect fit. Having infiltrated Julia's life, I know her best friend, Lanie, is looking for work and has been a nanny in the past. If I can get these pieces to fall into place, I might kill two birds with one stone, leaving me free to chase after Romero, and ultimately, Black.

I'm getting soft as I get older. I realized it when I started having trouble separating Trevor's and Dexter's lives from my own. I need to get these two settled so I can focus, and the only way I can do that is to get Lanie down here as Dexter's nanny. As close as these two women are, I have no doubt Julia and Trevor will cross paths once again.

Trevor made me swear to stay away from her. He doesn't think he can have her, but I've watched him die a little more every day since he lost her. Trevor needs her more than he knows, and perhaps she can once again be the distraction I need to keep him occupied while I take down his last living relative.

Resolve in place, I tell my agents to inundate Julia's computer with nanny agency ads and ensure her search engine shows Waverley-Cay as often as possible. Next, I place an agent on intercepting emails and phone calls from Lanie Heart. I've spent the last month watching these girls. Even if Trevor hadn't already fallen in love with Julia, I would have given them my seal of approval. Lanie's had a tough life, but given all Dexter's children have been through lately, I think she just might be what his kids need, too.

CHAPTER 22

TREVOR

"Hey, Loki," I say, answering the phone. I'm in no mood for bullshit. "Please tell me you have some fucking news already?"

"Major waves today, dude," he answers. This is Loki's way of telling me our line is not secure, so I have to play along.

"Yeah? Any hot surfers out today?" *Like I give a fuck about hot surfers.*

"Nah, just one hot piece. I'll be getting on that soon." It's code, he means he has information he'll be making a play for soon, I think. I'm not cut out for this cloak and dagger bullshit.

Loki told me in no uncertain terms about six months ago that my part of the mission was over. Now I have to sit and wait. I've been waiting for almost eighteen fucking months, and we've gotten nowhere. Romero is still walking free, as are the Black family up in Boston. My patience is running thin.

I'm not a violent man, but my entire adult life has been in limbo. I'm done being patient, and I think Loki can tell. He's been checking up on me a lot more lately.

"I'm almost at Dexter's. You headed there now?" he asks.

189

"Yeah, I'm getting in my car. I'll see you in about twenty minutes." We all received a text from Dex about an hour ago asking us to come over for beers, but I know better. Something's up with him; this is as close to asking for help as we get with him. So even though my mind is in the darkest of places, I drop everything to be there for my friend.

Walking into Dexter's new home, I regret not adding unpacking to Dexter's moving company order. There's crap everywhere. *He's lived here too long for it to look like this.* Following the sounds of voices, I find Dexter, Preston, and Loki in the den.

"What the hell, Trev?" Preston says. "You're the richest son of a bitch, and you look homeless."

Fucking Preston.

"Fuck off, Pres. I'm not in the mood. What's up, Dex? It's been a long time since you've sent an SOS, you okay?" I ask my friend while glancing around at the piles and piles of moving boxes everywhere.

"What SOS? I just got a text saying beers at his house! If you called us here to unpack for you, I'm going to be pissed," Preston says, annoyed.

Loki shoves him. "Fuck off, Preston. He didn't call us here to help unpack, but since we're here, the least we can do is help."

"He has three small kids, so stop being a prick and get off your ass to help," I insist.

Preston may be the first in line to help, but he prefers it to be a supervisory role. I only half listen as the guys continue to give each other shit. When they talk about Dexter's ex-wife, I tune out. She's the biggest bitch I've ever encountered. Taking a big swig of the beer Loki handed out, I turn and unpack the box in front of me.

A while later, I glance over and notice Dexter lost in thought, so I give him a nudge. The guy looks exhausted.

"You okay?" I ask.

Sighing, Dexter rests his head in his hands. "Nanny number three bit the dust two and a half weeks ago." I watch as he cringes and his shoulders sag.

Why the hell didn't he call me?

Before I can go off, Preston speaks up, "What? Why didn't you call us, man? We know what you have going on with your company. We would have been here in shifts to help. We love those kids more than we love you."

Pacing the room, pissed at myself because I didn't know my best friend was struggling so much, I listen as he explains an interview he just had with a potential nanny. I'm finding it increasingly difficult not to laugh right in his face, though. It sounds like this woman is a firecracker that's woken something inside of Dex.

Unable to contain my smile, I finally sit next to him. "You like her."

"What? I don't know her," he protests. "The interview was the biggest clusterfuck of my life. She swooped in here, took Harper from my arms, and got her to stop crying immediately, might I add. She essentially told me to shut up while she got my kids settled. Then and only then would she let me know when we could carry on with the interview."

Glancing at each other around the room, we all burst out laughing. You have to know Dexter to know what a real nightmare this must have been for him. He's always controlled, always calm under pressure. This fucking girl got to him in a big way, and it has me grinning like a fool even as my heart cries for Angel.

"She got Tate to speak," Dexter says, drying up the laughter as we take in what he just said.

"What?" I shout, shocked more than anything. My little pal, Tate, stopped talking when his twat of a mother up and left him.

"What do you mean what?" asks Preston. "She got him to speak!"

"Yeah, it wasn't like he opened up or anything. It was just a couple of words here and there. He liked helping her find stuff to get the girls settled. When she gave me shit, he burst out laughing," Dexter says, not even trying to stop the grin that appears on his face.

"So, where is she? Why haven't you hired her?" Loki demands harshly.

I try to give Loki a 'What the fuck?' look, but he ignores me, pissed off about something.

"She has some issues," Dexter starts. "This is just between us because I found out through Ryan." He pauses, staring at each of us. We all know Ryan is the owner of EnVision Security—a company he hired to keep track of his ex-wife. If Dex went to him for information, it has to be something serious. "She was severely attacked about a year and a half ago."

I find myself pacing again. Hearing about abuse in any form is a trigger for me. Watching my mother suffer at the hands of my father when I was too young to do anything about it makes the fact that I couldn't save her when she died that much harder of a pill to swallow.

As I'm glaring out the window, trying to calm my racing heart, I hear Loki ask, "You seem pretty confident in her abilities to care for the kids, what's holding you back?"

"I am. She was truly great with them," Dex says, staring straight at me. He's silently asking my opinion. He wants to know what I think because I've lived that hell before.

"Then what aren't you telling us? Do you think she has issues from her attack that would make her unable to care for the kids?" Loki continues.

What the fuck is Loki's problem tonight? He never pushes like this, and it makes me edgy.

I pace the room of Dexter's new home while I listen to him recount the events of his interview with Miss Lanie Heart. If I wasn't so distracted by Loki's bizarre behavior, I might have even found it funny. As it is, I'm lost in thought until Dex says something about her attack, catching my attention.

"I feel like I can trust her, but going through something like that has to change a person, right?" Dex asks, staring straight at me.

Sighing and attempting to keep the contents in my stomach from forcing an exit, I nod. "Look, man, you know about my mom. After everything she went through, she was still the best thing in my life. She would have done anything for me. What's your gut telling you about this girl?"

Dex doesn't hesitate in his answer, "It says to trust her."

Loki sits down next to him. "It looks like you have your answer."

That's how, a few days later, I find myself in Dexter's office, watching as Lanie puts Dexter in his place and whips his household into a home in a matter of minutes. For the first time in months, I laugh. This girl is going to give Dexter a run for his money, and it will be so fun to watch.

CHAPTER 23

JULIA

"Good Love" by Shy Carter

"*M*amamama." I hear Charlie babbling from the next room. I realize how tired I am when I try to roll out of bed to get him. I knew Lanie had helped a lot when she was here, but I guess I never considered just how much she actually did. "This is what single parenting is like," I say to an empty hallway. "It's really hard, but I've got this."

"Hey, handsome," I coo, lifting Charlie out of his crib. "What are you doing up so early?" He babbles away happily as I carry him through the hall on our way to the kitchen. Passing Lanie's room, he reaches for it. "I miss her, too, bubba." I kiss his cheek.

I'm really missing her lately, but she needed this. My best friend was suffering from night terrors and couldn't find direction after her life was almost taken so brutally. "We'll talk to her later, I'm sure," I tell Charlie. We've been Face-Timing every day, but it isn't the same. For the first time since finding out I was pregnant, I feel utterly alone in the world.

As if he can read my thoughts, Charlie whacks me across the face. "Motherfu-dge, Charlie, what the heck? No, buddy. No hitting," I scold him, and he laughs.

In the kitchen, I grab his bottle and fill it with formula. Plopping him in his bouncy seat, I go about making some much-needed coffee. While I wait for it to brew, I scan the mail that came yesterday and freeze. It's been a long time since I've gotten one of these letters, and I'm not in the mood for it right now, but I know the longer I put it off, the worse it will be.

Dear Ms. Julia McDowell,

After further investigation, we regret to inform you ...

I don't even bother reading the rest of it. I'll be stuck with Erick's debt for the rest of my life. "It's a good thing your mama is a genius, buddy," I say sarcastically. I make good money, but the debt Erick accrued in my name is suffocating. Add to that attorney's fees, and I'll be lucky if I can pay for Charlie's college in seventeen years. I could have asked my parents to help, but I was too embarrassed. I never even told Lanie all of it, and I've always told her everything.

I stare at Charlie, who smiles so innocently at me with his father's eyes, the color of whiskey and fireflies. He looks so much like his father; it's brought me to tears many times. I keep hoping I'll outgrow that. I can't blame the tears on hormones at this point, and people will notice if I don't get my act together.

As my front door bursts open, I jump off my stool and almost land on my ass. I hear the clack-clack-clack of ortho-pedic shoes and know GG's here.

"Jules? Where the hell ya at?" she yells from the front door.

"In the kitchen, GG." *Why in God's name is she here before seven?*

Tossing a bag on the counter, GG slaps the back of my head in greeting.

"Jesus, GG. Do you have to do that every time you see me?"

"Keeps you on yer toes, doesn't it, Sinny?" she cackles. "Now, let me get my hands on my little man here."

I have to admit, GG is batshit crazy, but she loves Charlie like her own grandson. I love her for it.

Watching as she picks him up and carries him to the couch, I grab my coffee and a cup for her as well.

"What are you doing here so early today?" I ask.

"Let's cut to the chase, Jules. Somethin' isn't right with you. Hasn't been in a long time. Now with Lanie gone, I'm worryin' a little more is all."

"Ah, GG, I'm okay, really. It's harder with Lanie gone, but don't you dare go telling her that. She's exactly where she needs to be."

"No argument from me there, girly, but you keep spending all your time looking after everyone else, you're gonna end up missing out on the life you were meant for."

Staring at Charlie, I can't help but smile. "I'm good, GG. How can I not be when I have the best gift a woman could ask for?"

"Mhm, we'll see. My money is bettin' you'll be singing a different tune before you know it. Jarrod down at the hardware store is teachin' me to read those funny fortune cards, and we read yours yesterday. You're in for a lot of changes, missy. Get ready."

I can't help but laugh. "Yeah, GG. Lots of diaper changes are definitely in my future."

"You sassy little twit," she scolds. Pointing a boney finger at me, she says, "Mark my words, Sinny, this will be your year. Now, the other thing I came for. Lexi is coming into town late tonight, and she'll have to stay with you. Hope that's okay? The inn is full, and the lodge has a wedding."

Lexi is Lanie's older cousin by two months. Their mothers were twins, and if you were to see Lexi and Lanie together, you'd think they were, too. The three of us were always close, but where Lexi was a jock, Lanie and I came up with every plausible excuse to miss gym class.

"That's fine," I tell GG. "I haven't seen Lex in over a year, how's she doing?"

GG tsks in a way that has my stomach twisting. "Something's going on with that girl, I just know it, but she won't tell me nothin'," GG complains. "This guy she's mixed up with, Miles, I think she said his name was. I just don't like him one bit. I'm worryin' for her."

GG is uncharacteristically subdued. She must be really concerned. "Have you talked to Lanie? Maybe she's spoken to her," I offer, feeling guilty for not having reached out myself.

"No, I have not, and don't you go doin' it either. Lanie needs to get her head on straight herself. The last thing she needs is to be worryin' about Lex."

"Okay, I'll see if I can talk with her when she arrives. Do you know what she's coming for? She hasn't been home in ages."

"No clue. Lex just said she'd be up for lunch tomorrow, but wasn't staying more than a night. I wanted her to stay with me, but the ice damage hasn't been fixed from the last storm yet, and the guest room is torn down to the studs."

"That's all right, GG. It'll be nice to have some company."

After handing Charlie back to me, she finishes her coffee. "I thought it might. Okay, I've gots to go! I was touchin' the ladies earlier. We're going to hit up the diner before that handsome cook leaves for the day," she says with a wink and a wave.

"Texting, GG. It's called texting," I tell her as she walks through the front door.

Laughing, I tuck my face into the crook of Charlie's chubby little neck. *God, he smells good ...* Right up until he doesn't. "Ugh, Charlie. You couldn't have done that for GG?"

Once I've changed him, we're headed to make breakfast just as my mom walks in to take over so I can go to work.

"Hi, Mom."

"Hi, sweetie," she says, kissing my cheek. "How are you doing without Lanie? I know it must be tough."

"Yeah, it was definitely easier with two sets of hands around here, but I'll be fine." *Someday that phrase won't be a lie.*

"So, what's my little guy—" She's interrupted by Madonna blasting on my cell phone. She smiles because she knows that's Lanie's ring. "Go ahead, check on our Lanes. I've got my buddy here."

"Mom," I say as I'm headed down the hall.

"Hm?" she answers, already distracted by Charlie.

"Love you."

She pauses to really look at me and smiles. "I love you, too, Jules."

I really am lucky to have such amazing parents. Turning up pregnant and alone could have been a nightmare, but they never once left my side, questioned my sanity, or made me feel like I'd messed up my life. Having Charlie and no father around is not ideal, but given a choice, I'd choose to have a piece of my Charlie with me always.

Pressing the green button on my phone, I wait for Lanie's face to appear.

"Jules," she hisses, "I haven't been here a week, and we're already flirting. *Me*, Jules, I'm flirting with a man!"

I try not to laugh. "Oh-kay, I know there are a million ways this could go sideways, but you're both consenting adults. As long as you both agree to put the children first, I don't see why it's such a big deal. I'm freaking ecstatic for you. You're finally on the road to recovery, my friend. If that hot specimen of a man can help you move on, I say go for it."

Lanie had told me earlier in the week how hot he was, but until I Googled him, I couldn't fully appreciate it. That man is definitely hot.

"It's not that easy, Jules," she complains.

Knowing she needs a little push, I ask her, "Answer me this. How would you feel watching Dex leave on a date with someone else? He's the first man in years you've had chemistry with. Would you honestly be okay with him dating someone else if you didn't at least explore it first?"

Lanie hasn't known this man long, but who am I to judge? I fell in love with a man in a matter of days. At least she knows this one's name. I can't help the sadness that washes over me as I think about Charlie. It hits in the most random of moments. I do my best to hide it. Lanie still feels guilty, even though it isn't her fault, and I don't need her dwelling on something that can never be changed.

I realize I'm still waiting for her to answer when she finally says, "I know, without a doubt, I'm in for heartbreak with this guy."

Run, run, and never look back. You'll never recover from it if you get hurt like me, I want to shout, but of course, I don't, and thanks to my new trick of curling my tongue, then biting it, the words don't slip out from my mouth unbidden either.

I choose my words carefully and will my voice not to break. "Sometimes, we have to have a little heartbreak to get to where we need to be. Maybe a little heartbreak will be worth it if he can help you get past what happened to you. Remember, you're the one who keeps saying you will only stay a year. You need to remember that. You aren't the only one risking heartbreak if you take things any further with him."

The sense of déjà vu washes over me as I remember Lanie saying almost precisely the same thing to me about my one-night stand rules.

"You're right, as always. Lord knows if I don't do something, I will end up as alone as my mother has always been," she says sadly.

"Lanie Kathleen Heart. You listen, and you listen good," I scold her. "You are not, nor will you ever be, alone."

"Thanks, Jules. I have to get going. Tate has to be at school soon. Luvs," she says, sending air kisses through the phone.

AFTER FINALLY GETTING Charlie in bed, I search for my phone. I don't know how it's possible to lose something so many times a day, but it's become a real talent of mine. Finding it in the couch cushion, I check the time to see it's getting late and Lexi still hasn't arrived.

I'm getting nervous, so I give her a quick call, but it goes straight to voicemail. Trying it one more time, I leave a message. "Hey, Lex! It's me, Julia. GG said you were coming up tonight, and since her roof still has ice damage, you'll be staying with me. I was just wondering what time you're coming. I'll be here all night, so when you get this, just let me know. See you soon. Luvs." As I hang up, GG's concerns echo through my head.

Around eleven, I realize I've been pacing for over an hour. "Ugh! Do I call GG and wake her up? Or just keep waiting? I don't want to worry her any more than she already is. Poor GG, she hasn't had an easy time of it lately with Lanie and now possibly Lexi." When I'm home, I don't have to pretend. I can talk to myself all I want and no one makes fun of me for it.

Plopping down onto the couch, I do what any reasonable, small-town girl would do. I call the fire department. Technically, it's the volunteer fire department, but since we don't have either a police station or a fire station, the volunteers are getting my call tonight.

"Hey, Jules, what's your emergency?" the voice on the other end asks. I recognize it as Suzette from my mom's book club.

"Hi, Suzette. Ah, I don't actually have an emergency, but Lexi was supposed to be coming into town today. GG said she was staying with me, but it's been hours, and Lex isn't answering her phone. I just wanted to see if anyone had reported any accidents?"

"No, sorry, hun. I haven't heard anything. Is she staying with you because of the ice damage out at the lodge? I thought we told Travis to get on that last week?"

This is both the blessing and the curse of living in a small town. Everyone literally knows every single detail about everyone. Rubbing my temples, I fill her in. "No, Travis couldn't get out to the mountain until later this week, I guess. GG said it was a guest room, but I haven't been to see it yet."

"Well, that's one way to put it. Rosa will freeze her ass off out there if someone doesn't get to her soon. The ice damaged a sizable portion of the roof. I can't imagine it's contained to just one room."

Grabbing my notebook, I write a quick note to myself to go check it out tomorrow. I wouldn't put it past GG to downplay it, but if there's actual damage, I need to make sure she's safe out there.

"My dad and I will run over tomorrow to take a look, okay? So, no word on Lex or any car accidents?"

"Sorry, no. Chester is here though. How about I send him out on patrol to check out the area? I'll give ya a call if anything turns up. Sound good?"

"Sure. Thanks, Suzette. I appreciate it."

"Anytime, kiddo. Bring Charlie by the station sometime this week. We just got some new swag," she says, stressing the word swag because that's what she thinks the 'kids do'.

"I will. Have a good night."

I grab my Kindle and sort through my backlog of Kindle Unlimited books. I only recently found out that these poor authors get half a cent per page, but only if you actually read the book. It makes me feel shitty about all the ones I've stockpiled on here, so I vow to make it through one of them while I wait for Lex.

〜

I HEAR a crash and bolt upright in bed, ready to run to Lanie's side, thinking she's having another nightmare. Except I'm not in bed, and it's not Lanie standing in front of me, it's Lexi. To be fair, most people would probably struggle to tell them apart, but I know instantly.

"What the fuck, Lex? You scared the hell out of me."

"Yeah, well? What are you doing sprawled out on the floor like that anyway?" she retorts.

Glancing around, I realize I'm on my family room floor with my Kindle stuck to my face. "Ah, I must have fallen asleep." When I look at the clock on the wall, I see it's one in the morning. "What the hell, Lex? Why are you strolling in like a teenager who missed curfew?"

"Sorry. I-I just had some things I had to take care of before I could leave."

She's not making eye contact with me, and she is fidgety as all hell. "What the hell, Lexi? Are you okay?" GG was right. Something's off with her; something's definitely not right.

Shutting the door behind her, she looks around. Anywhere but directly at me. "I'm fine, Jules. I'm just exhausted," she lies.

Standing, I march to her. Like Lanie, Lex is over six feet tall with beautiful, blonde hair. As a kid, it was always in a ponytail. Now, it's cut in a sharp bob that doesn't suit her. She's always been thin with an athletic build, but seeing her here, there's nothing athletic about this pile of bones. Where Lanie and I would have to work out, Lexi has always been toned from the sports she plays. Staring at her now, the only definition is the outline of her frame.

"Jesus Christ, Lex! When's the last time you ate some-thing?" I know I should be more tactful, but it's a shocking state to find her in. She's never had an eating disorder that I know of, and it isn't like it's been years since I've seen her.

Flipping on the light, I take a better look at her. She has big circles under her eyes she tried to cover with makeup, to no avail. Her clothes—an outfit Lanie would surely approve of—hang limp on her frail body.

"Don't look at me like that, Jules. I said I'm fine. Drop it," she demands.

"I will not just drop it, Lex. Look at you! What the hell is going on?" I ask, trying to control my voice so I don't wake up Charlie.

Sitting down, I watch the fight leave Lexi's body. "Miles isn't who I thought he was," she begins. "I-I came home to see if your parents could help me set some things up before … before I leave him."

"Lex, you aren't married. You don't own property together. What do you need lawyers for?" I ask, confused.

"He's into some messed up shit, Jules. I only found out by overhearing a conversation I wasn't meant to hear. I need your dad to help me make sure I'm not involved in any of it before I leave. Miles will not let me go easily."

The admission makes my spine tingle.

"Has he hurt you?" I demand. After everything I've just gone through with Lanie, what the hell are the odds of Lex being in trouble, too?

"No, not physically, anyway. He'll make sure I won't be able to work in Boston again, but if that's the only price I pay for leaving, I'll take it." She shrugs. "He certainly won't make it easy, but I can start over."

The entire conversation is reminiscent of my own situa-tion with my ex. I sit still for a few moments, wondering if I want to go here with her. Seeing how defeated she seems, I decide that telling her my story can only help. Even if it only makes her feel less alone.

"Lex, I've never told anyone this, not even Lanie, but I think we can probably help each other right now. Remember Erick?" I ask, stupidly. Everyone knew Erick.

"Jules, I'm tired, not a freaking moron," she replies, trying not to roll her eyes.

I've missed this girl. "Well, the truth is, I didn't break up with him." Her expression makes me cringe. "He took off, with close to a hundred grand in cash." I pause to see her mouth fall open. I haven't even told her the worst part yet. "And he opened almost four hundred thousand in credit cards and loans, in my name. I have no idea where he is, but I've spent the last four years trying to pay off his debt."

Gasping, she leans back into the couch. "Fuck me. Is it too late to open some wine?" she asks, reading my mind.

"Hell no," I tell her, already heading for the wine cabinet.

When she sits at the island across from me, I see the sadness written all over Lexi's face. "He isn't the man I thought he was."

Leaning across the counter, I pat her hand. "They never are, Lex."

Except, I know that's not the truth. Charlie would have been the exception, I know it.

"Why didn't you tell anyone about Erick? Oh my God, what did your parents say?" Her words have me cringing in shame. Again.

"What the hell, Jules? You didn't tell them either?" she shouts.

Shaking my head, I tell her the truth. "I was so embarrassed, Lex. I still am. My career is literally risk-management for this stuff. How was I so fucking stupid I didn't see a con coming straight for me?" Releasing a breath, I feel four years' worth of pent-up shame leave my body.

After pouring us both an enormous glass of wine, Lexi clinks her glass with mine. "Cheers. Here's to new beginnings and the fucked-up lovers who caused them."

Together, we laugh, then proceed to drink our faces off.

CHAPTER 24

TREVOR

"Monster" by Imagine Dragons

Sitting at my desk, I do what I promised myself I wouldn't. I scour the dark web for Angel. I do this from time to time, always coming up empty-handed because I have nothing substantial to go on. A few times, after more drinks than I care to acknowledge, I've been tempted to ask Loki. I know he has all the answers I need, but I don't. I can't. Almost two years later, as far as I know, we aren't any closer to bringing down my father. That means my life is still a shell of what it could have been. I have nothing to offer but heartache.

I toss a pen on the table and recline in my chair, noticing my hand has found residence over my heart again. A constant ache lives there now.

Fuck it. If I'm going to hurt, I might as well have a mark there to remind me just how close I came to having it all.

Trevor: You busy?

Loki: Depends. You going to let me help you with Angel?

Trevor: Fuck off. Meet me downtown, near O'Malley's, in half an hour.

Loki: Done.

Standing on Waverley Street, I look up at the sign, Redemption Tattoo. It's a great name, but there will be no redemption for me.

"What in God's name are we doing here, Trevor?" I hear Loki call out from half a block away.

My chest zings with the pain that's been there since Boston, and my fist involuntarily clutches the empty space.

"Give me a break, all right? Just come in and make sure this guy doesn't spell anything wrong while I'm not paying attention."

"Trevor, fucking hell. You're losing your goddamn mind. Have you even showered this week?"

I ignore him and open the door. "Are you coming in or not?"

"You don't have to live like this, Trevor," he barks.

"As long as Romero walks free, I do," I tell him, letting the door close again. "They need me. They need my software. Until we take them out, my life is not my own. I won't give them leverage. And that's what she'd be, Loki. Leverage to hell. If Dexter didn't fucking need me, I would kill them myself just to be done with this shit. To serve justice for my mother. But I can't. We're the only family he has right now, and I won't do that because I'm not Romero. I don't put my family in hell, why can't you fucking understand that?"

Before I get out my next breath, Loki has me jacked up against the wall, his forearm cutting into my neck. The fucker is strong.

"You asshole. Don't you think I know what you've been living through? Don't you think I've been doing everything in my fucking power to bring this to an end? You don't want to bring your family into your hell, but guess what, asshole? I'm your family, too. I'm here with you, and I'm telling you to get a fucking grip. You need Angel, and I'm telling you right now, she needs you, too."

Something in me snaps at his statement, and I shove forward with both hands, but I don't let up. I charge him as my fist flies through the air. "What do you mean she needs me, too? You goddamn asshole, are you watching her?" My fist connects with the side of his head.

His arms move quickly to block my next punch, and we tumble to the sidewalk. "Stop fucking punching me, you dick," he yells, rolling on top of me, using some martial arts trick to subdue me.

Bucking my hips, I'm able to roll us, but he's right. I'm losing my fucking mind, and I swing wildly. I've never been a fighter, and he's obviously trained. He dodges my next punch and gets one in himself, straight to my kidney, knocking the wind out of me.

"What the hell is going on out here?" asks a burly man who has exited the tattoo shop. Pulling me off of Loki, he stares between the two of us. "Are you two about done, or do I need to call the cops?"

Straightening his black T-shirt, Loki says, "Nah, we're good. This asshole here is your next appointment."

What the hell is wrong with me? "Loki, I—"

"Save it," he snaps. "We'll sort this shit out later, but from now on, fucking trust that I'm doing what I told you I'd do." He gestures for me to enter the shop, but I pause before going in.

I have to know. "Is … is she all right, Loki?"

Clapping me on the back, he leans in. "She will be, Trevor. But you have some choices to make. As much as you need her in your life, she might just need you more."

Fuck.

"You two knuckleheads figure your crap out?" the man from the tattoo shop asks.

"Yeah. We're all good." I hope, anyway. I've never brawled

like that in my life. Maybe I do need to reevaluate things. Now that I'm certain Loki has been keeping tabs on Angel, I know one thing for sure—I'll never get her out of my head again. I hate him a little for it.

Feeling the tattoo artist's eyes on me again, I glance up.

"So, what's it going to be today, guys?"

"Can you do something like this?" I slide a sketch I'd drawn earlier over the counter. It's the same image that comes to me every night. My angel. Her head is bowed so I can't see her face, and her wings are frayed. I replaced the bits of her halo that are left with the words, 'My Grace Is Gone' in delicate script. Her arms are wrapped around her middle, with her gown pooling at her bare feet. In the hem of her dress, I've written 'Where you end is where I begin.'

When I glance over my shoulder at Loki, I see him raise his brow. "What's this mean?"

"Grace is her middle name. My angel, *My Grace Is Gone*."

Pulling at his hair, Loki pushes off the counter. "I can't take this shit, man. She doesn't have to be. You're being a stubborn son of a bitch. If you would just trust me, you wouldn't be living in this fucking self-imposed misery. It's time to get your goddamned head out of your ass. I'm out, but mark my words, get your shit together or I'll do it for you."

"What the hell is that supposed to mean?" I bark, but Loki is already out the door.

Trying to shake off his threat, I stare at my drawing. "So, can you do this?"

"You got it. Take off your shirt and have a seat. Get comfy, you'll be here for a while."

Staring at the ceiling, I pray for every poke of the needle to take away some of the pain. Replace it, at the very least. I'll take a needle branding my skin any day over the ache I've been living with for the last two years.

Four hours later, I leave with Angel permanently affixed

to my heart, right where she was always meant to be. I'm heading to my car when my phone rings. Pulling it from my front pocket, I see it's Dex.

He's been in London all week for work, and I know he's calling to check on his new nanny, Lanie, and the kids. I promised him I'd keep tabs on her and I have. To be honest, she's freaking amazing. The kids love her, and she's been a blessing for Tate. Those two have a connection that he desperately needed after his mother left.

"Hey, Dex, congrats on the deal! You must be so relieved," I say, genuinely proud of all he's accomplished.

We talk for a while and find out Preston has been messing with him again. But listening to Dexter's concerns about the feelings he's having for his nanny, something in me snaps. He has a chance to be happy, and I sure as hell won't let him pass it up.

By the time we hang up, my body is shaking with emotion. I'd given him advice I can't take myself. *Don't let the fears of your past ruin your future.*

"For fuck's sake," I yell to an empty car. Throwing my phone on the passenger seat, I know I need to go find Loki.

Don't let your fears of your past ruin your future.

CHAPTER 25

JULIA

"Smile Like You Mean It" by The Killers

"Mom? Dad?" I yell as I enter my childhood home. "Where are you?" Propping Charlie up on my hip, I toss his diaper bag onto the couch.

"Julia?" my mother's voice calls from the hallway. "I didn't know you were stopping by," she adds, coming into view. "Lanie, I'll be ..." she starts, cocks her head to the side, then laughs. "Lexi, I swear you and Lanie will always fool me at first glance. Rosa told me you were visiting, but I didn't know we'd get to see you. How are you, sweet girl?" my mother asks, pulling her into a hug.

"I'm good, Mimi. How are you guys? I've missed you." The relief in her voice concerns me.

"Oh, we're good, just missing Lanie a little if I'm being honest. I hate that you girls are all over the place now," my mother says wistfully. As far as she's concerned, Lanie's her daughter as much as I am. "Now, what can I get you to drink?"

"I'm fine, but thanks. I was actually hoping I could speak

to you or Pete, privately." Lexi fidgets in place. "I think … I think I need a lawyer."

"Oh, dear, okay. Come this way. Jules, there's a snack in the kitchen for you and Charlie if you're hungry," she says, giving Charlie a big kiss on her way by. "My sweet boy."

"All right, big guy, what do you say we get something to eat? Momma's a little hungover and needs some food. When you're old enough to know what I'm saying, little man, I'll have to watch what I say. Until then, you get the job of being my outlet when the chaos comes." I kiss his chubby cheeks, and melt into a puddle of goo at the sound of his laughter.

Knowing Lexi could be in trouble definitely has the chaos coming. Mix that with the fact that I think my best friend is falling in love with her boss, and I'm a category four storm ready to touch down.

"Speak of the devil," I say, putting Charlie into his high-chair just as Lanie calls.

Pressing the green accept button, I hold the phone out so both Charlie and I are visible in the frame. "Hey, lady, what's up?" Noticing her swollen face, I hand Charlie a teething biscuit and pull the phone in close. "What the fuck happened to your face?" I demand.

"Ugh, Jules. You won't even believe it. The kid's mother happened. She showed up here out of the blue, yelling and screaming. Poor Tate was scared out of his mind."

"That doesn't explain why you have a handprint on the side of your face," I deadpan.

"I went outside to talk to her, and she boot-slapped me. Can you believe that? She actually slapped me. Knocked me right off my feet," Lanie explains as only she can. She never swears, and I got used to her terminology years ago, but I have a feeling it will take Dexter a while to get used to it.

It takes me a few breaths to calm down, but by the time she's done explaining what happened, I'm fairly confident that Dexter Cross has it handled.

I listen as she tells me all about Dexter, but my eyes are on my son. I can't help wondering if Charlie would have been protective. My gut says yes, and it makes me sad that I'll never know for sure.

"What am I going to do, Jules?" Lanie's question brings me out of my daydream.

"Lanes, you're both consenting adults. Just try to relax and see where it goes. But if he doesn't do something about that ex-wife giving you a smackdown, he'll have me to answer to."

She laughs, and I catch sight of Lexi coming down the hall.

"Hey, Lanes? Ah … I gotta go, okay? I'll call you later. Luvs." I hang up before she can answer. I can only handle one crisis at a time. Thankfully, it sounds like Dexter has made Lanie his business.

"You all set?" I ask as Lexi enters the kitchen.

Looking from me to my dad, Lexi says, "Yeah, I'll be fine," but I'm not buying it.

So I turn my attention to my dad. "Is she going to be all right?"

"Jules, you know I can't disclose client information like that, but we'll do everything we can," he says, smiling at Lexi. I notice his worry lines appear deeper—a sure sign he isn't telling me the complete truth.

"Lexi?" I try.

"I'm going to be fine, Jules. I promise. I have to go. I promised GG I'd have lunch with her before I headed back. Thank you," she says, giving us each a hug.

I may not know exactly what's going on with her. However, based on the expressions on my parents' faces, it's more serious than she led me to believe.

"I've got some calls to make," my distracted father mumbles. "These girls will be the death of me."

At least I know where I get my filter from.

"Try not to worry, Jules. We'll take care of Lexi, I promise," my mom says, kissing the top of my head.

"I'm going to head out, too. I have to get Charlie home for
a nap, and I've got some work I need to catch up on."

$\sim$

WITH WORK, everything fits into a nice, neat bubble.
Numbers make sense. Risk is manageable. I know what to
expect with spreadsheets and graphs. What I wasn't
expecting were the text messages I got that night.

Crazy-Town Group Chat.

**GG: There's a handsome young man that just checked
into the Wagon-Wheel.**

Julia: Not interested, but thanks.

GG: This one's not for you.

Julia: Then what are you telling me for?

**GG: Because Dexter Cross is coming to see you tomor-
row. Says he's goin' to see about a girl.**

And that's why I'm sitting at my parents' island at the ass
crack of dawn the next morning.

"Julia, you need to calm down. We don't even know what
he's doing here," my mother says. "It could very well all be
innocent."

"I'm not buying it. Lanie said he had a work trip come up
at the last minute, which means he lied to her to come here. I
don't like this one bit, and when I get my hands on him, I'll
give him a piece of my mind."

"Whoa, there, tiger. Slow down," my father says, laughing.
"Maybe I'd better wait outside and head him off before she-
wolf over here decapitates him," he tells my mom.

Rolling my eyes like a surly teenager, I grab another cup
of coffee. I'm on fire already, but the pot of coffee I've
consumed will really give me a boost when I rip into this
asshole. No one messes with my Lanes.

Forty-five minutes after Dexter arrives, I finally hear my father yell, "Okay, girls, you can come on out now."

Glaring at my mother for not allowing me to eavesdrop, I grab Charlie from his play mat and storm outside.

After handing Charlie to my dad, I stand directly in front of Dexter Cross. *God, Lanie was right, he's fucking hot as hell.* Regardless, I cut right to the chase. "What are you doing here?"

"I'm sorry, your son's adorable. I missed what you said," he states, staring at Charlie.

Trying not to smile because this man will not charm me, I cross my arms to guard myself against his sorcery. "His name is Charlie, and he is, thank you. What are you doing here, presumably behind Lane's back? If you're looking to fire her, so help me God, you'd better think again."

I can't help it, I'm a ball of caffeinated energy looking for a fight.

"Julia, just calm down for a minute and let him explain. I think you'll be happy with his answers," my dad says.

Dexter smirks like he has an ally, and I narrow my eyes at him.

"Just because you pulled the wool over my dad's eyes, with lawyer-speak I would imagine, doesn't mean I'll automatically trust you."

If I've pissed him off, he doesn't show it. Instead, he sounds more offended than anything.

"I'm not here to fire her. I'm man enough to do that to someone's face, not run to their family to do it," he scoffs in disgust.

All right, Dexter. Points for acknowledging we're her family. Fuck, I bet this guy's a major suck up.

"Then what are you doing here?" I ask again.

"I'm here for back-up, as strange as that sounds. I want to have a relationship with Lanie. Whatever she can give me, and I know it'll take work and a lot of convincing. I need help to make that happen."

I'm speechless. It's a rarity for me. "You sound like you love her. You haven't even been on a date yet. One kiss cannot have you head over heels already." Ah, hell, I feel my face flush red.

"Well, it was a perfect kiss," he says with a wink.

That smartass. We just might be able to be friends after all.

"Look, I realize I haven't taken her on a date yet, but I know how I feel. I know how hard it'll be to convince her to give us a shot, but, like I said, I'm committed. I'll put in the hard work. Will you help me?" He seems so sincere, so honest, so in love.

In this moment, I realize that Lanie may have found her puffin, and as happy as I am for her, my heart cracks wide open.

Forcing a smile, I say, "On one condition."

"Anything, name it!" he says, and I can tell he immediately regrets it. *Ha, if he only really knew me.*

"Tell me what you're doing to keep Bitchzilla away from our Lanie?"

The laugh that falls from him echoes in my ears. Lanie will be just fine.

What about you, Jules? Where's your puffin? My inner voice is going to get kicked right in the taint if she doesn't mind her own damn business soon.

CHAPTER 26

JULIA

"Lonely If You Are" by Chase Rice

"*M*om, I know it's only been a few weeks, but I think Dex might really be Lanie's puffin. Look at this," I tell her, sitting down at her kitchen island.

"Ooh, are these the text messages from the MLM?" she asks.

Dexter is a lovesick fool. He has seriously pulled out all the stops in his bid to win Lanie's heart. He's also annoying as fuck because he texts me and his three best friends every damn day. He even named the group chat MLM, which stands for Make Lanie Mine. I get it, it's cute … but come on, dude. Grow a pair.

"It is. He's really going to piss off his friends though." I laugh.

My mother sighs. "Julia, what are you going to do when Charlie's first word is fuck? You need to start watching your mouth, or he'll be the one to get kicked out of preschool for calling someone an asshat."

I'm momentarily stunned. My mother isn't a prude, but hearing her swear openly has me shaking with laughter.

"I'll try to do better, Mom," I tell her, snorting.

"Good grief, Jules. Okay, let me see these messages," she says eagerly.

"Here you go," I hand over my phone, "knock yourself out. I'm starving. Do you have any cookies?"

"You know I do. In the pantry," she says, distracted by the text messages she's already scrolling through.

Dexter: Day 1 of MLM: Mission in process. LED flood-lights are being installed in her room as we speak. She never has to worry about the dark again.

Preston: It's early in the day for word games. What is MLM?

Julia: Obviously, it's Make Lanie Mine. Should I expect these updates daily?

Trevor: Who has the 802 number?

Trevor: Also, little bit creeper-ish here, man. What happened to chocolate and flowers?

Julia: A guy gives me flowers and chocolate, I'll kick him in the taint all the way back to his car.

Trevor: Noted. Again, who is 802?

Dexter: 802 is Lanie's best friend, Julia. Julia, meet the guys, Trevor, Preston, and Loki.

Preston: Is she hot? The friend?

Julia: Another douche-canoe? Come on, Dex, I thought you were better than this.

Trevor: I think I'm in love.

"Julia Grace! How often does he send these updates?" my mother asks.

"Every freaking day. Why, how far have you gotten?" I ask, shoving cookies into my mouth.

"I'm just finishing day one, I guess. Oh my, Jules. This is something else." She holds her hand out for a cookie. "I can't wait to see what he does next. Good Lord, GG would have a field day with these."

"Oh, she's aware," I tell her. "GG has the entire town

taking bets. The odds are in Dexter's favor, ten to one."

"No way," she says, awed.

"Yup, you better get to The Convenient One and place your bets soon, you never know when GG will declare a winner." I laugh. "GG is camped out at that store from seven to eight every morning taking the bets," I say with a smile. "Okay, keep reading, it only gets better."

I try to hold it in, but explaining how my best friend is falling in love makes me break down completely.

"Aw, Babycakes. I know this is hard for you, sweetheart. You really miss Charlie's dad, don't you?"

"More than I should, considering I knew him for less than a week. B-But I think he was my puffin, Mom," I cry.

My mom holds me while I let it all out. "Julia?" she asks, waiting for me to look at her.

"What? Did I get snot on you?"

Laughing, my mom gets serious. "No, sweetheart, and it would be fine if you had. It wouldn't be the first time. I just want you to know that you're the best thing I've ever done in my entire life. I'm so proud of the woman, the friend, the mom you've become. I know you've always felt like you were lucky to have Lanie as a friend, but I'm telling you, you both lucked out in the friend department. You, my dear, are one incredible human being."

The tears start anew, but I'm able to choke out, "Thanks, Mom. Keep reading. It only gets better."

I concentrate on her reactions as she reads and can almost pinpoint the exact messages as she reads them. Dexter and Lanie are going to have one hell of a love story.

A FEW DAYS LATER, I'm realizing Dexter is going to need more help than I thought when I get a text from his friends.

Loki: Okay, guys, I'm about to take off, but these

two dipshits, as Julia so eloquently puts it, will need some help. I'm not there, and Preston will be useless for this, so I suggest the two of you work together to make sure Dex and Lanie don't fuck up their happily ever after.

Trevor: What are you? A fairy godmother all of a sudden?

Loki: Can you do it, asshole? He deserves to be happy, and I think Lanie will be the one to get him there.

Trevor: You're right. You up for this, Julia?

Julia: Fuck yes! I've got my girl. You take care of Dex.

Trevor: Consider it done. Be safe, Loki.

Julia: I've always wanted a spy friend. I think I'd make an excellent spy, just an FYI.

Loki: Noted. Help our man get the girl. Don't fuck it up.

∿

Julia: Okay, Trevor. You ready to do this? Get your ass over to Dexter's and calm him the fuck down. I'll deal with Lanie.

Trevor: Yes, ma'am. Are you always this bossy?

Julia: I like to consider myself organized, but you can call me whatever you want.

Trevor: That, my *friend*, is a dangerous proposition.

Julia: (Rolling eyes emoji) Just take care of your boy, huh?

Trevor: On it.

∿

I'm washing dishes as my mom pretends to play with Charlie, but really, she's scrolling my text messages for the latest on Lanie and Dexter.

"How often are you texting with Trevor?" my mom asks, and I drop a plate into the sink.

"Well, considering Dexter texts us an SOS almost daily, we talk a few times a day, probably. Why?" I can already feel an inquisition coming on.

"No reason." Her smile tells a different story, though.

"Yeah, right? We're just texting, Mom, to help Lanie. We don't even talk on the phone, and definitely no FaceTime," I tell her.

"Why not, honey?"

"Because …" I pause, stalling for time. "Because I have Charlie." It comes out barely a whisper.

"And you're still heartbroken over Charlie's dad," she surmises.

"And I'm still heartbroken over Charlie's dad," I echo.

"It'll get easier, sweetie, I promise." She pulls me in for a hug, and I let her.

"God, I fucking hope so," I mumble and feel her tense.

At least she doesn't scold me again. If ever there were a time for F-bombs, it would be now.

∾

TREVOR: **You asleep?**

Julia: **Yes.**

Trevor: **Good. Want to play a game?**

Julia: **It's after midnight. What are you doing up?**

Trevor: **I've got a lot going on, I haven't slept well in months.**

Julia: **Want to talk about it?**

Trevor: **On the phone?**

Glancing down at a sleeping Charlie, I debate carrying him to his own crib. Part of me is so curious to hear Trevor's voice. *Fine*! I admit it, I'm lonely, but peeking at Charlie again, all I can see is his father. And as much as I love the

221

banter Trevor and I have, it still feels like I'd be cheating. *Am I always going to feel like I belong to him?* The thought is upsetting. I'm in for a long, sad life, if that's the case.

Julia: I can't. But I can text anytime.

I feel like his reply takes forever.

Trevor: No worries. So, you want to play a game?

Pulling up my game folder, I send him an invitation to Words with Friends.

Julia: Get ready, Trev. I'm about to whoop your ass.

Trevor: Bring it on, sweetheart. Bring. It. On.

$\sim$

JULIA: **What's wrong with your friend?**

Trevor: You'll have to be more specific than that. I could make a list for Preston and we would be here for days. Loki's away, so that leaves Dex. What did he do now?

Julia: I am a HUGE fan of lists.

Julia: He sent Lanie an MLM message about Sylvie babysitting tonight, and now she's blowing up my phone like a crazy person.

Julia: I can't lie for shit, so I'm having to ignore her and she's going to be pissed.

Trevor: I'm a list-making kind of guy myself.

Trevor: Fucking Dexter. I'm heading over there now. I'll make sure it's all smoothed over.

Julia: You're the best.

Trevor: Right back at ya.

$\sim$

JULIA: **OMG! Did you hear Dexter finally got laid last night?**

Trevor: No shit?

Julia: Yup, our babies are growing up.

Trevor: It's about fucking time. Jesus. At least one of us won't have blue balls anymore.

Julia: Aw, poor baby. You're not getting any action these days?

Trevor: You could say that. I'm "Holding Out for the One".

Trevor: What are you wearing? (Winky face)

Julia: Oh no you don't. I've tried the one-night stand. It didn't end so well for me.

Trevor: Now you have to tell …

Julia: Forget it. My one and only one-night stand is off-limits. What about you? Tell me about your conquests.

Trevor: I'm offended you think I'm that kind of guy, Jules. Only one one-night stand for me, too, and the damn girl broke my heart. Not looking for one of those again. Hence, the blue balls.

Julia: I know the feeling.

Trevor: What do lady balls look like?

Trevor: Send me a picture.

Laughing my ass off, I Google a gif for an extremely large gorilla who had just nursed a baby. The nipples alone need their own zip code.

Julia: (GIF sent)

Trevor: Jesus Christ, Jules. Not cool. Not cool at all. But since you started this, here you go. (Big donkey dick GIF sent)

Julia: I just threw up a little.

Trevor: Then we're even.

❀

Six months later

I'M SITTING on the floor with Charlie while he plays with some blocks when I realize for the first time just how sad I've been lately. Charlie's the best thing that has ever happened to me, and I love him dearly. I just can't help crying for all he'll never have—all he'll never know. This little boy, with the eyes of his father, watches me cry for the man I'll never know.

"Ah, child," I hear GG say from my doorway.

"Jesus, I need to start locking that door," I say through a hiccup.

She makes her way to me, sits next to us, and pulls me into her boney shoulder. "It'll get easier, Jules."

Wiping my tears, I ask, "What will?"

"Pretendin' to be happy," GG says knowingly as a sob escapes. "Tell me 'bout him, luv."

I could lie, pretend I don't know who she's referring to, but GG has been around this block one too many times. And honestly? I'm tired of fighting it. Sitting on the floor, with Charlie in my lap and GG to my side, I tell them both about the man I could have loved.

Sometime later, my tears have dried, I've placed Charlie in his crib for the night, and I find GG sitting on the couch with a bottle of wine. "You know, you don't have to babysit me, right? I'll be fine."

"Mhm, I know ya will," she says, handing me a glass. "I told you this will be your year, young lady, and I meant it. It's in the cards."

"Right. The cards," I say, rolling my eyes. "I can just picture you now at The Convenient One, reading peoples' fortunes."

"Ya know it." GG snickers. "I think this move will be good for you."

Since I really have nothing holding me here and we found out recently that Lanie is pregnant, I decided to follow my best friend to North Carolina. My parents have a beach house there that they're planning on retiring to, so eventually we'll all be down there.

"You sure you don't want to come with us, GG?" I ask, smiling, knowing there's not a chance in hell we'll get her off this mountain any time soon.

"Hell no! Ya kiddin' me? I'd melt in that southern heat. I'm not cut out for it, ya know?"

"Yeah, yeah, I know. You're a year-round mountain girl." I laugh, using the words I've heard fall from her lips for as long as I can remember.

"Damn straight. I know it's been hard on you, Jules. Watching Lanie fall in love when your own heart's so shattered, but I want you to know I'm damn proud of you."

What the hell is this? GG isn't sentimental.

"You've always put others first, Jules. I'm here to tell you, start putting yourself at the front of that line from now on. Life's too short to go on the way you've been livin'."

"GG, I'm not unhappy," I tell her, feeling defensive.

"You may not be unhappy, but you're not whole either. You think no one is noticin' you, young lady, 'cause that's the way you've always wanted it, but nothin' gets by me, you hear? You're not unhappy, but your smile's broken. It has been for a good long while. I want you to promise me you'll find a way to smile again and smile like you mean it. I know you've been touchin' with that friend of Lanie's man. Maybe he'll be a *pleasurable* distraction for you, huh?" she says with a wink.

Oh my God, she's so out of control.

"Trevor? Nah. I mean, we get along great, through text, GG, it's called texting," I explain for the billionth time. "But we just text, that's all it is. We've never even spoken on the phone. I've got Charlie to think about, and he has his own shit. There's nothing else there. It will be nice to have another friend once I get down there, though."

Then why haven't you told him you're moving?

225

"Mhm, mark my words, young lady. This move will change everything, just you wait and see."

"Ah, GG, what the hell am I going to do without you?"

"Buy your own damn condoms, that's what you're gonna do," she says just before she cackles in her own special way.

CHAPTER 27

TREVOR

"On Top of the World" by Imagine Dragons

Bang. Bang. Bang.

Checking the clock, I see it's five a.m. *Who the fuck is breaking down my door at this hour?*

"Hold on, I'm coming," I yell.

"Trevor, open up," Loki hollers back.

Fuck. I may have just been asleep, but I'm wide awake now. There's only one reason Loki would be here waking the neighbors like a goddamn lunatic. Unlocking the deadbolt, he bursts inside.

"Listen, man. It's happening. It won't be as fast as you want, but when I go dark this time, I won't be back until it's over. It could take a few months, so I need you to hang tight, but, well … shit."

Loki looks as unsure as I've ever seen him. *That can't be good.* He's a completely different man than the one who told us he was going dark a few months ago. This Loki is haunted. He's twitchy and agitated, but last time, he strolled out of here like he owned the world.

"Listen, Julia …" he starts.

Well, that's not where I thought this conversation would go. Letting out an enormous sigh of relief, I turn to make coffee.

"Trevor," he barks.

"What, Loki? What's so important about Julia?" I snap back. I shouldn't. This guy, this friend, is putting his ass on the line for me every single day, but fuck, it's five in the damn morning.

"She's here. She's moving here."

I stare at him, waiting for a bomb to drop, but he says nothing.

"Oh-kay," I say. "Loki, are you drunk?"

"No. Listen, Julia and her son are moving into Dexter's guesthouse," he repeats.

That gets my attention. "Julia has a son?"

I guess that makes sense. It's probably why the one time I wanted to call her, she shut me down. I've been so busy this month we haven't been able to text as much as we normally do, but I wonder why she didn't tell me? I'm trying to think of our text conversations when Loki speaks again.

"There's more," he says.

Knowing he's waiting for my undivided attention, I pull a stool out and take a seat at the table.

"What?" I ask once I'm seated.

"She, J-Julia, is Angel," he finally blurts, tossing a folder onto the table.

Shaking my head, I laugh. Surely, I misheard him. But, opening the folder, all the air leaves my body, and for the first time in my life, I feel faint. Turning around to face the sink, I vomit. When I'm done, I dry heave some more.

My brain is missing a connection, and I can't get it to focus. Loki hands me water, but my hands are shaking so hard it crashes to the ground.

"Trevor …"

"No. Loki, don't," I warn. I grab the folder and all of its

contents, then storm off to my office and slam the door so hard it falls off the hinges. Setting the folder on my desk, I take a seat. I don't know how long I stare at the back of the envelope like it will burn me, but when I finally open it again, my heart beats for the first time in almost two years.

"Julia is Angel." I say it repeatedly, but it doesn't compute. I sit there for hours without a cohesive thought. Finally, the pieces come together for me. The reason she was so adamant about a one-night stand, the reason she didn't do relationships. She couldn't, she had a kid at home.

I stare at the pictures again. I can't tell how old the boy is, these pictures must all be old. He doesn't seem much older than Dexter's girls. *I hope he looks like her.* Where the fuck did that thought come from? I inspect them closer, trying to see his face, but it's clearly winter in Vermont, and he's wrapped up or buried in her chest in every shot.

What the hell am I going to do? What's she going to do when she sees me? Will she feel the same as she did in Boston? It's been a long time. Loki said just her and her son were moving, didn't he? Does that mean she's still single?

What the fuck are you even saying, douche bag? What about Romero?

I try to remember what Loki said this morning. Something about him going dark again, but I know he said that this time when he comes out, it'll be done. Over. Is it possible for me to be with Angel again? Will she even want me after she learns the truth?

Fuck, what if Romero learns she's here? *Will he remember her?* I wish I hadn't stormed off like a juiced-up nut monkey so I could ask Loki these things, but I'm sure he's long gone by now. I can tell by the way he was dressed that he was leaving straight from here to whatever hell the Black family was dragging him into.

Pacing my condo while making a list, I can come up with

only one solution. I have to face Julia and hope she isn't about to put the final nail in my barely beating heart.

~

FLYING through Dexter's front door, I don't even bother with pleasantries. "She's here? Julia. She's here?"

Raising his eyebrow, he asks, "With as much as you guys text, I figured you knew."

"No, no, I didn't know. I've been in the lab day and night finishing something," I lie.

"Yes, Julia's here. Just not right at this moment. She went out to run some errands. Come on, let's grab a beer," he suggests, obviously thinking I'm about to have a coronary. Maybe I am. "What's the big deal? You knew she was Lanie's best friend. You had to know you'd run into her at some point. Are you seriously telling me you're still only texting? No phone calls? No FaceTime?"

"No. Strictly texting. It was best for everyone." I don't elaborate because I don't trust myself with words right now.

"What's best?" Lanie asks, walking into the kitchen.

"Nothing, Lanes," I blurt before Dex can say anything. "How are you feeling?"

"So far so good." She smiles, taking a seat at the island. I can't help but gape at her and wonder what Angel looked like when she was pregnant.

"La-aine, I've got just what you need, babes," I hear Angel's voice coming from the hall, and the world moves in slow motion.

I train my eyes on Angel as she enters the room. Her lithe body is entirely covered by the bags she's carrying in one hand and what appears to be an enormous jar of pickles in the other.

"Can you believe I had to go to five different stores for these pickles, Lanes? But trust me, they are so …" She breaks off as she lowers the bag to find Lanie, but meets my eyes instead.

Instantly clutching my chest, I feel the life beating again.

How had I been living? She jumpstarts my heart, and it's like being born anew.

"Charlie?" she whispers.

"Angel." Holy fuck, I didn't plan this very well. It cements my feet to the ground, and my mouth is so dry I can't form words. I just watch her as she stares, first at me, then at Lanie.

"Holy shit," is all Lanie gets out before a loud crash catches my attention.

Shifting my gaze, I realize Julia just dropped the jar of pickles and everything else in her hands. She's backing up when I realize there has to be glass all over the floor.

"Julia, don't move, you're barefoot," I hear Dex warn, but she's getting ready to run. I can see it in her body language.

Do something, asshole. Go to her. My head is screaming at me to fix this, but it's like a movie playing out before me and I can't move.

"N-No, I have the groceries. They. But. You? Not, Boston?" she mumbles, making no sense and visibly shaking. Before I can reach her, she turns and runs down the hallway with keys in hand.

No! She can't run. I move to chase her, but Lanie holds up a hand to stop me. "Hold on there, Boston, this is my fault. Let me explain while Julia gets her thoughts together. She won't be able to talk to you until she's cleared her head."

"What do you mean, this is your fault? What the hell's going on, Lanie?" I don't mean to yell, but Angel is getting away again, and I won't survive losing her a second time.

"Hey," Dex says angrily, "calm down! Yelling at Lanie won't solve anything."

Sighing, Lanie stands. "Come on, let's sit in the family room. This is going to take a while."

She leads the way, and I watch on with Dex as Lanie takes a seat. I pace impatiently in front of the windows of their family room. Just when I don't think I can take the silence for another minute, she speaks.

"Okay, well, right before my attack, Julia was scheduled to go to a conference in Boston. I was trying to push her out of her comfort zone a little. I got her to agree to a new wardrobe and made her promise she'd put it to good use. I just thought she needed a one-night stand, so I told her she didn't even have to use real names if she didn't want to. How was I to know you guys would keep the game going all week?" She twirls her hair around her finger like she's nervous, but I can only focus on Angel.

"I called her Angel, so she named me Charlie." Our first meeting is engrained forever in my head. I can't help the smile that plays, remembering that very first encounter.

"Right, and we called you Boston. Anyway, the day she left, she was already planning on telling you her name and exchanging numbers. You had dinner plans at the hotel that night," she reminds me.

"Yeah, but she didn't show up. I searched everywhere for her. It was like she disappeared." The familiar hurt is once again taking residence inside of my chest.

Dexter's head is going back and forth between us like a pinball machine. I know this is all news to him, and I feel like a dick, but we can make up another time after I have Angel back.

"Her not showing up was my fault, Trevor," Lanie explains with tears in her eyes. "About two hours before she was supposed to meet with you, she got a call from her parents letting her know that someone had attacked me. She wasn't thinking, she just left. She didn't even pack up her stuff from her hotel room, just grabbed her keys and left. I'm so sorry, Trevor. We've been looking for you ever since, but with no actual information to go on, we've had no luck."

"I'd say luck just smacked you in the face." Dex laughs. Then his face pales, and I worry for a moment he'll be sick.

"Holy fuck, Trevor! You're a dad. You're Charlie's dad. That's why he always seemed so familiar. He has your fucking crazy-colored eyes," Dex blurts, and my world spins on its axis.

Angel has a son named Charlie. My son's name is Charlie. I have a son?

I'm up and screaming so fast, the room literally spins. "What? Is that true, Lanie? Do I have a goddamn son no one told me about?" I can't control the way my voice raises as emotion consumes me.

Fuck. I think I'm going to be sick for the second time today.

"Trevor, I'll tell you one more time. Calm the fuck down. Did you just hear Lanes? They searched for you, but they had no way to contact you," Dexter says, moving closer to Lanie, afraid I'm about to lose my shit. Hell, I'd do the same thing, and I can't even promise I won't lash out right now.

"She needs to come back here. Now," I say through clenched teeth, trying to ward off nausea. I grab my phone and scroll angrily until I come to her name. Finding it, I press send, only to hear the telltale ring coming from the kitchen floor. "What the fuck? Did she leave without her phone?" I walk to the mess she left in the doorway. "And her wallet? What the hell?" I grumble. Glancing at the hallway, I notice her pink Chuck Taylor's. "She didn't even leave with shoes on. Where the hell could she be?"

Panic finally takes over, and I drop my hands to my knees, trying to catch my breath. "Julia is Angel. Charlie's my son. Fuck, my father! What am I going to do?"

"Trevor? Do you want some water or something?" Lanie asks, but it barely registers.

"Charlie? She named him Charlie?"

Lanie nods.

"And you've seen him?" I ask, staring at Dex.

"Yeah, man. H-He's a cute little bugger, too."

My mind whirls. "Where is he? Is he here?" I scan the room as if my son will suddenly appear. *My son.* The room spins and I close my eyes to center myself.

"No," Lanie whispers. "He's still in Vermont with Julia's parents."

Fear and relief war for top billing, and Lanie misinterprets my silence for anger.

"This hasn't been easy on her, Trevor. Not at all. I know she's been hurting since the second she realized she lost you, but she kept it to herself because I felt guilty. We tried, Trevor. I promise you we tried to find you. Your name wasn't listed in the hotel. The name she was able to find for your room in the hotel database was for a person that didn't exist. Or at least not someone she could find, and she's really good at what she does, Trevor."

My brain suddenly makes a connection. She must have been the presenter I wanted to see so badly in Boston. My lip twitches when I recall saying she must be homely.

I have so many questions I need answers to, but it doesn't feel right getting them from our friends. I need my angel. I need Julia. My body moves on autopilot back to the family room where I pace again under the watchful eyes of my hosts.

I stop abruptly as a thought occurs to me. If she flew here, she may not have a car.

Turning my attention to Dex, I pray I'm right. "Dex? Is she in Lanie's car?"

"Yes," he replies, pinching the back of his neck. A sure sign he's uncomfortable.

"Then you can trace her car. Tell me where she is."

"What?" Lanie shrieks. "You track my car?"

Embarrassed, he shrugs his shoulders. "It's a feature that came with the car," he says by way of explanation. Pulling out his phone, Dex presses a few apps, then scowls as he follows the dot. "Ah, I don't think she is coming back tonight."

Grabbing the phone from his hand, I try to get my bearings on the map before me. "Where the hell is she going?"

Lanie peeks over my shoulder and winces. "Ah, my guess is that she's heading to her parents' beach house in Corolla."

"How in the hell is she going to do that with no phone, no money, and no goddamn shoes?" I groan, returning to my spot by the windows to pace. "Give me the address, Lanie. I need it now. I'll have to go after her and bring her home."

The thought almost has me smiling. I'm going to bring my angel home.

"Trevor, I'm not going to tell you until you calm down. You can't go after her guns blazing. This wasn't her fault, it's … it's mine." Lanie's voice breaks, and I have to slow down and apologize.

"Lanie?" She brings her teary gaze to mine. "This wasn't your fault. It was a clusterfuck of epic proportions, but it wasn't anyone's fault. Th-There's stuff about my family. Stuff no one should have to deal with, but I am. I just need to bring her home, so she'll be safe."

"Wh-Why wouldn't she be safe? What the heck is going on?"

"Lanie, I promise you, I'll keep her safe, but I have to get to her before my father knows she's here."

I think, by Lanie's dazed expression, that I've stunned her into silence. I hope this won't be too much for her. I know her pregnancy is already a high-risk one.

"Go get her, Trev. Don't worry about Lanie's car. I'll send someone down to get it later in the week," Dex interrupts, bringing me in for a hug. "Just bring her home, okay?"

"Yes. Yes, go. What are you waiting for? Keep her safe, Trevor. Bring her home," Lanie screeches, shoving me toward the door.

"She's only been gone an hour. I'll make up the time on

the highway. If you get ahold of her, please don't say anything about my father. I-I need to explain that in person," I tell my friends as I run to my car.

Holy shit. It's time my angel heard what's on my mind for a change.

CHAPTER 28

JULIA

"Believer" by Imagine Dragons

"*J*'m a master, oh oh oh," I sing at the top of my lungs in Lanie's car. I'm trying to drown out everything happening in my head. I just have to get to my parents' beach house, then I can lose my goddamn mind. And I will. Oh, will I ever. The chaos isn't just coming, it's raging and swirling and threatening my sanity with every beat of the bass drum vibrating the car doors.

"How? How is Trevor my Charlie? Shit like that doesn't just happen. Right? It doesn't, I know it doesn't. I ran. Jesus, I've been living with a broken heart for almost two years, and the one man who holds the glue just found me. And I *ran*."

Pounding my head into the seat as I drive, I try to clear my thoughts, but it's useless. My hands beat the steering wheel in time with the music while my thoughts scream out, trying to be heard first.

It's too much. There's just too much. I'm on the verge of a nervous breakdown as I pull into the driveway. My parents built this home as a sanctuary, but tonight there's no peace. After shifting the car into park, I jump out and head to the

237

back of the house. Following the path over the dunes illuminated only by the light of the moon, I run—a dead sprint to the water's edge.

Falling to my knees, I set my pain free.

I don't hear him approach, but I feel him. I'm not sure how long I've been out here, but my heart skips a beat in time with his whenever he's near. It's the only reason I don't end up face-down in the ocean from fright when he finally speaks.

"Angel," he whispers on an ocean breeze.

Turning my head, I see him clearly for the first time in almost two years. My dreams didn't do him justice. His eyes glow with emotion, and I see all his insecurities in the tightness of his body.

I swallow, trying to speak, but no words come, just tears. When I nod to acknowledge him, Trevor steps forward. Wrapping his muscular arms around my body, he lifts me to his chest, cradling me like a child. That's when I break. Sinking into the sand with me in his arms, Trevor holds me as I cry.

At some point, I realize my hair is wet. Glancing around, I wonder if it rained. When I feel another drop hit my cheek, I realize Trevor's been crying, too. "My dad cries sometimes, too," I whisper, wondering if he'll know this song or if he's forgotten my quirks.

A sad chuckle escapes him. "Let me wipe your tears so I know you're real," he says, kissing my cheek. "You know, one of these days you're going to quote a song that I don't know."

"I hope not," I tell him, unsure what to say next. "There's no handbook for what to do when your one-night stand reappears and is so intertwined in your life it's hard to believe fate alone had a hand in it."

"I'm not sure I believe in fate, Angel. Destiny, maybe, but I think this fate had a name, and it was Loki," he sighs.

Pulling back in shock, I stare into his eyes. "We have so

much to talk about." It's the understatement of a lifetime, but it's also the most truthful thing I've said in a long time.

His gaze directed over my head, Trevor states, "You left with nothing, Angel. You scared the shit out of me. Then, and now." His voice breaks, and he coughs to clear it. "Do you even have keys to the house? You're covered in sand."

Watching as he attempts to brush damp sand off my legs, I try to take everything in stride, but that's just not my style.

"I wanted to tell you my name," I blurt. "I wanted to exchange numbers. I was even going to ask you on a date … an actual date. I've never asked a man out on a date before. Did you get my voicemail? I-I wanted what we had to be real. I wanted to believe it was real." Tears are making it impossible to see his face, and that's probably for the best. "What if he wasn't planning on showing up at dinner that night? What if he's only here because Lanie made him chase me down? Oh my God, Trevor, you're a dad, and you've never even got to meet him. He's the most amaz—"

Trevor's lips land on mine mid-sentence, his sand-covered hands rough as they hold my head in place. He angles my face in a way that suits him, and he deepens the kiss. Oddly, the kiss isn't sexual. This kiss is all about feelings and emotions. It's the single most intimate moment of my life.

"You told me once that people are always trying to shut you up. I'll never do that, Angel, unless I get to do it that way." He smirks. "We have so much to discuss, but let me clear up something else for you, Angel. Lanie did not send me. I'm here because I want to be here. I want you. I have so much to tell you, though, and when I'm done, you'll have to decide if I'm still what you want."

"Char— I mean, Trevor, there isn't anything you could say that will make me walk away from you again."

"Let's not make any promises, yet, okay?" He stands, taking me with him.

AFTER TYPING in the four digit-code to my parents' electronic door lock, we enter the home as familiar scents of summer engulf me. Walking through the house my parents built years ago, I notice all the little touches my mom has added since they stopped renting it out to vacationers. I'm reaching into the hallway closet when I realize Charlie … *Fuck. Trevor!* Trevor isn't behind me.

Backtracking, I find him in the family room standing in front of the mantel that's covered in photographs, and the air catches in my lungs. I'm witnessing the very first time Trevor is laying eyes on our son. Even though it's a photograph, there's no mistaking whose son Charlie is. He's the spitting image of his father.

Watching as he runs his finger back and forth over the frame, I'm reminded of the very first time I ever got to hold our little miracle.

"Jules, he's beautiful," Lanie cries.

My body is so tired from the anesthesia, I'm fighting to keep my eyes open. Then the nurse lays a little bundle across my chest, and I'm entranced. His olive complexion so far from my own, I know I'm holding a copycat version of his father. When he opens his eyes for the very first time, I realize I'll never love another person as much as I love this little man. And since no one but his father could ever come close, I acknowledge right then that my heart will be full and aching every time I look at my son for the rest of my life.

"What are you going to name him?" my mother asks.

"Charlie," I say firmly. "Charlie Gracen."

"Gracen?" my father asks. "That's an unusual name. I like it, Babycakes."

It's an unusual name, but knowing nothing else about his father, I'll give him what I can. Charlie Gracen McDowell is the new love of my life.

"You named him Charlie." Trevor's voice is a hoarse whisper.

"After you."

"After me." He smirks.

"His name is Charlie Gracen," I say, spelling out Gracen, so he understands my intent.

"You named him after me … and my mother?" he asks, emotion threatening to drown out his words.

Unable to speak, I nod. "I searched for you, Trevor. I've been looking for you every day. I've broken some laws hacking computers even, but I had nothing to go on. Nothing."

Crossing the room, still holding onto the photo, Trevor lowers his head. "Shh, Angel. I know you did. Lanie told me."

I shiver. Not because I'm cold, but because of the effect this man has on my body. He's standing inches from me, yet I feel him everywhere. Putting aside all of my questions, all of my hurt, I jump. Figuratively and literally, I launch myself, and he catches me quickly. Charlie's picture is still in his grasp as he holds me tight.

I'm climbing his body like a fucking lunatic, but I can't help myself. "Trevor," I gasp, before attacking his mouth with my own. I get lost in him. I kiss him as more tears fall down my face. Tears that I found him—tears that we've missed out on so much.

Breaking the kiss, he cradles my face in his hands. "Angel, sweetheart, we have to talk. If you keep kissing me like this, we won't make it back tonight."

Feeling desperate, I attempt to draw him nearer. "Then let's not go back tonight. Stay here with me."

The growl he emits soaks my panties, and I know he can feel the heat through my thin shorts. "Fuck," he groans. "Sweetheart, we can't," he protests, placing me on my own two feet again.

"Oh my God, what was I thinking? You probably have a

girlfriend now, or wife?" My head is spinning as I search for his hands. "I'm so stupid. Why would I think you'd still be single? I'm so sorry. I'll apologize to her, whoever she is. I'm so embarrassed. Let's just forget about it, okay? I know we have to talk, but this is a lot to process. Maybe you can head back to Waverley-Cay and I'll come back tomorrow? We can talk then. I won't get in your way, I promise. And I'll try not to make it weird. I mean, it'll be a little weird because my best friend and your best friend are together and we have Charlie, but I'll be cool, I promise. Just, oh sweet Jesus, does Charlie have a stepmom? I can't handle him calling anyone else mom, so we'll have to figure that out." I'm pacing the kitchen now. "I mean, he can call her by her name, right? Trevor, I don't think I can take any more heartache today, and I can't have my son calling another woman mom. I've heard horror stories … I know people do it, but please don't do that to me."

I finally look up to see him leaning against the kitchen counter, smiling from ear to ear. His arms are crossed over his chest and he's just watching me meltdown. Suddenly, self-conscious, I glance down at myself. I don't see anything misplaced.

"A little sand here and there, but at least I have a bra on. God, that would have been embarrassing. Can you imagine if I'd jumped a married man and didn't have a bra on?" Rolling my eyes, I keep them pointed at the sky. "I just said all that out loud, didn't I?"

Shit.

"Fucking hell, Angel. I've missed you." He laughs. "My heart is beating again for the first time since I lost you." His phone rings. Taking a quick peek at it, he silences the ringer. "What is it with you and married men? Was your ex married or something?"

"No! Maybe," I say, embarrassed. "I don't know, Trevor. He ran off without a word. All I know is he took half a million dollars, and I'm still paying it back. He could have ten wives for all I know." I hadn't meant to tell him any of that.

Why can't I keep that shit to myself?

Trevor's phone rings again and again. "Hold that thought, Angel. We can add it to the list of topics we need to cover. I have to get this." Turning his back to me, he walks toward the wall of windows that face out over the ocean.

"Loki, what's up? … Slow down. What the fuck are you talking about? Why are you out of breath? Are you okay? What the hell is going on there?" Trevor asks in rapid succession. Turning to face me, I watch him pale, then his expression turns hard. Dangerous.

"We're leaving now," I hear him say. "Well, what the fuck are we supposed to do, Loki?" His eyes never leave mine as he listens. "How long until they get here? Loki? What the fuck was that? Loki?" he screams. As he pulls the phone away from his ear to check the connection, I notice his hands are shaking.

"You have less than five minutes to get whatever you need from here, and we're leaving," he barks.

He must sense that I'm about to argue because, in a few quick strides, he's in front of me again. "Don't argue with me about this, Angel. We don't have time. I'll explain everything when the car arrives, but for now, just know this … I'm not married. I've never been married, and there has been no one in my life since you. Since the day I met you, it's only ever been you. Here," he points to his heart, "and here," he taps his temple. "My heart stopped beating the moment I lost you and didn't start again until just now."

"Huh."

Raising an eyebrow, he smirks. "I just bled my heart dry for you, and all you can say is huh?"

I'm saved from having to answer by a commotion in the driveway.

"Fuck, let's go," Trevor says, taking me by the hand.

Holding up the photo of Charlie that he's still clutching, he waves it in the air. "I'm keeping this, all right? I'll replace it for your parents if they'd like, but I need to keep it with me tonight."

My heart just freaking exploded. "I'm sure they'll understand," I promise as he drags me to the front door.

Outside, I'm shocked by the sheer amount of people. Observing the controlled chaos, I realize there have to be ten men all suited up in SWAT gear. Trevor keeps me mostly shielded by his body, but I can't help trying to sneak a peek.

What the fuck is going on?

"Mr. Knight, right this way, sir. Do you have keys for the other vehicles?" one of the men asks.

"Angel, where are your keys?" His eyes search mine, but my brain is scrambled.

"Ah," I look around. *Crap, where did I put them?*

"We found keys in the SUV, sir," another man informs the one I assume is in charge.

Trevor shakes his head while staring at me, but smiles. Handing over his own keys, he shuffles me into a waiting car.

"Hey, I can't just leave Lanie's car here with strangers," I shriek.

"Angel, they work for the government and with Loki. You can trust them. Besides, Dex told me to leave the car behind, and he'd get someone to pick it up. Just get in the car. Please," he adds as an afterthought.

Unless I plan on single-handedly taking out a dozen armed men, I have no choice but to comply. Sliding into the car, I watch as Trevor exchanges a few tense words with another man, then climbs in after me.

CHAPTER 29

TREVOR

"Every Other Memory" by Ryan Hurd

I slam the car door shut, and the car takes off almost immediately. Angel has slid as far across the seat as she can get, curled into the door of the car. I can't blame her, but fuck do I hate the fear I see in her eyes. How the hell do I explain all this to her? Luckily, I see her own chaos looming, so it gives me a few minutes to collect my thoughts.

As much as I try to focus, all I can think about is Loki. Something was wrong when he called. His voice was weak and strained, and I swear, just before something disconnected us, I heard gunfire. So much fucking gunfire. My gut rolls, and I pray for the second time in as many months. I pray that my friend is all right.

I'm startled from my thoughts when Angel places her small hand in mine. Entwining our fingers, I stare at them as my breathing slows.

"Trevor, I need you to tell me what the hell is going on." Her voice is steady, but I feel anxiety radiating from her like a volcano about to erupt.

"Fuck." Rubbing a hand over my face, I try to decide where to begin. Angel doesn't rush me; she doesn't have to. We both know we're trapped in this car for hours as we head back to Dexter's house, so taking a deep breath, I go back to the beginning.

"When I was in college, I got a phone call from my mom. She wanted me to come home for the weekend. She had something she needed to talk to me about, but Dex and I had planned this enormous party at our fraternity house, and I told her I couldn't go." I gaze out the window, remembering that last phone call with her.

Without looking back at Julia, I tell the story I've never wanted to repeat.

"She called me that Saturday morning. Asked me to reconsider, but I refused. She was in the car, driving out of Waverley-Cay, when she went into the tunnel. I stayed on the phone with her, assuming we'd get cut off, but we didn't. She only made it halfway through the tunnel when she was ambushed. I heard her scream. She told me she loved me. Then I listened to the gunshot … just one. I found out later, one was all it took. The man who picked up her phone told me I was next unless I joined my father in his company. I don't remember much else after that. I know Dex was with me, and Preston got his mother to fly us all home. I identified her body. I saw the single bullet hole. They executed her at close range."

"Oh my God," Julia whispers, but doesn't let go of my hand.

"I spent the first five years avoiding my father and the last five trying to take him down."

"And Loki's involved?" she asks.

Nodding, I confirm, "He works for a specialized unit within the U.S. Military. He says it was dumb luck that got him assigned to my father's case, but I'm learning nothing is as it seems with Loki."

"I-I heard you on the phone. Is he okay?"

Swallowing thickly, I tell her the truth, "I don't know. He's gone dark, which means he's undercover. When I met you in Boston, that was the start of his assignment. You met him once, at the baseball game. He introduced himself as Lance. Anyway, we were there knowing they would watch me and attempt contact. How much do you know about the Black family?" I ask, and watch as her beautiful mind goes into overdrive to make the connection.

"The Black family? You mean, like the Black family in Boston? The one rumored to have ties with the mob?" she finally asks.

"Not rumored, Angel, and not ties. They are the mob— the newest, most dangerous crime family since Whitey Bulger," I tell her, and watch as her little body goes rigid.

"Y-You're part of the mob?" she squeaks, trying to release my hand, but I refuse to let her go.

Not this time.

"No!" I nearly shout, startling her. "No," I say more softly, "I'm not, and have never worked for them or my father. I decided long ago that I would die before I let that happen."

"Trevor, we have a son. A little boy. I-I can't be part of this, he's my entire life." Her words cut deeply, but I have to make her understand.

"Angel—"

"Don't. Don't call me that," she snaps. "What the fuck? I need to think, Trevor. I need to think, and I can't breathe in this car. Please tell him to pull over," she begs almost hysterically.

"Ang— Julia, we can't do that. We have to keep moving. I'm sorry, but please let me finish," I beg. Julia's breathing is becoming erratic, and she's looking like a caged animal. I hate that she's trying to get away from me, but I understand her fear.

"Mr. Knight?" the driver interrupts. "I think she may need this." He hands me a paper bag.

Fuck, he's right. She's seconds away from hyperventilating.

"Angel, take this," I say, bunching up the top of the bag for her to breathe into. "Place your head between your legs and just try to take deep breaths." I'm pleased when she does as I suggest.

Because I'm a selfish bastard, I use the opportunity to run my hand up and down her back. Under the guise of comforting her, I let my hand run rhythmically, using the contact to calm myself down, too.

I lose all sense of time as we sit, and the silence is deafening. Eventually, Julia sits up. Squaring her shoulders like she's going into battle, she brushes the hair away from her face and turns to me. "What does this mean, Trevor? Do they know about Charlie? Is he … are we in danger?"

"Ma'am," the officer in the passenger seat interrupts, "as of now, we have no reason to believe that they know about you or Charlie, but considering the damage done to Mr. Knight's home this evening, we have to assume it's only a matter of time. The fact that Mr. Knight didn't know about his son until this afternoon will buy us some time, but everything will need to move quickly from now on. The best thing you can do is let us do our job by following instructions as best you can. Loki Kane is the best man we have, and if he trusts Mr. Knight, I'm comfortable saying I'd trust him with my life, too."

He gives me a curt nod, then faces forward again. I never thought I'd be so thankful for a stranger sticking his nose into my business, but right now, I could kiss the fucking guy.

Julia is quiet for a while, trying to process things, so I don't push. When she's ready to talk again, the questions come rapidly.

"What does this mean, then? What am I supposed to do?"

"Loki is in the field right now." *I hope.* "He told me this morning things were going down, that's when he told me about you," I cringe, "and Lanie."

"What about Lanie?" she demands.

"I'm not entirely sure, but I think Loki had a hand in getting Lanie to North Carolina."

"That's impossible," she scoffs. "I very clearly remember the day she decided to come here and interview with Dex. We were sitting on her bed when I suggested nannying." She pauses and frowns for a second. "Motherfucker. Is he the reason my computer was bombarded with nanny ads in Charlotte for months?"

Shrugging, I'm assuming that answer is yes, but I won't tell her that until it's confirmed. "I honestly don't know. I had no idea he fucked around in our lives like this."

"Hmmm. Then what? What's he doing now?"

"I don't know."

"Is he okay?" she asks.

"I don't know," I say again, but my throat feels like sandpaper.

Tapping the man in the passenger seat like she has every right to do so, she asks, "Is Loki all right?"

"Ma'am, he is in the field. We don't get updates until he returns to base." He answered her question, but it seemed strained. If I didn't know better, I'd think he's worried about Loki, too.

"You, my friend, are a liar," she says, pointing at him, then turns back to me.

"What happened to your house?"

She's back to rapid-fire questioning. It makes me love her even more. *Holy shit.* But I do, I love her. If I'm honest with myself, I've known that since our very first kiss on the dance floor. I realize I'm smiling like a fool when Julia snaps at me.

"What. Happened. To. Your. House?" she says as if talking to a child, and I wonder what she's like as a mom.

"It blew up." Okay, maybe I should have been a little more tactful there, but this woman has my brain all scrambled.

"It blew up?" she screeches, and I watch as she folds in on herself again.

With her arms cradling her midsection, she rocks in her seat, and I remember something she told me at the baseball game. This is her trying to calm her chaos when the world is too much. Without thinking twice, I reach over and unbuckle her. Before she can object, I've dragged her across the seat and into my lap, so I can hold her.

"Let me calm your chaos, Angel."

"I'm not sure I can chase away your darkness anymore, Trevor," she tells me sadly.

"But you already have, Angel. You're my guiding light in a world that was dark. The moment you came back, I knew I'd walk through hell to be with you. I'll fix this, Angel. I promise you, I'll fix this."

She finally leans in, allowing me to comfort her, and soon, the questions start again.

"Tell me about your father. How did he get involved in all of this?"

Blowing out a breath, I debate how to answer. Truthfully, he's the last person I want to think about, let alone waste air on. I want to end all this and just hear about Charlie, my son. *My fucking son.* But I know she needs these answers. I need to give her these answers if we have any chance of moving forward.

It's funny though. Until this very moment, I'd never questioned whether we would be together. However, as I explain the fucked-up situation I've dragged her into, I realize there's a very distinct possibility Julia will run from me as fast as she can the very first chance she gets. The thought has me holding on to her a little tighter.

Leaning my chin on top of her head, I tell her about my father.

"He wasn't always a terrible person; at least, I don't think he was. When I was younger, he was a great dad. He showed up to every game, every practice. We went fishing on the weekend. When I was around ten, something in him changed. He started drinking all hours of the day. By the time I was thirteen, he'd began abusing my mother. I was too small to do anything about it at first, but one day, I found him over her, ready to kick her while she lay bleeding on the ground. I charged him, and he never touched her again … at least not that I knew of. The verbal abuse never stopped, but as far as I know, he never hit her again. I honestly don't know how or why he got in bed with the Black family, but I don't think he was always the man he is today." It's a hard admission when everything in me wants to believe he's always been the devil.

We're silent for so long, I wonder if she's fallen asleep. I use the time to take her in. I would never have guessed this morning when Loki woke me up that I'd end the day with Angel in my arms, but here I am. My heart is beating in time with hers. I decide then and there to do whatever it takes to have this for the rest of my life.

"How can you be sure Charlie will be safe?" she asks in a choked voice. I realize then that she's crying.

Placing a finger under her chin, I raise her face to mine. "I can be sure, Angel, because I will die before I let anything happen to either of you. I'm alive for the first time in years. You've brought me back to life, and I'll move heaven and hell to make sure you're never taken from me again."

I hope she can hear the sincerity in my voice because I've never meant anything more in my life.

A smile I've never seen comes over her beautiful face as she asks, "Do you want me to tell you about Charlie?"

"Holy fuck, Angel, more than anything in the world."

For the rest of the drive, she tells me everything she can remember from Charlie's first months of life. I soak it all in, committing it to memory, and vowing to never miss another moment of his life.

CHAPTER 30

JULIA

"Stand By You" by Rachel Platten

We pull up to Dex and Lanie's home, and even though it's late, all the lights are on.

Shit.

"Trevor, what are we going to tell Lanie?" I ask on their doorstep. "She already has a high-risk pregnancy, if I tell her this, it'll send her to the hospital for sure."

Clasping my hand, he waits for me to calm down. "We'll only say what we have to, okay? At least until I hear from Loki. We just need to get to Vermont and pick up Charlie. All they have to know right now is that I can't wait a second more to meet my son. I've got you, Jules. We'll get through this."

He called me Jules. As much as I love Angel, hearing him use my proper name puts a smile on my face and a sense of calm washes over me even in the middle of the biggest shit-storm of my life.

Exhaling more loudly than necessary, I follow Trevor as he pushes open the door and walks into my best friend's new home.

Following the sounds of voices, we find Dexter and their friend, Preston, in the family room.

"Doll," Preston says, opening his arms wide for a hug.

"Didn't I tell you to watch your balls if you called me that again?" I ask.

Over Thanksgiving last year, I'd gotten to know Preston and his crazy brothers when they came to Vermont with Dexter. His bid to win over Lanie made huge strides with that trip. And although I'll never admit it, I think Preston's a good man.

Cupping his dick, he backs away. "I forgot, sweet cheeks, forgive me," he says with a wink.

I said he's a good guy, I didn't say he wasn't an asshole, but something about his playful nature sets me at ease. I can almost forget the clusterfuck I learned about in the car.

"You," Dexter says, pointing to Trevor. "Sit the fuck down and start explaining."

Dexter's pissed.

Playing dumb, Trevor says, "Well, we met in Boston—"

Dex cuts him off, "Try again, fucker. I know all about Boston thanks to Lanie. You could have told me you've been searching for someone for almost two goddamn years, asshole. But that's not what I'm talking about. Start with why the hell your house was blown up," Dexter whisper-yells.

I try not to laugh. I know he's doing it so he doesn't wake up the house full of kids, but I have to wonder if he is keeping this from Lanie, too.

"Dex," Trevor exhales, staring at the floor. Gripping his neck, he continues, "Listen, it's more shit with my dad. I'll explain as soon as I can, but right now, we need to get to Vermont. I have a son to meet." The smile that comes over his face makes the entire room go silent.

"Fuck yeah you do," Preston finally says. "What are we waiting for? Let's go get that little sucker."

"Can you not refer to my son as the little sucker?" Trevor says dryly. "My son," he repeats in awe. "Holy fuck."

"Yeah, holy fuck is right," Dex says, dragging Trevor off the couch into an embrace.

I know after a year's worth of texts that Dexter is the biggest romantic on the planet, but to watch him tear up with happiness for his friend is too much, even for me.

"So, when are we leaving?" Preston asks.

We all turn to him. "What do you mean we?" Trevor asks.

Holding up his phone, he says, "Mom's plane is ready and waiting. If you think I'll miss out on a chance to get some of Mimi's cookies, you're out of your fucking mind." Turning serious, something that is not usually in Preston's DNA, he says, "Plus, whatever the fuck is going on with your dad, I have a feeling the faster we get you guys back here to Waverley-Cay, the safer everyone will be. What's faster than a private plane?" He grins in a way that screams troublemaker. "My brothers are packed and waiting at the airport, so I'll ask again, when are we leaving?"

Preston is an enigma. He's also the oldest of five boys. If he means they're all waiting at the airport, my poor hometown of Burke Hollow is about to get railroaded by a pack of Westbrooks.

"All your brothers are at the airport?" Trevor asks incredulously. "What if we hadn't come back until tomorrow?"

"Then they would have slept on the jet," Preston says, shrugging like that's an everyday sentence. *Maybe in his life, it is.*

"Dex, what about Lanie?" I ask

"Preston's mom will be here at the crack of dawn to help. For now, let's just tell her that Trevor couldn't wait to meet Charlie, okay? I hate having to lie to her, but her blood pressure is already high. I'm worried this will be too much for her."

"Do you not remember what happened the last time I

tried to lie to her?" I ask, recalling when I had attempted to be his wingman when Lanie first moved here.

"Oh, I remember perfectly well, thank you. You almost blew it for me before I'd even been able to turn on the charm," he says, teasing.

"Yeah, well, nothing's changed," I mutter. "Lanie will know I'm hiding something."

Coming up behind me, Trevor wraps his arms around my middle and rests his chin on my head. "Love, you're not alone. We'll get through this together, okay?"

Fuck me. Lifting my head to look into his eyes, I know I'm about to walk into hell for this man. "I'll stand by you."

Smiling, he says, "And I'm going to stand by you."

Less than two hours later, I'm on a private plane for the first time in my life. A flight so full of fiery men I feel like I'm in the middle of a dirty movie because this cannot be real life. I met all the Westbrooks when they came to Vermont last time, but there's so many of them I don't even attempt to keep their names straight. They're all carbon copies of Preston, each with a slightly unique personality.

Curling into a ball in my seat, I try to sleep, but my mind is spinning. As much as my heart hurts living without Trevor, can I be with him? I have to put Charlie first. Right now, I don't have any other options. We have to get Charlie and bring him to Lanie's house. After that, though, I'm not sure what I'll do. What kind of mother would I be if I stayed in a situation like this?

As I'm grabbing AirPods out of my purse, I hear Trevor ask Dex, "Have you heard from Loki today?"

"No, why? Should I have? Is he involved in this?" Dex asks.

I turn on iTunes to drown out the answers and pray to God that Loki is okay. What kind of life could I give Charlie, raising him in a world where I have to pray regularly that one of our friends is alive?

~

I WAKE with a start as we touch down on the runway in Vermont, but I don't stay awake for long. I'm vaguely aware of being lifted into the air and hearing Trevor say, "She's exhausted. I'm surprised she hasn't had more of a breakdown today." My world then goes blissfully black and I'm again in a dreamland where mobs and guns and explosives don't exist.

~

"JULES? WE'RE HERE," I hear someone say.

Opening my eyes, I suck in a breath. "Charlie," I whisper. It takes only a second for the events of today to catch up with me. "Trevor, sorry. I-I ..."

"Shh. It's all right, Angel. You've been through a lot today. But we're at your house. Where are your keys?" he asks.

"Keys?" I ask him. Then I remember they don't know how things work around here. "We don't need keys for the house, I don't even have locks." Stepping out of the car, I hear a commotion and stick my head back inside of the car. That's when I notice the officer that was with us on the way back from the Outer Banks. "Ah, hey. What are you doing here?"

"Jules, this is Seth. He'll be with us until we hear from Loki. As far as anyone needs to know, he's a friend just like Preston or Dex," Trevor explains.

I have a bodyguard. It makes this situation that much more real, and I hate it. Having a bodyguard makes it impossible to pretend.

"Fucking hell," I mumble.

"Good to see you, too, ma'am," Seth says dryly. "What do you mean you don't have locks on your doors?"

"Just what I said. I don't think this house has ever even had locks."

"Julia," Trevor scolds, "you live in the middle of the woods by yourself. How the hell do you not have locks on your doors?"

"I don't have locks because I know every goddamn person in this town," I seethe. I'm looking for a fight, and I know it, but I can't help myself.

"So, listen," Preston cuts in, "I have to piss like a fucking racehorse. If there are no locks, is it all right if I just let myself in?"

"Go ahead," I tell him, with my eyes trained on Trevor. "It's down the hall, first door on your left."

"Thanks, sweet cheeks." Out of the corner of my eye, I see Preston take the front steps two at a time.

Trevor and I are in a staring competition, neither budging until we hear Preston scream, and the reality of my situation rushes me like a linebacker.

Seth is at a dead sprint before I can move a muscle. Preston's backing out of the house, his hands in the air before Seth makes it to the porch. Preston is followed by the barrel of a shotgun. A shotgun I recognize. I'm stomping toward the house when I see Lexi step outside.

"What the fuck are you doing, Lexi?" I'm at my limit now. Watch out, world, I'm going to lose my goddamn mind any second.

"Jules? What the hell? Do you know what time it is?" Lexi asks with the gun still pointed at Preston.

"Do you know you're in my freaking house? For God's sake, put the gun down before you shoot Preston."

"Julia, I love you, girl, but who the fuck is this, and why does she have a gun?" Preston asks.

Lexi finally lowers the gun and turns on the porch light.

"Holy fuck, it's Lanie," Preston says.

"Ugh, no. This is Lexi, Lanie's cousin," I tell everyone.

"B-But are they twins?" Preston asks, his hands still in the air.

Seth, who looks like he could murder someone, takes the gun from Lexi's hands.

"No, you idiot. What part of cousins don't you understand?" Lexi retorts.

"In all fairness, you look exactly like Lanie," Trevor offers.

"Lex, what are you doing here?" I ask, trying to keep us on track.

"Me? Mimi said you'd be gone all week. What are you doing here?"

"This is my house, Lexi." Shaking my head, I walk to her. That's when I notice the bruises on her arms for the first time.

Aware of what I just saw, she grabs her robe and pulls it tight. "Mimi said I could stay here this week. I-I just needed a place to crash while I figure some stuff out." Lexi lies about as well as Lanie and I.

Too exhausted to take on anything else tonight, I pull her into a hug.

"Okay, guys, I guess it's one big sleepover tonight," I call over my shoulder.

The inside of my house is in disarray. I'd already packed most of my things for the move to Lanie's, so it'll take some maneuvering to find a place for eight grown men to sleep. I'm overwhelmed and ready to break down just as I hear a truck come barreling up my driveway.

"Oh my God, I cannot take one more thing today," I yell as Seth goes careening down the driveway.

I have to laugh when I see GG walking toward my house with a gun pointed at Seth.

Fucking GG.

"Stand down, GG. Jesus, what is it with you Heart women pulling guns on people tonight? This is not real life. Where are the cameras?" Glancing around, I'm waiting for someone to jump out and say, "Gotcha!" but it doesn't come.

"Jules?" GG asks. "What in Sam hell are you doing here at one in the morning?"

"Jesus, GG. *I live here!*" I want to scream, but at this point I know it won't do any good.

"Well, that's enough yellin'. Get your asses in the house and tell me what's goin' on. Last I heard, you were with Lanie, and Lex was staying at your house. What the hell are all these menfolk doing here?"

"GG, it's been a long-ass day. You can go home, and we can talk in the morning, okay? How did you even know we were here?" I ask, already knowing the answer.

"Benny on Route 12 told me he saw a caravan of cars headed this way. I figured I'd better check it out to make sure Lexi here was safe," she says like it's the most obvious thing in the world.

Turning to Trevor, I can't help but gloat. "This. This is why you don't need locks on your doors in this town."

"Well, I'll be damned," GG says, walking to Trevor as fast as her old legs will carry her. "I've been waiting for you, young man. I told Jules here this was her year, nice to have you back."

We all gape at her like she's crazy.

"What? I told you, I've been readin' those cards. He kept comin' to me, the upside-down King of Hearts. Good to see you found your way, handsome. Your little Charlie will be so happy to meet you."

"GG?" I hear Dex say from behind me.

"Ah, Dex. My handsome boy. Tell me, how's my Lanie girl?" GG shifts to get better access to everyone.

"I-I can't take this shit. Seriously, someone please wake me the fuck up!" I shout, storming farther into the house.

"Oh, dear. I know Jules. Whatever you've done today, it's too much for her." We all watch as GG takes charge. "Okay, well, Dex, you and you four," she directs, pointing at Preston's brothers, "you come with me. I'll put you up in the lodge. The rest of you stay here and get some sleep. I'll be back in the morning to sort ya all out."

Like the whirlwind she is, GG sweeps in, grabs an army of men, and is gone before I can count to ten. Lexi, Trevor, Preston, Seth, and I stand in the driveway, staring at each other.

"What the fuck just happened?" Seth finally asks.

"That was my grandmother," Lexi explains. "You never leave her company without wondering what the hell just happened." She twines her arms through mine. "Come on, chica, let's get you to bed. You look like your head might explode."

"I think it already did," I tell her honestly. I don't fight it as she walks me to my room, tucks me in, then heads back out to deal with the guys. I listen in while she directs everyone to different rooms. When the house finally goes quiet, I let out a long sigh.

I'm almost asleep when there's a soft knock on my door, and I know it's Trevor. The door creaks open and he slips inside. Without a word, our eyes connect, and I raise the blankets, silently inviting him in.

I swear I hear him whisper, "Thank fuck," but I can't be sure. He slides in and pulls me close. We're silent for a long time before he breaks. At first, I think he is trying to speak, then I realize he's crying. With my back to his front, he holds me as tight as he comfortably can.

"I'm so sorry, Angel. I tried to stay away, to keep you from this hell. I really did. Loki found you. He followed the security footage from the ballroom the day you found out about Lanie. He traced you almost immediately, but I wouldn't let him tell me anything. I didn't want this life for you. We didn't know you were pregnant. When he found out you had a son, I figured that's why you only wanted a one-night stand in Boston. If I had known Charlie was mine, I would have come to you sooner. I would have found a way. I'm so, so sorry. I can't even promise that everything will be okay because I can't get ahold of Loki. I'm so scared that they killed him. I'm so scared that they'll take you from me, too, and I-I don't know what to do because now I know I can't live without you."

I take in his words. They roll around in my head, but all I can think is, *Have I even been living without him?* I've felt dead inside for a long time. I finally felt my heart beat when I saw him in Lanie's kitchen. But there are so many unknowns. I don't know what to do. Choosing the only viable option, I say, "We'll just take it one day at a time, Trevor. Together, we'll take it one day at a time."

As our breathing regulates, we fall in pace with each other. Our heartbeats sync, and eventually, with Trevor wrapped tightly around my body, we fall into a deep sleep.

CHAPTER 31

TREVOR

"Tell Your Heart to Beat Again" by Danny Gokey

Buzz. Buzz. Buzz.

I open my eyes, and it takes only a second to know where I am. Angel is still asleep in my arms, and the relief that washes over my body is instantaneous. Peering around the room, I take in my surroundings. The house is silent, so everyone must still be asleep. That's when I hear it again—the buzzing sound. Trying to slip out of bed without waking up Julia, I root around the floor for my jeans. Finding them, I pull my phone from the pocket.

Loki. Thank fucking God. Taking the phone and slipping into the hallway, I creep to the back door and step out onto the porch. It's fucking freezing, but I don't want to wake anyone.

"Loki. Thank God, man. Where the hell have you been?" I ask, forgoing any greeting.

"Trev," his voice is weak. Too weak for a thirty year old, and I feel the panic rising.

"Where are you?" I demand.

"Trevor," he rasps, "I'll be okay. I-I'm hurt, though. I won't be home for a while."

"Loki, this is my fucking fault. Where are you?" I beg. "We'll come get you. Pres has Sylvie's plane, just tell us where—"

"Trev, listen. I'm not out yet. I need you to know …" He coughs, and I hear the pain in it. "Romero will get immunity, I'm sorry. It's the only way. We got everyone else, but Romero has to testify." He breaks again, and I hear his labored breathing. "Black's youngest son is free, too. We couldn't connect him to anything, but everyone else is in custody. There's a problem I haven't worked out yet, and it involves the girls."

"What? What girls? Loki?" I ask before I realize the phone has gone dead. *Where the fuck is he?* I need to find Seth. Storming into the house, I don't care who I wake up at this point.

Julia's house isn't big, but it's cozy. I clutch my chest, realizing how many firsts Charlie had here that I've missed. I'm standing in the kitchen when I notice a painting hanging on the fridge. It's a complete disaster of blues and greens, but she's written "Charlie's first finger painting" at the top, and I suddenly think it's the most beautiful artwork I've ever seen in my life. I'm running my finger across his handprint when I hear something that makes me pull back. It takes me a second to recognize the muffled voice as Preston's.

If you know Preston, you know he doesn't get worked up, and he definitely never yells at anyone. Judging by his tone, he's pissed, so I go running toward the front of the house. I'm stopped by Seth, who's standing at the door.

"You can't go out there," he tells me.

"What? Why not? Who the hell is Preston yelling at?"

Seth steps in closer, physically blocking me from the door, and I feel uneasy. I know Seth is on our side, but the way he is blocking me from my friend has me tense. I'm

264

about to go ballistic when the front door slams open and Lexi comes storming through it, followed closely by Preston.

"How the fuck was I supposed to know that was your boyfriend?" he bellows.

"Ex-boyfriend, and it doesn't matter. I don't need you barreling into my life like a jacked-up prince. Happily ever afters are for fairy tales, and the last thing I need is another alpha male stepping in to take over my life," Lexi yells back.

What the hell just happened?

"Well, where I come from, honey, when a man has his hands on a woman like that asshole just did, you step in, whether you like it or not," Preston screams back.

"Don't you dare call me honey, you condescending prick."

It's like watching a tennis match.

"Okay, sweet tits ... is that better?" Preston snaps, just as Julia comes barreling out of her room.

"What the hell is going on?" Her hair's disheveled. She has what seems like drool dried on the side of her face, her shirt has risen over her hipbone, and her tiny sleep shorts just might be on backward. She's never looked better.

"I woke up to your friend here being manhandled like a zoo animal, so I stepped in to help, and she freaked the fuck out," Preston informs us.

I'm taken aback. I've never seen Preston react like this before, but I know if I'd been out there first, I'd probably be in jail, so I let it go.

"No one asked you to step in, you dick," Lexi screeches.

"Whoa, whoa! Everyone, take it down a notch or ten," Julia says.

I watch as she assesses the situation. Even with everything going on, she's trying to fix this. She's trying to fix everyone, take care of everyone.

Who's been taking care of her?

"Lexi, you know I love you, but if those bruises on your

arms are from the asshole that was just outside, I'm on Preston's side," Julia admits.

"What bruises?" Preston asks, and I watch in shock as he crosses the room and lifts the arms of Lexi's T-shirt to reveal a bruise in the shape of a hand. "What the fuck is this?" He's barely able to contain his rage.

This is something I've never seen from Preston before. He's always the happy-go-lucky, no care in the world guy. To see him lose his shit over a girl like this is bewildering.

"Get off of me, you twat. No one asked you to save me," Lexi shouts, slapping at his hands.

Julia and I stand there, staring at each other. I'm about to jump on board with her; this is too much. I go to say something when Lexi speaks again.

"Miles Black is my ex. I left him. I don't need some pompous asshole coming in on his white horse, telling me what to do. I know he's a fuckwad. That's why he's my ex," she tells the room.

Loki's words come back to me, *"Black's youngest son is free, too. We couldn't connect him to anything, but everyone else is in custody. There's a problem I haven't worked out yet, and it involves the girls."* I'm willing to bet Loki's problem is Lexi, and it brings me to my knees. How is it possible to be this intertwined? How can our worlds overlap like this and still be real life?

Julia must think the same thing because she's grabbed a duffle bag and thrown it at Lexi. "Pack your shit, you're coming with us," she tells a perplexed Lexi.

"Wait," I say. "Just … everyone, wait."

But Julia's already grabbing her phone.

"Hey, Mom," I overhear. "Listen, I'm home with Charlie's dad. It's a long story, but it's Dexter's friend, Trevor. I can't explain right now, but can you bring him over here?"

Facing the room with her hands on her hips, she tells me, "We are ending this shit, now, together."

Dumbfounded, I nod. "Okay." Then I watch as she smiles the first genuine smile I've seen since Boston.

~

AN HOUR LATER, I'm pacing Julia's small kitchen. Her parents are due here any minute with Charlie. I've never been more nervous about anything in my life.

"Hey," Julia's voice drifts through the kitchen, "are you okay?"

My expression is full of honesty. "No," I admit. "I'm about to meet my son and your parents for the first time. I'm freaking out, and I think I might be sick."

"Don't worry about my parents. Dex and I will talk to them while you get to know Charlie. I should warn you, though, he's kind of like me. He doesn't take to new people easily, so I don't want you to take it personally. Dex has met him a few times, and Charlie still screams every time he comes into the room."

"Fuck."

"Julia?" I hear a woman call from the front of the house.

Jules places a hand on my jaw. "Just relax. This will be an adjustment for us all. He'll come around, just give him time."

"Okay," I sigh, leaning into her touch. "Let's do this."

I'm not prepared for the audience I see as I walk into the family room. But Dex and Preston's brothers are here with GG. They must have shown up at the same time as Julia's parents. I'm searching the room when my eyes land on an older woman who can only be Julia's mom. On her hip, she has a mini-me. I stand stock-still, staring at him as he babbles.

His chubby little fist is shoved so far into his mouth, I'm afraid he'll choke, but he's laughing and making faces at Julia's mom. The second his eyes meet mine, the world falls out from below me. It's like tunnel vision. All I see are my eyes staring back at me.

"Whiskey and fireflies," I hear my mom whisper.

"Whiskey and fireflies," I repeat.

Without missing a beat, Charlie takes his chubby little fist out of his mouth and shocks us all when he lifts his arms to me. "Dada."

My head flies around the room, seeking out Julia, when I hear it again. "Dada."

My legs move of their own accord. I'm heading straight for Charlie. I make eye contact with Julia's mom for a moment, and I see the love in them as she hands me my son for the first time.

The room is so quiet. The expression you could hear a pin drop is accurate. Even Charlie has stopped his baby chatter as I hold him. I stand there, Charlie and I staring at each other when he places a wet, chubby hand on my scruffy jaw and laughs. I swallow multiple times, trying to compose myself, but it's useless. Finally, I just sink to the floor, holding him to my chest. When we're seated, I release him just enough, so he's resting against my bent knees. Leaning in, I kiss his drool-covered face. "Hey, buddy, I've missed you. My entire life, I've missed you."

"Dada."

"Yeah, buddy. I'm Dada," I choke out on a sob.

Slowly, the world comes into focus around me. I'm aware that Julia has sat down beside me, resting her head on my bicep while I stare in awe at the perfect little human she and I made. Our friends and family have made themselves scarce while I connect with the son I never knew I had.

There's still so much unknown. So much danger lurking around every corner, but for these few moments, my life is more perfect than it's ever been. For the first time since I lost Angel, a song comes to me, and I sing to Charlie, "The Luckiest" by Ben Folds. *Because I am the luckiest son of a bitch in the world today.*

The day passes in a blur, and Charlie never leaves my side. It's pretty freaking amazing. Around seven, Julia finally takes him from me.

"It's his bedtime, and we sort of have a routine," Julia tells me.

It cuts a little that I'm not part of it, but I know it'll take time. While she's putting him to bed, I seek Seth out. I need some answers. As if expecting me, I find him sitting on the porch.

"You have some pretty amazing friends, you know that?" he asks.

"I do," I say.

"Dex faced an intense firing squad for you with the McDowells' today. Did you know that?"

"I didn't, but that explains why Pete didn't kick my ass as soon as he saw me," I say, then get right to the point. "Seth, I need to know if Loki's okay."

He nods like he was waiting for this question. "He's alive, but that's all I can say for sure. He was in seriously deep cover, Trevor. He was solo. It was the only way he could infiltrate, and he knew the risks."

"Why are you talking like he won't get out?" I ask.

"I'm just trying to be honest with you. We've had no communication in twelve hours. We know he took some heavy gunfire. I'm sorry. Until we get word, there's just no telling."

"I spoke to him this morning," I blurt.

"What? When?" Seth looks shocked.

"He called around seven. I figured everyone knew, but he sounded so weak. Loki wanted me to know that he got everyone and that my father would get immunity. He also said he couldn't connect the youngest Black son, and that there was a problem with the girls."

"Fuck," Seth curses, standing suddenly. "What number did he call from?"

"My phone showed his name, so he must have been calling from his own," I tell him.

"Did he say anything else?" Seth asks.

I try to remember our conversation. "No, just that he wanted me to know. I feel like he was trying to tell me that Angel, I mean Julia and Charlie were safe, but he was talking about a problem he hadn't solved yet. Something about it affecting the girls. Seth ... I know who Miles Black is. I don't know how it's fucking possible that Lexi is mixed up in this, too, but is that what he's talking about? Do we need to worry about her?" I ask.

Seth has already pulled out his phone and is typing away. I worry for a split second if I should trust him, but remember that Loki assigned him. There are few people I can trust more than him, so I brush that thought aside.

"Honestly, Trevor? Until we can touch base with Loki ourselves, I would plan on everyone having security around the clock. I have to go call into HQ. If he called from his cell, that means he's on the move and he's not secure. The faster we can locate him, the faster we can help him," he tells me as he gets up to leave.

Shit. Why didn't I think to talk to Seth as soon as I got disconnected from Loki?

"So, you're the boy that doesn't know how to use a condom, are ya?"

Turning in my seat, I see the infamous GG walking up the steps with a cucumber and a box of fucking condoms.

"You're not serious?" I ask.

"As a heart attack, young man. At my age, you don't fuck around with heart attacks, so let's get to it," she says, handing me the cucumber and a condom.

Who the hell is this woman?

Chuckling because my day cannot get any stranger, I

place the condom on the cucumber like a twelve-year-old boy.

"Good enough," she says. "Now, what are your intentions with my Jules? She hasn't had an easy time of it, ya know? She was heartsick over you. Then she had to put on a cheery face while Lanie fell in love. I'm not sure what all the mess you've gotten yourself mixed up in is, but that girl is needing her fairy tale. Whatcha' gonna do about that?"

"Everything I can," I say confidently, just as Preston walks out onto the porch with two beers.

"You best have one of them for me," GG says.

Stifling a laugh, he scoffs, "Of course, GG. You know me better than that." Winking, he hands her a beer and me the other.

"All right then. Now that I've got this one squared away," she points at me, "it's time to talk about you," she tells Preston.

"I'm squared away?" My eyebrows raise in confusion.

"You gonna take care of my Jules and little Charlie?"

"Absolutely. For as long as she lets me and for the rest of Charlie's life," I promise, acknowledging that Julia and I still have so much to discuss when it comes to us.

"Good, you'll work it out, I know it. I read your cards this mornin' ya know, and your king was finally centered. You need her as much as she needs you. Just keep her centered and you'll be fine. It's this one I'm worried about," she says, narrowing her eyes on Preston.

"Me?" he asks incredulously. "I'm good."

Pointing her finger right in his chest, she says, "You have a broken heart."

I chuckle. I've known Preston most of my life. He's never let anyone close enough to have a broken heart, but when I see him grimace, I wonder if he's hiding something.

"Ah, no," he finally replies. "No broken hearts here. I'm

not in the market for heartbreak, so I keep things casual." His words ring true, but his voice is strained.

Without missing a beat, GG says, "I didn't say you had heartbreak. I said you have a broken heart. There's a difference, young man, and you know that better than most."

Laughing but visibly uncomfortable, Preston replies, "Heartbreak, broken heart? It all amounts to the same thing, right? I'm going to grab a beer. Who needs one?"

"I'm good," I tell him.

"Mhm, conflict is coming your way, Preston. It'll also be what heals your broken heart, so take it in stride," GG tells him.

"Yeah … okay. Thanks?" Preston heads for the front door as fast as his legs will carry him.

"What was that about, GG?"

"That's Preston's story to tell, not mine. But mark my words, that boy is in for a hell of a year. You'll want to keep a close eye on him. You're gonna have to tell his heart to beat again. Mark my words, he'll need you." She speaks cryptically yet confidently, and I almost go chasing after him, but she changes the subject so fast, I'm spinning.

"So, where ya goin' to be living now? I hear your house got blown up while you were away. Not judging, but you best get thinking about that sooner than later."

Fuck, my life really has shattered into a million pieces right before my eyes, and surprisingly, there's nowhere else I'd rather be.

"I'll get right on that, GG. It's on my list of shit to do," I tell her, smirking.

CHAPTER 32

JULIA

"Single Saturday Night" by Cole Swindell

*R*unning my hand over Charlie's dirty blond hair, I sigh. I've been rocking him in the rocker for over an hour, but he fell asleep the second I sat down. I've needed some time to myself. It sucks knowing I hurt Trevor's feelings when I told him Charlie and I have a routine. But today has been too much, I needed some normalcy. Nothing brings you back to the present like rocking a tired baby to sleep.

After a while, I know I need to face my reality. I've spent this time thinking about Trevor and Charlie. Myself. GG was right, I haven't been living. Something died inside of me when I lost Trevor. I feel it stirring—I feel it knowing he's just in the other room, but I'm scared to death. What we're living through right now is not normal. As easy as it was to sweep it under the rug when I was watching Trevor with Charlie this afternoon, the reality is, there are very dangerous people out there. People who killed his mother. People who wouldn't think twice about killing me.

I'm about to lay Charlie in his crib when there's a soft

knock at the door. Expecting it to be Trevor, I whisper, "Come in." Turning, I jump when I see Seth in the doorway.

"Sorry," he apologizes. "Can you come with me for a minute?"

Looking between him and Charlie, I shrug. After laying a final kiss on Charlie's head, I follow Seth out of the room. I'm surprised by how quiet the house is until we round the corner and I hear GG's cackles followed by Trevor's laugh on the porch. The thought of them bonding warms my heart.

When we get to the kitchen, Seth turns and hands me a phone. "This is going to ring in less than three minutes. Answer it and follow every instruction, or Loki's blood will be on your hands."

I'm so startled, I almost drop the phone, but Seth grabs it and places it firmly back in my grasp. "Fuck, I'm sorry. I'm not good at this shit. It'll be Loki that calls. I just mean, he isn't in a good way, and he can't come into HQ. Whatever he asks you to do, just do it, please. I owe him my life. He's an excellent agent, but he's in deep here and is adamant that he needs to speak to you."

I don't have time to think as my hand slices through the air. We're both startled when my palm makes contact with his cheek. When the surprise wears off, my anger reaches a boiling point. "You fuckwad! You just scared the shit out of me. I thought you were a double agent and had turned us in. Work on your motherfucking bedside manners or whatever the hell it is spies are supposed to have. Jesus. You moron. What the hell is wrong with you?" My tirade is interrupted when the phone rings. Giving my best glare, I take the phone and stomp off to the back porch.

"Hello?" I answer tentatively.

"Julia," comes a male voice.

"Yes." *How am I supposed to know this is Loki again?*

"You're wondering how you can trust it's me, right?"

"Well, it had crossed my mind."

"Babycakes is a good name for you, but I think Charlie was spot on calling you Angel."

I gasp, but I still need more. "Who did I meet at the baseball game?"

"Lance. Nice to meet you, Angel McDowell."

"You don't sound good, Loki. Are you okay? Trevor said you were shot?"

"Jules, I know you have a tendency to talk a lot, but right now, I just need you to listen, okay?"

"All right, I can do that *after* you tell me you're okay," I counter.

"I will be," he says weakly. "First, had I known you were pregnant, I would have forced Trevor to see the light much sooner."

"Yeah, I've heard you have a habit of interfering in your friends' lives."

"Little nudges, Julia. Little nudges. Listen, I'm running out of time. I've followed you enough these last couple of months to know that you're thinking you need to run from Trevor, but I'm telling you, you don't. I wouldn't have put my life on the line if he wasn't worth it. I won't lie to you either, though. It'll be a tough road for you guys. You'll all have bodyguards, but you're not in any immediate danger. With the big players taken out, everyone is scrambling. You'll all fall off their radar as a new boss steps in."

"Loki, why are you calling me?" I finally ask.

"Because I recognize how your brain works, Jules, and I want to tell you to shut it down. Trevor's an honorable man who finally came alive for the first time in ten years when he met you. I've watched you, too, and I know you've been miserable, even if you hide it well. Let me take care of this shit, and you focus on the family you guys can be. Can you do that?" he asks.

Ignoring him, I ask, "When are you coming home?"

"I have an additional problem to fix. Once that's taken

care of, I'll be back in Waverley-Cay. I can't get out until all innocents are secure," he answers vaguely.

"You really are a spy, aren't you?" I ask.

"Give this life a chance, Jules. You both deserve it."

"Wh— Loki?" I look at the phone, but the line's gone dead.

Walking back into the kitchen, I find Seth with an ice pack to his face, so I chuck the phone at his head.

"Fuckwad," I say as I pass.

"Crazy bitch," he replies.

"Glad we understand each other," I reply, then storm past him.

Unable to take a second more of this day, I go to my bedroom, only to find Trevor sitting on the edge of my bed with a photo album. It contains every picture of Charlie I own, and he's cradling it like it's the most precious thing on the planet.

"I hate that I missed all this," he says without looking up.

"Me too," I tell him. Padding across the hardwood floors, I stop at my nightstand to grab a notebook I've never shown anyone. I take a last glance at it, then hand it to Trevor.

"I don't want you to read this right now. But I want you to have it. I wrote you a letter after every milestone Charlie reached. I started when I was pregnant and scared. I used it to feel close to you. Once he was born, I realized how much you'd be missing, and I hated myself. I did my best to write how I felt about every detail, thinking if we ever found you, you'd know how sorry I was … and how great Charlie is."

"Angel," he says with sadness in his voice just before he rips his shirt over his head. At first, I'm confused, then I see the tattoo. A tattoo that was most definitely not there when I met him in Boston.

Walking closer, I feel my throat close up. When I'm standing in front of him, I let my gaze stray to his heart.

Trevor's heart is now decorated with a broken angel. "Grace is gone," I whisper.

"Julia Grace, you've been etched into my heart and mind since the first moment I met you. My heart hurt every day after I lost you. Every day, I ached because, without you, I was dead inside. I found myself clutching my chest and needed you there. You've been with me every single day. I need you with me, always."

Overcome with emotion, I lean down and place my lips on his. It's a kiss I've waited so long for. A kiss that wakens me from my darkest days. The kiss is slow, exploratory … until it's not.

"Angel," he says, pulling back. I'm standing between his legs, and he places his hands on my hips. Trevor rests his forehead against my stomach and kisses it. "I don't want to miss another moment with Charlie, or you."

The emotion radiating off of him drowns out all my earlier worries. This connection we have? It doesn't come along every day. I know that now. Can I stand by him through whatever shitstorm is coming? Can I trust him? Loki?

My heart is screaming, *Yes, you nutbag*. And for once, I follow my heart, not my overcrowded brain.

"Me neither, Trevor. I need you," I tell him.

Peeking up, he asks, "Do you need me now, or always, Julia?" The vulnerability in his voice has me spiraling.

"Both," I finally say.

Moving like a jaguar, Trevor has me off my feet and onto the bed in less than a second. Hovering over me, he stares deep into my eyes, waiting for permission.

In response, I reach between us and undo his belt. The growl escaping him is the only warning I get. Swatting my hands away, he lifts my shirt over my head and tosses it somewhere in the room. When he presses some of his weight into my body, I feel him, long and hard. I *need* him with an urgency I've never experienced.

"Trevor, please."

"Please what, Angel?" He blows warm air onto my exposed nipple, causing a rippling sensation to roll through my body.

I arch into his touch, and he accepts my invitation. Sticking out his tongue, he slowly draws circles around my stiff peak just before he bites down gently on it.

"Argh ... holy, Trevor."

"I know, Angel," he says cockily as he lays open mouth kisses down my center, stopping just above my jeans where he licks from one hip bone to another.

Never taking his eyes off of me, Trevor undoes my pants. He hooks his thumbs into the waistband, then slowly lowers them to my knees. My body heats as I watch his gaze travel from my eyes down to my exposed body. I hear him gasp just before he runs a finger along the C-section scar that runs above my pubic bone.

"Fuck, Julia ... is this from Charlie?"

Biting my lip, I nod. My body isn't the same as it was when we first met. Charlie was an enormous baby, too big for my little body. I hadn't ever given them much thought, but now, with Trevor staring at me, I'm feeling self-conscious of the stretch marks and scars.

"Thank you," he says, confusing me.

"Thank you?"

"Julia, you carried our son, thinking you'd never see me again. Your body went to war for him. I can see it here ..." He runs his finger along the jagged line. Moving his other hand up my sternum, he stops just above my heart. "And I can feel it here."

I can't help the tear that escapes, but I'm thankful when Trevor glides back up my body to kiss them away.

"I want to be here, Angel, to kiss away all your tears. To

stand beside you as you fight your battles. I want to be a partner to you and the best fucking father to Charlie you've ever seen. I want to be part of your bedtime routines, and I want to hold your hand when your chaos comes. I want to be the one you turn to for comfort, the one you count on when life gets messy. I want to be with you always." His face is just inches from mine, and his body involuntarily grinds into me.

A smile takes over my face as I stare up at him. "You want to be my puffin?"

"Your puffin?" He looks at me quizzically, then glances around the room like he's missing something. "I think for the first time, I have no idea what song you're talking about."

Shaking my head, I say, "Never mind, doesn't matter."

Staring at me for one more minute to make sure I'm okay, he leans down for a kiss. Just before our lips meet, he whispers, "I want to be your everything, Angel. Forever."

I WAKE to the noises of a full house. I flop my arm to the other side of the bed, and finding it cold, I sit up immediately. Peering around the room, I see Trevor's shoes on the floor, but his clothes are gone. Attempting to wipe the sleep from my eyes, I strain to hear what everyone's saying. It's a full house for sure. I think I can hear at least ten people talking.

Finally, reaching for my phone, I squeak when I see it's after ten a.m. *What the hell?* When was the last time I slept past seven? Scrambling to untangle my limbs from the sex-scented sheets, I land on the floor with a thud. Trevor is barreling through the door in less than a second, Charlie attached to his back like a monkey.

"Angel?" It's a one-word question that has his sexy, crooked grin on full display.

"What?" I snap.

"Whatcha' doin'?" he asks playfully.

"I-I'm getting up, why?"

Now he's laughing fully, and Charlie is laughing with him. "Did you fall out of bed?"

"No," I lie.

"You sure?" he asks, coming closer.

"Yup, just sitting here thinking about my day." I stare at my fingernails as if I'm bored.

"Uh-huh. Okay, up you go." Trevor lifts me to my feet, twirling me as I go to untangle the sheets that trap my legs. "I never noticed in Boston, but you sleep like a cyclone. At one point, I was freezing my balls off only to find out you had twirled in the blankets like a burrito. I think I'll have to get my own from now on."

From now on? Is that what I want?

Once I'm free, I take a step to the side to give Charlie a kiss. "You did a good job with this baby backpack," I tell him. "He's getting too big for me to carry him in it, but he does love it."

"I like having him close," Trevor says sheepishly. "I'll carry him like this every morning. It definitely makes cooking breakfast easier."

The weight of his words slams into me. *Every morning.*

"Every morning," I repeat.

Noticing the change in my tone, Trevor places his hands on my shoulders, bringing me in for a hug. "We have to talk, Julia. I need to know what you're thinking, but I'll tell you what I want first."

Nuzzling into his hard body, I nod. "Okay."

"Well, I don't want to miss another minute with Charlie, I've told you that. In an ideal world, I'd scoop you both up, buy a house, and live happily ever after. Any other circumstance and I know this would probably be too much too soon, but the reality is, I don't have a house to go home to right now."

"Oh my God, Trevor. How could I have forgotten? Do you know how bad it is? Is there anything left?" I ask.

"Ha. It's been a crazy couple of days, sweetheart, but Seth said it's pretty much all gone. But, Angel? None of it matters, it was just a shell, it wasn't a home. I haven't had a home in over ten years. When I'm with you, I'm home. That's all I need. You and Charlie are home to me now."

We stand there, embracing each other until Charlie pounds on Trevor's back. Reaching behind Trevor, I grab hold of Charlie's chunky little thighs and tickle. Charlie's delighted laughter fills my heart in a way it hasn't been filled before. Peering up through thick lashes, I see the same contentment in Trevor's eyes. He's my future. This is my future, my family.

"Will you stay with Charlie and me if it's all right with Dex?"

Trevor laughs, and I feel his anxiety leave his body in a whoosh. "If it's not okay with Dex, I'm getting a new best friend. I'm never leaving you again, Angel. Never again."

Two days later, I stand in the middle of my family room, looking around. We have packed all my belongings up and carried them out to the moving truck. I'm leaving all the furniture so Lexi can stay here while she plans her next move. Turning around to find her, I try one more time.

"Are you sure you won't come with us?" I whine for the thousandth time.

"Jules, I'll be fine here. Plus, your dad said it's probably better if I stay here, anyway." I know he did, but it doesn't mean I like it.

"But Seth is worried, Lex. I really wish you'd reconsider," I plead.

"GG and your parents will check on me multiple times

a day, I'm sure. I'll be fine, Jules, I promise. Now, get going, everyone's waiting on you." She tries to shoo me away, but I lean in for one more hug before I hear Trevor.

"Ready, sweetheart?" he asks, carrying Charlie.

"You know, you have to put him down sometimes or he'll never learn to walk," I say in my best mom voice.

"He has plenty of time for that. Plus, I'm not ready to let go of him yet."

Shaking my head, I smile. "I always thought Charlie would grow up here."

Hugging me from behind, Trevor rests his chin on my head. I've noticed he does that a lot, and it's starting to grow on me. "We can always come back, Angel. Once things are settled, I don't care where we live. As long as you let me come, I'll follow you anywhere."

"I appreciate that, Trevor. I do. However, with Lanie in Waverley-Cay and my parents moving to the beach in a few months, it wouldn't make sense for us to be here. Lexi will check on GG, and my parents will come back for the summers. Plus, Lanie's getting enormous. They'll have five kids under the age of seven before we know it. They're going to need me. Us," I correct myself.

"Holy shit. That's a lot of kids, isn't it?" He laughs.

"Yeah, when Lanie has the twins, she said they'll hire a night nurse to help, so that'll make it easier, but I want to be there for my nieces and nephews," I tell him. "Lanie's as close to a sister as I'll ever have, so you can bet your ass I'm claiming the name of Auntie."

"Does that make me an uncle?" He grins, knowing full well that Tate already calls him Uncle Trevor.

Rolling my eyes, I laugh. "You know it does, I—"

"You're the most stubborn woman on the planet. I was only trying to help," Preston bellows from the kitchen as Lexi storms toward us.

"I love you, Julia, but are you getting these meatheads out of here soon?" Lexi asks through clenched teeth.

"Meathead? Are you serious? You're the most controlling, obnoxious woman I've ever met. I was just trying to hang a shower curtain she had laid out when I went to take a piss," Preston complains.

"I don't need you to do things for me," Lexi retorts.

"You need someone to do something to you," he mutters under his breath. "You're stiffer than a wedding dick."

"Are you always this stupid?" Lexi demands.

"Are you always colder than a witch's tit in a brass bra?" Preston fires back.

"Uh … hey, guys? What's going on?" Trevor cuts in.

I'm too busy watching these two volley insults at each other to do anything.

"She could start an argument in an empty house," Preston sneers.

"He's the most conceited man-whore I've ever met in my life," Lexi spits.

"At least I'm getting some. Maybe you'd chill the fuck out if you'd take the icicle out of your ass and get laid."

Preston is on fire.

"Whoa, guys. Okay. Everyone calm down."

"She's impossible. Like a hemorrhoid, she's a pain in the ass when she comes down and a fucking relief when she leaves," Preston grumbles as he storms out of the house.

I catch Trevor's eye, and he bursts out laughing.

"How is this funny?" Lexi demands.

"Lex, I don't know what the hell you did to get him so worked up, but I've only seen Pres drop colloquialisms like that one other time. It takes a lot for Preston to get pissed off, but when he does, his southern boy comes out in spades," Trevor tells us.

"Whatever, I didn't do anything. He's seriously the worst." Lexi groans while leaning in for a hug. "I'm glad I don't have to be confined in an airplane with him. I'd probably take up sky-diving just to get away."

"He's a good guy, Lex," I tell her.

"Yeah, right. I'll take your word for it."

"Ah, I'll take Charlie out to his car seat and have Dex show me how to work the stinking thing." Trevor smiles, and I watch him walk away.

"He's good for you, Jules," Lexi observes, eyeing me carefully.

"I think he is, isn't he?"

"Whatever shit you guys have to work through, do it. I've never seen you like this before. I'm happy for you," she says while looking anything but happy.

"Lex, are you all right?" I ask. Her appearance is still unsettling to me, but at least she has some color back in her face.

She swats my arm just like GG would. "Oh, don't you worry about me, I'll be just fine. Thank you for letting me stay here, though. I really appreciate it. I'll be able to give GG a hand while I'm here and make sure the lodge is up to par."

I know she's trying to change the subject, and since her smile seems so sad, I let her off the hook. "Well, if you need anything, Lanes and I are just a phone call away. Promise you'll call if you need anything?"

"I promise. Now, come on, let's get you out of here. I can't take another minute with Preston in the same state." Taking my arm, she ushers me out of the house.

Part of me wonders if, under all that animosity, there's a schoolgirl crush happening. All that changes as soon as I see their reaction to each other in the driveway. They would never work. Glaring at each other, they may as well have spat in each other's faces.

"All-righty then." I turn Lexi away from him. "Give me a hug."

Spinning in a circle, I don't see Trevor or my dad, and I feel myself tense up.

Dex comes up beside me. "Your dad asked to have a word with Trevor in private. They're in the back." He smiles mischievously.

"Not that long ago, my dad met you with a shotgun in his lap," I remind him.

"Oh, I know. What kind of talk do you think Trevor's getting right now?" He laughs.

Oh no!

Dex must see the moment I panic because he chuckles again and pulls me into his side. "Relax, Jules. Your dad's just doing his job."

"That's right, you lil' hussy, that's a daddy's right ya know. Dex, you best be takin' notes," GG says.

"I'm back to being a lil' hussy?" I ask.

"Oh, I'm no prude, young lady. You've got that glow 'bout ya. You got yourself some man meat last night. I can see it written all over your face," she tells the group.

We all stand in silence for a minute. I've decided I'll never get used to the shit that comes out of this old bat's mouth.

Preston's the first to break. "God, you're crazy, GG. I love you."

"Come here and give me a hug, Broken Heart."

We all watch as he stiffens but follows orders.

"Remember, I didn't say heartbroken. I said broken heart. You go about getting that fixed, you hear me?" GG commands.

"Yes, ma'am," Preston replies with none of the playfulness I've grown accustomed to with him.

Glancing at Dex, I watch as he just shrugs his shoulders. He doesn't know what that was about either.

"Okay, Dexter. You take care of my Lanie girl, you hear me? Mimi and Pete said they'll bring me down to see her once those babies are born."

"You got it, GG," Dex replies as Trevor and my dad come walking around the corner.

"Ah, everything all right?"

"Oh, yes, Babycakes. Trevor and I just had to come to an understanding is all." My dad nods his head with a twinkle in his eye I know all too well.

Trevor just nods, appearing a little shell-shocked.

"Ah, guys? Let's get going! My brothers have the moving truck handled so the plane will be a lot less crowded on the way home," Preston explains.

"Aw, the poor little rich boy had to share his private plane," Lexi says in disgust as she waves to us over her shoulder.

"Ugh, that girl is so stuck up, she'd drown in a rainstorm," Preston mutters as he climbs into the car.

"What the hell is it with the two of them?" Dexter asks. "I haven't heard Preston use terms like those since we were fifteen."

"No clue," Trevor says. "But it's fun to see him riled up for a change."

Laughing, Dex claps him on the shoulder. "Come on, let's go calm our pretty boy down."

Turning to my mom and dad, I give them another hug. Eventually, I'll have to explain everything in more detail, but for now, it's nice to see them happy for me.

"I'll see you at Lanie's in a few weeks, right?" I ask them.

"You know it, sweetie." My mom nods with tears in her eyes.

"We love you, honey," my dad chimes in. "We'll need to spend more time with Trevor, but from what we've seen and what Dex has told us, well, I'm just happy you found your way back to each other."

"It's a little crazy how this all worked out, isn't it? You two must have a guardian angel out there somewhere." Mom squeezes me tight.

"Yeah, I think his name is Loki," I mutter. After giving them both another hug, I pile into the packed car next to Trevor, who insists on sitting in the middle so he can be near both Charlie and me.

Resting my head on his shoulder as the car starts to move, I savor the end of our beginning.

PART III
THE BEGINNING OF OUR FOREVER

CHAPTER 33

LOKI

Three Months Later

"With a Little Help from My Friends" by The Beatles

*F*uck, my leg is throbbing today. Black's fucking sidekick did a number on me before I could escape. It was worth it, though, because all the people I care about are safe. Or they were, until this latest intel came through.

"What the hell could Romero need Trevor for so badly that he's willing to risk his life to get in touch with him?" I whisper to an empty room.

Not that I'll ever let that happen. I vowed to keep these guys safe the day I found out my own flesh and blood was trying to ruin them. It's what sent me this route. I'd always believed I'd be a surgeon. The thought makes me laugh now.

I threw plans for becoming a surgeon by the wayside the second I heard my older half-brothers discussing how best to take down the Princes of Waverley-Cay. It didn't take long to figure out they were talking about my three best friends. At fifteen years old, I didn't know yet that my family was dangerous. I didn't realize I was being groomed to one day help take over the wicked world of my father's business. I definitely didn't know that because I was my father's bastard child, they'd turn on me the first chance they got.

I'd hoped Miles was different. That he had been young enough to be spared. But combing through the file on my desk, I now know that was wishful thinking on my part. The only way to ensure the innocent lives of my friends and their new families is to take out the rest of my own.

Is this a lonely life? Yes. But it's one that I chose to keep innocent people safe. Dexter and Trevor often talk about chosen families. They, along with Preston, are mine. Since I have now inherited their wives and children as well, the pressure is on. I'll stop at nothing to ensure their safety. They never asked for this life, they never did anything to deserve what my family wants to do to them either.

I'll admit, the girls are a hiccup I wasn't expecting. Lanie and Julia, yes. I orchestrated every part of their current relationships. I wasn't prepared to find out that one of their own, Lanie's near-identical cousin, was engaged to my half-brother, Miles Black. This is a complication that needs to be handled delicately. I just haven't figured out the best way to do it yet.

What I do know is that I need to speak with Trevor as soon as possible.

CHAPTER 34

TREVOR

"Monsters" by Eric Church

"Trevor!" Julia's exasperated voice interrupts the chat I was having with Charlie. "He has to feed himself. You can't keep doing everything for him," she explains ... again.

I know he needs to figure things out on his own, but I've missed so much. Perhaps I'm overdoing it a little, though. Placing his pasta on the tray of his highchair, I step back with my hands in the air. "Okay, okay, you got me," I joke.

When she walks to me, I open my arms and embrace her. Our life is remarkably normal right now, and I've never been happier.

"What do you have going on today?"

"I have to go see Loki, but I should only be gone about an hour."

Loki finally made it home a few weeks ago, but won't talk about where he was or what was going on. He's walking with a slight limp now that most people wouldn't notice, but those of us who love him do. Whatever he went through, his body hasn't fully recovered yet.

"What about you, Angel? Are you going to the hospital to see Lanie?"

"Yeah, Preston and his mom are coming by to watch the kids, and my parents will come over in about an hour, then I'll head over. Can you believe the babies will get to come home soon? I'm thankful they're doing so well."

Lanie has had a brutal pregnancy. Guilt eats away at me every time I think of Julia going through that without me. She promises she had an easy pregnancy, but I'm learning my angel has a way of taking care of everyone else and sugar coating her own needs.

Kissing her head, I fight the urge to hold her longer. "Me too, Angel. Give them all kisses for me. I'll be back in a couple of hours to help with the kids."

Between Lanie and Dexter's three at home, their two recent additions, and Charlie, this property is exploding with children. I keep meaning to talk to Julia about getting our own place, but we've been putting it off. There's too much happening around us at the moment. Soon, though.

PULLING up to Loki's building, I give the security guard my name and he lets me through. After parking next to his car, I take the elevator up to the tenth floor. Preston lives in the penthouse of this building, which always makes me laugh. These two could not live more unconventional lives if they tried.

I raise my hand to knock, but he opens the door before I can make contact.

"Do you have cameras in every inch of this building or what? You know it's creepy as fuck when you do shit like this, right?"

"Yeah, yeah. Whatever. How are you? How are Charlie and Jules?"

"We're all good," I say, walking into his condo. "What about you? You look like you're moving around a little better?"

He flinches but composes himself in the same breath. He hates being reminded of what he considers a weakness. "I'm fine, but I need to discuss some things with you. Have a seat."

"Fuck, Loki. Why does this feel like the conversation we had a few months ago?" I can already feel the dread creeping into my bones.

Peering around his condo, I notice again just how sparse it is. He's a minimalist by nature, but save for a single picture of him with Dexter, Preston, and I, and a picture that little Tate drew, there's nothing personal here. If you removed that picture frame from the mantel, this place could pass as a model home. You'd never even know he'd been here. Thinking about it now, I realize that's probably by design.

"It's not as bad this time." Loki winces. "At least not for you."

"What the hell does that even mean, Loki?" I hate it when he talks in riddles.

"It seems the Black family has its new leader. Apparently, Miles Black wasn't as in the dark about the family business as we thought."

My mind immediately goes to Lexi.

"Jesus. Is this nightmare ever going to end?"

Suddenly serious, he uses both hands to run his fingers through his hair roughly. Thankfully, he has a military cut, high and tight, or the poor guy might have ended up bald already. After a few deafening seconds, he crosses his arms over his massive chest and turns to me.

"Trevor, I will end this, don't doubt that, but I need your help again."

Fuck.

"Has your father contacted you?" Loki asks, and I'm instantly wary of where this conversation is heading.

"Yes, but I blocked him. He may have weaseled his way out of jail time, but he's dead to me." Uneasy about why he's asking, I study him skeptically. "Why are you asking, Loki? Please don't tell me he's messed up with them again?" I plead. I'm not sure how much more of this shit I can take.

"From what I can tell, he's rebuffing their requests, but it'll be increasingly difficult for him as Miles Black builds his army." Loki turns to stare out the window.

I notice the worry lines etched in his face are more prominent today, and I feel for my friend. This shouldn't be his battle, but he's taken it on, for me, and it's a humbling reminder of just how lucky I am.

Forcing my thoughts to stay focused on the issue at hand, I ask, "What does any of that have to do with me? I thought I was in the clear now?"

"As far as I know, you are. There are just two loose ends I can't figure out." His posture tells me whatever he can't solve is eating away at him.

"Those are?" My leg bouncing rapidly is a dead giveaway that I'm getting impatient, even as I acknowledge none of this is his fault.

Loki's jaw ticks as he stares at me, then with a quick nod of his head, he fills me in. "The first is why your father is so desperate to contact you. He's going to impressive lengths to get your attention, and I can't figure out why. You're not seeing most of it, especially if you've blocked him because you're holed up in the safety of Dexter's compound most of the time, but I'm telling you, he's a desperate man. Whatever it is he's trying to get to you, he's willing to risk his life for it."

My mind races as I try to figure out what the hell could be so important from a man I haven't spoken to more than a handful of times over the last ten years. Remembering Loki said two things, I ask, "What's the other thing?"

This time when he speaks, his rage nearly knocks me over. "Lexi Heart."

My eyes whip to his so fast I'm surprised they aren't rolling. "What about her? She's staying at Julia's house, but she left Miles months ago. She isn't mixed up in this, is she? There's no way! It's all too much of a coincidence for her to be involved as well."

Shadows cross Loki's eyes as I speak, and I wonder just how involved he is in all of this. Then I want to bitch-slap myself. This is my friend, a friend that has put his life on the line more times than I can possibly understand, and he has never once asked for anything in return.

"I'm trying to figure it all out, Trevor, but I'm running out of time. We have to find out what Romero wants with you, and I'll have to extract Lexi."

That doesn't sound good.

"What do you mean extract? From where? Isn't she at Julia's?"

"For now, but I know Miles is working on a plan to take her back by force, if necessary. She'll have to come to Waverley-Cay." His voice is strained, and now that I look closely, I can see every muscle in his body is wound tight. He's more on edge than I've ever seen him.

I'm spiraling. Holy Christ, we're going to have a full house. "Where is she going to stay?" I ask, my brain jumping from one problem to the next. "Lanie's bringing the babies home soon. Julia and I are busting at the seams already in their guest house. I've been meaning to talk to Julia about getting our own place. Maybe I need to rush that?"

"Slow down, Trevor. You and Julia have to stay put for the time being. There are still too many unknowns for you to be branching out. I have Dexter's place locked down, so you're safest there." I've known Loki a long time, so I know he's fighting hard to appear calm, and I hate it. The guilt I feel for the pressure he lives with daily is insurmountable.

"Then where is she going to stay? She has to be somewhere safe? Will she stay with you?" I ask, suddenly liking the idea of Loki having a house guest and not being alone.

"No, she won't be able to stay here. As soon as I have her, I have to take another assignment to ensure everyone's safety." He isn't making eye contact, and his shifty behavior has my anxiety spiking to an all time high.

"Loki? Is there something going on I don't know about?" I finally ask.

"More than you could ever guess, but you have my word. I'll never let anything happen to any of you. Leave it at that, Trevor. That's as much as I can tell you." The way his expression hardens, I know it's his truth.

"Where will Lexi stay then? The girls will freak out if she isn't somewhere safe." I'm already mentally calculating our options. Preston's mom and brothers come to mind, but Loki's solution is the worst of them all.

Sighing, he pinches his neck as a rueful smile crosses his face, then he stares at the ceiling. "I know. There's only one place I can put her, and neither party will be happy about it."

Oh, shit. He's thinking of sticking her in Preston's place. Somehow, I just know it. "Y-You can't be thinking about putting her in Preston's place? Dude, they'll kill each other. Without a doubt, they'll kill each other. You should have seen them in Vermont." Just remembering it makes me shiver. "It was ugly. Preston pulled out old southern sayings I haven't heard in fifteen years."

Smiling like the devil, he shakes his head, trying not to laugh. "I know. But we don't have another choice."

"If I didn't know better, I'd think you're some kind of crazy fucked-up match-maker." I narrow my eyes as his grin deepens.

Patting me on the back, he doesn't even try to tame his grin. "I've been called worse. Much, much worse."

I'm distracted momentarily by Julia's ringtone, Jack Johnson's "Better Together".

"Please tell me you're kidding?" Loki asks disgustedly. "Did you lose your fucking nutsack along with Dex?"

"Screw you." I chuckle, fishing my phone from my pocket.

Julia: Lanie's bringing the babies home today! Meet us at the house in an hour.

Loki holds up his phone to show me he received the same message. "Maybe we need to rename this group chat Pussies R'Us."

"You do that, and Julia will have your balls next," I tell him, but his face has gone stone-cold.

This is a side of Loki I always imagined had to exist, but none of us have ever seen it. Pushing away from his desk, he points to me, barking orders. "Don't move. Stay right there, I just need a minute."

"Loki, wh—"

"Trevor, just sit there and shut the fuck up for a minute," he seethes. Pulling a phone from the drawer, I watch as he boots it up.

"Kane," he speaks into the phone with a deadly calm control that has sweat trickling down my neck.

Something's wrong.

"Heading there now. Knight's on his way, keep him informed. Lock them down. I'll leave for Boston now. Have Westbrook's apartment prepped, I'll deal with him when I return." Loki throws the phone across the room with such force it shatters, leaving a hole in the sheetrock.

"Get home, Trevor. Now. Grab Julia and Charlie, and bring them back here until they have the perimeter secured. Dexter's family will be safe there, but I need you and yours here until you hear differently." His words sound fuzzy as the world tunnels in around me.

I'm out of my chair and sprinting to the elevator before my brain can even catch up. Julia will not be happy about leaving Lanie right when she gets home, but if there's anything I've learned lately, it's to trust Loki with my fucking life.

Speeding through Waverley-Cay, I try to call Julia multiple times, but she doesn't answer. The tingling sensation in my heart is picking up, and it's scaring the hell out of me.

She's just busy helping Lanie with all the babies, that's it. It has to be.

Finally, pulling into Dexter's driveway, I'm pissed I have to park so far from the house. Everyone and their mother are here, but I have one mission—get Julia and Charlie to Loki's.

I sprint from my car and rip open the door to Dexter and Lanie's home, almost taking out poor Lanie in the process.

"Julia," I blurt. "Where is she? We have to leave. Now."

"Trevor, what the hell is going on?" Dex asks, staring at me with concern.

"I don't have time to explain. Where is she?" Making my way through the house, I call for her, "Julia?"

Julia's dad comes around the corner holding one of Dexter's daughters. "Trevor? What's going on? What's the matter with you, son?" The use of the endearment has my heart skipping a beat. It's been a long time since someone has called me son and I've welcomed it.

"Mr. McDowell, I apologize. I don't have time to explain. Please. Please tell me where Julia is?" I beg, as my body shakes in fear and rage.

A group has formed around us now, and Julia's mom steps forward, wrapping me in a hug. "Whatever is going on, let us help." Her voice is soothing but does nothing to ease the tension threatening to tear me apart.

I'm overcome by emotion. The capacity for love that this family has is overwhelming. "I-I'm sorry, I just can't right now. I really have to get to Julia. Is she here?"

"She just ran out to the guesthouse to get some clean clothes for this little guy," Preston says, holding Charlie.

Walking forward, I reach out to touch Charlie's cheek. "I'm so sorry, Charlie. I'm trying to fix this for you, for us." I lean down and kiss him on the nose. Turning to everyone else, I say, "I'm sorry, I can't explain right now," and then take off through the kitchen to the guesthouse.

I'm to our front door in seconds, but I already know she's gone. My chest aches and I grasp it like someone has stabbed me. That's when I see it. The note in my father's handwriting taped to the doorframe.

Trevor,

I'm sorry it had to be this way, but I need to see you, son. I'll send instructions soon. You know better than to go to the police. I'm not looking to harm her, Trevor, but desperate times call for drastic measures.

Your Papa

I don't recognize the sound that comes from me as I fall to my knees. *What have I done?* This will never end. "My angel, my Julia, my angel." The words fall from my lips on a loop as my chest attempts to crack wide open. Sweat gathers at the base of my spine and my stomach threatens to revolt.

Seconds later, I hear feet barreling across the lawn. When I look up, I feel the instant my fear turns to rage.

I will kill my motherfucking father.

Lanie hands a baby over to Preston's mom, Sylvie, but I can't see who it is through my anger. She's on the ground next to me seconds later.

"Trevor? What's going on?" Gazing past me to the guest-house, I know she's searching for Julia, and the guilt throat punches me as I gasp for air.

"He took her. My father took Julia, and I'm going to fucking kill him," I explain, clutching the note in my hand. The venom in my voice is toxic to my own ears.

Behind me, I hear everyone talk at once, but it's Dexter's voice that cuts through them all.

"Stand the fuck up, Trevor. This bullshit has gone on long

enough. Mimi, come get the baby, please. Preston, grab your brothers and take them to the guesthouse. Trevor and Lanie, you too. Mimi, I know you're worried, but Trevor's father won't hurt Julia, that I can promise you. Please just take care of the kids while we fix this."

"Dexter, this doesn't concern you. You have a family to take care of, go do that. I'll fix this," I command.

"Trevor, I've had enough of this shit. For two years, you've done this on your own, but now my family's involved. Julia will be my sister-in-law. She's Lanie's sister and best friend, and now things have gone too far. I don't care if you want our help or not because you're getting it."

"Absolutely not," I yell, but Dex interrupts me with a hard shove to my chest.

"Shut the fuck up," Dexter bellows. "Fuck you, Trevor. Fuck you for not coming to us sooner and fuck you for keeping us out. The time of you doing this alone is over. We'll do this together. Now get your ass into that house and fill us in so we can get Julia home and finally put your piece of shit father where he belongs."

I hang my head, knowing I can't do this to him. "I can't ask you to do that, Dex."

Reaching his breaking point, Dex lurches forward, grabs me by the collar, and shoves me against his guest house. "Then it's a good fucking thing you're not asking," he barks as he shoves me through the front door. We're followed by all the Westbrook boys.

Dex goes outside once more to make sure the grandparents are all set. *Julia's parents must be a fucking mess.* Storming back into the house like a man on a mission, he heads straight for me. I'm such a mess that he gets a good right hook in, and before I can protect myself, I'm flat on my ass on the hardwood floor.

"Dexter," Lanie gasps but stops the second she sees the determination in his eyes.

"Start talking, Trevor, or so help me God, you won't like where we end up. And just so you know, I fucking meant it when I said the days of you doing this," he sweeps his hands around the room, "alone are over. We are your goddamn family, and it's time you start treating us that way. Do not leave a detail out or so help me, Trevor ..." He breaks off when Lanie places a hand on his forearm.

The innocent gesture has my gut clenching painfully. "What if he hurts her?" I let slip without thinking.

Taking a deep breath, Dex lowers his voice. "That right there is why you're going to start at the beginning and not stop until we know every last detail."

With nothing left to lose, I do just that. I start at the beginning, with my mother, and don't stop until I was in Loki's office an hour ago. The only thing I leave out is the fact that Preston will soon have a houseguest. I don't think I can deal with his tantrum right now, and make no mistake, there will be meltdowns of epic proportions when he and Lexi find out about their living arrangements.

As I'm finishing, the front door opens and in walks Seth.

Loki sent him.

Peering around the room at all the stunned faces, he wastes no time "Am I right in concluding you've filled everyone in?"

"Yes, I-I didn't have a choice. Has Loki taken off?" I ask, wishing more than anything I could talk to my friend right now.

"He did, but we've appraised him of the situation. To say he's pissed is an understatement. He wants you to know he's taking care of it, but because he's in the air, it'll take a few hours. I know it's hard, but you all have to sit tight. If Loki Kane says he has it under control, I'll bet my life he'll come through." Seth makes his way into the guesthouse as everyone else stares on.

"So, we're just supposed to sit around and wait while the mob has my best friend?" Lanie cries.

I'm happier than ever I didn't mention Lexi in my synopsis. I don't think she could have handled it.

"Lanie," I say. "I'm so sorry I didn't get here in time, but Julia will kill me if she thinks you're not taking care of yourself. She's been so worried about how little sleep you're getting between all the kids. Maybe you should go to the main house with the grandparents and try to rest a little?"

"Maybe you should fuck off," she bites back. With her hands on her hips, she glares straight ahead, daring me to argue.

If you know Lanie, you know she doesn't swear. Ever. So, the fact that she just dropped an acid laced f-bomb brings everyone in the room to a screeching halt.

Taking that as his cue, Dexter cuts in, "Lanie, sweetheart? I know you're worried, but maybe Trevor has a point. There are five kids ... well, six until we get Julia back, that need you. You won't be any good to them if you can't function."

On a sob, Lanie cries, "But sh-she's my puffin. I mean, you're my puffin, but she's my puffin, too. She was my first puffin; I can't do this w-without her." The anguish in her voice causes my throat to close up.

Taking Lanie in an embrace, I hug her as we both cry.

"Lanie, I-I don't know what the fuck you're talking about with the puffins, but Julia asked if I was hers. I am, I mean, I want to be, and I don't even care what the fuck it is," I tell her.

"Puffins mate for life, dude," Preston says as if that's common knowledge.

Every head in the room turns to him with a *what the fuck* expression, but he just grins back. I know without looking that we're all wondering how the hell he knows about puffins.

"Huh," I can't help the smile threatening. "Okay, I'm her

puffin, and so are you," I whisper into the top of Lanie's head. "I promise. I promise you I'll get her back, and then I'll put an end to this once and for all."

She squeezes my middle, then pinches me, hard.

"Ouch, what the fuck, Lanie?" I shout.

"You forgot one thing, Trevor. *You* will not do anything. We. From here on out, it's *we*, you hear me? Julia and I are a package deal. We're a family now, you're my family now, and I've had a pretty fucked up example of family life. We'll do this right. Got it?" she asks, pinching and twisting my side painfully one last time.

"Jesus, Lanie. Ouch. Yes. All right. We. We," I submit.

"What am I, chopped liver?" Preston asks. "Do I have to marry your uncle to get in on this family?"

"No, just her cousin," Dex jokes, and we all watch as he cringes.

If they only knew what was coming!

Glancing around the room, Lanie takes in all the males. Dexter, Preston, and I, plus Preston's four brothers who are still looking a little shell-shocked by the events of the night. To their credit, though, they're all still sitting, waiting for instructions because Lanie was right. We're all family. Not the kind through blood, but the kind that matters. The kind that will sit vigil with you while you wait for instructions from your secret military friend so you can get the love of your life back.

"I haven't even told Julia I love her yet," I say, realizing for the first time how important those three little words are.

Preston is by my side in an instant. Putting an arm around my shoulder, he assures me, "You will, man. When we get her back, you can spend the rest of your life telling her, but I have a feeling she already knows."

It's so un-Preston like that I actually take his words to heart. This is the Preston we used to know before we all went to college. He wasn't always the booty-calling player he presents now. I forgot how much I missed this side of him.

"Thanks, Pres," I say, a little choked up.

"I just hope she isn't scared," Lanie whispers, sobering us all to the moment.

"Come on, Lanes, let's get you home, okay?" Dex wraps an arm around her and leads her to the house.

Once she's settled, Dexter joins Preston and me on the couch. Preston's brothers—Easton, Halton, Colton, and Ashton—are spread out throughout the house. I give them credit. Not a single one of these guys had to stay, but they did. As grateful as I am, I'll owe these guys more than I can ever repay.

CHAPTER 35

JULIA

"Not Afraid" by Eminem

*I*t's dark when I wake up. "Holy fuck, what the hell did I drink last night? I haven't been this hungover since the night Lanie made me ride that damn bull, and I broke my finger when I fell off."

"I'm sorry, my dear, you're not hungover. I'm afraid that's the sedative we were forced to give you." It's a male voice I don't recognize, and I force myself to focus.

My head may be foggy, but my fight-or-flight system is just fine, and it's telling me to fight like hell. Trying to jump from the bed I'm in, I fall to the floor with a thud.

"Julia, please take it easy. The sedative will take a while to work its way through your body. I promised my son I would not hurt you, but I can't be held responsible for what you do to yourself by being stubborn," the voice says.

"Motherfucker," I curse trough clenched teeth. I try to pull myself back up to the bed, but it's nearly impossible. My legs are dead. Using the little upper body strength I have, I finally drag myself up. Glaring around the room, I try to make sense of the shapes, but I can't see anything.

"Where are you?" I demand. My throat hurts like hell, though, and it comes out on a rasp.

The light flickers to life and it takes my eyes a few moments to adjust, but when they do, I realize I'm alone in a bedroom. "What the hell?" I mutter, turning my head from left to right.

"Yes, you're alone, my dear," he says again.

I'm racking my brain for his name, but everything is so fuzzy. I feel like someone clobbered me over the head a few dozen times.

"To your left, you'll find a bottle of water and some aspirin. I suggest you take them to help with the headache you're sure to have. I do apologize for that. Had I known you were such a little hellcat, I would have planned for more help. As it is, you're lucky I didn't crash the car when you attacked me. Because of your behavior, I've had to *modify* my plans. I had hoped to meet with you face-to-face, but I no longer think it's in our best interests tonight."

The night comes back to me in a rush. I was in Lanie's guesthouse when he cornered me. I fought, but he drugged me with something. When I woke up, we were in the car. You'd think I would have been scared, but one look into his eyes and I knew exactly who he was, and I got fucking pissed.

"Well, asshole, stop kidnapping women, and we wouldn't be forced to attack you to get free," I growl.

"Sadly, I agree. However, in this instance, I had no other recourse. Someday, I only hope you'll be able to forgive me."

Forgive him? Is he out of his goddamn mind?

"Where the hell is his voice coming from?" I mumble.

"There's a monitor on the nightstand to your right. Should you need anything, you only need to ask."

Romero! That's his freaking name.

"How hospitable of you," I bite out.

"It's late, my dear. Drink your water—"

"So, you can drug me again?" I interrupt. "No thanks."

"I thought you might say that. You'll find I have not broken the seal on the water nor the pain killers. As I was saying, drink your water and get some sleep. We have a lot of ground to cover tomorrow, and you'll want that brain of yours in tip-top shape," Romero says just before I hear the telltale click of the line going dead.

I attempt to move my legs because I need to find a way out of here, but they're still numb and my eyelids are heavy. I try to fight sleep, but it takes over before I'm ready.

When I wake next, the sun is shining through the cracks in the drapes. Blinking a few times, my eyes finally open, but they feel like sandpaper. Using my tongue to lick the roof of my mouth, I almost gag. This is the worst case of cotton-mouth I've ever experienced.

"It's from the sedative, the water will help," Romero says, and I realize he sounds way too close to be over a speaker. Grabbing the water bottle, I hurl it in the direction his voice came from.

When my eyes have focused, I see he has it in his hand and is walking it back to the nightstand just as his henchmen come into the room. If it was just Romero, I'm confident I could take him. He's built like Trevor, but frail with old age, and I'm scrappy and pissed as hell. His henchmen are another beast entirely. They would crush me like a bug without breaking a sweat. Changing tactics, I slide up the bed to rest on the headboard.

I don't say anything, I just glare at Romero.

"Are you hungry?"

"No."

"Julia, I promise I don't plan on drugging you again. That was a last-minute decision based on time. We're here now and not going anywhere at the moment, so if you're hungry, my chef will make you something."

My traitorous stomach growls at his words, but I remain defiant.

"I said I'm not hungry," I grumble. "Plus, I haven't had my coffee. Life does not start without caffeine."

I narrow my eyes as he smiles, and I know I just gave away my coffee addiction. I bite down hard on my tongue so nothing else slips past. God, I would make the worst spy. I'd be giving away secrets left and right. Maybe that's why I'm here. *Oh God, does he know I'm incapable of keeping my mouth shut? What could I possibly tell him, though?*

"My chef will bring you coffee and some breakfast. There's an attached en suite through that door, and we have provided clothing. Make yourself at home. We'll talk this afternoon." Romero makes his way to the door. Pausing, he turns to look around my prison cell. "This was Trevor's room. I haven't changed anything in here since he was a boy."

With that, he turns and leaves the room, followed by his personal ogres. Listening, I hear the door click and know they locked me in. Scrambling from the bed, I'm thankful my legs are finally working properly. I rush to a window first and look out. *Holy shit, we're up high.* Giving it a tug, I realize it's a lost cause, anyway. Even if I get the window open, there's no way for me to get down without breaking my neck. I turn in place, scanning the room, and see so many doors.

Opening one, I find a walk-in closet and am pummeled by the scent of a teenage boy. "What the hell is that stank?" I plug my nose and make my way into the cavernous closet, finding it full of sneakers, cleats, and jockstraps. Basically, anything a teenage boy would need for every sport imaginable. Pulling open a drawer, I see it's overflowing with various medals and awards. I spend more time than I should snooping through everything. "I wonder if he knows this is all here?"

Exiting one closet, I open another door only to find

another closet, exactly like the first. This one only smells of stale air, but it's as full as its twin. I run my fingers across the clothing, all hung by color and item. "It's like he packed a bag one day and walked right out of his life."

"He did," comes a soft-spoken voice. Poking my head out of the closet, I see an older woman with a tray. "Come on now. I don't bite, and your food will get cold if you don't eat soon."

I eye her suspiciously, but the food smells incredible. "You take a bite first," I say, feeling proud of myself for thinking of it.

She very daintily rolls her eyes, but opens the silver cover and takes a giant bite of egg. I watch as she chews and swallows, then she hands me a cup of coffee.

"That too," I say, letting her know I want her to taste everything in front of me.

"Oh, dear. You're a smart one. No wonder Trevor's so smitten." She takes a sip of the steaming mug of coffee.

I want so badly to ask who she is. Why is she here? How does she know Trevor? But thankfully, biting my tongue seems to work for now.

"He left for college and never came back," she explains. "His room has stayed just as he left it. I come in and clean once a week. Otherwise, this room sits empty."

"Hmm," it's all I say, even though I desperately want to know more.

"All right, dear, I'll let you get ready for the day. I placed clothing and any toiletry items I thought you might like in the restroom. If you need anything at all, you can just press number two on the wall and it'll connect you right to me. If you don't have any requests for lunch, I'll bring you whatever Mr. Knight is having."

"That's fine," I say. "Thank you. Ah, I'm sorry, what's your name?"

"Jenny." She smiles. "My name is Jenny."

"Thank you, Jenny."

She pats my arm and leaves quietly.

I woke up raging against the world, against Romero, and now I'm just confused. This is not what I thought being abducted by the mob would be like. Deciding to trust Jenny, I devour the food she prepared. I guess I never had dinner last night, and apparently being abducted sure can make a girl hungry. I roll my eyes at myself. I'm ridiculous, even in these circumstances.

Taking my coffee, I mosey into the bathroom and am again assaulted by the scent of Trevor. He hasn't been here in over ten years. *How can it still smell like him?* I turn the shower on, then dig through his drawers. I laugh when I come across his stash of condoms. There are at least six full boxes—not one of them is opened.

IT FEELS like hours since Jenny was here. I've paced every inch of this room and rummaged through every drawer. I don't even feel guilty about going through Trevor's belongings; it was nice to see this side of him. Plopping myself down on the bed, I let my head hang over the edge and I notice a secret drawer in the bed's frame.

I practically dive-bomb the floor in my rush to open it. I'm expecting it to be locked or, at the very least, stuck, but it opens easily. Inside, a shiny, decorative box catches my eye. It sits alone in what I find is a large compartment.

I lift it out, finding it's heavier than I expected since it's only about the size of a child's lunch box. Hefting it to the bed, I climb up and look around. At the last minute, I turn the monitor Romero speaks through over. He may have cameras over every inch of this room, but since I only know about that one, I place it face-down.

Running my hands over the platinum box encrusted

with jewels, I take in the intricate detailing. That's when I notice the engraving, *To my precious Grace Juliette, Love Daddy*.

My hand covers my mouth as I gasp, "This was his mother's?"

"It was." Romero is standing at the doorway of my room. I was so absorbed in my treasure hunting that I didn't hear him enter. "I kept waiting for Trevor to come and retrieve it after she passed, but he never did. Lately, I've wondered if he's forgotten about it."

"You knew it was here?" I ask before I can think better of it.

"Oh, yes. Trevor was always hiding his most prized possessions. When he was about nine, I had his room outfitted with all kinds of secret storage spaces. The one in the bed was always his favorite. I told you I haven't touched Trevor's room. I've left it almost exactly the way it was when he left. The only exception is a few additions to that box, things I thought he would want," Romero says, nodding to the box in my hands.

Suddenly, I'm not feeling so sure about opening this beautiful treasure.

"Go ahead, open it," he encourages, as if reading my mind. He crosses the room and sits in the large armchair in the corner.

"Jesus." I shake my head.

"Julia, it's all right. When you leave here, I hope that you'll take it with you for Trevor. It belongs to him."

Sighing, I open the lid carefully. The inside is full of pictures, letters, and two small jewelry boxes. I notice the first few letters are addressed to Trevor, but sealed. Lifting them out, I inspect them.

"Two of those are from Grace. She wrote them before she passed. In the event anything happened to her, she had things she wanted him to know. I've tried over the years to get them to Trevor, but he, rightly so, has kept his distance from me," Romero admits.

"And this one?" I ask, noticing the handwriting is different.

"That one is from me."

He gives no further information, so I set the letters down on the bed. I remove the two jewelry boxes but don't open them. Underneath the letters and jewelry are stacks and stacks of pictures. Pulling them out, I examine them one by one.

"Holy hell," I gasp, tracing the photo of the little boy in my hand.

"Charlie looks just like him," Romero agrees, and my blood flies to my head in a rush, making me dizzy.

He knows about Charlie. "Fucking stupid, Julia," I mumble.

"I understand your fear, Julia. While I wish I could know Charlie, I'll never disrespect your wishes."

"Goddamn liar," I hear myself spew. *Jesus, Julia, bite your freaking tongue before you get yourself killed. This is a man in the mob, after all.*

I hear Romero sigh, but I don't make eye contact. I simply sit, staring at pictures, waiting for him to make his move.

"The day I met Grace was one of the best days of my life," he begins. "The second best was when Trevor was born. I wasn't always this monster you see before you, Julia. At one time, I had hopes and dreams for my family, like any other man."

I tried not to engage with him, but like most times, I have no control over the words that fly from my mouth. "How can you say that? You beat Grace. You hit her in front of your son."

I watch as he nods his head in shame. *He feels shame?* It's shocking to me.

"Let me start at the beginning, Julia." There's a lengthy pause while he collects his thoughts. "I have two regrets in this life. Perhaps I should have more, but when I reflect, I made two decisions I wish more than anything I could take back."

Scooting up on the bed, I raise my knees to rest my chin on them. I wrap my arms around my shins, curling into a ball. Keeping my eyes on Romero, I settle in for whatever it is he has to tell me.

"When Trevor was a young boy, I worked a lot. I was building a business, but I wanted so badly to be the dad at every game he played. I was greedy. I wanted it all. I'd just purchased this home, and we were growing accustomed to the lifestyle that comes with having money. Work was steady, but I was burning the candle at both ends. Eventually, Grace and I took on a partner. I say Grace and me because, in those days, we made every decision together. No marriage is perfect, but ours was very close." Eventually, he lifts his head to meet my eyes.

"There isn't a day that goes by that I don't wish I could turn back time and choose another partner. Anyone but Loki's father, Antonio Black," he says, and my brain fights to make the connections.

"Wait, are you saying that Loki Kane is the son of Antonio Black? There's no way! Loki is single-handedly taking out that family. Fuck, why can't I keep anything to myself!" I panic that I've just outed him to the mob, but Romero puts my fears to rest.

"I know he is." Romero smiles. "Antonio would never have guessed his bastard son—his words not mine, mind you —would be the one to take down his empire."

"But Loki's last name is Kane. I saw yearbooks in Trevor's closet that have him listed as Loki Kane," I say, attempting to piece this fucked-up puzzle together.

"Kane was his mother's maiden name. When he was around three, she married his stepfather who raised him here in Waverley-Cay with his mother. Antonio had them killed in a car accident when Loki was seventeen. He spent his senior year living with Sylvie Westbrook and her boys," he tells me.

"Oh my God," is all I can manage.

"Anyway," Romero continues, but it takes a few seconds for me to listen. I'm still processing how Loki could be related to the family that killed Trevor's mother.

"Trevor doesn't know about Loki's family?" I interrupt.

"Not that I know of. When the boys went to college, something changed with Loki. I know now that he went into a secret branch of the military and has spent his career doing dangerously heroic things. My suspicions are he's spent his adult life trying to make up for the sins of his family."

I nod, running facts through my brain like a computer.

"My second regret is that I started drinking when I realized who Antonio Black was. By the time I made the connection, it was too late for me to get out. Antonio threatened the lives of both Grace and Trevor anytime I tried to leave. While it's not an excuse, I believe if I'd never started drinking to deal with the stress, I never would have laid a hand on my Grace. She was … *is* the love of my life. I'll carry the burden of that pain for the rest of my days.

"When Trevor had been in college for a few months, Grace and I decided to tell him everything. We would go to the FBI, do whatever it took to get out, even though we knew that would mean jail time for me. I deserved it. A stronger man would have done it the second he found out about Antonio, but I was scared. I was weak. Grace called Trevor several times that week, begging him to come home. Once we made the decision, we knew we had to move quickly. In hindsight, it was a blessing Trevor refused to come home. Antonio found out about our plans. He killed Grace himself as a warning to me. He said Trevor would be next. I lost my wife and my son that day, and there was nothing I could do about it."

"Romero," I attempt, but my throat feels like I swallowed razor blades. "Wh-Why are you telling me this?"

"Because I know what Loki's half-brother, Miles, is planning. If he succeeds, Trevor and Loki will be in grave danger. I have a plan to stop him, but I'm afraid technology is not my area of expertise."

"And you want Trevor to help you? Why not go to the police?" I ask.

"I've tried to get ahold of Loki, but they have thwarted every attempt. My only chance of helping my son now is if I'm face-to-face with him," he explains.

"And you think kidnapping me is the way to do that? He'll tear you apart before you ever have a chance to explain anything."

"It's a risk I have to take," he states simply.

I think for a few minutes. I know Trevor's brilliant with software and tech in general, but I have an exceptionally high IQ as well. Knowing Trevor will never listen to his father, I make an executive decision and hope he'll forgive me later.

"Trevor won't help you. His rage will take over, and I think there's a very distinct possibility that he'll kill you before you ever get a word out. That being said, tell me your plan, give me a computer, and I'll see if I can do it for you," I say reluctantly.

"You?" he scoffs. "No offense, Julia, but I think we need Trevor for this. While Miles is not nearly the intellect Antonio was, we need to be very careful. This is not the time for trials."

Romero's words ignite my rage.

Standing from the bed, I stomp toward him. "Listen to me, you pea-brained, misogynistic asshat. Trevor and I may work in two different fields, but I graduated at the top of my class with three degrees before I was twenty-one years old. By the time I was twenty-three, I was making six-figures. I won't argue that Trevor has a brilliant mind, but the one fucking thing I've always been sure of is that I am the smartest goddamn person in any room I enter. If you think Trevor can do this, then I'm here to tell you I can do it better and faster. If you don't believe that, then you can just fuck off and let Trevor come 'fetch' me and see where that leads, you cocksucker," I fume.

Leaning back in his chair, he steeples his fingers and a crooked grin takes over his face. I swear I'm about to knock that smug look right into next week with a throat punch when he agrees. "Okay."

"Okay?" I ask, dumbfounded.

"It's been a long time since I've seen a fire like that, Julia. And the last person to call me a cocksucker was my Grace." He smiles. "I think you two would have gotten along very well."

Feeling my own smile appear, I nod in agreement. "Well, all right, then. Let's get started. Tell me what you need."

Don't ask me why I'm trusting this man; I'm running solely on gut instinct here. If I end up being wrong about Romero, I hope Trevor will forgive me.

CHAPTER 36

TREVOR

"Counting Stars" by OneRepublic

I'm standing on the beach as Julia walks down the sandy path toward me, her flimsy, white gown blowing behind her with the ocean breeze. I can't see her face clearly through the veil, but I can tell her smile matches my own. As she gets closer, I notice she's barefoot, and I'm acutely aware I could never love anyone more. She's the most beautiful woman I've ever seen. Glancing to my left, I see Dexter holding Charlie, and I feel the first tear fall. I'm about to make these two my family, and then I'll be able to love them forever.

"Trevor, I got an email from Julia," Lanie screams as she bursts through the guesthouse door, startling me awake.

How the fuck did I manage to fall asleep when Julia is missing?

Fully awake in less than a second, I spring from the couch. "What do you mean? Where? Let me see!"

"I'm not sure what it says, it's in our secret code, but I have my cheat sheet, so it'll just take me a few minutes to decipher it," she announces.

"Lanie, what are you talking about, sweetheart?" Dex asks, looking uncomfortable.

We're all thinking that perhaps the lack of sleep all these weeks has finally taken its toll on this new mom.

"When we were in college, Julia set up this account with a website she built and fake emails. Anytime I went on a date, I would have to text her. If I said it was going *well*, she would know to send an email that would arrive with all kinds of alerts and buzzers showing it was a work emergency, and I'd have my out to leave." Lanie pauses to look up and finds us all staring at her.

"That's a little fucked-up," Preston says, echoing all of our thoughts.

"You just wait and see if you think that when you all have teenage daughters. It's about being safe," Lanie informs us with a hand on her hip.

"Back on track, guys. Can I see the email?" I ask.

"Sure, you'll be able to decode it faster than I can anyway." She hands over her phone.

"Tell me how the code works."

"Okay, well, the first number will show where to start in the alphabet." She looks over my shoulder. "So, her first letter is I because she starts with the number nine, and it's just the word I because it has an ^ after it. 9^ is the word I. Then there's a backslash, so it's telling you to go back 8 letters followed by the number 12^. So, 9^\8.12^ says, I am."

"Okay, what are the other directives?"

"An asterisk means you need to jump ahead ten letters. Periods are number or letter spacers. The and sign means a new sentence, and the forward slash means move ahead that many letters from the last one used," Lanie explains in one breath.

"Jesus, that's really fucking complicated. She couldn't have just called you?" Preston asks.

Rolling her eyes, Lanie continues, "This is the dumbed-down version for me. She had all kinds of tracking software incorporated into this email account in case I ever got abducted on one of my dates, but I could never follow the code she originally had. Even this one takes me an hour to decode."

"Holy shit. Julia has more than just tracking on this account," I tell everyone. "She's a freaking genius."

"Actually, she really is. She's been a member of Mensa since she was fourteen," Lanie says, catching my attention.

"Seriously?" I ask. *How did I not know that?* "Jesus, she really was the one giving all the presentations in Boston that I wanted to see but couldn't get into," I mutter, working through memories out loud.

Lanie grins. "My girl's a rockstar."

"She really fucking is." Once again, I'm in awe of my girl.

"So, how's it feel to be the second smartest in the family?" Dexter teases.

"As long as I get her back in one piece, I'll gladly bow to her superior intellect any day of the week," I tell him. "Hmm, give me a minute to work through her email."

Fifteen minutes later, I sit staring at the message she's sent, trying to make it compute in my brain and my heart.

I am fine. At Romero's. Tell Loki Miles knows about him. Miles is hunting Loki. Warn him. Setting a cyber trap for Miles. Do not retrieve me for three days. Systems running follow it.

"I don't get it, is she working with your father?" Preston asks, reading over my shoulder.

"I-I don't know. Get Seth, though. We need to get a message to Loki."

"What does she want you to follow?" Dexter asks.

"I think she set up this program so I can follow all the activity between Romero and Miles Black. I-I have to get acquainted with her programming before I'll have any other information."

Seth comes barreling through the door. "What's going on?"

"I think Loki is in danger," I tell him.

"What? Where is he?" Lanie asks. This poor woman, I don't know how much more she can take in her state. Dex must be thinking the same thing, because the next thing I know, he's trying to usher her out, reminding her she needs to nurse the twins.

"He's collecting a-a package," I say before she leaves, hoping that'll ease a little of her anxiety for the time being.

Seth passes them on their way out. "What do you know?"

I spend the next ten minutes filling Seth in, then watch as he takes out multiple phones and starts shooting off messages left and right. I know Julia hates this man, but something tells me he's loyal to Loki in a way that doesn't just happen. I'm convinced there's a story here, but it's not mine to question.

"Trevor," Seth yells across the room, "Loki thinks you're the best to follow Julia's path. Is that correct, or do I need to bring in some guys?"

"No," I say determinedly, "I've got this. Preston, grab all my screens from the bedroom. I need to set up a war room. Dex, I'm going to need some extension cords and a tower server. You have one in your office, right? Can you bring that down here?"

"We got you, dude," Preston says as he starts collecting items and clearing space at the kitchen table.

"Trevor?" I hear. Peering up, I see Preston's youngest brother, Ashton. I've been so caught up, I forgot that all five Westbrook boys were here.

"What's up, Ash?" I ask while trying to set up various monitors.

"This is kind of my thing," he mumbles so no one else can hear.

Ashton is seven years younger than we are, so I'm not as

close with him as I am with the other four Westbrooks, but he's one of us, and I see how badly he wants to help.

"Yeah? How so?" I don't want to shut him down if there's something he can actually help with.

"I'm on par with Julia." Then, leaning in, he whispers, "I've been hacking for Loki since I was sixteen."

This catches me entirely off guard, and I chuckle. "What the fuck?"

He nods, staring at the ground with his head bowed. He seems embarrassed to admit that and it makes me smile.

"I can't believe it. Little Ash is all grown up," I say, feeling lighter knowing I have backup. "All right then, dude, grab a chair, we'll get you set up."

He smiles and holds up a bag I know contains his own supplies. "I've got it covered."

No shit.

"Let's get started then, brother. Welcome to the chaos, huh?" I chuckle, slapping him on the back.

For the next two-and-a-half days, I watch, log, and reroute items as they come in. Julia's fucking brilliant, and I'm beginning to suspect Ashton does a lot more for Loki than just hacking. The system Julia's set up monitors Miles' every move. I'm pissed that I can't just storm my father's house and take Julia back, but she's sending updates every four hours, letting me know she's okay. Unfortunately, she had to disable incoming messages from me, but I get it. Leaving that line open would be an easy trace should Miles get suspicious.

The amount of shit we have collected is enough to take Miles down, but she's waiting for something. Something big, and I'm afraid it has to do with Loki. We haven't been able to get ahold of him in over twenty-four hours, and I have a pit in my stomach that says something is wrong. The fact that Seth is also on edge isn't helping the tension that's settled over the house.

I'm staring at the computer screen when we hear Lanie scream Julia's name. I'm out of my chair and through the front door at the same time as Dexter. Both of us panic at the sound of the scream.

Standing at the door of the main house is Julia. With Charlie on her hip and a bag in her hand, Julia smiles the second her eyes meet mine. *I will marry this fucking girl*, is the last thought in my head before I'm sprinting across the lawn.

Wrapping her and Charlie in my arms, I lift her off the ground.

"Dada," little Charlie babbles happily.

"Yeah, Dada, little man," I reply while searching Julia's face. "Where's Romero? I'm going to kill him."

"No, you won't," she stops me. "We have a lot of ground to cover, but before I fill you in on everything, I need to talk to Preston."

Her words take me by surprise. "Preston? Why?"

Julia cringes a little, and I know she's aware of the *package* Loki's collecting.

"Oh shit."

"Yeah, we need to get him home with Seth so they can finish setting up security." She fidgets awkwardly.

"Ah … I'm not telling him who the package is," I whisper, slightly terrified of his reaction.

"Fuck no. That's a job for Loki."

Following her across the lawn to the guesthouse we call home, I chuckle. "I couldn't agree more."

The next hour goes by in a flash.

A perplexed Preston finally left with Seth. All of his brothers, except for Ashton, followed suit. This kid really knows his shit, so he stays behind to keep tabs on all the files we're watching. Dexter goes back to his house, and after a brief dinner with her parents, Julia and I are finally left alone.

CHAPTER 37

JULIA

"Hey Brother" by Avicii

Sitting cross-legged on the couch, I watch Trevor closely. I just dropped more bombs than any one man can process at once, and he hasn't said a single word. Not one.

"Trevor?" I nudge cautiously. "Are you okay?"

Raising his eyes to meet mine, he says the last thing I'm expecting. "Marry me. Right here, and soon. If you want a big wedding, we can do that, but I don't want to wait one more minute to make you mine. Please, Julia, marry me?"

"I … Trevor. What? Did you hear anything I just said to you?"

"Yes. There are letters in here from my dead mother. Loki is related to the Black family. The family he's currently taking out. My mother and father took on a partner who happened to be the mob and Loki's biological father. They tried to get out, and they killed my mother for it. Marry me," he says in one breath.

"Your sky just fell down, and you want me to marry you?"

"For you, sweetheart, there's not a thing in this world I wouldn't do," he sings. "But yes, I want you to marry me. I knew the first time we danced I wanted to marry you. When you were taken from me for the second time, I decided I wouldn't let that happen ever again. Marry me."

"Wh-What about the letters? Your d-dad? L-Loki?" I stammer.

"The letters aren't going anywhere, and I'm not ready to read them. Someday maybe, but not today. I've been living in chaos for long enough. You once told me you would keep my darkness away. Do you remember that?" he asks softly.

"Of course I do."

"Then marry me. Be my guiding light for the rest of my life. As for my father? I-I really don't know, but he isn't a priority for me right now. And Loki? I'll kick his fucking ass as soon as I get my hands on him. He should have come to us years ago instead of going vigilante, putting his life on the line day after day while we were clueless," he roars.

"He did what he thought he had to, Trevor," I argue.

"Exactly. What he thought he had to do, but what about us? He never gave us the option to help him. Who the hell is he to decide all this?"

"It was his family, Trevor. He sent his brothers to prison for life, and he very likely had to kill his own father. Isn't it the same exact thing you were doing by not talking to Dexter and Preston? You thought you had to handle it all yourself because you didn't want them involved?"

It's a reminder that's hard to acknowledge.

"Fuck." He lowers his head to his hands. "In some ways, it's the same, yes. But, Jules, I had him. I had Loki to help me and be there for me. Who the hell has he had? He should have told me, and we should have told the others."

"You're right. As far as I can tell, you're all a bunch of pig-headed asshats."

Laughing, he lunges for me, lifting me easily into his lap.

Resting his forehead against mine, he brings his hand in between us. That's when I notice he's holding a ring box I know was in his mother's engraved case.

"This was my grandmother's." He pauses to take a deep breath. "My mother gave it to me when I turned eighteen and told me to hang on to it until I met the woman that lit up my nights like the Fourth of July and filled my days with a love I could never have imagined."

Opening the box, he pulls out the ring. "Julia Grace McDowell, I've spent the last ten years living in a nightmare. The day I met you, I woke up. You're the sunshine I need to live. You make me want to do better, be better. You make me believe in happily ever afters when I've lived in a horror show most of my life. I want the happily ever after now, with you and Charlie. Please say you'll marry me and be my light forever?" he begs.

"How could I say no to the only man who has ever calmed my chaos?" My tears flow freely as I wrap my arms around his neck.

"Is that a yes, Angel? I really need to hear you say it."

"Yes, it's a yes," I sob.

Trevor leans in to kiss me, then pulls back suddenly. "Oh crap, hold on. I'll be right back."

I stare at him, confused, as he sprints from our house to the main house. After twenty minutes, I'm getting pissed off when I hear cheering and yelling coming from Lanie's open door. Staring out the window, I see Trevor come running back across the yard.

He busts through the door, drops to his knee, and asks me again, "Angel, now that I've gotten your family's approval, will you marry me?"

I can't help but laugh along with him. "Yes, yes, I'll marry you." As soon as the words leave my mouth, I'm rewarded by cheers from the doorway.

"We witnessed Lanie's proposal. I figured it was only fair

they got to see ours, too." Trevor shrugs.

Bending forward, I kiss my fiancé. The most ridiculous year of my life has also turned out to be my best one yet.

CHAPTER 38

LOKI

"Memories" by Maroon 5

*C*rouched down in the bushes of my biological father's home, a home that now belongs to my half-brother, I go over the intel in my head one more time. They're holding Lexi in my old room. Not that I ever lived here. Miles did that to send a message, I'm sure of it.

Thanks to Julia's intel—intel I'm fucking shocked she could get—I know they're waiting for me. I have every inch of this place mapped out in my head. After all, it wasn't that long ago I raided it. The event sent three of my half-brothers to jail and ended in gunfire. My father left in a body bag.

Of all the Blacks, Miles had been the one I was closest to the few times they forced me to visit. He's younger than me by six years, and I had really hoped that by being the youngest, he'd been spared. Now I know differently. There's no brotherly bond connecting us. It's good versus evil, and only one of us can win. For the sake of my friends, it has to be me that wins.

I know my guys have taken out the cameras on the east side of the house, so after giving my signal, I sprint in the shadows to my entry point. Using the grooves in the old stone, I scale the side of the building, stopping when I've reached just below the window I'll need to enter. Hanging flush with the building, I wait for my signal. My guys will use heat sensors to ensure Lexi's alone before they let me enter.

After what feels like an eternity, I finally see the flash of light across the treetops to my left. Just as I'd hoped, so does Miles' security team. The second I hear them exit the building, I lift myself up enough to break the lock. Technology is amazing. The lock pops with barely a sound. As silently as possible, I raise the window and heft myself through it.

Listening, I'm relieved when I hear silence. I know what I'm about to do will scare the shit out of this poor girl, but after all she's been through in the last few days, I'm hoping the scare will be minimal.

I place a hand over her mouth so she can't scream, and using my weight to hold her down, I see her panic. But I need her to listen so we can both get out of here alive.

"Lexi, listen to me. I'm on your side. I'm a friend of Dexter's and Trevor's. I'm here to get you out, but you need to do exactly as I say and not make a sound. Blink twice if you understand," I tell her.

Blink. Blink.

Thank fuck. "Before I let you go, I need you to understand something. If you scream, we're both dead. Do you understand?" I ask again.

Blink. Blink.

I release her, and she sits up in bed. "They know you're coming. You're Loki, right?" she whispers.

This can't be good.

"Yes, we need to move," I say as the door swings open and I come face-to-face with my half-brother. Covertly pressing the button embedded on the ring I'm wearing, I signal my guys that they've found me.

"Brother, I've been waiting for you," Miles says, raising a gun to my chest.

As planned, the flare gun goes off, distracting Miles for a split second. It's quick, but all the time I need to dive for him. Thanks to Julia, I know he doesn't have as many goons hanging around as my father did, but he has at least six men, so I need to make every move count. A quick jab to his throat blocks his airway, and he drops to the ground, the gun sliding across the floor.

Before I can make a move for it, Lexi picks it up, pulls back the safety, and points it at Miles. "You stupid idiot, do you not even know how to use a gun?" she scolds.

"Fuck you," he says, spitting on the floor.

"Lexi, you know how to handle a gun?" I ask, surprised.

"Dude, I grew up in Vermont. They taught gun safety in second grade," she scoffs.

These Vermont girls keep surprising the fuck out of me. Confident Lexi knows what she's doing, I walk over to Miles, pulling the handcuffs from my back pocket as I go. Just as I'm leaning down to cuff him, he lunges for me, plunging a knife I hadn't seen deep into my flesh. The fucker was aiming for my heart, and he may have gotten it had I not been wearing a Kevlar vest. Lifting my knee to his groin, I push him off of me just enough that Lexi's able to take a clear shot. He crumbles to the ground with a loud thud as his head hits the hardwood.

"Fuck," I say, removing the knife. I turn to Lexi, expecting her to be a mess, but she appears calm. *Perhaps she is in shock?* She moves to the dresser and pulls out a T-shirt that she rips apart. I watch for a second, then realize she's making a tourniquet and sling out of her shirts.

"Another life lesson learned in the deep woods of Vermont?" I whisper.

"You know it." She smirks.

"The gun had a silencer, but it won't be long before we're surrounded again. We have to move," I tell her.

Removing my vest, I instruct her to put it on. She shrugs me off while applying pressure to my wound.

Staring into her eyes, I see conflict in many shades.

"Thank you," I tell her when I realize she has packed my wound the best she can.

"Eh, everyone needs a little help from their friends sometimes."

"That's usually my line," I mumble.

Suddenly, I wonder if this is how Dexter and Trevor feel. Having someone to rely on like this is something I've never had or wanted, quite frankly. I shake the thought from my head as quickly as it came. In my life, there's no room for distractions of any variety.

Placing the vest around Lexi, I make sure it's secure, then lead her from the room. "Just stay close to me," I whisper. Glancing at my watch, I know we have another thirty seconds before my team surrounds us. We make our way down the hall, and I pull Lexi into a room the maids once used. I know there's a secret passage in this room that will lead us to the underground tunnels. I just have the hidden door secured when I hear the gunfire go off.

Pop. Pop. Pop.

It's like fireworks no one ever wants to see.

"Loki, we really need to get you to the hospital," Lexi says for the nineteenth time since we boarded the plane.

"Lex." The nickname rolls off my tongue far too easily. "Lexi," I try again, "this isn't over. There's always someone else waiting in the wings to take over. It doesn't just end because you shot Miles," I try to explain to her. "We have to get you to your safe house, and you must stay there until I tell you otherwise. You'll all need security for the time being, but at least you'll be close to Lanie and Julia."

"Am I staying at Lanie's?" she asks hopefully.

Pulling at my shirt collar, I answer, "No, but you'll be able to see them anytime you want. That's the silver lining in all this." Trying to change the subject because I do not want to spend another two hours on a plane with her once she finds out about her new living arrangements, I say, "Lanie's babies are adorable." Women and babies, I'm hoping the stereotype holds true.

I watch as a longing smile slides across her beautiful face. *Bingo!* I'm still not accustomed to how nearly identical she and Lanie are.

"I saw some pictures before douche-canoe took me from Vermont," she says wistfully. "They're pretty damn perfect, aren't they?"

"I'm not really a kid person," I admit, "but the few times I've seen them in the NICU, they've been amazing."

Thankful the distraction worked, I lay back in my seat and try to rest a bit before I walk into my second firestorm of the night.

THREE HOURS LATER, I'm pulling up into the apartment building that Preston and I share. Well, where Preston lives now. I've sublet my apartment, knowing I'll have to take leave from my friends to shut down the rest of the Black organization once and for all.

Ushering Lexi into the elevator, I pull out a keycard that'll take us to Preston's penthouse apartment.

"Ooh, penthouse! Fancy," she says, rolling her eyes.

I can't help but chuckle. If she only knew. Rolling my shoulders, I grimace as pain shoots through my shoulder and down my arm.

"I saw that you know. When are you going to get that looked at?" she asks.

"As soon as I drop you off," I tell her as the elevator doors open into Preston's foyer.

Giving Lexi a gentle nudge, I make sure she's far enough from the elevator doors so they can close before we go searching for her host. I can't have her making a run for it, and I know she'll try. Imagining her attempting an escape has me smiling.

We're walking down the hallway when we hear, "Loki? Is that you?"

"Oh no, Loki. You cannot be serious?"

She's attempting to back up, but I've blocked her path, gently urging her forward. She comes to a dead stop the second Preston walks around the corner.

"Fuck no," Preston curses. "You're out of your goddamn mind, Loki."

I can barely hear him because, at the same time, Lexi's screeching, "I am not staying with this asshole, Loki."

"Me? I'm the asshole?" Preston stands with his hands on his hips. "You're the one who's had her knickers in a knot since the moment I met you."

Jesus, Trevor was right. Preston hasn't pulled out these sayings since we were kids. This woman is getting under his skin in a way I hadn't thought possible. I almost burst out laughing, but for the sake of keeping my nuts attached, I rein it in.

"Knickers? In a—" Lexi fumes, but I interrupt her.

"Hold on," I bellow, attempting to break through their nonsense. "There's no other option. You two will have to learn to get along for at least a few months."

"A few months," they both squeal at the same time.

"Yes, a few months," I repeat.

"Why can't I just stay with you?" Lexi asks with pleading eyes.

"Yeah, that's a brilliant idea. He lives a few floors down, you can stay there," Preston agrees happily.

Raising my hands to shut them both up, I explain our situation. "I've sublet my apartment. As I was telling Lex," *Fuck, there it is again*, "this fucked-up situation isn't over. I'm only here to drop Lexi off, then I'm back in the field."

"Loki," Preston says, his voice already filling with concern. "You don't have to do this on your own, let us help."

"I love you, Preston, but this is what I've trained for. Until all of Black's organization is taken down, none of you are safe. I can't live with that, so let me do what needs to be done. Alone."

"Jesus, man. Why are you so fucking stubborn?"

"This is my fight, Pres. I need you to do your part by staying with Lexi. That goes for the both of you," I say, turning my attention to Lexi, whose face is almost purple with anger. "The best thing either of you can do is find a way to get along for the next few months. I can't be worrying about you while I'm in the field. Can you do that?"

"Fine," Lexi grumbles.

"Preston? Can you at least try to be happy about this? We're all alive, and there's an end in sight."

"Oh, I am. I'm as happy as a dead pig in sunshine," he says before turning on his heel. "Come on, your room's this way."

I watch as Lexi reluctantly follows him. For the second time today, I find a tiny piece of me wishing I could have what all of my friends have found—happiness and love. Unfortunately, that ending was written out of my life the day my mother conceived another son of Antonio Black's.

EPILOGUE

PRESTON

"*T*revor, I know this is your big day, but there has to be another option. I'm already living with Lexi. If we have to partner up for this entire wedding, we'll kill each other," I tell him.

"Sorry, man, it is what it is. Grow a pair and deal with it," Trevor replies. "Dexter will cut off your sack before he lets you walk down the aisle with Lanie, so that leaves you and Lexi."

We both grow quiet, acknowledging we're down a man. No one has heard from Loki in weeks, and the more time that passes, the more disheartening it is. He's never gone more than a month without checking in with someone. We're getting dangerously close to that month marker now, and my gut roils with worry.

"I hope to God Loki isn't dead," Julia says, walking into the room. "Because I'm going to fucking kill him myself when he comes home."

It's a thought we've all had, but Julia might be the one to act on it. She was madder than a wet hornet when she found out he dropped Lexi off with me and then vanished.

"Come on," she says, grabbing both our arms, "we have choices to make. The first one will be the specialty cocktail."

Julia is the least girly-girl I know, but she has taken to wedding planning like the beast of Waverley-Cay.

Allowing her to drag me through the house, I follow her to the tables set up in Dexter's yard. "Are we cake testing, too? Please tell me we are?" I say, trying to lighten my own mood.

"There will be cake," Julia says happily before breaking away to meet the girls.

Eyeing the bartender standing alone at the table, I'm about to take my chance and speak to him privately when Trevor says, "I found Erick."

"Erick? Like Julia's ex, Erick?"

"Yup," he says, obviously satisfied with himself.

"Ah, do I want to know what you've done?" I ask.

Smirking like the devil himself, he says, "You mean besides turning him into Loki's guy at the FBI?"

"Oh, no, Trevor. What did you do?"

"Julia said I wasn't allowed to go near him, so I did the next best thing." He shrugs.

"Which is?" I hate it when he draws stuff out like this.

"I buried him in shit just like he did to my angel."

"Funny, Trevor. Seriously, what did you do?" I ask, annoyed that I may lose this chance to corner the bartender.

Laughing now, he says, "I literally buried him in shit. As we speak, there are fourteen dump trucks headed to his house to dump pig feces. I paid more to make sure they got it all the way to the front door."

I stare at him in disbelief before laughing right alongside him.

"I don't understand, though. Why fourteen?" I ask.

"That dickwad took out fourteen loans in Julia's name. I figured the symbolism was a nice touch."

"Yeah," I say, still laughing. "Fuck, Trevor, that's messed up."

"I know," he says as he watches our group of friends.

"Listen, I'm going to get us a drink. I'll meet you over there," I tell Trevor, encouraging him to go with Julia.

"Thanks, Pres. I didn't realize wedding planning would be such a big freaking ordeal," he says, pulling at his tie.

Chuckling, I clap him on the back. "I'll be over in a minute."

Crossing the lawn, I glance around to make sure no one is nearby. "Hey," I lean in, reading the guy's name tag, "Mark? Listen, I've got a minor problem."

"He sure does, it's called being an arrogant prick," Lexi's voice grates from behind me.

How the hell did she sneak up on me so quickly?

"Seriously, Lex? You don't get enough of me at home, you have to nag me here, too?" I groan.

"I do not nag," she exclaims. "If you wouldn't be such a stuck-up man-whore, I wouldn't have to remind you to do shit all the time."

The fact that she thinks I'm a man-whore is comical, considering the truth. But, since I'm the one letting her believe that I do, in fact, have a woman over every night who only stays for a couple of hours, I can't really argue with her.

You could try telling someone the fucking truth, I hear in my head.

"You're in my home, sweet tits. My home, my rules," I say, knowing I'll piss her off enough to go storming back to our group. It worked, but now I have to figure out how I'll get out of tasting these drinks. With everyone eyeing me, I leave the bartender and go to join my friends.

"Do you have to set her off every time you two speak?" Dexter asks.

"She started it," I sulk.

I know with all the secrets that came to light in the last few months, I should just come clean. I won't, but I should.

My secret will only ruin whatever time I have left with them. I'd prefer to spend the rest of my days having fun with my friends, my crazy ass brothers, and my loving mother. I worry about her most of all. I know when they find out about my broken heart, it just might be the end to hers as well.

EXTENDED EPILOGUE

TREVOR

"7 Years" by Lukas Graham

"Are you going to just stare at them again tonight?" Julia asks as she sits in my lap.

Nuzzling into the crook of her neck, I inhale deeply. This woman calms me in ways I can't begin to describe.

"I don't know if I'm ready."

Turning in my lap, she wraps her arms around my neck. "Trevor, you've been staring at those letters for months now. I know you want to read them, what's stopping you?" she asks.

I've been asking myself the same question for weeks now. Squeezing her a little tighter, I say, "I think I'm worried my mother won't be the woman I remember her to be." Putting a voice to my fear makes it more real.

"There's only one way to find out, you know? And if something in that letter changes your opinion of her, it doesn't have to change your memories. You said she was an exceptional mother, that she did anything and everything for you. A terrible person wouldn't have put you first like that,

Trevor. Did she do some things you might not like? Probably, but haven't we all?

"Someday, Charlie will realize you weren't there when he was born. He'll question why there are no pictures of you at the hospital, but that doesn't make you an awful person or a terrible father. It makes us human. We all have things in our lives we wish we could change, and after listening to your father, I think you owe it to yourself and to her memory to read them. Would you like me to do it?"

Swallowing hard, I finally say, "No, just stay with me?"

"Always," Angel says, and I know she means it.

With a heavy heart and a boulder in my gut, I reach for the first letter. I spend a minute running my fingers over her handwriting. I've stared at it every day, but tonight I can envision her sitting at her desk that always had fresh flowers in the corner, writing it. It makes the letter feel alive, and I almost chicken out again.

Sensing my hesitation, Julia places a hand on my thigh in silent support. I take another deep breath, then slide my fingers under the seal of the aging envelope. Gently removing the pages, I hold it for a moment before I get the nerve to open the pages. When I do, I feel all the emotions I've been holding in release. Anger, fear, helplessness, sadness, and heartache all escape my body through my tears as I read.

My Dearest Trevor,

If you're reading this letter, our plan did not go accordingly. Don't hold this against your father. It was a joint decision from the beginning. By now, you know our biggest mistakes, and I'm sorry we could not correct them before they caught up to you, my beautiful boy.

I know you'll never forget the way your father mistreated me at times, and you shouldn't. It was reprehensible. But I have forgiven him, Trevor. Because with forgiveness, you find peace. We found ourselves in a situation we never expected, a situation no one could have predicted, and we did the best we could. At times, the stress became too much for your father, and I took the brunt of it, yes.

As your mother, Trevor, I want to say I'm sorry. I'm so sorry I couldn't protect you from this. I'm sorry I won't see you grow into the man I know you'll be one day. I'm so sorry I won't see you become a father. One day, you will be the most amazing father, Trevor. Never let your fear hold you back. You are so much more than our mistakes.

The day you were born was the best day of our lives. I wish I could explain to you the feeling we had holding you for the first time. Well, I hope one day you'll experience it for yourself. Until that day, just know, I spent every breath I took from that day forward loving you with everything I had. You're the best pieces of me, Trevor, and I hope one day, when you find the woman you'll marry, she sees you in all your glory.

Please, never lose your caring nature, your loving soul, or your curious mind. Continue to grow into the man we dreamt you would be. Love with your whole heart, and when given a chance, accept love in the same way.

You, my baby boy, are my greatest creation. My love for you will never die, and I'll live in your heart for as long as you'll have me.

With all my love,
Mom

"Fuck." I wipe angrily at my tears. After handing Julia the letter I just read, I reach for the next one before I chicken out.

Opening it, I feel dizzy. *She thought of everything.*

With a heavy heart, I hand the second letter to Julia. "It's for you."

"What? How?" she says but goes silent as she begins to read.

To the woman who captured my lovely boy's heart,

Thank you. Thank you for loving Trevor just the way he is. For accepting him and all his perceived faults. Thank you for reminding him of the good in the world and thank you for bringing him back from the dark.

If you're reading this, my heart is full. It means that Trevor has learned to love again, and I know I only have you to thank for this. His father and I made mistakes that I have worried would ruin him. If you're reading this, then my soul can finally be at peace.

Love him with all you are, but remember to put him in his place from time to time. Men need that, you know, even in the hardest of times. Be a team. A team that cannot be broken. I feared for a long time that we'd broken my handsome boy. If I make it to heaven, I'll be crying tears of joy when I see you reading this.

Take care of him. He's strong in so many ways, but like any selfless hero, he needs support. Be that for each other. Never take your life for granted and never go to bed angry. That seems like a no-brainer, but we all forget sometimes.

I'm sorry I never got to meet you, but if my son loves you, I know I would have, too. Take care of my son's heart. He may not show it often, but he is a gentle soul who once had the biggest capacity for love. I hope you can bring that side of him back to life.

With all my love,
Grace

"Wow," Angel says, wiping away tears. "I was not expecting that."

Pulling her into me once more, I admit, "Neither was I."

We sit for a long time just staring at the last letter—the

344

one written in my father's handwriting. "I don't think I can do his letter tonight," I finally say aloud.

"This was a lot," she agrees. "It isn't going anywhere. I think it's okay to open it another day."

We didn't know it at the time, but 'another day' came much sooner than we were prepared for.

ACKNOWLEDGMENTS

There are so many people to thank for helping me with this book—first, my family. To my husband, my daughter, and three sons, thank you for your support. A lot has changed in the last year, and everyone is adjusting to having a working-stay-at-home Mommy, but we are figuring it out (with minimal complaining even!). Thank you for loving me and believing in me.

Rhon, your talents know no bounds and I would be lost without you. Your support on this journey is more helpful than you could ever know. The encouragement, kicks in the ass, and your friendship are what has helped get me this far. For that, I'm eternally grateful!

Beth, my dear friend, who reads my books quickly, so I don't have a panic attack and, overall, just keeps me in line. I can always count on her to find my over-used words! You truly are amazing, and I cannot thank you for all that you do. My books wouldn't be the same without you! XOXO

Denis at Weekend Publisher, without you I would still be wasting hours of my life posting in every Facebook group known to man. Thank you for helping me get to the next level and for tirelessly going over Amazon Ads with me!

Brooke & Valerie, thank you for being my naughty-word connoisseur's, research assistants, and all-around helpers. Your texts always give me the push I need just when I need it.

My Beta-Readers, Jennifer, Gina, Melissa, and Cheryl, thank you for helping make this book everything it could be. Your honest opinions, suggestions, and edits are more helpful than you could ever know. Thank you.

Last, but definitely not least, **YOU**, my readers. Thank you for taking a chance on an **indie author** and for loving my stories as much as I do. I can't do what I do without you, and I appreciate all the love and support you've given me. I hope to have lots more stories for you, so be on the lookout! **LUVS!**

Editor: Melissa Ringstead, https://thereforyouediting. wordpress.com/

Cover Designer: Emily Wittig @ Emily Wittig Designs. https://www.emilywittigdesigns.com/

ABOUT THE AUTHOR

A New-England girl born and raised, Avery now lives in North Carolina with her husband, their four kids, and two dogs.

A romantic at heart, Avery writes sweet and sexy Contemporary Romance and Romantic Comedy. Her stories are of friendship and trust, heartbreak, and redemption. She brings her characters to life for you and will make you feel every emotion she writes.

Avery is a fan of the happily-ever-after and the stories that make them. Her heroines have sass, her heroes have steam, and together they bring the tales you won't want to put down.

Avery writes a soulmate for us all.

Avery's Website www.AveryMaxwellBooks.com

ALSO BY AVERY MAXWELL

Standalone Romance:

Without A Hitch

Your Last First Kiss

The Westbrooks Series:

Book 1 - Cross My Heart

Book 2 - The Beat of My Heart

Book 3 - Saving His Heart

Book 4 - Romancing His Heart

Book 5 - One Little Heartbreak - A Westbrook Novella

Book 6 - One Little Mistake

Book 7 - One Little Lie

Book 8 - One Little Kiss

Book 9 - One Little Secret

Made in the USA
Las Vegas, NV
15 May 2025

22221575R00208